Notorious

LESLIE MCADAM

Copyright © 2024 by Leslie McAdam

All rights reserved.

No part of this book may be reproduced in any form or by any electronic or mechanical means, including information storage and retrieval systems, without written permission from the author, except for the use of brief quotations in a book review.

❦ Created with Vellum

About this book

Picking up your favorite adult film star at a bar in Vegas is a bad idea—especially when you wake up the next morning married to him. Ask me how I know.

Before I met Velvet the Cowboy, the public knew me as an innocuous guy who was running for office.

Now I've gone from boring to notorious in twenty-four hours.

The hot stranger's ring on my finger puts a damper on my political ambitions, since his day job isn't voter-friendly. An annulment is a no-go, and a quickie divorce would make me look unreliable.

In any case, when I find out Velvet's dark plans, I know I can't let him out of my sight. Which means I'm taking a gorgeous, 6'6", slow-talking cowboy home with me to protect him from himself.

Being with him might light my career on fire. I'm just not expecting it to do the same to my heart.

Notorious *is a stand-alone contemporary romance about Johnny Haskell, a cowboy turned adult star who stops to pet every good dog (and they're all good dogs), and Kurt Delmont, a senatorial candidate who wants to save the world. It features recovery from a mental health crisis, healing from old wounds, and love that takes these two by surprise. This book contains sensitive themes; a detailed description of the contents is in the author's note in the book preview. Happily ever after guaranteed.*

Playlist

"Midnight Rider's Prayer" — Brothers Osborne
"Sleep with the Lights On" — The Wanton Brothers
"Zen" — X Ambassadors, K. Flay & grandson
"Eulogy" — grandson
"It's the End of the World As We Know It (And I Feel Fine)" — R.E.M.
"Yes, I'm A Mess" — AJR
"Demons" — Imagine Dragons
"Car Radio" — twenty one pilots
"Institutionalized" (feat. Bilal, Anna Wise & Snoop Dogg) — Kendrick Lamar
"Paper Tiger" — Beck
"If I Ever Feel Better" — Phoenix
"Always" — Isak Danielson

https://music.apple.com/us/playlist/notorious-johnny-and-kurt/pl.u-qxylA3aFDYoyo

To my demons: Fuck off. I won. You have no power over me anymore. But if you can inspire someone else to slay their own demons, then ... thanks?

Content warning | Spoilers | Author's note

Notorious includes descriptions/depictions of: suicidal ideations, attempts at self-harm, a loved one's death by suicide, violence and gore, violent sexual assault (not by either of the two romantic leads), sex worker shaming, homophobia, recreational alcohol and drug use, vomiting, hospitalization, mental illness, chronic illness, and financial instability, as well as the usual explicit sexual content and swearing. If I've missed a content warning I should include, please let me know at info@lesliemcadamauthor.com. Same goes for typos—rather than report them to Amazon, please email me so I can fix them.

If you're feeling suicidal, please seek immediate professional help. In the United States, one resource is the 988 Suicide and Crisis Lifeline, which you can contact by texting or calling 988 or chatting at 988lifeline.org.

* * *

Dear Reader,

Please forgive the overly personal author's note, but I want you to know what you're getting into with this book and why it matters.

This story is inspired by my own experience being strip-searched and locked up in a behavioral health hospital due to suicidal ideations. "That was when I learned I had several mood disorders, including depression," she says. (I can imagine my editor wondering why I switched to the third person in that last sentence. I feel vulnerable, so I need to distance myself. I'm still raw, years later. Humor helps. So does portraying my experience through the lens of a tall, drawling, porn star cowboy. Then I can pretend it's fiction.)

Anyway, after about a year and a half of intense care, I recovered. *Completely*. If you're interested in the details, I've talked about it a lot on my blog at www.lesliemcadamauthor.com/blog.

Part of my recovery included realizing that the only thing I'd ever wanted to do was to write—and then letting myself do that. It's not an exaggeration to say that writing is literally a life-or-death issue with me, and I'm grateful that after lots and lots of help I'm now strong enough to tell Johnny and Kurt's story. I wasn't when I started out. I wasn't a year ago. I've also become an advocate for taking the stigma out of mental health issues, which means I talk about them often.

But just because I'm in a space to finally write this story does not mean that you're in a place to read it. Like they say on the edge of old maps, *hic sunt dracones* (here are dragons). **_Please do not read further if it will harm you in any way_**. Part of taking care of your mental state is knowing when to *stay away* because it's safer. Only you will know the answer to that question for yourself, but if you're in doubt, don't read this book. This story includes depictions of sexual assault and suicide attempt(s) that were uncomfortable to write, so I'm going to assume they're uncomfortable to read. Skip this book if you think they might harm you. Just because I think they're essential to the plot doesn't mean you have to read them. I'm harping on this because your mental health is of paramount importance.

I mention my past because my inpatient experience in a mental hospital—where, yes, the mountain lion encounter Johnny describes *really happened*—will not be someone else's experience navigating the territory of mental health. This is my truth, my experiences, my recovery, told through fiction; I'm *not* saying that anyone else's journey would be like mine or Johnny's or that this depiction is universal. *It clearly is not*. Humans are complicated, and this variation in experience is what I find fascinating. Don't assume that because I portray these characters experiencing mental illness and recovery in a certain way means I think that some other way is invalid or couldn't happen; I don't.

An additional warning on tone: There is teasing in this book about suicide. If that will offend you, stay away. As someone who got close to suicide, I don't think it's a topic to take lightly. But I also don't believe we need to shy away from whatever coping mechanisms we need to talk about our problems, and humor can be one of those mechanisms—at least it is for these two love bugs. But again (*again? again!*), if that portrayal will cause you harm, please pick a different book.

On a separate note, as far as reality goes, I intend the *IOU* series to be comfort reads, meaning a relatively low-angst series of M/M novels where generally nice people get their happily ever afters in an environment with minimal homophobia. Unfortunately, that is not the world we live in, and it's become my routine to request that you suspend some disbelief in the fictional world that I'm creating. I could provide you with a list of things in this book that I've stretched reality on, but let's just round up and say *all of it*. If you're going to get distracted by details like election timelines, procedures for getting married in Las Vegas, or where on the map Kurt's home could actually exist, this will not be the book for you.

But if you want to read about two broken men who fall sweetly in love ... by accident ... and you feel this story won't be harmful to your mental health—then keep going. This *is* the book for you.

Regardless of whether you keep going or stop here, thanks for checking out *Notorious*. This is the longest and most emotional book I've ever written, and I intend it for the people who don't feel seen. Who suffer from the harsh things they tell themselves, like "you aren't enough" or "you don't do enough" or "you can never be enough."

I see you. You are enough.

My love and best wishes to you all.

Love,

Leslie

P.S. This book includes many Easter eggs, including Johnny's therapist, who appears in my debut novel, *The Sun and the Moon* (M/F). With Johnny's story, things come full circle.

CHAPTER 1
Kurt

I'm dead.

Or maybe I'm about to die. That's a distinct possibility, too. One way or the other, I'm pretty sure I won't live to see the rest of today. Death has to be preferable to whatever invisible demon is rubbing sandpaper on my brain.

I attempt to open an eyelid, but it's crusted shut, so it takes me a moment to pry my lashes apart. I'll probably need a crowbar for the other eye.

My limited vision informs me that I'm in a dim but downright pleasant bedroom. It's grand, with modern chrome-and-white furnishings and a sitting room off to the side with a sleek but comfy-looking couch. Tall ceilings make the space airy and fresh. Although the curtains are drawn shut, daylight peeks through around the edges. An enormous bouquet of pink roses with a small white card poking out the top sits on a round table. My drool is decorating a fluffy white pillow with a seriously high thread count.

Using careful logic, I deduce I must be in a suite in a fancy hotel.

Then it dawns on me that I must still be on my trip to Las Vegas.

Problem is, this isn't my suite.

I manage to open my other eye so I can see more of the room. My cell phone is lying next to another one on a dresser by the TV. A plain black roller bag with jeans spilling out of it rests on the floor by a pair of well-used cowboy boots. A white cowboy hat is thrown on the couch.

Except for the cell, none of this stuff is mine. I don't own a cowboy hat or boots. My luggage is classic red T. Anthony.

What the actual hell happened?

Moving my bare arm wakes up more of my body, and a once-familiar horrible feeling comes over me. Bile starts in my stomach and rises up my esophagus, making me want to dry heave.

Ugh. A hangover. I haven't had one of these since college.

I hold still. Am I going to puke? I scan my body quickly. Stable. I think. I just feel like absolute crap. I need the bathroom, then to drink some water and take pain relief, and maybe I'll survive after all.

My rusty joints creak when I attempt to move again, but I manage to turn my head to the other side … and stop dead.

As I should've suspected, there's a man in my bed. Or, wait, I'm a man in *his* bed. Anyway, he's a very, very large man. His big frame takes up a significant portion of this king-size mattress. He's got light brown hair that's buzz-cut on the sides but longer and wavy on top, and I have a close-up view of his wide, buff shoulders and smooth back. His rounded muscles make me stare. The sheet has dipped down below his midsection, displaying an expanse of golden tan skin. By the way the linens are tangled around his hips, I'm guessing he's naked.

Come to think of it, now that I look down, *I'm* naked, too.

I freeze again and check my body for any aches down there.

Nope. Okay, then.

Who is he?

I'm trying to think of a way to find that out without waking him, when he turns and gives me a sleepy smile—or maybe it's a grimace.

I'm distracted from trying to analyze his expression by the awareness that I *know* him (or at least recognize him)—and in a rather intimate way. I've watched his videos more times than I can count.

I'm naked in bed with Velvet the Cowboy, my favorite porn star.

My skin tingles at the same time my stomach lurches, and I gulp and scold my belly, telling it to get itself under control. The curve of Velvet's ass is barely covered by the sheet, and his skin is just so ... touchable. My gaze moves to his messy hair and drowsy bedroom eyes, which are blinking rapidly.

Since this is a top-tier fantasy come true, I just wish: (1) I felt better, (2) I remembered how I met him, and (3) I remembered what we did.

If anything.

As he moved, the sheet slid farther down, so his famous—and quite large and hard—dick is now exposed, thwapping against his lower belly. My brain helpfully notices that he doesn't have any tan lines, and I briefly imagine him beside a pool, all stretched out—and nude. The man's just plain huge, with long legs, a defined torso, and burly arms. I'm 5'11". While I'm not tiny, he's a giant compared to me.

He flinches back slightly, and his eyebrows squish together. Then he narrows his eyes.

I'm still trying to figure out what happened. I'm ruling out any kind of sex, since there's no crusted come on my belly. My jaw's not even sore. The only ailments I have relate to this damn hangover.

That's disappointing.

Why am I here with him—and, more importantly, why are we naked, if we didn't do anything? Is this a practical joke?

It's sabotage.

A chill goes through me, followed by a wave of nausea that I can't blame on whatever I drank last night. Did Santangelo set me up? Are there hidden cameras in this suite? Or is it extortion?

Photos of me naked in bed with a porn star would be a sure way for me to end up in the tabloids and not in a Senate seat.

Or, *shit*. Did one of my *mom's* enemies set this up? That'd be even worse.

Tremors rack my body. Gasping for air, I scramble away from Velvet and fall backward out of the bed, taking the sheet with me and landing on my ass with a thud.

I look around for my self-respect, but I appear to have misplaced it.

Dammit.

Velvet pushes himself up, army crawls over on his belly, and peers down at me. A lock of his hair flops over his forehead.

Oh my god, is he *handsome*, even first thing in the morning. He has ... not quite a baby face, but close. Despite his chiseled jaw, high cheekbones, and narrow nose—and despite the very, *very* "adult" situations I've thoroughly enjoyed viewing him in—there's an element of innocence about him. Thick lashes rim his wide blue-green eyes. And then there's the rest of him. Hair dusts his veiny forearms, and his biceps bulge without him even trying. I've seen his physique on my screens often enough to know that he's beyond perfect. The way the videos show his ass in Wranglers? *Yum*. And when he dips that Stetson to greet people—before he fucks them into the mattress. I shiver.

I think he was wearing the hat last night.

I think he dipped it at me.

Velvet gazes at me with concern as he, too, appears to be putting the night together. At least, that's how I interpret the scrunch of his nose. His sleepy eyes register genuine bewilderment.

"Hey, darlin'," he whispers, his iconic voice deep, with a hint of a drawl. "Are you okay?" He rubs his temples.

"I ... don't know," I admit, drawing my knees to my chest and wrapping my hands around my calves. As I do, I notice something amiss. Well, something *else* amiss.

My naked companion nods, as if my words make perfect sense. "Yeah. Last night must've been wild, since I'm not entirely sure how I got back here." His eyes dart to his left hand, and he squints. "What in tarnation?" Then he looks at my hand at the same time I pull it up to my face to inspect it.

A ring circles the fourth finger. A shiny platinum band without any scratches or dings.

I don't wear a ring on that hand. I don't wear jewelry, period. I glance back at Velvet and confirm that he's got a ring on his fourth finger, too.

I blink.

He blinks.

I furrow my brow.

He does the same.

"Um," I rasp, staring at my ring, then gesturing to his. "Do you know where these came from?"

Velvet starts to shake his head and then frowns. A light dawns in his now fully awake eyes. He cocks his head as he studies his hand. He blows out his cheeks, then releases the air. "Well, heck," he says. "I think we might be hitched. What's your name again?"

CHAPTER 2
Johnny

THE NIGHT BEFORE

I take a slow, steady breath and put my hand on the doorknob. Am I gonna go with plan A or plan B?

Plan A means I make it through this event here, then go back up to my hotel suite to do the deed. I've explained everything to my fans in a video that'll go live tomorrow. Plan A has a certain poetry to it, what with this evening's award. Plus, most importantly, it'll get the job done: Mama will have what she needs.

With plan B, I get a little bit of payback along with taking care of Mama. Plan B's the pistol in the holster under my dinner jacket—and I haven't decided who's going to be on the receiving end of its bullets. I have to admit, Plan B has more flair. With plan B, they'll *really* be sorry.

Decisions, decisions. If only I could figure out who deserves it more—them or me?

Why not both?

With my mouth dry and my heart racing, I saunter into the

crowded dining room of the swanky Las Vegas hotel. I'm entering a den of my industry peers who are gathered, at least in part, in my honor. What a joke.

I'm a failure.

The noise level's about the same as a stampede of a couple hundred head of cattle, so everyone's shouting to be heard over the loud, sexy music and the other boisterous conversations.

My muscles tense as I wind my way around the circular dining tables covered with lavender tablecloths and fancy china. It's Saturday night. I'm wearing my best white cowboy hat, a rented tuxedo, and my favorite boots. I'm a lot taller than most folks, and the boots and hat make me taller still, so I stand out. More than a few conversations stutter when I lope past, but I'm used to everyone's eyes being on me.

Get a good look while you can, folks. One way or another, I'm finishing things. Tonight.

My chest tightens.

You'd think I'd be soaking it all in—the gaudy colors of my porn star peers' evening wear, the heady floral arrangements with decorative glass dildos as accents.

In reality, I've got tunnel vision. I've been that way ever since The Incident.

After tonight, though, I won't have to think about The Incident ever again, which is a second blessing on top of fixing my primary problem. *Not that I deserve any blessings.*

My mama's sweet voice tells me cryin' about the past wastes good tears. She's right. And I've wasted plenty.

Enough's enough.

That sad violin is playing in my head. Its plaintive, ripping-out-my-heart sound haunts me, like always. Instructing me to do more, fix things for her. The violin's been overwhelmingly loud lately, but it'll be silent soon enough.

My stomach's tight, and my jaw hurts from clenching it. I need to make my way toward my table at the front with the other honorees, but that means passing by a lot of people I'd rather not talk to. I draw in another heavy breath, let it out, then nod at the folks I like and ignore the ones I don't. I'm doing my best not to glare, but I'm not sure I'm succeeding.

As Mama always says, we can disagree, but we needn't be disagreeable about it.

At the opposite end of the ballroom, I spot the last person I'd ever want to see. Gary Pinkerton sneers at me and deliberately turns his back. Nausea hits me again. I need to get the heck outta here.

But that would mean they got the best of me, so I grind my teeth and rub my wrists.

They're not bound. I'm okay.

Well, I'm not okay. I'm sure a vein in my neck is popping. I make a fist, and my fingers itch to pull the trigger.

I've never been a particularly violent man, but there's an exception to everything, and he's the one who gets my blood boiling. I have enough presence of mind to hold my horses, though.

Which is more important, Johnny, saving her ... or vengeance?

She *can't* die. Vengeance may be just a fantasy on my part.

Plan A it is, then.

A tiny whirlwind of energy invades my space. "Velvet!" Tawni flings her arms around my waist, knocking me out of my thoughts. I'm way too tall for her, so she can't reach my neck too well. She and I don't do scenes together, since I don't fuck women, but our paths have crossed more than once, and she's a real sweetheart, which is rare in this predatory industry. Raven black hair, dark brown eyes, pretty face. She's got a great smile. I'm gonna miss it.

Gonna miss *her*.

"Hey, darlin'." I side hug her and brush a kiss to the top of her glossy head.

"Congrats on your award!" she gushes.

"Thank you, thank you." I have to make an effort to get my lips to work but give her a crooked grin. *When did I last smile?*

Before The Incident.

Tawni pokes my chest teasingly. "I havta say, getting a *lifetime* achievement award, Johnny? You're not *that* old."

I hook my thumbs in my pants pockets. "No, I ain't."

"How old are you, anyway?" she asks, twirling a lock of her long hair.

I tell her.

"That's my point!"

"You're too kind," I say, scratching the back of my neck.

"Aww, no. *You're* kind. You're actually *the best*." Someone calls out her name, and she turns to them and waves. Then she turns back to me and chirps, "Congrats, babe! Love you," and squeezes me again before zipping off to go squeal at someone else before I can say it back. Damn adorable woman.

She managed to distract me from my dark mood, but it returns like the tide. I smooth down my jacket and bite down on my bottom lip. *Get through this.*

Ace Dalton, my agent, approaches and shakes my hand. "Congratulations, Johnny. This is a big night for you!"

"Yeah, thanks, Ace. Appreciate it."

"Did you get the flowers I sent?"

"I sure did. Thank you much." He sent a bouquet of pink roses along with a generic note, likely dictated by his assistant. The thought counts, I guess.

"You doing okay? Seems you've been down in the dumps."

I keep myself from barking out a laugh. Dumps? The dumps look like paradise from where I am. "Yeah, okay, I guess."

Ace gives me a hard look. "Your mom okay?"

Fuck. "Dialysis sucks. Takes away her quality of life something fierce. She's ... going to be better."

"Oh? You get some good news?"

"No, but any day now," I say. *If I have anything to say about it.* "I'm sure she'll get a transplant."

"I'm pulling for her. And for you, of course. I've been shopping you around," he says, "but no luck so far."

"Well, thank you."

"Stay camera ready. We'll find you a new project soon enough." He opens his mouth to say something else, but the emcee gets up and asks us to take our seats. I heave out a breath of relief. I timed getting to this event perfectly and managed to miss having to mingle too much.

I'm seated with nine other honorees at a highlighted front table. We're served a salad, some kind of chicken with vegetables, and fancy-shaped potatoes, but I don't eat much. My nerves are too jangly.

They start the award presentations during dessert. Since mine will be last, I have plenty of time to consider what I'm going to say. This is my final chance to open my mouth and tell these people what I think of them. My lawyers told me to keep my mouth shut, but I have to give a speech of some kind or another.

Ideas war inside my head. Do I simply say thank you and zip my lip? Do I tell them exactly how rotten some of them are? Or do I take this opportunity to make things better and share my ideas to improve the industry?

Well, I hope it'd be making things better. Heck, maybe I'd make them worse if I opened my trap.

I'm a damn disappointment.

When it's my turn, jitters go through me like a tornado through a trailer park.

The emcee has slick black hair and is wearing a shiny silver tuxedo. "Our final honoree is someone who needs no introduction, but I'm going to do it anyway," he says. "A pioneer in many different online formats, he's starred in films for the past seventeen years and has among the most streaming views of all male entertainers. He's hot and popular, and the fans voted him to receive our highest honor, a lifetime achievement award. Please join me and put your hands together for Velvet the Cowboy." He gestures toward me with an open palm, as if to say "Ta-da!"

Finding my smile and pasting it on, I rise and wave at the crowd. While people at a few tables, including the one that I'm at, are giving me a standing ovation, some in the back and on the sides have dour expressions, arms crossed over their chests.

Well, I don't want or need their approval, and after tonight I'll never have to see them again.

I don't deserve an ovation.

I climb the stairs to the stage, legs trembling and boots heavy, receive the heavy clear acrylic award, and shake the emcee's hand. Then I step up to the microphone and clear my throat. Tawni's looking at me expectantly, and a few other friends in the audience shoot me encouraging smiles, unlike the bastard—bastards—glowering in the back. "Thank y'all very kindly," I say. "I'd especially like to thank the fans for this award. It means a lot to me that y'all appreciated my body of work."

Say more. Say more, say what you really think, say it.

But my lawyers' admonitions echo in my ears. Danny put it bluntly: "Don't fuck up the case, Johnny."

So instead of telling the truth about the people in this room who deserve to be called out, I pivot. "With this award, I'm announcing my retirement."

There's a collective gasp. Tawni's hand flies to her mouth. Ace's eyes protrude like a cartoon character's, and his face reddens. I probably should've mentioned that to him first. A little late now.

I can never do anything right.

I stand there awkwardly for another moment. I've got nothing else to say that isn't skewering all the people not clapping. So I tip my hat, give them my best smirk, and say, "I thank you again for the recognition. Now, if you'll 'scuse me, I'm going to go do something else tonight. Good night, and"—my voice cracks—"goodbye."

Award in hand, I flee the stage, exiting out the closest double doors, hearing a low but rising rumble of voices at my back.

When I step into the hallway, my nostrils flare and I sweep my arms out wide, almost hitting a trash can with the award. I want to punch something. Or kick something.

I don't.

It's time for plan A.

I take the elevator to my suite and drop the award in my bag. Then I sit down and write a note on the hotel's stationery.

When I get halfway down the page, I reread it.

Dear Mama,

I'm sorry you've been sick and I haven't been able to help you get better. That's the one thing I've tried to do right in my life—get you healthy. Maybe this time, I can succeed.

Please take the life insurance money and get the kidney. That's what I want most. You have to get better.

You've taught me all the good things. The bad things were all on me.

Should I say more? Or less?

I'm not a poet. I scribble:

I love you and May Ella. Thank you for all you've done for me.
Love,
Johnny

I put the note in an envelope, seal it up and write her name and address on the outside, and set it in my luggage.

Then I stare at the bathroom door, knowing what's waiting for me inside. Pills to dull the pain. The gun'll finish the job.

Mayyybee I need some liquid courage to get me started.

I keep the tux on. Might as well get my money's worth on the rental. I go downstairs, walk quickly through the lobby, and leave my own hotel, with its numerous bars. I wanna avoid seeing anyone from the ceremony. Wanna avoid answering questions about my retirement. Or anything else.

The casino across the way is quieter than the one I came from, and the first watering hole inside is upscale, with a restrained interior for Vegas—soft lighting, fresh flowers, black leather seats—and a few spaces at the bar. I park my ass in one of the seats and wait for the bartender, who's busy with a couple at the end.

She comes over to me and asks, "What'll it be?" as she sets down a thick paper coaster.

"What do you suggest for someone who's just hammered the final nail into the coffin of their career?"

She gives me a sympathetic smile. "I'll get you a triple shot of whiskey."

"Sounds good." I watch her pour the drink and keep a careful eye on it as it goes from her side of the bar to mine.

I give her my debit card, open a tab, then down the liquor.

I'm gonna need all the help I can to make it through the rest of my evening.

The last one of my life.

CHAPTER 3

Kurt

You want to do this, I tell myself for the seventh time in the past ten minutes. *This is a way to help people. Think of all the lives you're going to make better. You're going to effect positive change in the world.*

Although if I have to keep reminding myself why I'm going through this crap, it may not be exactly true that becoming a politician is meant to be my life's work.

Better than not having any purpose.

Better than doing nothing when I should've done something. *Maybe this time I won't be too late.*

I'm standing in one of the ballrooms of the Las Vegas hotel I'm staying in. A string quartet in the corner plays classical music. Given how dressed up everyone is, the exuberant flower arrangements, and the empty dance floor, it's like a very weird wedding—one that costs $20,000 a plate and where a silent auction offers the use of a staffed yacht for a week and rare bottles of wine.

These people live so far above upper middle class, they've forgotten what it's like to lack anything. *Remember your roots, Kurt.*

I need to remember more than that, since I've forgotten the

name of my companion. She's a potential donor at this fundraiser run by an LGBTQIA+ super PAC that's giving major funding boosts to various campaigns in the upcoming elections. But it's a popularity contest.

I smile at the short-haired woman and say, "Still. I can't stand by while more and more of this homophobic, transphobic, misogynistic, racist, xenophobic, ageist, ableist, anti-immigrant, classist ... okay, I could go on, but let's sum it up as political *bullshit* ... keeps happening, threatening people who don't deserve to be threatened."

"I agree," she says. "That's honorable."

"I know I'm ... not favored, because going up against an incumbent is always a long shot. Even with the top-two system, I'll be lucky to make it past the primary. But I don't think Santangelo is doing enough, and maybe I'm an incurable optimist. I just feel like someone could do much better than him, and it might as well be me. He's been at this for thirty years. He should give someone else a shot."

"Do you think you have a chance?"

I shrug and give her my winningest grin. "While I've never run before, I'm passionate about the political process and current events, and I've been developing a plan for once I'm in office. Plus, I mean, I'm electable. No skeletons in my closet."

At least none that anyone could ever find.

A lump forms in my throat, but I swallow it down.

"I'm sure your political connections will help you," she says.

"They definitely will," I say. "Gotta use every advantage." My momther's the lieutenant governor, with all the Sacramento connections I could ever want. (Not "monster," as the autocorrect on my phone wants, but "momther." I came up with that in my late teens, and it's stuck. Most of the time, she's not distant enough to be "mother" nor is she cozy enough for "mom," so "momther" is my solution.)

"I wish you luck," my companion says. She shakes my hand

and walks off, leaving me standing alone, surrounded by people I don't know. What should I do next?

I need money for ads and posters and signs and office space and mailings and all the other shit involved in running for office, and it doesn't seem great to self-fund my campaign, even though I could. I'd like to have outside support to validate my choice of running for office. Is that too much to ask?

I hadn't reckoned with all the stresses of the campaign, though. My brain's so full, I almost can't deal with life. Nonstop events, ceaseless self-promotion. I'm tired, and, as I look around at everyone else having a fucking fantastic time at this event, I want to throw up my hands in frustration.

Approaching people at political events and charming them was so much easier when I had Sam by my side.

I adjust the bow tie of my classic black tuxedo and approach a group of snazzily dressed men who appear to be in their forties and fifties. They're standing near my seat, which is my ready excuse, but I believe they're all potential donors.

"I'm Kurt Delmont," I say, shaking the hand of the first man, who's wearing a skintight dark green plaid tuxedo. "I'm running for the US Senate in California. Love the suit."

"Thanks, isn't it fab? And it's nice to meet you." He tells me his name, the names of his companions, and that they're all techies from the Bay Area. Despite my best efforts, I immediately forget every one of their names. I have to work on that, or I'll never be a good politician. "The Senate's ambitious."

I nod. "Yes, but I'm from an ambitious family. My momth—er—mother is Melissa Delmont."

They all say, "Ahh," in recognition, since she's got her sights on the White House. That election is still a couple of years away, but the various potential nominees are jockeying for position. Meanwhile, I've got a primary in March.

"And how is Melissa?" asks a man in a burgundy paisley tux

jacket. I bristle, because using her first name makes it seem like he knows her, but I'm sure he doesn't.

"She's good. Sixteen points ahead, last I heard."

"Great. She'll be a breath of fresh air if she can make it to DC," another one says. He's wearing a gold vest under a black tux. "She'll be supportive of gay rights, I presume."

"Yep," I say. "Fighting for the cause is one of the main points in her platform. All those PSAs from a few years ago were her idea. I went along with it, though it's a bit embarrassing now."

"Oh yeah, I remember seeing those posters on BART," green plaid tuxedo says. "You and your boyfriend. Or … ex?"

"Ex." I hide my wince, because the story's complicated. Sam Stone, the other guy in the photos, and I were never actually going out. As far as the public's concerned, though, Sam dumped me for Julian Hill, one of the biggest pop stars on the planet.

"So sorry Sam broke up with you," burgundy paisley says, again as if he knows Sam. I need to get used to this familiarity people assume with us. Sometimes I forget that I'm already something of a public figure—and many of the people I spend time with definitely are.

I chuckle, but it likely sounds strained, since this is the fourth time I've had to explain the circumstances tonight alone. Although, to be fair, this time I brought it up. "Well, if I'm gonna be dumped, at least it was for someone like Jules."

I wasn't dumped. We weren't together. I am datable. Dammit.

Not everyone kills himself after being with me. Sometimes they just find the love of their life.

I can't say any of that, though, so I shrug as gold vest says, "I'd do anything just to be in the same room as Julian Hill."

"He's pretty hot," I agree. While it's true, my nose wrinkles as I say it, because this conversation feels so superficial. I'm much more interested in talking about the real issues: fighting to take back rights that are being eroded and ensuring they won't be jeopardized again. Entertainment gossip isn't interesting. "He's been instrumental in some important charitable work," I say, attempting to bring the discussion around to the things I care about, and for a moment they play along.

"I'd heard about that. All the more reason to love him. So, why are you running?" asks green plaid.

"I thought we'd made strides, but every time we accomplish something, some hate group comes out of the woodwork to tear it down. I'm sick of it. So I'm going to do something about it."

They nod. We talk for a bit longer, but they're clearly bored with me, so I excuse myself and move on.

This event is like speed dating, without the goal of taking someone home. I do my best to stay focused, but with all the people I've met and hands I've shaken, I'm exhausted. My brain's overfull of things to do.

Worse, at the end of the night, I'm not announced as one of those who've secured major funding grants.

My brain says, "You're a failure. You're an impostor."

I tell my brain to fuck off and decide I need a drink, and fast.

As I'm leaving the ballroom (more slowly than I'd like, thanks to the crowd), my phone buzzes with a text from my momther asking how things are going, but I'm not interested in licking my wounds with her right now. I text back that I'm going to call it quits for the night and regroup when I get home tomorrow.

Shoving my phone into my pocket, I make my way to the only empty seat I spot at the nearest bar. It's right between the wall and a big, muscled cowboy in a dusky blue tuxedo. He's staring into his glass, so I don't really look at him. Even though I want to, because he's hot. But someone wearing a Stetson at a bar is likely straight. No?

I take the stool next to him and order a martini.

That's my first mistake ... er, *choice*. Whatever. I don't usually drink martinis, and I'm really not cool enough for hard liquor. I can handle beer and wine, but the bitter taste of some of those harsher drinks just isn't for me.

But the past few hours have sucked, and I want to forget the super PAC representative announcing all the names of the people who did get their backing. Sulking because I'm not as popular as the other kids is pointless and foolish, but it feels horrible to be told that you're not good enough in someone else's eyes, no matter the context.

My drink comes: cold, clear, slightly oily, and with two fat green olives on a stick. I sip the martini, pretending I'm James Bond but trying not to grimace. I end up downing it, then chasing it with a few nuts from a dish the bartender sets before me.

The bartender asks me if I want another, and I say yes, and after that, everything becomes looser. That's better.

The cowboy up-nods the bartender, who brings another whiskey—a big one—without him saying anything. She places it in front of him, and he puts his hand over the glass, half covering the top, but doesn't pick it up.

"How did she know your order?" I ask, which is a goofy question, because she must've brought him the same as what he had before. But it's an excuse to talk to the cowboy. I've always liked cowboys.

"I've been sittin' here drinkin' a li'l while," he slurs, his voice deep and guttural—and familiar. "And she's plenty smart."

Okay, that voice is *really* familiar, and I turn to face him and gasp. "Oh my god, you're ..."

I get the full effect of the smirk he's famous for, though his blue-green eyes are bloodshot. "I'm who, precious?"

"Velvet," I whisper. "The Cowboy."

The guy whose confidence on screen lights me up.

Whose deep voice and sexy drawl encourage the men he's fucking to give themselves over to him.

Whose intense eye contact makes me wish I were one of those

guys—being wrapped up in his gaze like it's a net when he murmurs "I got you" and "Come for me."

Who kisses like he needs someone else's lips to breathe.

This is *that* Velvet the Cowboy. In other words, the man of my dreams. My body's lit up just from being this near to him.

Velvet nods, and he's pretty loaded, because he seems to be having trouble focusing on my face. "You are correct." He picks up his glass and clinks it against mine. "Nice to meet you."

"Are you here by yourself?" I blurt.

"Well, yessir. I've heard tell you should never drink unless you're alone or with someone."

I snort. "Okay. I mean, I'm alone. Or, I guess I'm with you now."

Shut up, brain. Shut up.

"That you are," Velvet says. "Are you from the good town of Las Vegas?"

"No. I'm here for an event."

Velvet nods, lips pressed together. "So am I."

"I hope you were more successful at yours than I was at mine," I mutter.

"Got a lifetime achievement award."

"Well, then yes, you were." I hold up my glass, and we clink again. "Congrats."

He downs his shot and sets the glass on the bar. "Thanks," he says in a flat tone. He stares down at his empty hands.

I want to hug him, but that doesn't make sense. "What are your plans tonight?" I ask.

Velvet takes a really long time to answer my question. Did he not hear me? Before I try repeating myself, he lifts his head and gazes at me. "I s'pose right now, my only plan is to have a drink with you."

"That sounds perfect," I say, all warm inside—from the alcohol and from his words. My breath quickens, and something shifts near my heart.

"Yours? I mean, what are your plans?" he asks.

I snort. "Plans? None. I'm drowning my sorrows."

"They swim," Velvet says absently.

"Sorry?" It's not that loud in here, but I didn't understand what he said.

He gestures at his glass. "You can't drown sorrows. They swim."

Now I laugh for real, because he's right. "That's one of the wisest things I've ever heard. Sorrows most definitely swim, even when you try to drown them."

"Yep."

Images of all of the scenes I've watched this man in interrupt my brain's processing. His dick is *large*. While porn stars don't have to be enormous, he is, and seeing guys take it ... My ass clenches in sympathy. I stealthily look at his crotch, and I feel my face get red. Or maybe it's the drink making me flush. I'm extremely aware of my own heartbeat, and the hair's rising on my arms and nape, despite the fact that the bar's kept at a pleasant temperature.

"It's just really surreal that I'm sitting next to you," I blurt. I'm definitely feeling the martinis. "I mean—"

Velvet turns to face me, his long legs widening so he's kind of straddling me, and I check him out—up and down, my fingers tingling with the need to touch him.

Damn, he's hot—broad shoulders in the tailored western-style tuxedo jacket. Muscular thighs stretching the fabric of his slacks. Intense eyes. The only thing bothering me is how gloomy he looks.

Maybe I can cheer him up.

"I take it you've seen my work?" Velvet asks.

"I'll say," I mutter. Then, louder, "Yes. I'm a fan. Is Velvet your real name?"

He smiles, and it's the first real smile I've gotten from him. Then he tips his hat. "No, 'course not. My mama named me John, but most everyone calls me Johnny." He holds out his hand. "Johnny Haskell. Nice to meet you."

I shake his hand. It's firm and makes me crave his touch even more. "I'm Kurt. I've shaken a lot of hands tonight, but yours is the first I actually wanted to."

"Well, then, precious. That's an honor. Can I buy you another drink?"

CHAPTER 4

Johnny

When the cute man sits down next to me, he looks familiar, but I can't immediately tell from where. So I take a second peep at him.

He's got boy-next-door good looks, and even in my inebriated haze, I can tell he's something special. There's this aura about him —like he's going places and determined to get there no matter what. Though something's happened to make his shoulders hunch. And I still don't know who he is.

"You say your name's Kurt?"

He nods. "Yeah. Kurt Delmont."

Ah. The light goes on, and I connect at least some of the dots, because Delmont's a big political name in California, where I live, and Kurt's handsome face used to be on promotional billboards and posters all over for LGBTQIA+ awareness and advocacy. Always thought he was cute.

Just my luck to have a politician join me. I don't have much use for politicians. They seem like vipers to me, waiting to strike after their next election.

Not that literal vipers get elected, but you get my drift. I don't trust 'em. Not since what they did to my mama, making the rules the insurance companies used to deny her transplant.

That's gonna get fixed, though. I'm gonna fix it.

But I'm feeling off-kilter, since this is my last night on earth, and he's amusing me. There's nothing saying I can't have some fun before I check out, and Kurt's exactly my type. Boy next door, yes, but with soulful brown eyes that have seen more than they let on. I like how he's not small or delicate. He's not as tall as me, but he's, I don't know, lean but solid. Average size, but his looks are way above average. Dark hair that's stylishly trimmed but intentionally messy on top. Spectacular, actually. Looks a bit like that one guy on the historical romance show on Netflix, only without the breeches.

I'm lightheaded, though I'm not sure if it's from the whiskey or Kurt. My eyes dart over to him again, and the shiver that goes through my body is more pleasure than I've felt in months.

Him. It's him.

I want to erase the distance between us, which is ridiculous, since I just met him.

When we're both done with our fresh round of drinks, we look at each other. "Another?" he asks. "Or do you want to go for a walk?"

"Walk sounds mighty fine," I drawl, and signal the bartender. Kurt pulls out his wallet, too, but I tell him, "I got it." I have a little bit left, so I might as well spend it on him.

I *want* to spend it on him. I'm flooded with warmth as I check him out, with his snappy tuxedo and pretty-boy face.

He looks at me for a moment, then swallows and nods. "Thank you," he says quietly.

We walk out of the bar shoulder to shoulder, out onto the Las Vegas Strip.

It's a cold October night, and the desert doesn't hold the heat this time of year. That doesn't stop people from wearing very little.

We don't get far before we see showgirls in G-strings and pasties, their huge feather headdresses and lack of clothing attracting all kinds of attention.

"You ever seen a show like that?" I ask, indicating them with a nod.

Kurt shakes his head. "Not too interested in ..." He trails off, waving his hand vaguely. I get distracted by that hand. What would it feel like on me?

"Women?" I ask.

"Yeah. I've got plenty of female friends, and I love them. But I don't wanna stick my dick in one. Just men. And with them, I prefer to be on the bottom."

I laugh for real, because Kurt has good manners and looks polished. Hearing him say something so crass hits my funny bone.

Also, okay. Saliva floods my mouth as I picture him spread out naked before me. My toppy self's even more interested in him.

"What about a male strip show?" I ask. "Ever been curious about one of those?"

He shrugs. "I dunno. Those kind of things feel fake to me. Like people are just doing it for the money. If someone ever performed like that for me, I'd want it to be because they like me. Not because of my wallet. But maybe I'm too much of a stick-in-the-mud."

I wanna move closer to him. "Sticks in the mud are okay in my book."

"And I realize I'm being hypocritical, because I say that and yet you should see the amount of porn subscriptions I have," he says. Then his eyes widen.

"No judgment from me on that," I say, holding my hands up. "For obvious reasons."

Kurt smiles, and it relaxes something inside me. The violins get a little quieter.

Since he sat down next to me at the bar, I haven't been berating myself. Instead, I've been interested in figuring him out. So I'm grateful for the distraction.

Even if I don't deserve it.

Anywhere but in Vegas, two men in tuxedos—me especially tall and in my cowboy hat—out together would be quite the sight. Here, we blend in with the bachelorette parties and college benders going on all over the place.

Supercars stuck in traffic rev their engines as we keep walking, listening to a busker play the saxophone and watching people hand out cards to the closest brothel.

One offers me a card, but I thank him politely and decline. "Not so interested in women, I hope y'all don't mind." I take Kurt's hand and squeeze it for emphasis.

A zap of electricity passes through us at the connection point. *Damn.*

Kurt looks down at our joined hands and doesn't pull away. The promoter doesn't miss a beat, saying, "We've got men, too."

"Thanks anyway," I say, and tip my hat, keeping hold of Kurt.

We don't get far before we have to stop and talk with a woman walking a German shepherd puppy with a leather collar. Or, well, maybe I'm the one who has to stop for every good dog—which is all of them. After getting the owner's permission, I crouch down and scratch the puppy behind the ears. "You're such a good ... girl?"—I look up at the lady, and she nods—"... good girl, aren't you?" The puppy licks my hand, and a true chuckle escapes me.

"I swear that dog is smiling at you," Kurt says, a hand over his mouth as he tries to hide a grin.

"Dogs are good for what ails ya," I say and thank the lady for letting me say hi. Then I take Kurt's hand again—and feel another frisson of energy pass between us.

Kurt and I walk inside the next casino we reach and are assaulted by all the noise from slot machines and craps tables packed with people trying to win. With alcohol still coursing through my veins, the scene is blurry but manageable.

"Fascinating. All these folks trying to get one up on the house, even though the odds are stacked against them," I murmur into Kurt's ear, and he shivers as my lips brush his skin.

That's even more fascinating.

"Vegas is powered by unfounded optimism," Kurt says, looking around. Scantily dressed people wearing lots of sparkles sit next to people wearing sweats and T-shirts who might've been in their seats for a week.

"That's a good observation," I say. "But is there such a thing as founded optimism? Or—sorry, I'm drunk. I mean, justifiable optimism. Is it ever justified to be optimistic?"

"I think if we aren't optimistic, we'll die," Kurt says. "At some level, when things aren't going right, we have to believe that they can get better."

Well, shit. That's where he loses me. Because I *don't* think things can get better with me around. Or rather, they can only get better if my mama gets my life insurance, which by definition means I've gotta go.

Good riddance to me, anyway.

But my venomous thoughts won't stop me from having a final night of fun with him. He's too cute for words, even if we don't agree on the optimism question.

I don't have to agree with him to spend a few hours with him. To hold his hand.

Maybe I want a little comfort before I end things. Maybe I need *him*, specifically.

"Wanna keep hanging out?" I blurt. "But maybe get out of here and go downtown? I like downtown better than the Strip. Downtown feels funkier. Less ... fancy. More real. I dunno."

"Sure," Kurt says with a smile. "I didn't have any plans. I'm not here with friends or anything. I was just going to go back to my hotel room and lick my wounds."

I consider asking if I can join him in his hotel room to help with the licking—but while I was at that bar longer than he was, it's clear he's feeling the booze, too. Sleeping with someone who's intoxicated is my hard limit. After all the shit I've been through, I'd be the biggest hypocrite if I weren't absolutely scrupulous about consent.

I'm not opposed to kissing or being affectionate while intoxicated. I'm not a saint. But beyond that? Getting naked? Hell no. That's where I draw the line.

Hanging with Kurt fully clothed sounds like the best idea ever, though. "Then let's go," I say easily.

My blood heats in my veins at the prospect of getting more time with him. He's as pretty as they come, and while I've spent lots of time with hot guys on set—and I'm not a fan of politicians, as I said—there's something about Kurt that draws me to him. Maybe it's the furtive way I spy him looking at me. As if he doesn't want me to catch him at it. It's cuter than a newborn colt.

And the way he listens to me—he gives me all his attention. I don't think it's the martinis, either. He just seems to be a good listener. Like if you tell him something, he'll remember it for the rest of his days.

I admire his optimism, too. I've lost that like a white rabbit in a snowstorm, but he's making me remember that some people still have ideals. So even if I don't have hope, I can leave this world to folks who'll take better care of it than I have.

Kurt interrupts my thoughts by pulling out his phone. "Let me order a Lyft," he says, and a few minutes later, we're climbing into the back of a Nissan Pathfinder driven by Nadine and hurtling toward downtown.

As we speed away from the Strip's superhigh buildings, throngs of people, and dizzying amounts of lights, Kurt sits near me and doesn't bother with a seatbelt, so I sling an arm around his shoulders. I like the way he feels next to me, and I like the way he smells—faintly of expensive cologne. I'm getting preoccupied by his scent and the way he's curled up against me, and I briefly fantasize about stripping off his clothes. With my teeth.

This isn't the way I planned tonight going, but I can delay my plans a tad. He's too fascinating to let go. As long as I take the pills before the video goes live tomorrow, I'm good.

Well, I'm never gonna be *good*. That horse is outta the stable. But it'll do the trick.

As I tug him to me, he moves his butt closer, then stiffens and looks at me quizzically, drawing back. "Is that ..." he asks in a loud whisper, running a finger along the holstered gun under my armpit.

"Cowboy," I say, pointing a thumb at my chest. "Don't worry, darlin'. It'll stay put."

With a serious expression on his drunken face, Kurt nods. "It goes with your hat and boots."

"It does, precious." I squeeze him tight. Everything fades except him as he cuddles into me.

The driver stops at the edge of the Fremont Street pedestrian area. Kurt and I thank her, get out, and head over to watch a cover band that's playing Led Zeppelin. Not my style of music, but it's pleasant enough for a few minutes.

There are so many people hanging out, it's hard to move, but I again hold on to Kurt's hand. Girls in sparkly dresses and guys dressed up in suits (or in gold lamé shorts) make it so, again, we don't stick out too much in our tuxedos, even though this part of town is definitely less fancy. And while walking around in this getup makes me feel like we escaped from a wedding, it seems that's what a lot of people come to Vegas for, judging by the number of "I'm the Bride!" sashes we see on women walking by.

We make our way through the crowd to an open area, and then Kurt stands up on his tiptoes, his lips brushing against my ear.

I want to turn and kiss him, but I don't know if that's what he wants. Although I'm pretty sure he's attracted to me, based on his reaction when we first met. Still, I can wait and see if the time is right.

Apparently it isn't, because he says, "Stay right here," and lets go of my hand. It oddly aches at the loss.

A few moments later, Kurt returns with two plastic cups of something that looks alcoholic and fruity. Given my past, I should be suspicious of him handing me a drink, but it's too hard to go through life and not trust people at all. Kurt's not giving me any vibes that I shouldn't trust him. While, yes, he's a politician, he hasn't said anything that makes me think he's using me for anything.

But I gotta be smart. "I'm tryin' to remember the rules for drinking," I say as a means to stall and see whether he drinks his. "It's been a while since I've really had a night out. Liquor before beer, never fear? Is that it?"

"Yep. Beer before liquor, never sicker." He clinks my glass. "Since we're sticking to hard alcohol, we're good, right? This has, I think, vodka? Not sure."

"Did we get the same thing? Wanna try mine?" I hold it out to him.

He takes a sip of it and says, "They're the same."

I relax and down the drink, then tug on his hand when he's finished with his. "C'mon. Let me get you another one."

But as we head over to where he bought the drinks, I catch sight of a bar with men wearing G-strings dancing on the tabletops. Lady Gaga thumps loudly from the speakers, and rainbow flags fly on every possible surface. It's gaudy as hell, but if it isn't Vegas, I don't know what is.

"Wanna go in there?" I whisper in Kurt's ear, and he lets out a little breathy noise.

Lord, he's responsive. He'd be fun to play with.

Sober.

"Abso-fucking-lutely," he says. "Lead the way."

We walk up to the bar and show our IDs to the bouncer, who tells us there's a two-drink minimum. After paying and entering, we order our two drinks, and I go find the bathroom while Kurt locates a booth for us. When I come back, I cuddle in next to him, getting another hit of his delicious scent as waiters in half shirts and booty shorts swish by with trays laden with tons of drinks. It's loud and fun ... and distracting.

This night's going very differently than I expected. Not sure what I think about that.

But for a moment, the violins are silent.

CHAPTER 5
Kurt

Tonight's so fucking surreal. It started with me (badly) wooing donors for my political campaign, and now I'm curled up in a semicircular Naugahyde booth with my absolute favorite porn star.

Who's so much more than that. He's charming and sweet. While he has undeniable sex appeal—that face, that height, how muscular he is—that's not what's most attractive about him. Plenty of people are good-looking. He's got something inside that pulls me to him like a magnet. I succumbed to his siren call when I watched him on-screen, but in person he's irresistible and overwhelming.

He feels a little dangerous, too. He's carrying a gun, but I'm not nervous about it. I think it's just part of his cowboy persona—hat, boots, gun, drawl.

Velvet's—er, *Johnny's*—strong arm is flung over my shoulders, holding me securely to his side like he doesn't want anyone here to think I'm available. Fine by me. A thrill passes through me at how easily he claims me.

I snuggle into him, noticing his thick thighs against mine, the bulge under his fly, his flat stomach. His left hand toys with a drink, while every once in a while the fingers of his right trace circles on my shoulder or bicep. His hat sits on the seat next to him, and when he talks, his lips brush my skin, making me flush.

My nerve endings are going wild, wanting more, more, more. It doesn't help that we're surrounded by sex—gyrating hot men, guys kissing in booths, some really seductive dancing off to the side. None of it compares to the big guy I'm plastered to.

I think he likes me, too. He's leaning into me because this place is loud, but I *love* it. His tongue darts out to lick his lips, and it's distracting. He's holding me close, his touches lingering.

He's not trying anything, though, which is a bummer.

But we're sitting close to each other, and the solid warmth of his body feels like home on this cool night. Even though we're inside, the doors are all open—which is a good thing, because it'd be stifling otherwise.

"You're so damn hot," I blurt. The latest drinks are getting to me.

He grins, squeezing me to him. "So are you, precious."

I can't seem to stop my mouth from drunkenly asking, "Do you want to fuck me?"

Johnny's face gets serious, and he turns to face me more squarely. He runs a finger down my cheek. "Yeah." His voice gets husky. "I really do, but I have rules, and that means not fucking you when you're intoxicated."

A thrill passes through me at his admission. "I'm not that drunk. Am I? Okay, that's the alcohol talking, which probably proves your point. But you're just so ..." I shiver. "I want you so bad. What about a little bathroom blow job?" I whine.

"Nope." He says it with a smile, but he's firm. "Later, maybe. When the booze wears off." His deep voice drops even lower. "I want you, too."

"Fine," I grumble. But then I return his smile. "I do have to take a leak, though. I'll be just a sec."

He nods as I get out of the booth. On my way to the bathroom, I look over my shoulder, and his eyes are tracking me. Like he's got my back, even though I know he's gotta be as drunk as I am—he was slurring his words when I first met him.

When I return from the sticky, dark, but functional bathroom, a guy in booty shorts and a hot pink fishnet shirt is hovering over Johnny, who looks a bit uncomfortable. My blood heats with possessiveness that I shouldn't feel about a man I just met, until I realize the guy's asking for an autograph. Johnny signs a napkin with a polite smile as I sidle up beside him, and he immediately tugs me close.

"Thanks, Velvet!" the guy coos. "You're my favorite."

The fan takes off, and I ask, "How often do you get recognized?"

"In LA? Not that much, unless I'm in WeHo or Silver Lake. In a place like this? I'd bet more than 90 percent of them know who I am."

And sure enough, the dancer must've spread the news, because five minutes later, there's a line of people wanting to take photos with Velvet the Cowboy.

"Want to go to another bar?" I ask, after he poses for the tenth photo.

He nods. "Sorry 'bout this."

"No worries." I kiss his cheek. Then I halt. "Oh my god, I'm sorry. Is kissing part of your no-no list while drunk?"

Johnny gazes intently at me. "Kissing ain't on the naughty list. I just don't wanna do more while in-tox-i-cated." He says the word slowly like he's mulling it over.

I swallow hard, staring at his lips. Wondering what they would feel like on my skin. Wishing I could make the first move. "Good to know."

He slowly looks me up and down, checking me out as much as I'm checking him out. I hold my breath.

Finally, he nods. "Let's go."

"Come on." I get up from the booth and offer my palm, which he takes.

We set out together into the increasingly chilly night, and Johnny keeps his arm around my shoulders as we walk down the crowded downtown thoroughfare. People separate around us so we don't have to break apart.

Johnny's cowboy hat shields me from the wind as he cuddles his cheek against the top of my head, and I get a whiff of his delicious scent—like cloves and orange. Spicy and sweet.

This man. He's *real*. He's not just on my screen.

And he's with *me*. No one else. I pull my shoulders back and puff out my chest. "Where'd ya get the name Velvet?" I ask.

"Joel McCrea movie from the 1950s. It was the name of the bad guy in the movie, but I thought it was cool."

"It's *so* cool," I gush. "You have the coolest name. I've always thought it was special. I've always thought you were special."

The alcohol is making me blabber way more than I usually do. I'm not hating it, though—the freedom to say whatever the hell I mean for once.

After we stop at a sidewalk bar for two more shots each, the night starts getting very, very fuzzy.

I'm aware of lights—the kind on a dance floor. Strobe lights. Pink and yellow and blue and purple. I like Johnny's face in all of them, but when the clear white light is on him, he looks rugged and handsome, and I think about the way he gazes at men when he fucks them, and I wish that could be me. Lights from phones and people taking selfies with Velvet. I might be in some of them.

The soft fabric of his jacket against my cheek when we dance to a slow song. His rough hand in mine. The way I slip on ice from a discarded drink and he holds me up so I don't fall.

Bitter alcohol. I'm not even sure what I'm drinking anymore. Only that it keeps me going.

The odors of cologne, cigarettes, spilled drinks, vomit, and weed. The vapes smell sweet. But plenty of people still smoke weed the old-fashioned way, and at some point, someone hands me a blunt. I don't often indulge, but I take a hit, and it burns down my throat. Johnny does, too, and I'm mesmerized by the way his meaty chest expands as he inhales.

He blows out a plume of smoke and passes me back the blunt, and between us, we finish it off.

The night was already muzzy, but now it's tilted at a forty-five-degree angle. I'm not out of control, I tell myself. But the world doesn't look quite the same way that I'm used to, and I'm pretty sure I'm wrong about still being in control.

I'm holding Johnny's hand, and I like the way it looks and feels in mine. Since he's an actor, I'd have figured his hands would be soft, but they aren't at all. He has calluses. Maybe from working out? Because you don't get muscles like he has naturally.

Or do you? Maybe real cowboys do it roping cows or whatever.

"Are you a real cowboy?" I ask.

Johnny's lips brush against my temple as he murmurs, "Yes."

"It's not just a porn name, is it?"

"It's a porn name, but I'm really a cowboy," he assures me.

"How did you get these calluses? Roping horses?"

"Not anymore. I lift weights."

"Do you like horses?"

"I do," Johnny says. "Very much."

"Did you grow up on a farm?"

He stills. After a moment, he says, "Yes, till my mama couldn't work there no more. She was the cook for a big ranch."

He opens his mouth to maybe continue, but then he stops and doesn't go on.

And I suppose he doesn't have to. There's no reason why he needs to tell me his life story.

I open my mouth to say this. That he doesn't owe me anything, and that I'm sorry I pressed. That I can be pushy when I really want something.

That I really want *him*.

And somehow he leans down, and I reach up, and we're kissing. A drunken, high, sloppy kiss. While the world's fuzzy, this kiss is coming through loud and clear. My body's lighting up like it's one of those fireworks displays that goes off sequentially, the electricity sparking from where our lips meet down my spine and onward to my legs, my arms. I'm *alive*.

Our lips are magnetized, tongues reaching into each other's mouths, teeth clacking.

I grunt and wrap my arms around his neck, and he pulls me closer, holding my ass securely as our lips press together harder and our tongues dance more. I'm trying to climb him. To wrap my arms and legs around him. To be one with him.

He smells so damn good.

He kisses like a dream.

He tastes like weed and liquor, yes, but also like some kind of arousal drug. I want him.

I've always wanted him. When I watched him on the screen, I wanted him.

But now, in the middle of Fremont Street, with people and lights and noise and smoke and smells everywhere, my world narrows down to the freckle at the corner of his eye. The slight rasp of his stubble against my skin. His subtle cologne. His hot tongue inside my mouth. His bittersweet taste.

I fucking love it.

And the way his biceps squeeze me to him. The way his hands knead my ass cheeks. The way he sounds as he groans into my mouth.

I have just enough self-control to understand that I'm in public and shouldn't drop to my knees.

But I want to. I want to suck his cock. I want to see all of him.

He's so dominating right now. I want him to dominate me.

I want to fuck him and mess around with him and keep kissing him.

I've always liked the man he is on-screen.

I like him even more in person.

"We should go find a room," I murmur in his ear as he sucks on my neck. I'm getting so hard that if I were sober, I'd be embarrassed. But I'm not, so I'm not.

It's late.

We're drunk. Lights flash around us.

"Okay, darlin'. If that's what you want. But we're still not fucking when y'all are drunk. *We're ... we're* drunk." He's slurring, but it comes out firm.

I pout and put my hands on my hips. "Is this because you don't know me?"

"It's my rule. For everyone."

"Whoever has you for real," I say, "has a true treasure." I think about it. "So you're saying, even if I were yours, you wouldn't fuck me when I'm drunk?"

"Yep. I'd want you to remember all of it."

"I'll remember it," I insist. Even though minutes have slipped away tonight that I'm sure are lost forever. That I don't and won't remember. "What if we go back and sleep and then wake up and fuck?" I ask.

Because I want him so badly. I don't know when I'm ever going to have another chance to be with my hotter-than-the-sun crush. And he's just so sweet, besides.

"Yes, precious. That's okay." He yawns. "Sorry, darlin'. I was up early. Guess I'm a little tired. Wanna head back to the Strip?"

"Sure."

"Share a Lyft again?"

"Sure." I look around drunkenly. We can't get a car here. They aren't allowed in the pedestrian area. "We need to get to a place where they can pick us up. Then I'll order a ride."

We head in what I'm pretty sure is the right direction, but stop at a place selling shots and each take two more because the buzz is wearing off.

Then, when we're almost to the street, we pass a twenty-four-hour wedding chapel, its doors open and the wedding march playing loudly from speakers. A group of ten people walk out, and a happy couple is kissing on the steps.

"Oh my god," I whisper. "Look! We should do that!"

"Get married?" Johnny's eyes are wide as saucers, even though they're reddened by alcohol and smoke. "Why?"

"When in Vegas! Come on, Johnny Haskell. Marry me."

"Are you serious?"

I nod.

"Why?" Johnny asks.

"I like you. And we're in Vegas! We'll be married, and then we can have our wedding night, and you can fuck me anytime you like."

He widens his stance. "Darlin', I've fucked plenty of men without being married to any of them."

"But I want you to only fuck meeee," I slur.

His eyes latch onto mine. "You've never fucked me. What if I suck?"

"I hope you do suck," I say, and waggle my eyebrows, which makes him chuckle.

And he relents. "I guess, if this is the last night of my life, I might as well get hitched," he mutters, low but audible.

What does he mean? This isn't the last night of his life.

Maybe he's talking about living each day to the fullest, and all that, because you never know what'll happen.

I learned that lesson with Andrei.

What's he doing in my brain? No, drunk brain. No!

I don't know why I'm so insistent on us getting married. Except that I want to lasso Johnny. Strap him to me and keep him. I like being in his presence. I like the way he lights me up. I want to be with him.

It's not just *like* or *want*—it's an overwhelming *need*. I *need* this man. I *must* have him.

I walk triumphantly into the wedding chapel holding his hand. *Velvet the Cowboy is mine, motherfuckers.* Although, if I'm marrying him, I should only think of him as Johnny.

Johnny Haskell is mine, motherfuckers. That sounds better.

Inside, the chapel is ... okay. Chipped paint and white decor. Lots of silk flowers. It's fake nice. Not real nice.

But a wedding is an excellent idea. In fact, it's the best idea I've ever had.

People ask us questions. We answer them. We sign documents. We buy rings. I think I maybe pull out my credit card. Someone holds up a camera, and we smile.

And then we say, "I do."

We kiss, and it's as electric as the one earlier. Maybe more so, because I knew it was coming.

More photos.

And when we pile into a Lyft to go back to Johnny's hotel room, I almost immediately fall asleep in the car.

He's shaking me awake, and I'm stumbling out into the night.

An elevator door.

The lurch of the elevator moving.

The hallway holding me up.

Johnny's hand on mine.

He fumbles for a key and lets me into a room.

I take off my clothes.

And bed.

Bed looks very good.

I don't remember anything else.

CHAPTER 6
Johnny

It's the morning after I apparently got hitched, and I'm studying the man on my floor. The one I woke up lying next to.

"Um," he says. He's super cute and kind of familiar—familiar beyond whatever happened last night, that is. He also looks hungover, with a gray tinge to his skin, his hair rumpled, and his eyes red from booze. My fingers ache with the desire to touch him. Soothe him. Make him feel good. "I'm Kurt Delmont."

"That's right. Now I remember." I get this strange, swirly, sinking feeling in my stomach when I hold up my left hand again. "Do you think this is for real?" I try to not sound too disgusted. I don't want to offend the man. I don't even know him.

I do *want* him, though. I don't know how I know that, but I do.

I want him like a cold drink of water on a hot dusty day.

Flashes of the night before are coming back to me. How I started drinking at a bar and ended up partying with Kurt all night.

How he derailed my plans entirely.

Shoot. *Mama.*

"I have no idea what the hell happened," Kurt whispers. He

winces, his hand going to his head. "Sorry, I'm pretty damn hungover." He gets up, grabbing the sheet he took with him when he fell out of bed and wrapping it around his waist. It's fine with me if he wants to preserve his modesty, but I have no problems with nudity. Obviously.

Precious man. He's so cute. No wonder I wanted to keep him, if even for one night.

Guess I'm taking the "till death do us part" vow literally.

Kurt finds his tuxedo pants by the front door. After a moment's searching, he comes up with a pair of black boxer briefs and slips them on. I crawl out of bed, not bothering to cover up—although my morning wood's wishing us all a good day—so I can rustle up my own clothes.

I've got a feeling Kurt's fixed an eye—or both—on me but doesn't want to admit it. A small flame of pride flickers through me. Even though I make my living based on my looks and my body, I still like the validation.

Scratching his belly and yawning, Kurt pads over to the cluttered nightstand. His behind looks real pretty in his tight boxer briefs, and I stifle a groan. He doesn't need to know I'm perving on him.

I shuffle to my suitcase and find a pair of cutoff gray sweats under my award. I slip them on. I'll spare him from being confronted with my erection, which is the size of a spruce. My body can't help its attraction to him.

Truthfully, I'm happy my body's attracted to *anyone*. It's been pretty much broken since The Incident.

He turns to me. "You okay?"

"Yeah. Just feeling last night." While I have a headache from all the booze, I'm plenty awake now. I crack open a bottle of water and down it.

That's better.

Kurt tilts his head and fishes an official-looking piece of paper out from under my cell phone and wallet. He swallows hard and then glances at me. His morning stubble is flat-out gorgeous, and the hard angle of his jaw is so sexy, it could start bar fights. Possibly turf wars.

I join him and peer over his shoulder at the document, which says "CERTIFICATE OF MARRIAGE, CLARK COUNTY, NEVADA. This is to certify that John Huckleberry Haskell and Kurt Arden Delmont were united in marriage ..."

It looks pretty darn official.

"Shoot. We're really married?" I say in wonder, touching the blue signatures on the paper.

Kurt inhales sharply and turns toward me. His bare chest is broad, although not as broad as mine. He has soft-looking skin that's asking to be kissed and caressed. Heat radiates from him, and I'm attracted to it like a lizard to a sun-warmed rock. But I can keep my hands to myself.

Especially when my husband is a virtual stranger and his mind is very obviously racing. "Yeah. I think so. Shit. What happened?"

"I think I got very drunk," I say, rubbing the back of my head.

He snorts, then flinches. "Yeah. Me, too." He leans against the table while I stare at the paper some more.

Other parts of the night come back to me in short bursts. The convention. My award. All the faces glaring at me. Going to the bar to drink away my sorrows before I—

"Okay, I'm sure there's a way to get it annulled." Kurt taps the paper with a slim finger and interrupts my thoughts.

For some reason, his suggestion annoys me. It's irrational—after all, we don't know each other—but a rejection's a rejection.

I guess it don't matter none, though, seeing as how this is it for me. I can sign whatever he needs me to sign.

Except ... I want him. My hands reach for him without my volition, but I pull them back.

"You want to do that?" I ask.

"Definitely. We *can't* stay married. I've got an election to win.

I've thrown my hat in the ring for a Senate seat. The primary is in March, and I can't be married to a ..."

He doesn't finish the sentence, but I get the gist of it. He can't be married to a porn star. That'd be bad for his image.

Kurt catches my pinched expression. "Oh my god, I'm sorry. That came out totally wrong, and it made me sound like a jerk. I didn't mean it like—"

I hold up my hands. "Don't worry. I don't care much for politicians, either." Then I feel bad for saying it so plainly. "'Cept you, of course."

His Adam's apple bobs. "That's not what I meant. I'm not going to shame sex workers. Not at all. And I certainly don't want to shame *you*. I'm a fan. I think you're amazing. I just don't know you. Or, rather, I don't know who you really are."

"Not many do," I say lightly.

Ain't that the truth.

"We really can't ignore this"—he gestures at the marriage certificate—"no matter how much I might want to."

"Yep. Mama says runnin' from a problem's the best way to slam into a new problem."

Kurt keeps shifting his weight. It's adorable, actually—sweet man trying to find a way to get out of being married to li'l old me. If he was a better politician, he'd be used to saying whatever lies he needs to and hiding how he really feels. Politicians act just as much as any professional actor.

The fact that he's not doing a great job of it makes me like him more. Kurt's no liar, even if he wants to be a politician.

"I'm completely accepting of adult stars," Kurt insists. "I just don't think it works with the image I'm trying to portray. And my mom's looking at a White House run." He bites his lip and does a little dance. "You know what? I'm making a mess of this conversation, and I'm sure part of that's my fault, but another part is because I'm hungover and really need to pee. Lemme have a few minutes in the bathroom, and then can we try this again?"

I squeeze his shoulder. "Of course, darlin'."

Kurt gives me a shy smile, and his gaze lingers on my face. I have the strongest desire to lean down and kiss him, but I don't. He heads into the bathroom to put himself to rights, grabbing his tuxedo shirt on the way.

As I watch his pert butt scoot in there, I shake my head and try to remember what the heck happened last night. Other than me getting hitched to a stranger, that is.

Shit. How am I supposed to go through with my plans if I have a husband? Mama needs her money. The faster we get this here marriage annulled, the better.

A thought strikes me, and my stomach bottoms out. There's no way *he'd* get the money, right? Now that he's my husband? I think they have to send it to whoever I say, but I'd better be sure. The violins wail in my brain. With my heart pounding, I do a quick Google search that confirms he won't get my life insurance, but that doesn't calm my brain down much. I need to check in.

> JOHNNY
>
> How are you feeling this morning?

MAMA

I guess I've been better, but you know that.
Don't you worry about me.

> JOHNNY
>
> I'm always gonna worry about you.

MAMA

I know, son. But we'll get the money somehow.
It's not your responsibility. You already do too
much for me.

> JOHNNY
>
> No such thing. Yeah, you'll get the money. I'll
> make sure of it. I love you, Mama.

MAMA

I love you, too.

Kurt'll need something to settle his stomach, so I order room service. A big pot of coffee, a greasy breakfast and a healthy breakfast—I'll have whichever one he doesn't want—a big pitcher of orange juice, and some toast. Hopefully something in there will soak up the alcohol and make him feel better. While I'm hungover, I'm not as knocked out as he seems. Maybe because I've felt so bad for so long that alcohol don't matter none.

Normally, I'm saving every penny to help Mama out, but the organization in charge of the award paid for my trip, and the room came with an allowance that I haven't used. So I can afford to spoil Kurt a bit. Besides, I don't think we should go anywhere until we figure out what we're going to do next.

One thing I know for sure: A failure like me doesn't get to keep a cutie like him.

CHAPTER 7

Kurt

When I see my reflection in the bathroom mirror, I startle at the sheer mess that is my face and barely refrain from shrieking. "Oh, fuck no," I hiss. "You look like nasty chewed-up gum on the bottom of a shoe."

My ears burn red, and I start to sweat. Here I am with a dreamboat of a man, and I look like hell sent me back because I was too messed up for admission.

Speaking of that warm place ... what the hell have I done?

I groan and drag my hands down my cheeks. I've jettisoned my political dreams to outer space. Pretty sure that a wannabe politician who woke up in Vegas married to his favorite porn star is not a candidate the average voter will embrace wholeheartedly. Before, the only thing marring my goody-two-shoes image was having been dumped by a safe, sensible boyfriend for the most famous pop star in the world. How much more of a fall from grace can I have in one night?

I don't want to answer that question.

Moreover, given that my momther's planning on running for president, she'll likely have a valid opinion on her only son drunk-marrying a guy whose job includes fucking naked men wearing ball gags or cock cages (or both) on camera. And I don't want to hear that valid opinion.

My chest caves, and my chin dips down. I sigh. I take care of business, wash my face with the hotel soap, and swipe some toothpaste from a tube sticking out of a Dopp kit, using my finger to clean my mouth while my mind spins out of orbit.

Fuuuuck. I need to come up with a way to get out of this. But now that I'm thinking about it, if we annul this thing or get a quickie divorce, and then somehow word gets out about the marriage—which, let's face it, oppo research is going to make sure happens—would I seem even more flighty? Maybe I need to stay married.

That might not be a hardship, because let's not ignore the fact that my new husband is, after all, my absolute favorite porn star. Maybe there's a plus hidden here.

If he's into me, that is. I'd never force myself on him. But if he doesn't object, then could there be an upside? Not that my queasy body wants any form of sex at the moment.

He seemed to like me last night, though. I think? As I set myself to rights, slipping on my tuxedo shirt so I'm at least sort of covered, bits and pieces of the night that Johnny and I spent with each other come to me in shards, like a kaleidoscope. A glimpse of clinking my glass to his in a bar. Listening to a tribute band downtown. Lyft rides. Kissing. There might be a coherent picture, maybe, if I twist it ... Nope, it's gone.

There's no doubt I've fucked things up more than usual. Can I win the election if I stay married? Can my momther?

Or have I tanked two political careers with one careless night?

After I down several handfuls of water from the sink, I start to feel less like a desiccated corpse and more like a simply damaged human being. My hair appears to be a lost cause, but there are worse things—like being cruel on the inside.

Do I have more of a rebellious streak than I've ever let out to play? Because while I've led a pretty boring life in my adult years, get me smashed one night, and I've taken off all my clothes, put a lampshade on my head, and danced the Macarena.

Or, you know, drunk-married a porn star.

I glance down at my ring finger again.

What the hell did I do? Rather, I know the *what*, but the *why* is an open question, other than that marrying my porn star crush apparently seemed like an outstanding idea to my extremely intoxicated self.

Who lets drunk people get married, anyway?

I answer my own question: How many people who get married in Vegas are completely sober? I'd wager not that many, and it's not like they administer a breathalyzer before you say "I do."

Time to face my ... *husband*.

I can't deny that the word sends a thrill through me. My drunk self wanted him, but I'm pretty sure my sober self wants him more.

I open the Dopp kit to put the toothpaste back and—slightly more awake, now that I've hydrated a bit—notice bottles and bottles of medication in transparent orange containers with white tops. It's none of my business, but is Johnny sick? This seems excessive.

I take a closer look. They're all the same prescription: eight full bottles of sleeping pills.

While I don't always follow my gut, I've learned the hard way not to ignore my intuition, and it's pinging loudly right now. Because I'm pretty sure this is a problem. Abuse or ...

Dizziness washes over me, and I start rocking, because no, fuck no. *No no no.*

Images from seventeen years ago flash through my brain. Fuck, no. Not *again*.

I can't let this happen to another person if I have the ability to stop it.

I shake my head and try to evaluate the situation logically. Maybe Johnny's ... sick.

But no one needs this many sleeping pills. I turn the bottles around and read the labels carefully. The dates they were filled are a month apart. Like he's been hoarding the medication.

Am I wrong?

I can't be wrong again.

It's none of my business ... but how many people have silently cried out for help and gotten no answer because they've kept things private that needed to be discussed?

Johnny might hate me for what I'm about to do, because it's nosy AF, but I can justify it in a number of ways. I discovered the pills by accident, I'm curious, and he's my damn husband.

Most importantly, though, I'm not going to fuck up by missing signals again. I don't know how I could've prevented what Andrei did, but that hasn't stopped me from wishing I had every single day for the past seventeen years.

If Johnny needs help, I'll help him. Even if he doesn't want it. More important to stop him and risk being out of line than to stay quiet and wish I'd said something.

If I'm wrong ... god, I *hope* I'm wrong. I'll gladly take that outcome over the alternative.

I take a deep breath and open the bathroom door.

"Hey, Johnny?" I ask, walking out wearing a tux shirt and no pants, holding up three orange bottles of pills. "Are you feeling okay?"

He's sitting on the couch looking out the window. When he sees what I'm carrying, his bare shoulders stiffen. I don't lose eye contact with him, even though I'd normally be distracted by his pecs.

Finally, after a moment, he says, "Yeah. I'm fine."

"Then why do you have eight full bottles of"—I say the name of the drug, trying not to let my shaky hands rattle the containers.

He glares at me, crossing his arms over his chest, making it harder to not look at it. "That's really none of your business."

I set the bottles on the bed. My phone buzzes on the table, and I ignore it. My pulse is pounding in my ears. "I know it isn't. But I

... I couldn't live with myself if those pills were ... I know this is awkward, and it's not my place. I didn't mean to pry. I just ... It seems weird that you have them. Because aren't those for sleeping? Why do you need so many?"

Johnny sighs and bites his lip. Then he startles and says, "Shit," and grabs his phone. He swipes and scrolls, then clicks a few things, and his shoulders relax back down.

"You okay there?" I ask.

He nods.

Not a good answer. I'm pushing him. If he has some kind of prescription drug problem, well, since he's my husband, don't I have the right to know? Even in this fucked-up situation?

My phone buzzes again. I ignore it again, figuring it's better to run roughshod over things that aren't my business than have someone end up overdosing. "Johnny, we don't know each other, but maybe that could make it easier for you to talk to me. Why do you have so many sleeping pills?"

Johnny gives me a hard stare. I think he's debating whether or not he's going to open up to me. He's really got no reason to. Finally, he seems to come to a decision. His next words are quiet, and his eyes are full of pain. "I was going to take those last night."

"A dose?" I ask, my brows furrowing.

"All of them."

My knees buckle, and my stomach plummets to the ground floor of this high-rise hotel. "Two hundred and forty pills?" I whisper. "That's enough to kill a horse." My phone sounds insistently, and I pick it up with a huff, silencing it. "Fuck, not now."

Johnny's voice is raspy. "I'm not as big as a horse, but yeah, that's the idea."

No. Absolutely not.

No wonder he was treating last night like the last night of his life. Because in his mind, it was.

Fuck.

I'm going to hyperventilate.

Paige, my campaign manager, is texting me. I hit ignore again and try to control my breathing, when really I want to let out a primal scream. I pad over to Johnny and gingerly sit down next to him on the couch, feeling like he's a bomb about to go off. I want to comfort him, but would he let me?

Does it matter, though? Because even if he doesn't want anything to do with me, I don't care.

Johnny Haskell's not killing himself on my watch. Not now. Not ever.

And, if I'm being honest, this isn't only for his sake.

I can't go through another suicide.

I'm sweating, and I squeeze my eyes shut, seeing black spots. "Why?" I whisper, opening my eyes to study him.

He sits staring at his hands for a long time. Then he looks up at me. "My mama's on dialysis. She needs new kidneys. But her insurance company denied coverage, even though she was on the transplant list. So I found someone ... I found a supplier, so she won't have to wait on the list again. And my life insurance is enough to pay for it all."

"You were going to kill yourself so your mom could live," I say flatly, not entirely believing him. But everything about him exudes sincerity. "On the night you got a lifetime achievement award," I add, one more fragment of memory coming clear.

He nods, his eyes empty and sad.

This changes everything.

CHAPTER 8
Kurt

I reach out and take one of Johnny's hands. Fuck, what do I do? Is this all stemming from desperation over his mother, or is there something else wrong? I have no idea.

One thing's for sure: He's going to need help beyond what I can offer, professional help. But I can stay with him until he gets it.

We sit, silent, for long moments, because what the hell do you say to someone with the means and the intent to kill himself, who thinks the world will be better off if he's not here? He's wrong, of course, but I don't know how to convince him of that. I'm a graphic designer and a senatorial candidate, not a therapist.

But. I can't mess this up.

I'm not missing anything this time. I thought I was doing the right thing with Andrei—I thought I cared, thought I was helping. I never believed he'd go through with it.

I learned I can never know what's going on inside someone else's head. They may seem like everything is okay, and it could be the furthest thing from the truth.

Johnny's my responsibility now.

Nausea threatens to swamp me, but I have to get control of the situation and make good decisions.

"Do you think that your mom would want you to stay alive?" I ask.

"I'm worth more dead than alive," he mutters.

If *I'm* hurting at hearing him say that—and more importantly, *believe* it about himself—I wonder how much pain *he's* in?

"Did you see if you could be a donor?" I ask, thinking he could get over the list issue while we deal with insurance.

"Not a match." His voice sounds hollow.

"How far?" I swallow hard. "How far along on this plan were you? Besides getting the pills. Did you do anything else?"

Again, Johnny looks at me for a long time before answering. "I moved out of my apartment. Got rid of my truck, sold all my shit, and put almost all the money in an account for my mama. She'll be set for a long time. I spent most of the last of my own money last night on booze. I recorded a message for my fans and had it ready to go live on Ad/VICE after things were done." He coughs. "Mind, I just deleted it, so at least there won't be a big fuss over me faking my death. I had it all arranged so she'd know what to do. All the information she'd need to collect on my life insurance. So she could finally be healthy. It's all in an email I was going to send after I took the pills. I wrote her a note. And the obituary: 'John H. Haskell was born in Odessa, Texas. Attended high school in Fresno, California. Became a porn star in the San Fernando Valley. And died in Las Vegas, Nevada, saving his mama.'"

His words make my eyes burn and my insides clench. Johnny has some serious mental health issues that I don't know how to fix.

But I can keep him in my sight at all times until I can get him help.

"I'm so damn sorry you feel that bad," I reply unsteadily, knowing that my words are utter crap but not knowing what else to say. "Have you talked with anyone about it?"

Johnny shakes his head. "Ain't nobody's business."

"Don't you have any friends who'd want to know what's going on?"

He scoffs. "I have a lot of acquaintances, and some friends, but there ain't no one I'd trust telling this to."

Okay, then.

Johnny's health crisis is fucking *immediate*. And it sounds like he has no support system. I find that hard to believe, but sometimes people who are popular are just as lonely as those on the fringe. Or maybe he's isolated himself.

My phone rings, and I send it to voicemail. I square my shoulders and make a decision. Because of course I still want to be a politician and am going to run my campaign and do all the things I said I was going to do—I'm not giving up on the election—but Johnny's *mine*. I couldn't bear it if this beautiful man killed himself.

And he's my husband. Whether or not we were in any shape to make that kind of decision last night, whether or not we want it to be true long-term, right now my heart is telling me that means I get to keep him. He's also my responsibility—morally, and likely legally.

"Did you keep a copy of the video on your phone?" I ask.

"Yeah."

"May I see it?"

Silently, Johnny opens his phone, scrolls, and hands me his phone open to a video. I hit play.

Johnny's sitting in this hotel room wearing his white cowboy hat and tuxedo from last night. The vase of pink roses is to his side. He clears his throat.

"Hey, y'all. I wanted to hop on this here social media and let all y'all fans know how much I appreciate you. Tonight I got a lifetime achievement award, and I owe it all to you. You gave me a career, and with that career, you made it possible for me to help my sweet mama." He blinks and looks to the side. "She's real sick, though. She's been sick for a long time, and while my sister and I try to help her, it ain't been enough. I wanted y'all to know how grateful I am for everything you've done. Because of you, I was able to buy a life insurance policy years back, and it has enough on it to pay for my mama to get better. I'm gonna take care of her now. Just ... thanks to all y'all for everything. Be good to each other. Goodbye."

My eyes burn, and I feel sick. I hand the phone back to him.

"Can I ask you something?" I say quietly, squeezing his knee.

"Sure." He says it easily, but he wrinkles his nose.

I look into his pretty eyes, and he slumps in his seat and covers his face with his hands. I want to hold him, but I'm afraid it might not be welcome. "Would you come back to California and stay with me for a while?"

Dropping his hands, Johnny stares at me as if I've told him *he* should be the one running for office. Finally, he says, "Thanks for the invitation. That's mighty kind of you. But no."

My phone rings again. "Fuck," I mutter. "I'm sorry. They aren't going to go away unless I take this." Johnny makes a waving, go-ahead motion, and I feel shitty, because he's more important than my campaign manager. "What?" I hiss. "This better be essential."

Paige hisses back, "What did you do?"

I stay silent, trying to figure out what, exactly, she's referring to.

"The news is all over social media. 'Senatorial candidate marries porn star.' Really, Kurt? *Really*?"

Oh, god. But that isn't the most important issue at the moment.

"We'll have to deal with it later," I snap. "I can't talk right now."

"Don't hang up—"

I hang up.

"I'm sorry," I say to Johnny. "But—"

"You don't have to apologize for answering the phone," Johnny says. "But I'm not going with you." His jaw is set.

I scoot nearer to him. "I'm afraid I'm not taking no for an answer."

"Too bad, darlin'. It's not your decision."

My hand goes to my hip. "It kind of is my decision, because you're my fucking husband, and apparently that fact is all over social media."

Johnny's face blanches, and he stands, pointing to the door. God, he's glorious—bare chested, in cutoff gray sweats and nothing else. His tone is firm. "I think you should go."

I stand, too, and cross my arms over my chest, feeling ridiculous with no pants on. "No."

"Anyone ever tell you that you're pushy?" he says.

I take a step closer. "All the time."

We stare at each other in a standoff.

He chuckles mirthlessly and turns his head to the side. "Why do you even care what I do?"

"For fuck's sake, I can't let you kill yourself!" With a finger under his chin, I turn his face back to me and give him a weak smile. "Besides, you're my husband now. You're mine to look out for."

"Oh, no," Johnny says. "No, that's not okay—"

"Babe," I say, the endearment coming out naturally, since he is a babe. Since I like him. Since I want him to feel better. Since I ache for him. "That's not going to cut it. While you're like this, I'm not letting you out of my sight. You're *not* taking your life on my watch. We'll find another way to get your mom help." My voice is pleading. "I promise you."

Johnny opens his mouth like he wants to argue with me, but he holds his hands out helplessly. "I can't," he whispers.

I want to push him. I'm gonna push him. But I have to do this delicately, because the last thing I want is for him to storm off and shut me out. Or ... finish things.

Yes, I barely know him, but it doesn't matter. He's my husband, at least for now. It's my job to keep him alive, at a minimum. And I've never been satisfied with doing the minimum. "You said it yourself: You sold all your possessions, right? And you gave up your lease?"

"Yeah," he says slowly. "It was just an old apartment in the Valley. Nothin' special."

"Then come home with me. I recently moved to the Palisades, and the condo has enough room for both of us. We can find you a place to go where you can get some treatment—"

"I ain't got medical insurance—"

"I do. I work at a big graphic design firm. And we're married," I remind him—which reminds *me*. "My friend was telling me how one of his coworkers married a guy to get him health insurance. The same thing can work here."

He holds up his hands. "I can't take advantage—"

"And I can't have your death on my conscience, John Huckleberry Haskell," I say fiercely. I squint at him. "Is that really your middle name?"

Johnny shrugs and looks fondly into the distance. "Mama's a character."

"Well, good. Fine. But ..." My voice drops. "Will you do it? Will you come stay with me? Just for a little while. We can work out the details of everything else later."

Johnny looks over at the pill bottles on the bed. We're gonna have to get rid of those, stat. And anything else that he could use to self-harm. Shit ...

"Where's your gun," I demand.

Johnny doesn't pretend not to know what I'm talking about, and to my relief, he doesn't argue about it. He points to the holster that's under his suit jacket. I take it and hold it on my lap for now. I don't know what the hell I'm going to do with it.

"Was the gun for ..." I ask.

"Plan B," he says. "Well, also plan A."

I want to ask, but I think I can guess.

"Why?" Johnny asks again.

"Why what?"

"Why do you care?"

The forlorn note in his voice makes my eyes sting. "Because every human life matters. That's why we send massive search parties to find children who get lost in the woods. We care. Your life has value, Johnny. I'm going to show that to you." I blink. "But this isn't about some human in the abstract. It's you. *You* matter, Johnny. You've affected so many people you don't even know."

"I'm just porn."

"No one is 'just' their job. And besides, that's a very judgmental attitude, Mr. Haskell," I say, my tone snippy, though I hope he can hear the teasing in it as well. "Sex has an important place in the lives of most adults. Don't let the haters shame you for providing a service. Don't let them make you doubt your self-worth."

I'm not sure where the soapbox I'm standing on right now came from, but apparently it's what Johnny needed to hear, because he's looking at me with soft eyes. He opens his mouth to say something, but then he closes it and looks around the hotel room, clearly defeated. Moments pass while he bites his lip. I keep my attention focused on him.

"Do you think you're depressed?" I ask.

"I dunno. I've been going about my days just fine." He winces. "Or as fine as I'll ever get. There's no other choice if I'm going to take care of my mama."

"There is a choice. Let me help you. We'll figure out a way to get her the money she needs. I have to fundraise anyway, for my campaign. I'll talk with the promoters and see what we might be able to do." I tilt my head. "How much are we talking about, anyway?"

He tells me, and my chest constricts. "I have that in my bank account. It's yours."

"I'm not gonna let you give my mama your life savings."

"It's family money," I correct. "And even if you won't let me pay for all of it, I can do *something*. Does she need surgery this very minute? Is she in a lot of pain?"

"It can wait a little. It's more a quality-of-life thing right now. I just want her better."

"Okay," I say. "We'll make that happen. Just come home with me."

Johnny drags his nails down his cheeks and then curls his arms over his face, shaking his head. My heart breaks a bit more for him.

"Let me get you some help. And let me figure out a solution for your mom."

"What are you going to get out of this?"

"Besides the satisfaction of helping a fellow human being?" I say. *Besides not wanting you to be another Andrei?*

He nods.

A thought crosses my mind, but I don't want to voice it, because it would make it sound like I think this situation is transactional, which it most definitely is not.

But I like Johnny a lot, and I really wouldn't mind banging this beast of a porn star—my all-time favorite.

That's minor, though. It's obviously more important to help him and his family. If I never touch him, because it's not what he needs, I'll fully respect that.

"That satisfaction is enough," I finally say. "And you matter to me."

He gazes at me. I think he's going to nod, but he doesn't.

Then something else dawns on me, and I don't feel guilty using it to manipulate him, because Johnny doesn't seem to be motivated to save himself. Saving me, on the other hand ... that might work.

"And there's another thing to consider, *husband*." I emphasize the word. "It's bad enough for my political career that I drunk-married a porn star. How much worse would it be if said porn star killed himself the next day?"

Johnny's jaw drops, and his hand cups his mouth. "Shit," he mutters.

"Yeah. Shit." I look at him, crossing my arms over my chest. "And my mom's going to run for president. How's it going to look for her?"

He closes his eyes. "Goddamn."

"Right. So come with me for a little bit, at least. I mean, you gotta help me, man. I can't deal with this by myself."

Johnny swallows hard and nods.

The lightness in my chest makes me feel like I won something major. Maybe I did.

"Cool," I say faintly. "So now what do we do?" I shouldn't be asking him. I should be taking care of him. He's at the end of his rope, and I need to not put any additional demands on him right now.

"Um. I'll get dressed, and then we can—"

There's a knock on the door.

"Breakfast is here," Johnny says. "Maybe we start with that."

As I watch my tall, handsome husband open the door for room service, I question how I'm going to deal with this. I was already overstretched, with work and the campaign.

But this isn't optional. I can take on something else when it's as important as this is.

As *he* is.

CHAPTER 9
Johnny

Well, hell. My plan didn't work. Whatever the opposite of a plan coming together is, that's what happened. A falling apart. A failure.

That's what I am. A failure at my plan to fix my mama.

Do I even trust Kurt? I've known him less than a day, and most of that time, we were both drunk. How can he do what he's suggesting? Is he just saying whatever he can to save his own ass?

The violin wails in my head. *I should've just shot myself, with or without the pills.*

We're sitting at the dining table off to the side of the hotel suite. He chose the greasy breakfast, so I pick at a plate of egg whites and veggies while he's having bacon and a cheesy ham omelet. I hold up my hand, the metal ring on it shiny and unfamiliar.

"Are you sure y'all don't wanna get this thing annulled?" I say, watching Kurt bite into a piece of toast. His lush lips press together as he chews, and his throat works when he swallows. I'm tempted to move closer to him, to touch him. To feel his skin against mine.

We kissed last night. I want to kiss him again.

A weird feeling settles in my stomach that has nothing to do with the hangover. Part of me *likes* the symbolism of the ring on my finger.

A lot of me likes *him*.

Kurt's shoulders stiffen in reaction to my words, and his gaze goes distant. I wanna kick myself for making him sad. "It's probably what we *should* do. My fucking strategist is having kittens, and I'm afraid to think what my mom—er—mother's going to say. But you're more important than any of that."

He says that so easily, but I plain don't believe him. No one runs for office and then says the election don't matter. The election's *all* that matters.

"Now, I'm a skeptic," I say slowly, "and I think most politicians are just in it for the notoriety and to promote themselves. I get the feeling, though, that you're going into politics thinking that you're gonna make better decisions than the last person in that position."

"Of course," Kurt says, sounding like he's not sure where I'm going with this.

"In other words, you're thinking about the good of society. Right?"

"Right."

I almost scoff, but I don't want to offend him. "So you're telling me that you're idealistic enough to get into politics to help others. That you're civic-minded. But you'll set that all aside, and you're perfectly willing to sacrifice those good laws or whatever you might be able to achieve ... for me?"

To his credit, Kurt doesn't look annoyed. He must be used to people challenging him. So, hmm. Maybe he would make a good politician, because he can keep his cool.

He puts down his toast and leans in. "Have you seen *The Last of Us*?"

"That a TV show?"

He nods.

I shake my head.

"Then I'll do my best not to spoil it. All right ... there's a scene in the show where the protagonist has to choose between saving all of humanity—maybe. Or saving a little girl—maybe. And the episode is about what decision he makes."

"Okay," I say slowly.

Kurt looks at me intently, willing me to understand something that I'm not getting. "It's a very powerful moment, and no matter what, some people will think he makes the wrong choice. What he ultimately does, I think, is perfectly in line with his character. All I'm saying is, I know the arguments about the good of the many and society and wanting to serve, because that's what's been drilled into me by my parents, and that's what got me interested in running. Now, though, when I'm faced with the decision—do I let you go so I can maybe win an election, or do I stay with you and see if I can help you?—*I gotta choose you*. It's simple. Your life is more important than some abstract concept I can barely articulate."

"You don't even know me," I mutter, my cheeks heating at the idea that anyone on the face of this planet besides my mama and my sister, May Ella, would choose me.

No one ever has.

"In some ways, it doesn't matter that I don't know you," Kurt says, and I see some feistiness in him that I hadn't noticed last night. A backbone. It's sexy. "I've made the decision that we're keeping you alive, because you clearly can't be trusted to look after your own best interests."

"Ouch." I sit back in my chair. "I don't know. I ain't entirely sure what's what and how things are supposed to be. I've always been a planner and then just followed the plan. Now that I've thrown the plan out with the pig slops, I'm ... lost."

I should just die. Kill myself. Put all of us out of the misery.

Kurt looks at me with dark, compassionate eyes. "I understand that. I like plans, too, and I get on edge when they change. When we're all set to do something and then ... *nope*—it's unsettling. But I can help you. Step one is to get you to a therapist."

"Whoa," I say, holding up my hands. "I didn't say that was okay—"

"No, you haven't. And we'll talk about all of this. But I wanted to let you know that's what I'm thinking. There's no shame in going to a therapist, Johnny," Kurt says. "I go to a therapist." He rolls his eyes. "I've had more therapy than you can imagine, and one thing I've learned is that mental health is just the same as any other medical condition. If you broke your arm, you'd go to a doctor for a cast, right?"

"Yeah," I sigh, seeing where he's going with this.

"This is no different. Brain chemistry is a real, physical thing, and you having these suicidal thoughts is related to that. At least I think it is. That's why we're going to get you help."

I don't reply. I ain't got the money to get my brain fixed. My mama ain't got the money she needs to get her body fixed. That's the whole point.

But Kurt seems like he's not going to take no for an answer, and while part of me wants to challenge him, part of me wonders if he's so stubborn nothing can change his mind. And I'm just so tired. He's offering a solution, and I don't know if I have the energy to keep arguing.

Money doesn't seem to be an issue for him, either.

Mama says a fool and his money are soon ... *married*. Appears that Kurt's the fool in this scenario, though I have no intention of exploiting him.

Still ... it's tempting to let someone else take charge. Even though I know that's only a temporary solution.

"Since I've burned my bridges employment-wise," I say carefully, "I need to be clear that I ain't in a position to be able to contribute financially. Like, *at all*, at least until ... until I find work."

"Burned bridges? You're not going to—"

"Keep doing porn? No. I announced my retirement yesterday, but the way I see it, it didn't matter. No studio had given me work in months. Not since the lawsuit."

"Lawsuit?"

I pinch the bridge of my nose. "There's so much we don't know about each other."

"Right." He sips his coffee. "You don't have to tell me."

But I want to tell him. "I'm suing my former studio. I mean, it's been going on for ... seems like forever, though my lawyers tell me everything's moving along as fast as can be expected."

"I'm sorry to hear that. That sucks." He frowns. "Wait a minute, I heard about that. Not any specifics," he adds quickly. "Just that they represent you. Weston & Ramirez, right?"

"That's right."

Kurt grins a cute, toothy smile that distracts me from my mood. No matter what, I like being around this man. "I know Sam Stone," he says. "He works there, and he may have mentioned you being in the office." He blushes. "He teases me that I was less starstruck when he ditched me for Julian Hill than when he told me about seeing you in person."

I hadn't put those pieces together last night, since I'd been a wee bit sauced. But now that I think about it, I remember those posters around town showed Kurt and Sam together, looking mighty friendly. In a way, it's reassuring to know that Kurt really—probably—is one of the good guys. Everyone I've met at Weston & Ramirez seems to be trying to do the right thing, even if they are lawyers, so if Sam was with Kurt, that backs up Kurt's story about wanting to help people.

I ... enjoy being with him, even if he's fucked up my plans to get Mama money.

Maybe that blame rests squarely on me. *I'm the fuckup here. I'm always the fuckup.*

Still, there's a burning sensation in my chest. Kind of like ... *jealousy*? Because I don't like the idea of Kurt giving his heart to someone else.

Kurt seems to read the look on my face. "Sam and I were never really dating," he says.

"No?"

"No. We used to mess around some when we were first stuck together," he admits, "but he and I are really just good friends. We got along great and photographed well, so we were good public faces, but I never felt about him the way I'd want to feel about a potential partner. Our relationship was something our relatives made up because it played well to suburban liberals." He takes on a mocking tone. "'The governor's grandson and the lieutenant governor's son are in a long-term relationship. Look how stable same-sex couples can be. Isn't that nice?'"

I relax at the news that they weren't dating, and his words make me chuckle despite everything. "You sound slightly cynical."

"I'm more than slightly cynical." He gives me a tentative smile. "It wasn't the best idea. But your plan was worse. Killing yourself's not the answer."

"I thought it was the best solution."

"But you know that's not true, right?"

"I'll allow that convincing myself a bad idea's a good idea is a *very* bad idea," I mutter. "But I'm stuck. How else can I help her? I can't let her die. Not when I could get the money to save her."

"We'll figure it out," he says. "I'll help you."

My face, neck, and ears go impossibly hot at the idea of having to rely on anyone, but not so much that I refuse his offer. Because I'll do literally anything for Mama. Even set aside my pride.

Maybe that's my problem. Maybe my pride has gotten in the way of me listening to a few good ideas.

I'm a loser whether I have pride or not.

It's not like being with him is a hardship. He's gorgeous, and he's not at all an asshole. Not huge praise, sure, but I've been in the dating desert so long that the lizards know my name. Kurt's fresh rain on dry earth.

He's more than that. He might be my salvation.

"So you'll come home with me?" Kurt asks again.

After a long moment, I nod at him.

He smiles and nods back.

CHAPTER 10
Johnny

After we eat breakfast, I get up to take a shower, but before I can get into the bathroom, Kurt slides past me, grabs the rest of my pills out of my toiletry bag, and puts all of them, along with the derringer, in the plastic laundry bag provided by the hotel.

"Leave the door open, okay?" he says. "I'll be in the next room if you need anything." Like I don't know how to shower on my own.

I feel lower than a snake's belly when I realize that he doesn't trust me to be alone. But I s'pose I've earned that lack of trust. I get him back by coming out in nothing but a towel and getting dressed in front of him. Serves him right for giving me no privacy.

His eyes flare with interest. So, okay. He's attracted to me. Maybe he'd want to mess around—if the time was right.

A flicker of heat ignites inside me. I can't remember the last time that happened. Everything's been so dull for so long, but with Kurt, it's like there's this candle lighting up something I thought was gone forever.

Even feeling bad, I can dream and wish.

For *him*.

While I was in the bathroom, Kurt put on his tuxedo pants, shirt, jacket, and shoes. Looks like the tie and cummerbund are in the laundry bag he's holding.

Classic walk-of-shame attire ... just with an extra gun and some pills.

"Do you have anything else on you?" he asks. "Anything that you could use to self-harm, I mean. Knives, razors?"

I think about it and shake my head. "No. I use an electric."

"Would you tell me if you had anything?"

I nod, my head spinning. "What good would it do to hide stuff from you? You already know everything."

"Hardly. But tell me if you remember something else."

"Deal."

After taking a final look around and checking out remotely, I pluck Ace's note from the flowers, slide it and the marriage certificate into the front of my bag, and leave the hotel key on a table.

What the hell am I gonna do now? I have nothing. Literally nothing but a suitcase and Kurt's vow to help.

The ride down in the elevator is different from what I remember of the drunken one last night. Kurt and I look at each other, not talking, as various people crowd in there with us. What's there to say? My chest feels hollow, and my pulse is as sluggish as molasses.

On our way to his hotel, he spies a huge pharmacy on the Strip. "Hang on," he says, "I bet they have pill disposal."

My heart sinks—all my plans gone—but he's probably right. It's dangerous to have that much medication on me. I've proved I'm not making good decisions these days.

If I ever did. *I should grab those pills and the gun back from him and be done with it all.*

He marches up to the pharmacy counter and places the pill bottles in the red disposal box off to the side. After it's shut and secure, we stand there a moment, staring at it. My arms feel too weighty to lift, my legs too heavy to move.

He reaches out and touches my wrist, and I flinch. "Hey. You okay?"

Out of habit, I nod, and he stares at me.

Might as well be honest.

I shake my head.

"Hey," he says, and he wraps me in a hug. It surprises me, but I hug him back, liking the way he feels against me. He smells like weed and cigarette smoke and coffee, with something underneath that's faintly musky in the best way. It's comforting. I hold on to him a bit longer than I should.

Kurt feels *right* against me.

We break apart, silently walk out of the pharmacy, and cross the street to his hotel.

It's nice in a different way than mine. While mine was Vegas chic, his is more old-world. It's starting to dawn on me that *he's* from a different world than me. The reference to his bank account and "family money" probably should've been a tip-off.

I go with him, wheeling my small suitcase that contains everything I own, feeling like I have no purpose whatsoever. He opens the door to a spacious suite, about as nice as mine but with a more classic feel. I'm wagering Kurt wasn't comped this room, though. Again, different worlds.

He stashes my handgun in the hotel safe before he showers, again with the door open so he can keep an eye on me. I resist the urge to peep in at him, even though I know from this morning that I'd like what I'd see.

Kurt locking the gun up makes me feel like the muck you pick out from a horse's hoof. I should feel better now that I've got someone helping me with Mama, but I don't. If anything, I feel shittier.

I can't even kill myself properly.
I'm a total loser.
She's gonna die because of me.

"You feel up to a five-hour drive?" Kurt calls, the water muffling his voice.

"Sure, darlin'," I say, fiddling on my phone.

"Did you fly here?"

"Yep."

"Are you going to cancel your return flight?"

"Only booked a one-way," I admit.

"Did you rent a car to get around town?"

"No, I used a Lyft from the airport."

As he scrubs, Kurt keeps up the chatter like we're at a church social.

Shucks. He's forcing me to talk so he knows I'm still here. He's also keeping me from fixating on all the junk in my brain.

It makes my sour heart get a little sweet on him. Heck, it was already more than a little sweet on him.

As we gab, I scroll through social media and come across some photos of Kurt and me from last night.

We look like we belong together—two men in tuxedos grinning at each other. Kissing. Hanging off each other. Drinking.

He's prettier than a speckled pup. *Damn.*

It's more than his looks, though—it's the way he treats me like I'm someone special, even though I don't deserve it. I can't deny I like it, though. Can't deny I want him. I save the images to my phone.

Then I stumble on the aftermath of my speech. I'd forgotten that I'd essentially tossed a grenade but left before it detonated.

There are all kinds of stories about my lawsuit against the studio. Reactions from performers, fans, and studio brass about my retirement. Even some comments from politicians—both those who condemn porn as a scourge on society and those saying that we need stronger laws to support and protect the actors.

I throw my phone down, still shooting the breeze with Kurt about his favorite restaurants in Las Vegas and where we should stop for lunch on the way back to LA. I busy myself with poking around his room, but he doesn't have much here that reflects him other than some red luggage with black piping.

He emerges from the bathroom wearing a dress shirt and slacks. If that's what he wears for a drive through the desert, I wonder what it takes to get him to go out in only a T-shirt. His hair is slicked back, and he's freshly shaved.

Damn.

I wanna *devour* him.

But I leave him alone, because he's all gussied up, and I shouldn't mess with that.

He packs quickly and calls down for the valet, but when we step out of the elevator in the parking garage, we're confronted with a horde of paparazzi.

Flashbulbs go off, photographers jostling to get the best images of us.

Oh, damn. It's getting real.

"So it's true you married Velvet the Cowboy, Mr. Delmont?" one reporter says, shoving a microphone at Kurt, whose eyes widen to the size of spare tires.

"What are your future constituents going to say when they learn you married a gay porn star?"

"Have you seen your opponent's reaction?"

"What does Melissa Delmont think of your marriage?"

"Is this in response to Sam Stone being in a romantic relationship with Julian Hill?"

Kurt's gobsmacked. I whisper in his ear, "Put on your sunglasses."

He nods and pulls them out. He seems to be frozen, and while I don't want to make things worse for him, I want to move this along. Something clicks inside me. I guess I'm more used to invasive press questions than he is.

I throw an arm around his shoulders. Then I flash my big aw-shucks smile, turning on my charm. "Thanks for your interest in Kurt, but he's not going to be answering any questions right now."

Kurt melts into my side, reinforcing my decision to take care of this for him.

"Photos have surfaced of you partying last night," another says. "What do you have to say about that?"

I tip my hat to the reporters. "Folks who have no vices have very few virtues."

"What about you, Velvet? You announced your retirement last night. What are your future plans?"

"Dunno. Enjoy being married, I guess." I hold up my hand. "I'm pleased to report this here ring's cut off my circulation."

There's a pause, then a few laughs and some confused expressions.

"It fits fine," I say with another grin, and make a point of squeezing Kurt to me. "I'm just no longer available."

More camera flashes. Someone asks, "How long have you known each other?"

"Thank you," I say, and steer Kurt over to the valet station, where they tell him his car is almost here.

A driver pulls a shiny black BMW to the curb, and we throw our luggage in the trunk, get in, and take off, leaving the paps behind us.

Kurt's hands tremble as he turns right out of the parking garage.

"Hey, darlin'. You okay? You wanna pull over and let me drive?"

"I'm fine."

I'm tempted to roll my eyes. "Okay, I think we need a few ground rules. You called me on my horseshit this morning. I'm going with you to your house, because I can see that it's for my own good, and while I'm a stubborn so-and-so most of the time, I've decided I'm going to try to not be stubborn about this situation here. I can't think of any way to help my mama, but I'm smart enough to recognize that maybe you'll have a better solution. Now, your hands are shaking, and I'm thinking that the paps got to you because you woke up with a hell of a hangover and found out you were married to some fella you don't know."

Kurt glances at me and turns left to head to the freeway.

"So maybe one of our ground rules is honesty. I was honest with you that I was gonna take those pills. And that I'm feeling numb and useless. How are you feeling?"

"I'm panicking," he admits, and pulls sharply into a gas station, parking to the side and cutting off the engine. He bangs his forehead on the top of the steering wheel. "What the fuck are we doing? I married the man of my dreams, who's also a porn star. Please know I'm not judging you, but it's political suicide. Fuck, wrong word. And—"

"And I'm a disaster," I supply. "Sorry, don't mean to interrupt you, but I ain't gonna make you insult me when I can do it just fine."

"You maybe have some big issues that we need to solve," he says gently. He blows out a breath. "I was startled out there, and I didn't know how to react. My mind's going a mile a minute. Whatever happened to 'What happens in Vegas stays in Vegas'? That doesn't apply to us? What the hell?" He throws up his hands.

"Also, 'man of your dreams'?" I ask, thinking back through what he just said. The tips of Kurt's ears turn pink. *Interesting*.

"I told you I'm a big fan."

"You really are precious," I say, affection for him rushing over me in waves despite my numbness. He's still shaking, so I go back to my initial point. "I'm a good driver. And for some reason, I'm not feeling as hungover as you. So why don't you let me drive until we get the hell out of here and you get settled. We can switch back whenever you like."

Kurt glances at me, then stops to really study my face. "In your, um, scenes, you tend to take over, take charge. Is that what you're like in real life?"

I want to kiss his cute button nose, but he looks too upset for that. Plus we don't need any more photos—even though no one seems to be paying attention to us right now. "I do like doing that," I admit. I love it when I get to play a soft pleasure dom, because it's in line with my personality—my usual personality, at least. This present funk isn't like me—although it's been a long time since I've felt like my old self. But I don't tell him that. I also don't tell him how focusing on him makes the noise in my head go away. "C'mon. You're upset. There's only one highway until we get closer to Los Angeles—it's not like I'm going to get us lost."

"I hate to ask, but are you okay to drive? You're not going to go hurling us into oncoming traffic?"

Damn. I'm horrified that he has to ask that, but under the circumstances, it's a reasonable question. "I promise I'm going to drive like a normal person and not do anything rash. I'd never hurt you."

I *know* I mean that. I'll not hurt a hair on his head. Ever.

Kurt nods and opens his door, and so do I. We walk around the car and meet at the trunk. Before he can pass me, I grab him and hug him. He clings to me a moment, then nods and proceeds to the passenger side. I settle into the driver's seat, wondering if he's been wanting someone else to take the wheel of his life for a while.

Meanwhile, I need someone to help me out of my predicament.

Maybe this unplanned marriage can help us both.

CHAPTER 11

Kurt

I gaze out at the muted earth tones of the western Nevada desert as Johnny and I drive toward the state line. He's changed the radio station to some kind of twangy vintage country music, which normally I wouldn't listen to, but I'm finding myself lulled by it. It suits him. It also gives me space to think.

"I should've expected all the commotion," I mutter. "I've been to plenty of press events. I've smiled for the cameras hundreds of times. So why did this get to me?"

"Maybe because it felt more personal?"

He's put his hat in the back seat, and his hair is mussed. I want to reach out and touch it. It's distracting me from the encounter with the paparazzi.

Flashbulbs. Questions. *Intrusive* questions. "Yeah. It triggered me. But I don't know why."

"Because you didn't have a ready answer?"

"That's probably it." Although it could be because it felt like I've been found out.

Now the whole world has had a glimpse into my sexual preferences, even if Johnny and I haven't done anything, because people will draw conclusions from my marrying a porn star. While, as a gay man, I've somewhat defined my identity based on sexuality—and that's not a thing that American society tends to view with a high degree of positivity—it's another thing to announce that I adore gay porn. Which is what it felt like to pop up out of nowhere married to a major star.

We pass a billboard for an adult store.

Maybe that panicky feeling was shame.

Shame is the opposite of pride.

Given all the therapy I've been through, I've had plenty of practice at reducing my thoughts and feelings down to the lowest denominator. And that is always some common theme—usually shame. Enoughness is a big one, too: that I'm not enough or haven't done enough. Like with Andrei.

I chew on my lip as I watch the barren landscape, dotted only with the occasional over-the-top casino in the middle of nowhere and a ton of billboard advertising.

I'd thought I'd gotten over any feelings of shame about my sexuality. When I came out, my momther sent me to a therapist not—she said—because there was anything wrong with me, but because she thought I might want to talk with someone.

But maybe *I* thought there was something wrong with me. Maybe I still do. And maybe I should be a little more patient with Johnny and how he doesn't want to see a therapist. Although I think I've talked him into it.

Still—there's shame around mental health, too. I imagine he's got a lot going on inside his head, if it's anything like what's going on inside *my* head: a jumble of too much to handle. I realized a long time ago that I need professional help to keep that jumble from getting too overwhelming.

My phone pings, and I see it's an email from the wedding chapel. They've attached our wedding photos. More evidence that Johnny and I are really married. The certificate is one thing, and the rings another. But photos?

I click through them, and boy, I look overserved. I'm also gazing adoringly at Johnny.

My heart beats rapidly as I view the images, but I also feel a sense of weightlessness and lightness I haven't felt in a while. Am I actually happy about this, despite all the reasons it's a mistake?

"What's your email?" I ask.

Johnny cocks his head. "Why? Y'all have somethin' you can't tell me right now?"

"Ha ha. I wanted to send you our wedding photos."

"Oh, that's ... hmm. Okay." He gives me his email address, and I forward them, then make my favorite one my phone wallpaper. We're standing at the altar in the cheesy chapel holding hands and staring into each other's eyes. I don't remember the moment at all, but we look like we're completely ...

Completely in love.

We weren't. Aren't. I know that. But the picture makes me happy anyway.

After that, I put my phone down. I need to search for therapists for Johnny, but this is a long drive, so I have plenty of time.

I go back to staring out the window at the monotonous desert and yawn. Last night's the first time I've slept well in a while, and that was only because I was too drunk and tired to do anything but pass out. Now, though, my brain's starting to get overloaded again.

My phone buzzes, and of course, it's my momther. I decline the call, but a text comes through immediately.

> MOMTHER
>
> Do you have something to tell us?

I'm a grown man and don't have to ask my parents for permission to live my life. I can do what I want.

None of that goes from my brain to my texting app. Instead, I decide to get it over with.

> **KURT**
> If you saw a story online about me, it's true. Yes, I got very drunk and married Johnny Haskell in Vegas. I'm driving with him now, so I can't talk. I'll call you when I get back home.

> **MOMTHER**
> Oh my god, honey. Who is this man? How long have you been dating him? How come you never brought him around to meet us?
>
> Or did you keep him secret from us because of his occupation? I like to think we're more open-minded than that.
>
> Although I do think Santangelo is going to use it against you.

> **KURT**
> He will. The wedding wasn't planned.

> **MOMTHER**
> If it's a mistake, you can see if you can get it annulled.

I pinch the bridge of my nose. Johnny glances over at me, then returns his focus to the road.

"My mom found out about our marriage," I say. "Figures."

He gives me a wary look. "How's she taking it?"

"I'm reading it as she doesn't know if she should be supportive or if the best thing is for her to recommend that we get an annulment."

"We still could do that," he says, but my stomach sinks.

"No," I say. "I don't think that's the right way to go."

"How come?"

I'm not sure if I can articulate why I don't want an annulment, but I give it a shot. "The reason to annul a marriage is so that it's a ... well, a nullity. Like it didn't happen. But word's gotten out, and people know that it happened." I wave my phone at Johnny. "So what's the point of pretending it didn't? I'll look even more volatile and untrustworthy if I do that."

"Perhaps you've got somethin' there," Johnny says.

"I think it's better if we stay married for a while—until the election, I guess. Then after that, we can quietly get a divorce."

My stomach aches as I say the words, and I realize that I don't think I want a divorce. Not right away, and not after the election, either.

Also, I hate the pained look on Johnny's face as I tell him I don't want him in my life permanently.

He swallows. "Makes sense."

But I have to look at this logically: My impulsive wedding to Johnny throws a big wrench into my plans. I decided to become a politician so I could do something great for society. I was going to devote myself to the cause.

Marrying Johnny was about the worst thing I could do in terms of my chances at the ballot box. And my brain starts spinning as I think about all the implications of our marriage and how they will affect the election.

I need a break from my own head.

That brain escape is part of the reason why I like my graphic design job. Even though most of the time I'm designing junk mail, I can get into the flow of fussing with kerning—the spacing between letters—or something like that, and I stop worrying about my life. Everything just falls away.

Which is how I felt last night with Johnny. All I cared about was being with him. I didn't think about the election once, and I don't think it was only because I was drinking.

I glance over at him. He's wearing a tight T-shirt and jeans with a thick belt, his big biceps naturally bulging as he drives. Fuck, he's sexy.

But he's also misguided. I'm so upset that he thought that ending his life was a good idea. And for what? To buy his mom a black market kidney? He didn't say that, but I don't know how else she'd jump a donor line. Are there places that arrange organ donations for the right price?

I don't know the character of Johnny's mental issues, or whatever it is that's making him act this way, and I don't want to trigger him. I probably should be careful with my words around him.

Except I also want to say what's on my mind. I clear my throat.

"What's up, precious?" Johnny says.

"You said we should be honest with each other."

"I think that's a good idea. Don't you?"

"Sure." I do my best to say my next words as gently as possible. "But then we have to talk about some tough stuff."

My attempt at a soft touch doesn't totally work, since Johnny seems to need to steel himself before eventually saying, "Fine."

"If you did kill yourself, don't you think that would hurt your mom more than the disease she's suffering from now?"

I watch Johnny bite his lower lip. "She can't die, though."

"Babe, everyone dies. That's a fact of life. And mostly, unless there's some kind of accident or other tragedy, parents die before their kids do." Maybe it shouldn't be so easy for me to call him babe, but every time I look at him, I get a rush of warm affection.

"Shucks. That's harsh."

"You don't have to like it, but it's true. It's the natural order of things."

"I don't feel like it's natural for her to have a body that don't work."

"Has she struggled a long time?"

"She's been sick since I was a kid. Got diagnosed when I was eleven."

Maybe I shouldn't press, but that hasn't stopped me yet. "What was your childhood like?"

He sighs. "Like I told ya, I grew up on a ranch in the middle of nowhere, Texas, where my folks worked. That's where I learned to take care of horses, rope cattle, all that. When I was fourteen, my mama couldn't work there no more. Owners kept her on as long as they could, but eventually, they had to let her go. They were gonna sell the ranch to some developers anyway. Times were tough all around. The ranch foreman had a friend with a line on some work she could do at a packing house in Fresno, so we headed out. Drove west. Lived in her car for months. I was in school and doing the best I could to scrounge up a few dollars here and there. But my baby sister plays the violin like a virtuoso—she started with the fiddle back in Texas. In Fresno, if you're a street musician, there ain't no subway to play in, like in New York City, say, so she'd just go stand in front of an auto parts store in a strip mall, pull out her beat-up amp and her too-small electric violin, and put up a cardboard sign that asked for help for our mama—for rent, food, medicine."

My heart seizes at the image.

"She'd play 'All of Me' or some Disney princess song, but this haunting violin version. People would stop to see her. Young girl, not yet a teenager. Brown hair parted down the middle." He gets a wistful smile. "But she was a violin prodigy. She still plays for fun, but most of the time, she's managing a Taco Bell."

"Why didn't she stick with the violin as a career?"

"Stuff like that costs money. Lessons, private schools, I don't even know." He sighs. "Anyway, she'd play, and we'd be able to get some food or whatever. I did whatever jobs I could, but I ain't very good at reading or writing." He pauses. "I just have a little trouble reading fast, that's all. When I turned eighteen, I left so Mama wouldn't have to pay for me no more. I figured I'd go make some money in Los Angeles and send money to them, since the jobs in Fresno sucked. I walked into town, and a porn producer found me in a coffee shop. I coulda said no, of course, but"—he shrugs—"I like having sex. I said yes, because the money he offered was more than I could make at any other job I was likely to get. And I guess the rest is history. I'm not ashamed."

"So you've been doing porn since you were eighteen?"

He nods.

"How old are you now?" His date of birth was on our marriage certificate, but I didn't study it closely.

"Thirty-five. You?"

"Thirty-two."

We fall quiet for a while. Johnny drives in a sure, confident manner. And, unlike some of my friends who get all distracted when they drive, his eyes stay on the road, paying attention to the drivers around him. I like that. I exhale and settle more comfortably in my seat.

Holy fuck, the past day has been ... unreal.

I burst out laughing.

"What is it, sugar?"

"It's all just hitting me. That I'm married to you. That I have to figure out a way to salvage my campaign. That we need to fix things for your mom. And you."

"You're a fixer, eh?" Johnny asks.

"Yeah."

"Well, good luck fixing me."

"I don't think you need to be *fixed*, exactly," I say. "More like help you to be a little healthier. You're not broken. You just have something going on that's got you off course."

That reminds me that I need to get things set up for when we get to LA. Right now, Johnny may look like he's functioning fine, but he had a plan in place to carry out his own death just a few hours ago. I can't let his charming demeanor make me forget that. He needs help.

I log into my job's employee site and download the benefit forms on my phone, and when we stop for gas and snacks, I ask Johnny to get our marriage certificate out of his bag so I can snap a photo of it to upload with the application. I'm glad he can get automatically enrolled right away even though it's Sunday. Next, I start searching for mental health treatment centers.

I'm sure the reason it's so important to me to help him is only partly about Andrei and partly about my longtime crush on

Johnny, but whatever. I can have crushes. I am worried about what will happen when we ultimately have to disentangle ourselves, but it'll be fine.

I hope I'm not violating the honesty thing that we agreed on when I tell myself that.

"Johnny?" I ask. "I need some information so I can put you on my health insurance."

"Y'all don't have to—"

I hold up a hand. "We talked about this: You need care. I can make it possible for you to get it. Please let me help. I think my work insurance will cover most of your treatment, and even if it doesn't, what do I have money for if it isn't to do the right thing? My parents invested in a little company named Amazon in the late nineties. They're set for life, and they created a trust fund for me. While I try not to dip into it too much, this seems like the perfect reason to."

Johnny's quiet for a moment. Then he tells me his birth date and other personal info, and I upload it to the benefits portal. I also enter his cell number in my phone, trying not to sigh audibly at having OMG Velvet the Cowboy's number. Instead, I keep searching for possible treatment options—I want him to get the best care. I make a tentative appointment with a therapist with great credentials whose online scheduling says she's available tomorrow and bookmark sites to discuss with Johnny when we get to my house.

I don't know why I care *so much*, given that I just met him. I feel like I know him to some degree, I suppose, having watched him on the screen. Maybe it's, again, that false sense of familiarity. I feel it with him the way others feel it with me and my momther and Sam and Jules.

But I also feel ... possessive. He's my husband. I'm going to take care of him.

He's *mine*.

After I accomplish all those administrative tasks—which takes up quite a bit of the drive—I make the mistake of checking social media.

Herb Santangelo, our incumbent senator and my opponent, says on his social media account:

"Kurt Delmont wants people to think he's an upstanding, trustworthy candidate—but his drunken antics in Las Vegas aren't the kind of leadership California needs. Check the photos and decide for yourself. Vote Santangelo."

And from one of my mom's rivals:

"Melissa Delmont is now the mother-in-law of a GAY PORN STAR. Keep her out of the White House."

Shit.

CHAPTER 12
Johnny

The apprehension in my belly's like a sidewinder slithering over hot red dirt, getting more wiggly the closer and closer we get to Kurt's house.

The farther I get from Vegas, the more my problems seem to pile up without any solutions in sight. Mama's still sick, and now I don't have any real plan to get her the transplant. Kurt says he'll help fundraise, but will that work? How long will it take? Will she make it? The possibility of her … not … is unacceptable. And I can't take his money, no matter how much he says he has.

I'm married to a man I don't know. Sure, he's cute (and pushy), but I probably should've left him at the hotel bar last night. I feel like a street urchin adopted by the local moneybags, and that's not me. I don't wanna rely on anyone else.

If I was gonna stay alive, I shouldn't have done that retirement speech. Now I've got no money and no prospects. I'm a five-cent head wearing a ten-dollar Stetson. Well, it cost more than ten dollars, but you get my drift. It's not like I have many skills. I've only been a porn star and worked on a ranch. No schooling past eleventh grade.

I've got myself in a predicament with no way out. I'm as jumpy as a cat in a room of rocking chairs.

The panicky feeling gets worse as the GPS directs me to a high-end part of Los Angeles. Sure, Kurt told me he's got money, but it's different to *see* it. I've always lived in the cheapest place I could stand, so I could send as much as possible to my mama.

How can I send money to her now? I set a lot aside for her, but without the life insurance money, it'll run out eventually.

You know what the answer is. Kill yourself. Then she'll have the money.

My blood pressure shoots even higher when I slow the BMW at the entrance to Kurt's gated neighborhood. There must be a sensor in the car, or a transmitter or I don't even know what, because the gates open automatically, and he directs me to the driveway of a three-story condo. It's not what I imagined when he said he lived in a condo—it's Southern California modern, up on a bluff overlooking Highway 1. From what I can see between the structures, I expect the interior will have unobstructed beach views. Given the location, the manicured lawns, and the perfectly maintained homes, this development has to be stratospherically expensive.

It's one thing for me to accept a nice hotel suite for a weekend as part of an award. It's quite another to, what, freeload off Kurt indefinitely?

I'm a loser, yet again.

When I pull into the three-car garage next to a brand-new Volvo, I turn off the BMW and stay put in my seat. The space is lined with shiny gray cabinets and black-framed racing posters, and it's so clean you could eat off the pristine floor. It looks more like a showroom than a garage. I grip the steering wheel and let out a breath.

"Johnny?" Kurt says quietly, turning toward me. "What's wrong?"

"Where's the closest Greyhound station?"

Kurt chokes out a laugh. "What? Why?"

"Because I can't do this," I say through clenched teeth. "I ain't a gold digger."

He pauses a moment before he asks, "Is that what you think I think?"

"I dunno what you think."

"Look at me," he orders, and I do. His pretty brown eyes are intense and pleading. "Johnny. You're *not* using me."

I shake my head. "Not intentionally, but this is still a bad idea."

"Can you be more specific as to what's the bad idea?" He chuckles and spreads his hands wide. "Because you and I have made a few bad decisions in the past two days—namely your whole plan to remove yourself from the planet and us getting drunk-married." He pauses. "Shit, that was insensitive. Suicide isn't a joke."

"I figure if we can't joke about it, we can't talk about it," I say. My heart is still beating halfway out of my chest, but it's maybe a little better than it was a minute ago. "I'm okay with you teasing me."

"Phew. But which bad decision are you talking about?"

"Me coming here," I start. "Putting you in this situation where you have to deal with the fallout of marrying an adult entertainer. All my ..." I wave at my head. "All of it."

"Okay, for starters, that's not all on you. Last night is pretty fuzzy, but I think getting married was my idea."

I rack my brain, trying to remember which of us suggested going into the chapel. It might've been him. I was in a 'Fuck it, it's the last day of my life' mood, which is why I went along with it. Though my drunk brain certainly recognized a man I'm attracted to. That's for damn sure.

I look at his sweet face. Even though I don't deserve him—he's rich and educated and a literal poster boy, while I work, *worked*, in the shadows of society—I still really like him. Really *want* him.

I shrug. "Don't matter whose idea it was. I ... I don't belong here."

He reaches out and touches my shoulder, and I can't help leaning into his touch. "Hey. This has to be a shock to your system—being with me when you don't know me, getting married, and everything else. Especially with all that's been bothering you lately. But do you think you could come inside? I don't want to make you uncomfortable, but I'm not going to let you fend for yourself right now. That's just ... No. So I don't mean to be holding you hostage. But I do mean to be helping you." He gives me a grin. "And maybe you can help me, too."

I'm not sure how that would ever be possible, but it's nice to imagine. "How could I do that?"

"If you're my husband, you may need to go to a few public events with me." He holds up his hands. "Not now, not while you're feeling bad. But maybe when you feel better. Would you consider it?"

Of course I'd consider it. Kurt doesn't owe me anything—in fact, I've caused a ton of problems for him—yet he's sitting here wanting to take care of me. Of course I'll do anything I can to balance the scales.

He's being reasonable. I'm the one who's being a butthead. I tell the wailing violin in my head to hush.

"Yeah," I whisper.

"Can I ask you one more favor?" His voice is wary.

"Anything."

"Promise me you'll stay alive today?"

Well, heck. Tension grips me, but ... one day. And it's already half over. "Yeah," I say again. "I can do that."

I can't even die right.

Kurt smiles, and he leans toward me, but then he stops. "Thank you. That's all you have to do. C'mon, let me show you around. I used to live in an older bungalow, but when this development got built, I had to get in on it."

I nod, and we get out of the car, leaving our bags for the time being. I follow him up a flight of stairs into the bright, open condo. Sure enough, there's an expansive balcony overlooking the beach. I take off my dusty boots and leave them at the door. The place is spacious, and it's immediately apparent that it's a bachelor pad—no pets, no kids, nothing to mess it up. After I get a better look at the leather furniture, colorful art, and clean lines, I want to turn right around and head back to the garage.

Kurt sees the look on my face as he removes his own shoes. "What's the matter?"

"Nothing," I say.

"Honesty," he reminds me.

"Just ... what we were talking about in the car. I don't belong here."

"Babe." My whole body relaxes when he calls me that, even if the peaceful feeling won't last. "We need to focus on you feeling better. Everything else is secondary."

"Why are you being so—" I gesture helplessly. "Like this. I'm a stranger. You don't know me at all. I know at times it seems I'm studying to be a half-wit, but even I can tell what you're doing don't make an ounce of sense."

A pained look passes across Kurt's face. "We already talked about this. But I guess there's one thing I haven't told you. One big thing." He starts pacing in front of a breakfast bar. I stand in the middle of his living room in my stocking feet, watching him. "My high school boyfriend, Andrei, killed himself. He used pills and razors, and when his parents found him, it was too late. He'd bled out."

"Oh, shit," I hiss, my stomach sinking.

Way to fuck up Kurt's life as much as you've fucked up everyone else's.

"It ... it fucking gutted me. No one saw how bad he was feeling. I didn't realize. I didn't stop him." He bites his lip, and his eyes well up. "I still see him in my nightmares."

"Fuck, I'm sorry, Kurt."

He takes a breath and seems to get ahold of himself. "Yeah. So. Time has made it ... less. It's dulled the pain somewhat, but that loss, that guilt has never gone away." He gets almost clinical, like he's repeating something that's been said to him. "Suicide has implications far beyond the individual. For the people left behind, there's a void that can't be filled."

"Okay," I say, feeling like I need to say something.

"I kind of fell apart for a while. Not that—I don't mean to privilege my reactions over the pain Andrei must have been in. Anyway, the whole experience made my parents sticklers for mental health care. After that, if the smallest thing happened, I saw a therapist." He lets out a rueful laugh. "I've had a lot of fucking therapy over the years, let me tell you."

"It sounds like it."

"All I'm saying is, mental health matters. It should matter to everyone. It definitely matters to me. So please, stay with me, and let's get you the help you need. Let me do this."

"I'm a stubborn bastard, and I don't think I'll ever get used to accepting charity," I tell him.

"It's not charity."

"How is giving me a free place to stay, arranging for me to get medical care, helping my mama—how is that not charity?"

"I'd call it just being a decent human being," Kurt says.

"It's so far beyond that—"

"By staying, you're helping me feel like I'm making amends for the way I let Andrei down."

I swallow. "I don't think you let him down."

"Will you at least try to allow me to help, anyway?"

While part of me wants to keep fighting him, I relent again. "I'll try."

CHAPTER 13
Johnny

Kurt gives me a tour through the gleaming kitchen filled with top-of-the-line appliances and the large open space that serves as a living room and dining area, and then we go up to the third story.

"This is mine," he says, gesturing toward one room, "and this is the guest bedroom. Sorry it's kind of cluttered; I use it as an office when I work from home." There's a large computer desk in front of a window and a full-size bed in the corner, plus an easel and art supplies neatly stacked on a table. "I hope you'll be comfortable in here."

"I ain't gonna kick you out of your office."

He puts a hand on his hip, and I receive his message loud and clear. "Let's get our bags," he says.

"Do you have everything you need?" Kurt asks once we're upstairs again and I'm rolling my tiny suitcase into the guest bedroom. "Clothes, toiletries?"

I'm wearing my favorite jeans. I was planning on being buried in them. I didn't bring much else—a few things for while I was in Vegas, along with workout wear.

I shrug. "I'll get by."

He huffs. "Don't want you just 'getting by' when I can do something about it. After we have a bite to eat, let's go shopping."

"Hate shopping."

"What about a place like Boot Barn?"

I shrug reluctantly, because he's right that I need more than I'm standing up in, and I'm beat down by his kindness. "Yeah, okay. Fine. Dress me up. But if you call me Cinderella, we may have to have words."

Kurt smiles. "I'm good with being your fairy godfather." He gestures. "Feel free to use the closet," he says, "and there's a laundry bin in the corner."

"Hate to be a burden, but I gotta return my tux." I open my bag, and an envelope slips to the floor.

"Of course we can return your tux." He looks at the envelope addressed to Mama. "Was that meant to go to her ... after?"

I nod.

"Can I have it?" He holds out his hand.

I don't really want to give it to him, but I'm also not sure I should have it on me. I stare at it for a moment, pick it up, and shove it at him. "What are y'all gonna do with my gun?"

"For now? Lock it up. I have a few locking cabinets in the garage. Later, when you're stable, we can decide if you want to sell it or whatever."

"Not a fan of being without it."

Kurt raises an eyebrow. "Big, strong man like you can protect yourself without it, and you've got to be kidding if you think I'm gonna let you have a weapon." He presses his lips together and shakes his head. Without another word, he leaves me, taking the plastic laundry bag with my gun in it and heading back down the stairs.

A few minutes later, he reappears. "Don't go looking for it."

I sigh, knowing when I'm beat. I mean, sure, I could ransack his house for the keys, but I don't have the energy for it—and it's starting to dawn on me that I might be depressed.

Maybe that should have been obvious, but I'm in territory so foreign I can barely describe it. How do I feel? Numb, yes. Hopeless, yes. Listless, sometimes. Confused, often. But I ain't never been depressed before—unless I've been that way for so long I don't know any different.

Well, damn.

I thought I was just pissed and hopeless on account of my mama. But maybe I'm pissed and hopeless for myself.

Because shouldn't I be over-the-moon happy? My mama's going to get help. I don't know how Kurt's going to make that happen, but I'm starting to believe him when he says he will. I've got a safe place to stay, and Kurt's got plans to fix all sorts of things.

Things I don't deserve.

My brain's still messing with me. I rub my wrists, reminding myself that I'm not trapped. I can move. Kurt's not gonna hurt me.

I tell myself all that, but I start breathing fast and my knees give out. I plop down onto the bed, and to my surprise, a second later, Kurt is crouching in front of me on the floor, his hands on my thighs. Seeing his pretty face helps calm my breathing. Some.

"Look, Johnny," he says. "I know you're uncomfortable about staying here with me. I heard you when you said it felt like"—he shrugs—"I don't know. Like you're relying on someone else's benevolence. But that's not how I see the situation. I mean, yes, I want you to stay so we can get you help. That's not all there is to it, though. It's tough to explain how much I'm into you. I really, really fucking like you. I'm attracted to you—*you*, not the guy I used to watch on my screen. I'm hoping maybe if you get to know me, you'll like me, too."

He's so sweet, and somewhere in my foggy brain, a wave of lightness flows through me at how he makes me feel. "I do. Like you, I mean. And I wanna get to know you, too."

Kurt's face brightens. "Excellent." He stands and claps his hands once. "Are you hungry? You must be hungry—I'm ravenous. And if you tell me where you rented that tux, I can have Wendy, my assistant, return it for you, so that'll be one less thing for us to worry about."

I *am* kinda hungry, given that we hadn't stopped for lunch.

I follow him back into the kitchen and realize how badly I've been taking care of myself when I see his fully stocked refrigerator.

Kurt pulls out bread and sandwich fixings, then puts them together on plates with some chips and apple slices. It kinda makes me feel like I'm in preschool, but I also kinda like him taking care of me. No one's really done that, even when I was little. Ever since I can remember, I was always trying to take care of my mama.

"What do you want to drink? Seltzer? Coke? Gatorade?"

I clench my fists. "Don't drink Gatorade." Absolutely never. "Water's fine."

As we eat, Kurt clears his throat. "So, like we talked about, I think you should start therapy. Maybe some medication, if the doctors think that's a good idea."

I don't like the sound of any of that, but I'm not sure there's another choice. At this point, I'm basically going along with whatever he says. I know when I'm beat.

"While we were driving, I went online and made you a tentative appointment for tomorrow. It's a therapist who's highly recommended. Do you want to go?"

I nod, because I know that's what I'm supposed to do. Then I scold myself, since I was the one who insisted on honesty. So I shake my head, and he gives me a gentle smile.

That smile makes me breathless.

"You know what they say," he says. "The only way out is through. And I'll help you through."

"That sounds like some wisdom to me. Thanks." I don't mean thanks for the appointment, but thanks for taking me under his wing.

After we clean up the kitchen and Kurt's assistant picks up my tux, we go to a nearby western wear store, where Kurt buys me a week's worth of clothes. The whole nine yards: T-shirts, jeans, boxers, socks, a few flannel shirts, and a jacket. I feel lower than an earthworm letting him spend a bunch of money on me, but I don't waste energy I haven't got arguing. I take the receipt and mentally add it to my tab. I'll pay him back with interest.

I'll admit I'm glad to have more than one pair of jeans. It'll be nice to be able to change my clothes. I talked him out of getting me new boots, though. The ones I have'll serve me fine.

When we get back, it's past sunset, and after a light dinner, we sit awkwardly on the couch watching the local news.

The awkwardness isn't like me. For one thing, I'm used to touching people I barely know. For another, he and I weren't awkward last night. We kissed and cuddled, and we slept in the same bed together. It all felt completely natural.

I'm drawn to him.

I find myself wanting to curl into him, but I don't know if I should. I'm not in a sexual mood. Until The Incident, sex was as natural for me as breathing. These days, not so much.

I want to touch him, though. Not just to feel the warmth of another human being, but to feel *him*.

I can't explain why I'm hesitant. Maybe it's just my messed-up brain.

He looks at me a few times, and it seems like he might be leaning in to kiss me. But he doesn't.

So when it gets late, I say good night, stand up, and aim for the bed upstairs in his office, praying that sleep will find me soon.

I don't get far, though, before Kurt hops up off the couch and follows me. He sighs and pinches his nose. "I'm sorry, I know this is weird. Now that I've thought about it, I'm not really comfortable having you be by yourself all night. It's not that I don't trust you—"

"I ain't done the right things to earn your trust."

Kurt gives me a sheepish smile. "Well, maybe. I just want to ensure you're okay. Would you consider sleeping in my bed? We don't have to do anything," he adds quickly. "I wanna keep you close, but I wouldn't, y'know, expect more."

While part of me is annoyed that I ain't adult enough to be left alone for a few hours, the greater part of me is getting all soft and melty, because he cares. And spending another night sleeping next to him won't rightly be a hardship.

Instead of saying anything—or arguing—I nod and, after I grab the bag of my new clothes to bring with me, follow him into his big bedroom.

It's nicely decorated, with black furniture, framed black-and-white photographs and colorful art, and midcentury modern lamps. It also has what I think is a view of the ocean.

"Um," I say, scratching my belly. "I'm going to take a shower before bed, if you don't mind. Is there a bathroom you prefer I use?" I'm not grimy from the drive or anything, but I want a moment to myself.

"Of course I don't mind, and use mine." He walks me in there to show me how to use the complicated handles and pauses. "Johnny, I'll give you the space to do that, but would you ... would you please not lock the door? Again, it's not that I don't trust you." He shuffles his feet, then looks me in the eye. "Okay, I *don't* trust you when it's your own safety at stake. You had a lot of scary plans just a few hours ago, and I'd rather be safe than sorry."

While I don't like hearing that, I don't blame him. And again, maybe the depression(?) is making me not want to fight. I nod. "Sounds like a deal to me."

"I'm not going to come in," he says in a rush. "I want to be sure you're safe when I'm not watching you."

Something about the way he's insisting on caring for me penetrates my frozen heart. "It's fine, precious," I say, taking a step toward him before stopping.

Even though he smiles at me, I don't give in to the desire to kiss him, though I'm pretty sure I'm seeing the same want in his eyes.

Before leaving the bathroom, Kurt opens a drawer and

removes a package of disposable razors, which he takes with him. "Do I need to lock up the kitchen knives?"

I wince. I hate that he has to ask. "No. I'm not ... I'm squeamish about blood." I touch his wrist. "I promise I would not consider using those to hurt myself. Not after knowing about Andrei. I'd never do that to you. Swear on my mama."

Kurt studies me a long moment. "I believe you."

He turns to go, and I follow him into the bedroom, take my toiletry kit out of my suitcase, and return to his bathroom. I turn on the water, then brush my teeth and step into the shower.

While I lather up, I think about the past twenty-four hours. What a mess I've made. I'm like a rhino in a rose garden, leaving destruction everywhere.

I've ruined Kurt's chances at the ballot box.

I've endangered my mom's life.

I've blown up my life.

I don't see how things can get any worse, and yet I'm afraid they will.

But something Kurt said to me repeats in my brain over and over again as the hot water sluices down my back.

"The only way out is through."

There's a hint there. A promise that, if I can just hang in there long enough, I might be able to get better.

Do I want to?

CHAPTER 14
Kurt

Johnny emerges from the bathroom in a cloud of cloves and citrus, my new favorite scent. I love it.

I wonder what it is—must be soap or aftershave or something. Maybe a combination of products. He should bottle it and sell it, because it makes me think of something sweet and sexy and a little old-fashioned. Which is Johnny. Well, it's how I think of him, but that's probably not the common perception, so maybe it wouldn't work.

He's got one of my plush dark blue towels wrapped around his hips, showing off his V-cut and his tanned, muscled torso. I've mapped out all of those abs many times on video, but seeing them in person does something to me—something like set fire to my bloodstream.

While he was showering, I ran downstairs to shut up the house for the night and turn off the downstairs lights, so I'm in my underwear and taking off my shirt when he returns to the bedroom. I ache with the need to hold him. To run my fingers over his bare skin. To kiss him.

"Feel better?" I ask, and okay, yeah. I'm checking him out. He's just so beautiful, and he draws me to him. When I used to watch his videos, the minute he was on-screen, my dick would start to harden like Pavlov's dogs start to drool. Even though he was nothing more than a bunch of pixels, he always looked so *touchable*.

Only now he's here in person, and sober.

Johnny looks me up and down, and his expression tells me that he wants me as much as I want him. He stretches his arms over his head, making the ladder on his belly pop. "Shower felt good, yeah." A drop of water trickles down his forehead and across his high cheekbone. His eyes heat, and he bites his lower lip.

"Jesus fuck," I whisper. Before I know what I'm doing, I take a step forward and crush my mouth to his, wrapping my arms around his waist. He stiffens and inhales sharply.

"Sorry," I say, pulling back but gently running my teeth along his lower lip. Against his skin, I say, "I should've asked first."

"Darlin', shut up," Johnny says. And then he takes over the kiss. I don't know if you've ever been kissed by a 6'6" cowboy, but they *really* take over. He tilts up my jaw and keeps one hand under my chin, the other on the back of my neck. The move's possessive. He's *claiming* me.

I love it.

And my mind races to say *You're not special. He does this for a living. He's like this with everyone.*

I can't help but love that he's this way with me, though. I can't help but be swept away by this kiss. His minty tongue's in my mouth. His hot body's against mine. My hands are reaching around him and clenching on the smooth skin of his back, not sure if I should do more. He takes a step forward, and I take a step back, and there's no doubt he's the one running this show now.

We've kissed before—just last night—but that was drunken, and this is not. That was out of my mind, and this is ... just *wanting*. My dick's hardening against his thigh, and I rut into him, almost without my volition.

"Can we have sex?" I blurt, when we break apart again.

Johnny traces a finger down my throat. "That could be arranged."

Excitement surges through every inch of my body ... except for a small, still-rational part that reminds me why Johnny's here at all. I force myself to try to think. "With how you've been feeling ... are you sure you're okay with it?"

"I don't need to be feeling good to have sex," he says.

Cold water douses my desire. "Yeah. That's ... that's a no."

Johnny groans. "Normally I'd be all over getting together with someone as handsome as you. Now I'm so screwed up that I can't even give you a good time."

"That's okay," I tell him, taking a small step back. "I didn't bring you here for sex. I'm sorry—I shouldn't have gone there."

"You have nothing to apologize for." He kisses me again, but it's a plea. "You're so sweet, and I do want you, even if I'm depressed or whatever it is. Just, if you don't mind, maybe not tonight. When I fuck you, it should be 'cause we're both into it."

"I can wait," I say. I don't want to acknowledge how much of a thrill his "when" sends through me.

"It could even be in the morning. I dunno. That okay?"

"Of course." I'm half-hard, but that's not the end of the world. "Can I ask a question that's none of my business?"

"That hasn't stopped you before."

"Yeah, okay. Fair. So ... depression affects libido, right? Which makes me wonder, why would you think you might be more up for sex in the morning?" I don't want to be negative with him, but his depression isn't going to just go away overnight.

Johnny stares at his feet. "It's not like I understand what's going on inside my head, but I've got good days and not so good and then some downright terrible ones—and it's not necessarily whole days, either. Sometimes I'm fine, and sometimes I can't move. Sometimes things give me pleasure, and sometimes they plain don't. I can't always come, but touching still feels good—usually, at least. I can't explain it better than that."

"Makes sense. Would you do me a favor, though? I can't see inside your head. Can you keep me informed—as best you can—about how you're feeling?"

"I'll try." He looks at the bed. "Do you want me to put something on to sleep in? I usually don't, but I can."

I want to moan. Because I've seen him naked. I *desire* him. But I'm not gonna be a creep. "I want you to be comfortable," I say, meaning it.

Johnny hangs up his towel and comes back to the bedroom, all naked and glorious, his dick huge and mouthwatering. But then he looks at the bag of new clothes and opens a package of boxers. "Maybe I'll just wear these."

I sigh, but I understand. "Whatever you feel best in. It's been a very long day. And you've got that appointment tomorrow."

Johnny looks at me, resigned. I can tell he doesn't want to go, but he can't muster the energy to argue with me—or he knows he shouldn't argue, even though the idea of therapy terrifies him. Either way, it breaks my heart. What's this man like when his brain isn't beating him down?

"It's fine, precious," he says, and he climbs into my bed.

* * *

In the middle of the night, I'm awoken by noise and movement.

Johnny's moaning loudly and thrashing around under the covers.

"Shh," I say, trying to calm him but not wanting to get too close, because he's a big man, and he seems to be having a nightmare. Or maybe some kind of episode? I have no idea.

He cries out, and the raw vulnerability in his voice makes my heart break. I turn on the light. Everything looks worse in the darkness. Ask me how I know.

"Johnny," I whisper. "Hey. You're okay. It's okay. You're here with me."

He thrashes some more, but then he sits up, eyes vacant, roaring, "Goddamnit, no!" But then he seems to come to. He's trembling, and a tear rolls down his cheek. He shakes his head and blinks blearily, then cocks his head. "What? Where am—? Aww, hell."

"Hey," I say quietly. "You were having a nightmare."

"Didn't mean to wake you." He looks down at his hands. His torso is sheened with sweat.

"It's okay," I say. I want to ask what he was dreaming about, except I've been pushing him all day, ever since I found out his plans. And while I'm not going to stop trying to take care of him, he doesn't have to tell me all his secrets. Us getting drunk-married doesn't entitle me to that. Heck, being sober-married doesn't necessarily mean people don't keep secrets, though I'd like to think it would. "Maybe you can talk about it with the therapist," I offer, hoping that won't piss him off ... but even if it does, he needs to learn that it's normal to go to a therapist and share your truths with them. It's not a sign of weakness.

Johnny huffs and turns onto his side, his back to me.

Well, shit.

I don't want to touch him if he doesn't want to be touched, but it's amazing how dejected a big man can look when he's curled up in the middle of a big bed at dark o'clock.

"Want me to keep the light on?" I whisper.

"I don't need to sleep with the light on," he snaps. "I'm not a child."

"Never said you were. But you've obviously got a few demons that need slaying."

"My demons respawn. Even if I get 'em, they come back." Johnny's back to sounding defeated.

I turn the bedside lamp off but go into the bathroom and turn that light on, then leave the door cracked so it serves as a nightlight. I can almost hear Johnny side-eyeing me, but he can deal with me being a mother hen.

When I crawl back into bed, I face him, so we're like a quotation mark. I still don't touch him, even though I really want to. I want to feel his big, warm body against mine.

But what matters is what *he* wants. What he *needs*.

Holding in a sigh, I turn onto my other side, so that we're facing away from each other.

A few moments later, Johnny rolls over and shuffles toward me. His lips tickle my neck. "I'm sorry," he murmurs. "I don't like anyone seeing me like this."

"I'm not going to judge you," I whisper.

"Yeah." He doesn't sound convinced.

I decide to just go for it. "If it might help keep the nightmares away, you can put your arms around me. I like having you close."

"Even with me flipping around like a fish on a pier?"

"Even then."

He hesitates for a moment, but soon one of his arms snakes under my neck, the other around my middle, as he spoons me. I relax instantly with his big, hot body tucked up against mine, and he seems to settle in, too. He rumbles something deep in his chest that sounds satisfied.

This. This is what I wanted.

Maybe it will make him feel better, too.

He kisses the back of my neck and my hair, and his fingers trace absent circles on my stomach. Not annoyingly. Gently.

Soon, his breaths are easy, and I fall asleep, cradled in his embrace.

CHAPTER 15

Johnny

I wake up again in a bed that isn't my own—and then I remember I don't have a bed of my own no more. I'm curled up next to Kurt. At least this morning I know his name, unlike yesterday.

Shucks, was it only yesterday? It feels like my life has gone completely cattywampus in the space of barely over a day.

Kurt's body is warm and muscular against mine, and my natural morning reaction is raring to greet the sun. I want to get off, and that hasn't happened for a while. Would he still be open to fooling around?

I kiss the back of his neck and then down his shoulders. He yawns, then grins into my bicep, where it's cradling him. "Morning," he murmurs.

"Morning," I whisper back, rubbing my hard cock against his ass and running a hand down his side toward his boxer briefs. "How are you feeling?"

"Horny."

That makes me smile. "That's good, precious. Me, too. You wanna fool around?"

"Yes." No hesitation.

I heft myself up and push him to his back, then settle between his legs, rubbing my erection against his. His eyes widen at how fast I moved him, but he's easy to haul around, even though he's not tiny. I lean down to kiss him, and he kisses me back.

Lord, this is nice. Even first thing in the morning, with not the best, most minty breath, I like the way he tastes. The way he smells, all clean and musky. The way he kisses me, like he means it.

His hands are roaming down my back, headed to my ass so that he can pull me tighter to him.

When we break apart, I look at him, ingrained habit making me all business for a moment. "So you know, I get tested regularly. I ain't been with nobody since the last time I worked, which was months ago. I'm negative, and I'm also on PrEP."

Kurt scrubs a hand over his face and looks away. "I'm negative, too, as of my last annual exam. Haven't been with anyone since then."

I kiss him again as I lean over him, one palm by his ear and the other hand lightly holding his throat. He seems to be okay with that, but it's not making him go wild, so I move my hand to his collarbone and shoulder, stroking his skin.

That makes him shudder.

Okay, then. He likes it gentle.

I follow the caress with a kiss on the dip above his collarbone while I thrust against his cock. He's rutting into me, too, and it starts as a sweet, slow, seductive dance on the bed.

Exactly the way I prefer it.

"Let's get these off," I mutter, pulling his fancy black boxer briefs down by the waistband. He lifts his hips to help, and then he's naked under me.

"Lord, you're gorgeous," I say, admiring the planes of his body —not a bodybuilder or anything but simply masculine and hot. "Just perfect."

He blushes, and that's adorable. He likes being praised. Nice, because that's my favorite thing to do in bed.

I kiss my way down his torso, stopping to suck on each nipple.

"That ... that feels good," he says shakily.

While I know he ain't a virgin, he's acting like he hasn't been touched in a while. Not sure I wanna know his history—even though mine has mainly been recorded for posterity.

I shake aside those thoughts, and when I get to his hard, pretty cock, I stop for a moment to admire it. It's long and lean, but not huge. Not too thick. It's darker than the skin on his upper thighs, and the head is a purply rose color. He's starting to leak precome, and I lean down to lick at the tip—little kitten licks, just for fun.

"Yes, holy fuck, yes. Yes yes yes."

I grin and take him in a little ways, loving the way he smells—earthy in a good way. Like sex.

He bows his back off the mattress when I suck hard.

"Gonna come fast if you keep that up," he warns.

"Do you wanna?" My voice is a low rumble. "Come fast, that is?"

He shakes his head. "I don't want it to be over yet. I'd like to make it last."

"Well, if we want, this doesn't have to be the only time I ever suck your cock," I say, and he lets out a helpless groan as I take him farther down my throat. I stick my hand inside my own underwear to stroke myself a couple times, then move my fingers to his balls, cradling and fondling them while I bob up and down on his dick.

"Stop," he chokes out, and I pull off immediately, holding up my hands.

"Sorry—" I start to say, but he interrupts.

"No, it's not— I want you to. I'm just too close. And I want to return the favor."

I shed my boxers and scoot up higher on the bed, kissing his lips and moving so my cock is close to his hand. "Have at me, precious."

He reaches out and grips me with confidence. As he does, a shudder passes through him.

"You okay?" I ask.

"So much better than okay," he says. "Just ... I've fantasized about this a lot of times, but I never thought it would actually happen."

That makes me smile, and now I'm kissing him deeper, thrusting into his fist as he strokes me with sure movements. "Oh yeah. That's how I like it. You're doing that so well. Yes. Oh, fuck."

I reach for his cock, and while it's slightly wet from my saliva, this would be so much better with some lube. Kurt seems to get the same idea, as he's reaching a hand vaguely for the nightstand. I open a drawer and find a bottle of premium lube—nice. I squidge some into my hand, then line up our dicks, taking over the stroking as I kiss him hard.

Kurt's hands are squeezing my ass, scrabbling at the mattress, running through my hair and his. I'm turning him into a wanton, needy thing. Heck yes. I want to do more of this. I want to fuck his cute little ass someday. But right now, mutual hand jobs are working just fine, and I focus on him.

I bite down gently on his shoulder as I stroke him harder, and he gasps, his cock stiffening even more, then starting to pulse as his warm come floods over my hand.

I grin, watching his face go from tense to blissed out.

When I move to jack myself, he stills my hand. "Please," he says.

I nod, and he grips me perfectly on the part of my dick that's the most sensitive—the top part, under the crown. And with his good pressure and rhythm, I'm not going to take long.

From years of doing this on camera, I'm used to holding back my orgasm so the scene can last. So when I don't have to, when I can let myself get off when my body's ready—that's a treat and a half.

Climaxing at all is a treat, since lately I haven't been in the mood. At times, even when it's only been me and my hand, I haven't bothered to finish. Maybe that's tied to what's going on with my brain.

Definitely not feeling a low libido right now, though.

I shudder and moan, my come painting Kurt's belly, and his expression turns even more satisfied. Like he's proud of making me come.

"Good job, baby," I say, kissing him.

He smiles against my mouth and kisses me back.

Then we flop next to each other on our backs, panting.

Well, this ain't so bad. If I have to be facing all this awful shit in my life, fooling around with a cutie like Kurt is a nice ... compensation probably ain't the right word. He's more than that.

My husband.

The rush of pleasure into my brain is making me feel better. It probably won't last, but I'll take what I can get. I've had a lot of sex in my life, but with Kurt, it's fresh and new, perhaps because he's so into it. He really is precious.

Eventually, Kurt stirs. "I'll get us some washcloths."

"I can do it," I say, but he's already up.

On his way back to bed, he opens the curtains, and the ocean I hadn't seen in the dark last night is gray and misty across Highway 1 below. I take the cloth he hands me and glance around at the art on the walls as I clean myself up. The photographs are mostly landscapes, but there are some bright political posters and a few paintings. One in particular stands out to me. It's of two men embracing, done in an impressionistic style—loose and rough, but emotional.

"That painting's awful pretty," I say, gesturing at it.

"Thank you," Kurt says quietly, returning to bed.

I turn to look at him. "You did that?"

He nods. "Yeah. I ... I don't get to paint much these days, but I like to."

"Too busy with the election?"

"That and with work and whatever else."

"It seems like you need a break."

"Yeah." He sighs. "But I can rest later, I guess. It's fine."

"I dunno," I say slowly. "You're all up in my business, making me work on my mental health. Maybe I need to return the favor."

I can tell he's about to deny that he needs help, but then he shrugs. "Maybe so."

Is there something I can do to take a burden off him?

"I hate to ruin the moment," he says. "But we should probably get dressed."

I sigh. The real world is waiting, outside our little bubble. I'm not really eager to leave that bubble, but I can pull on my britches and deal. And while I still feel crappy about needing help, I'm sort of ... honored that he's chosen me to take care of.

Feels nice, honestly.

CHAPTER 16
Kurt

What do you call it when you have sex with your dream man? Hashtag goals sex? Finally-OMG-I-manifested-him sex? I-pined-for-him-through-my-screen-and-now-he-sucked-my-cock sex? I don't know. I'm not a wordsmith like my speechwriter. There should be a name for it, though. Having Johnny's mouth and hands on my cock was a fantasy come true. I can't wait until we can do it again. It's more than the physical, though. He's the whole package—kind and caring and sexy—and I genuinely want to get to know him better.

As we get up, shower, and dress, we're more affectionate than we were last night. Our hips jostle while we brush our teeth and shave.

Johnny's hand rests on my waist as I make coffee, and he kisses the nape of my neck. I groan into his touch. "You keep that up, and we won't go anywhere today."

"I'd be all right with that," he says. I turn to look at him with an eyebrow raised, and his face falls. "Yeah, okay. I know."

My amazing housekeeper, Galen, stocks plenty of breakfast food, so we have a hearty meal. When we're done, Johnny helps me with the dishes, looking right at home in stocking feet with a towel draped over his shoulder. It's like having the partner I've always wanted.

But it doesn't mean anything. I need to remind myself of that. He's here because I refused to accept any other outcome. Him being in my house doesn't make us anything beyond slightly more than strangers in a fucked-up situation.

That doesn't stop me from checking out his ass in the new, tight, dark Wranglers I bought him. A few times, Johnny looks at me and seems to want to say something, but then he closes his mouth. I assume he's considering either apologies or something he doesn't want to say under our honesty policy. I don't ask. I've been pressing him a lot. I can give him a break.

We have some time before we need to head out for his appointment. "Do you mind if I make a few phone calls?" I ask.

He shakes his head, gesturing to the balcony. "I'll check out the view and give you some privacy." I like that idea, because there's nothing for him to hurt himself with out there. I suppose he could jump, but he seems calm.

Watching over someone else's mental state is so hard. Can I trust him with anything at all? I feel like I can, but I know I need to be careful. I compromise by staying in the living room. That means I can study his stance as he braces himself against the balcony railing, arms straight and ass out.

Damn.

Reminding myself that I'm not allowed to spend all day ogling Johnny, I turn to my phone. First up, my momther.

"Kurt! Why didn't you call last night?"

"Sorry. I've been busy."

"I'll say." She lets out an annoyed laugh. "Your father and I have been wondering what you were thinking. Marrying a ... a ... a total stranger?"

A stranger? When he's gazing at me, Johnny focuses so intently I feel *seen* for the first time in my life.

And I seem to please that big, sad cowboy.

"I don't really have a good answer for that, but I do like him. A lot."

Her pause tells me that's not the answer she was expecting. "Okay. So ... he's not simply a mistake you made while drinking too much?"

Yes. *No.* "I don't know yet." I cringe as I ask, "Has there been any impact on your approval rating?"

"Too early to tell, but predictions are that I'll drop eight points."

I recoil. "Oh, damn," I mutter.

"It could be worse." She sounds resigned rather than angry. "I'm more worried about you and your life ... and the primary."

My stomach dips. With all my concerns about Johnny's mental health, I'd set my own issues off to the side. But now they come roaring back. "I'm fine. What are they saying?" I ask. I'm not sure who I mean by "they." People who talk shit, I guess.

"It's ... not positive, honey. While you have some defenders, the majority of social media posts I've seen are about how your behavior doesn't show strong family values."

"For god's sake," I mutter.

"I'm sorry for passing along bad news. Your father and I love you no matter what, of course. You just need to find a way to convey your goodness to the voters."

The stress of the past few days is crashing down on me. My failure at obtaining funding. My decision to drink my cares away. My drunken marriage. My suicidal husband.

I want to scream. "I don't know how to do that."

"Talk with Paige. She'll have ideas. That's what you hired her for."

"I know." My voice lowers. "While it's unconventional, I really like him, Mom."

Another pause. "Then let me know what I can do to support you. And him."

I blink back unexpected tears. While part of me thinks she's being pragmatic—because a united front's always stronger than a splintered one—this is also her being more of a mom than a politician. I like it when she skews that direction. "Thanks, I appreciate that." I have to clear my throat before I can continue. "Can we talk more later? I need to take Johnny to an appointment soon."

"Of course. Oh, Kurt? Does he want to meet Dad and me?"

"At some point, we should do that, yes," I say. "But we have a few things to do around here first. When are you next coming down south?"

"I'll check my schedule and talk with Dad. Likely not for a few weeks."

Am I even going to be with Johnny in a few weeks? My gut tightens. I want to be. Does he?

He'll still be alive then, right? *Fuck*. He damn well better be.

"We'll see you then," I say, sounding more confident than I feel. We hang up, and I immediately call my campaign manager.

"You motherfucking bastard," she starts.

I cough a laugh. "Hi, Paige. I'm fine. How are you?"

"I am *not* fine. Do you know how many angry messages I've had to field via every medium possible—email, phone, direct messages on all possible social media platforms. Carrier pigeons. Town criers. I swear, Kurt, I thought you were boring, and then you go and do this."

"Not boring anymore?"

"No. It's going to take a lot of work from both of us to save your campaign. While politicians have come back from a lot worse things than an unexpected wedding, this is an unexpected wedding to a *porn star*." She quickly corrects herself: "Sorry, adult film star. You know I have nothing against people in unconventional professions. But a lot of voters aren't as enlightened." Her sigh's so loud I think it moves walls. "Just ... we need to come up with a way to turn the narrative back into something that we want."

"I'll meet with you soon," I say. It's important, but Johnny's all that matters right now. "Tomorrow or the next day. Will that work?"

"I guess," she whines, and despite everything, that makes me smile. She's got my best interests at heart, even if she's angry at me right now.

We say our goodbyes and hang up. Johnny is still on the balcony, but he's moved to sit on one of the couches. Though he appears to be gazing out over the water, I suspect that he's not seeing the waves or the Pacific Coast Highway but is lost in his thoughts.

I go out and sit beside him, and he wraps an arm around my shoulders. "You okay?" I whisper, leaning into his chest.

"Yeah." His voice is hoarse. "Well, no."

"Sorry, babe. How are you feeling?"

"I ... I dunno."

Is the stuff with his mom—his fears for her well-being, his frustration and sense of inadequacy—the only thing that's got him so messed up? Or is there more going on? Not that there needs to be more, but ... I feel like there is.

"Want to talk about it?" I ask.

"Not really."

I want to be here for him, and I hope he feels safe talking to me, but ultimately, that's what his therapist is for. "You sure?" I try.

He nods.

"Okay." I give him a smile and snuggle into him. He doesn't pull away or seem like he's uncomfortable. On the contrary, he tightens his arm around me, holding me close. He seems to like to do that as much as I like him doing it.

Maybe he experiences life through his body, needing touch.

I need touch, too. I've been wanting it for a long time.

Moving slowly, to give him time to indicate if he wants me to stop, I shift so that I'm straddling his thighs. His nostrils flare, and he puts his big hands around my neck and pulls me down for a kiss.

I shiver, and it's not from the cool ocean breeze. I love kissing Johnny. I love the scrape of his jaw against mine and how he tastes. How active he is. How single-minded he is when he kisses me. How his tongue delves into my mouth, taking over my body.

"Don't treat me like I'm fragile," he whispers when we pause to breathe. "This is helping."

"Do you think it's just dopamine?"

"Not sure what that is, but maybe. Or maybe I just like you." His strong hands palm my ass and knead my butt cheeks. I start hardening, wanting to grind against him.

"Fuck," I gasp. "You're so beautiful."

He gives me a crooked smile. "That's my line. You're the beautiful one, precious."

Johnny reaches between us to undo my jeans. He glances up at me, hopeful. I'm lusting for him and already raring to go. Fantasy life part two.

I look around, though. We're up on a bluff, but the balcony balustrade is glass—to preserve the view from indoors—and telephoto lenses exist. The last thing I need is sex pictures of Johnny and me hitting the internet. "Can we take this inside?" I ask, hopping off his lap and holding out a hand.

"Sure thing," he says, and follows me into the living room. Before I even turn around, he's dropped to his knees in front of me and is deftly unbuttoning my pants and tearing the zipper down, then bringing out my hard dick. With one rugged hand, he gives it a light stroke. Then he tugs me closer.

"Oh my god," I gasp as Johnny's lips close around my cock. "That feels so fucking ... fuck."

He lets out a deep chuckle from his chest, and I gently thrust into his mouth. He nods, and I slide farther down his throat. I try to be careful, not wanting to use him, but it seems he's good with this.

He pulls off me just long enough to say, "Fuck my mouth, darlin'. I want to feel you get off." Then he gets back to work—but not before sucking a finger wet so he can reach between my ass cheeks and go exploring.

This is a dream come true, and he's as good as I suspected he'd be. On top of that, the scenario is surreal. I've imagined him doing this so many times—and watched it on-screen—but feeling his hot, wet suction and tongue makes my knees weak.

His big hands pull me to him as I rut into his mouth. He doesn't seem to have a gag reflex, which is un-fucking-believable, and his finger is nudging my prostate, and I'm about to explode.

"Keep this up, and I'm gonna—" I warn.

He nods quickly, clear permission.

I get to the edge and let myself go over, coming hard with the extra-good feel of that internal massage. I keep thrusting gently even after I finish, needing the come-down, loving how he lets me use his mouth.

I kind of collapse to the floor, then get to my knees, pushing him down on his back, wanting to return the favor. I reach for his fly, but he puts a hand on top of mine, stilling it. "I'm good, darlin'."

I look at him quizzically. "You sure?" Because it feels like he's almost ... *shunning* me.

Johnny coughs. "Yeah. Not quite in the mood. I'm ... good. I don't always need to bust a nut."

I want to tempt him, but I can listen to what he's saying and trust that he knows his own needs. I tuck myself back into my pants, and we both sit on the floor. I tug him over and kiss him. "Hey." I smile against his lips. "You made me feel really good just now." I want to thank him, but that seems maybe cringey and clumsy—things I'm good at. I don't know. Maybe I'm overthinking this.

"I'm glad, darlin'."

CHAPTER 17

Johnny

Kurt's curled up into me here on the floor. I'd suck his gorgeous cock again in a heartbeat—anything to delay contact with the outside world. Plus, I like making him wild—he deserves some sexy experiences in his life. I can give him those.

Instead, I say something distinctly unsexy. "Can I admit I'm nervous about going to the therapist? It won't be like talking to you. I don't know how I feel about talking to a stranger." Some people might argue that Kurt is almost a stranger, but he doesn't feel like one. Not at all.

He smiles at me. "Want me to go with you to the appointment? I mean, I'm going to drive you, but if it would help, I could sit in on the session."

Usually, I'm intensely private. But look where being private got me: a gun and piles of pills. In many ways, Kurt's the safest person on the planet for me, because he doesn't know me and doesn't seem to be judging me. I'm not getting a pitying vibe from him, either. Just a genuine desire to help—and maybe a bit of a crush on me.

Which is fine, because I've got a big crush on him. Despite how blue I've been, he makes me ... not *happy*, but as happy as I can be under the circumstances. I want him, and he's one of the few things that breaks through the fog and pain.

"I reckon I'd like you to come in with me," I admit.

Too weak to handle my own problems.

Kurt nods and kisses me. "I'd be happy to. I promise I'll be respectful of anything you say, and I'll never use any of it against you. Ever."

There goes my heart warming up to him even more. The last place I want to go is to a therapist's office, but Kurt's right. I need to. He's talked me into having a sliver of hope that I could feel better.

Why do I believe him? Maybe it's because he's new to my life and has a fresh perspective ... and I've got nothing else to lose. I do have things to gain, though. I might be able to save my mama and be around to see her healthy again.

And maybe be able to spend more time with Kurt.

For Mama, and for him, I'm gonna do my best to fix what's going on inside my head.

We get tidied up, but we still have a little time before we need to leave. "Mind if I call my mama real quick?" I ask.

"No, of course not. I'll let you be." He heads out to the balcony while I dial her number from the couch, my eyes on the ocean outside—and him. Mama answers immediately.

"Hey," I say. "How are y'all?"

"I'm as pleased as a pup with two tails," she says, but she sounds even more frail than usual, and I know she's fibbin'. "Now that I hear your voice."

I ask her about her doctor's appointments and her caregiver and my sister. Once we've exhausted those topics, I can't avoid talking about me. "So, I have some news."

"Oh? What's that?"

"I met someone. A man."

"You did?" She sounds delighted. "Who is he?"

"His name is Kurt Delmont, and actually, we got married."

Her voice gathers strength I didn't know she had. "John Haskell, y'all did *not* get married and forget to invite your mama to the wedding."

I squirm. "I'm sorry, Mama. The wedding wasn't exactly planned. We were in Las Vegas, and one thing led to another ... I do apologize for not inviting y'all. If it makes you feel better, only strangers were there."

"I don't think it does make me feel better," she says haughtily, and her tone makes me smile. It also makes my heart ache.

"I'm sorry for springing this on you. Maybe we'll come up and visit sometime soon. Would you like that?"

"I'd love that," she says.

Kurt reappears, tapping his wrist where a watch would be if he wore one.

"Then we'll arrange it. Sorry, Mama, for the quick call, but we've gotta go to an appointment. I'll talk with you later. Tell May Ella hi. I love you."

"I love you, too, Johnny, and give that husband of yours my love as well."

"You haven't even met him yet."

"He's family. End of story."

Trust Mama to make things so simple.

"Mama sends her love," I tell Kurt.

"Then I do the same," Kurt says, his dark brown eyes wrinkling at the corners as he smiles.

My limbs feel light, and my heart expands. My new husband just accepted—more than accepted—my beautiful mama, and it makes me even sweeter on him. If I'm not careful, I could find myself really into this guy.

I pretty sure I'm okay with that, even if he's a politician. I can overlook a man's profession. He's overlooking mine, after all.

After I hang up, Kurt and I head to the therapist's office, which, it turns out, is up the coast a ways.

When we walk in, I learn from the sign on the door that the therapist is named Christian Gray, which makes me smile. I read those *Fifty Shades* books to get some ideas for scenes, though it took me a while, because I'm not a great reader. I liked them, though.

"Um, Dr. Gray?" I say.

She's an elegant Black woman with a kind manner. "That's me, though I encourage you to call me by my first name, Christian. Are you John Haskell?"

I nod and shake her hand. "Most people call me Johnny. This is my husband, Kurt Delmont. You probably know that, because he's the one who made the appointment. I'd like him to join us. Is that okay?" I ask. I trip over the word "husband," but I like the way it feels when I say it.

"If you'd like to have him here, then of course. If at any point there's a reason I want to talk with you on your own, we'll agree among ourselves and have him step out," Christian says. "Welcome. Please make yourself comfortable." She shows us into a small room with big windows and a view of the coast. It doesn't have one of those stereotypical chaise lounge couches like you see in cartoons, but there are a few comfortable chairs and a regular couch, along with side tables with boxes of tissues on them. It's a generic room, and that makes me feel better. Like being here ain't so weird.

Kurt sits down next to me on the couch, his knee pressed to mine, and it's amazing how much less alone I feel with that contact. I fill out a few forms, and Christian waits and watches.

When I'm done, she asks, "What have you come to see me about?"

The truth is, I don't want to talk with her about anything. Even though I'm trying to be positive, I don't actually believe I can get better.

"Um. Well. I dunno how to start," I say, wringing my hands and wishing I were anywhere else.

"Then why don't you just start with how you're feeling right now."

"Numb," I say immediately. "And ... shitty."

She nods and scribbles something on a paper. "How long have you been feeling numb and shitty?"

"Months," I say. "Maybe years."

Kurt goes still.

"Has the level of numbness and shittiness been the same over that whole time span, or has it changed?" Christian asks.

I clear my throat. "It got really bad the past few weeks."

"How so?" There's no judgment in her eyes. She doesn't know me. She's a professional. This is confidential.

I'm safe.

Kurt is here and already knows.

"I was planning on killing myself."

Christian maintains a professional demeanor and doesn't react. Kurt takes my hand and squeezes it.

"Did you have a plan in place as far as how and when?" Christian asks, putting down her notepad and studying me.

"Over the weekend. Yesterday or the night before."

Christian asks me more about what I meant to do ... and I tell her. How sick Mama is. How crushed I was when I found out May Ella and I weren't good matches to donate a kidney to her. And then how her insurance denied coverage for the surgery anyway. I'd remembered I had life insurance and checked to make sure that Mama was the beneficiary and would get the money. Since I'd had the insurance more than ten years, the suicide clause didn't apply. I'd checked around and found some unsavory people who said they could get her a kidney without having to wait. I'd worked everything out to the last detail, including what I should be dressed in for my funeral: my favorite jeans and boots. How I'd collected pills for months—more than enough to go to sleep and never wake up. But maybe I'd been putting it off until this last setback with my mama's care. When it all got to be too much.

When I'm done talking, I look over at Kurt, and his eyes are welling up. Like the therapist, his expression holds no judgment. Just sadness.

I'm sad, too, I realize. My throat and lungs are sore, my body's cold, and I have no energy. My chest aches, and my nose is running.

I hadn't been sad for months—just numb—and it almost seems like an improvement to feel *anything*. Even something uncomfortable.

Huh.

"That's a lot to go through," Christian says. "We'll have plenty to talk about in upcoming sessions. For now, are you still having thoughts of killing yourself?"

I shrug. "I mean ... yeah. All the time. I'm not gonna do it today. Kurt tossed my pills and took away my gun." I pause. "And he's talked some sense into me."

"It's good you have him," she says, "although I might not characterize what he did as talking 'sense,' since our feelings aren't necessarily driven by logic. How present is the desire to kill yourself right now?"

"Um. On a level of one to ten, it's like a four or five. Or six, maybe."

She nods. "That's still higher than I'd like. What was it two days ago?"

"Ten."

"Last week?"

"Eleven."

"Are you on any medication?"

"Other than PrEP, no. Nothing for my head."

"Okay, let's talk about your mood. Do you ever feel hopeless?"

"All the time," I admit.

"Have you lost interest in things you used to enjoy?" Christian's eyes are intelligent and assessing, but I still don't feel like she's judging me. More like evaluating. Which I guess makes sense.

"I can't even remember what I used to enjoy. I feel nothing. Or—I can't even say that, because feeling *nothing* would still be a feeling. It's like I'm ... empty."

"Empty," Christian repeats. "Have you felt empty for more than two weeks?"

I chuckle mirthlessly. "I can't remember the last time I felt anything other than ..." I pause. I don't wanna talk about vengeance. "Other than bad feelings." I squeeze Kurt's hand. "Sorry."

"Nothing to be sorry for," he says immediately.

"I mean," I try to explain, "it's not like I'm crying all the time. I feel sad about my mama, but that's not sitting around feeling sad. It's hard to explain."

"What about feeling irritated?"

"Not so much."

"Angry?"

"Yes." I hesitate. "More like guilt."

"Guilt," Christian repeats. "Do you know why?"

I study my boots. "Maybe because I can't help my mama."

"So do you feel helpless?"

"Yes," I say, and some vehemence comes out. "I feel stuck. Like I can't do anything right. I can't change anything, and I can't make anything better. And it's all gone to shit."

"You feel stuck," Christian says. "Have you had anything change physically? Lost or gained weight?"

I shake my head.

"Do you sleep well?"

"Not really."

"How's your appetite?"

"Don't have much of one," I say.

"And over the past month, how often have you had thoughts of suicide?"

"The past month?" I ask. She nods. "I'd say every five minutes or so. Maybe more. I couldn't shake the idea. *Can't* shake it."

"And before that?"

"Yeah, definitely before that, because it took me months of refilling the medication and not taking it before I got enough pills. As time went on, though, I got more and more ... bad. Just feeling worthless. Like the only value I have is if I kill myself so my mama can get better."

"I'm so sorry you feel that way," Christian says kindly. "You know that's not true, don't you?"

I shrug and bite my lip. Kurt's been trying to stay quiet and let this be about me—which I appreciate—but his hand tightens on mine.

"Your life has value whether you send your mother money or not. The idea that you can only be worthwhile or worthy if you kill yourself is simply not true," Christian repeats.

"No fucking way is it true," Kurt says.

"You can say that, but I don't believe it," I say, then look at my feet. "Just being honest."

"Please do be honest," Christian says. "Who do you have to talk about this with? Besides Kurt, that is?"

"No one."

"Over the past few months, have you isolated yourself?"

"Kinda. Maybe. I mean, yeah, I guess." I tilt my head. "Is all of this depression? I thought depression was sitting in a dark room and crying. I go for runs. I ... function."

"Depression can manifest in many ways," Christian says. "Yes, I'm inclined to think you're experiencing a major depressive episode. Especially given your recurrent thoughts of suicide. Besides work, do you do things you enjoy?"

I laugh mirthlessly. "No. Can't think of any. Shoot, I'm not good at this. I dunno how to talk about it."

"You're doing just fine. Men can be less likely to discuss their feelings and seek help, which means their issues are more likely to go undiagnosed and untreated. But you're doing a great job right now. Keep it up."

"So what do I do about all this? Are you gonna put me on drugs?"

"You seem fairly stable right now, and I can see your partner is supportive, but given the degree of planning you described, I think a short inpatient stay would be beneficial for you while we figure out what, if any, medication may be appropriate. What do you think about inpatient care? It would give you an opportunity to really focus on your recovery. Is that something you're interested in?"

"No," I say, and Kurt stiffens his back and starts to cross his arms over his chest. There's my pushy husband. "But I'll do it anyway." I put my head in my hands for a moment, then look up, my eyes stinging. "I gotta be up-front with you. I'm tired enough to try anything."

She gives me a compassionate smile. "I think you'll be glad you did." She turns to Kurt. "Will you be okay managing without your husband for a few days?"

We haven't told her that we just got married or any of that, and it feels like she doesn't need to know. For now, Kurt's mine, and that's all that really matters. He's acting like a husband should, and I'm beyond grateful for that.

"I'll miss him, but I'll support him in anything he needs," Kurt says. I believe him. He's done nothing but be supportive of me since he found my pills. I wonder how different our lives would be if he hadn't.

Would we have gotten our marriage annulled?

Would I be dead by now?

I shudder.

"What's going on in your head?" Christian asks.

"Just thinking about my choices."

"Everything you do is a choice," she says. "Do you understand that?"

"I do. Just sometimes it feels like I have no choice."

"What does having no choice feel like?"

"Hopeless." Hot tears sting my eyes.

"Do you want to feel better?" Christian asks softly.

Do I?

I told Kurt I'd go along with this, but I'm not sure I've made the decision deep down. In the back of my head, I always knew I could ditch him and kill myself somehow. But ... I can't go on like this. That's clear. And if the doctors can help, then, "Yes. I wanna feel better," I say, and Kurt lets out a breath.

I mean it, I think, for the first time.

Fucking loser.

"I'm very glad to hear you say that," Christian says. "The most important thing for your recovery is that you *decide to get better*. That's it. I'm not saying there won't be a lot of work ahead, but deciding is the key to everything. It comes from the Latin word decidere, which literally means to cut off. You're cutting off all other options. *There's no going back, Johnny.* Are you okay with that?"

"Yeah." My voice is barely above a whisper.

"Good. That's the essential first step."

Christian tells us about a facility close by that she recommends. "You can go inpatient for a few days—they'll decide how long based on your evaluation and how you respond once you're there. After that, there's a two-week daily outpatient care program where they come and get you and you attend sessions for a half day. Then we could go into a more commonplace therapy schedule, maybe once or twice a week at first. How does that plan sound?"

"It's overwhelming," I admit.

She nods. "I can understand that it's a lot to take in. But you don't have to tackle it all at once. Just take it one step at a time. What do you think about checking in tonight? I'm concerned about your suicide plans, and I think the best choice for you and for your husband is to move forward with treatment right away."

"Wait, you mean, like, right now? I'm not packed or anything. Well, I ain't got that much stuff—" Panic starts to hit me, but at the same time I'm so numb it don't really matter.

"You don't need to pack. They'll provide clothes and whatever else you need. You don't have to bring anything with you."

Going into a strange place with nothing is somehow more frightening than voluntarily selling all my worldly possessions. Because it's just me and ... that's it. Not even Kurt.

Christian tilts her head, studying me. "I'll call over to the hospital and see if they have a free bed. Hang on." I'm boarding a train that's already moving down the track, and I just found out there are no brakes. Kurt squeezes my hand, and I focus on that to try to calm down. Into her phone, Christian says, "Hello, this is Dr. Gray. I have a patient who's interested in inpatient care for depression and suicidality. Do you have a free bed right now? Great. I'll let them know. Thank you." She hangs up. "Systems are go. So, what do you say?"

Shit damn fuck holy fuck what am I doin' shit oh my Lord in heaven I ain't got a clue.

"Check me into the mental institution," I say, hoping I don't come to regret that decision.

"Behavioral health hospital," she corrects gently. "Kurt, if I give you the address, will you take him?"

Kurt nods. "Of course." He leans over and kisses my cheek. "You got this, babe."

"Thanks," I say gruffly.

"Wonderful. Then we don't need to call emergency transport." Christian gives me a reassuring smile. "This is the first step on your way to recovery, Johnny. I think you're making the right choice, and I look forward to helping you as you progress on this path." She stands up, and so do we.

"Thank you, ma'am," I say, and realize I'm not wearing my hat. But I bow my head.

She smiles and shakes my hand. "You're going to feel much better soon. I know it."

Her confidence is heartening. Kurt hands her his credit card to pay for the session, which makes me feel all kinds of weird—I mentally add it to my tab—and once that's taken care of, we're on our way.

CHAPTER 18
Johnny

As we set out for the hospital, I'm bombarded with emotions and sensations, all of them contradictory. Calm panic. Intense numbness. Hopeful despair. I don't understand how I can feel so many confusing things—and nothing—at once, but I do.

What's going to happen? Is this going to work? It had better work. I can't get worse.

But Christian was right: Making the decision to get better feels like a cornerstone to build my recovery on. I now have a goal.

I keep going back to that. Got nothin' else to hang on to.

"Before ..." Kurt clears his throat. "Yesterday, you promised me you'd stay alive for the day. Can you promise me you'll stay alive until I see you again?"

Can I?

He's looking straight ahead at the road.

My voice is gravelly when I say, "Yeah, I promise."

Liar.

"Good. Spoiler: I'm going to keep asking you to make that promise."

"Whatever it takes," I say listlessly.

Kurt lets me pick the radio station, which I appreciate. He's full of little kindnesses, and each one makes me like him more. He doesn't say much else, and neither do I, choosing instead to look at the hills and the Pacific Ocean as we head north past Malibu.

After about a half hour, we turn off on a windy road and eventually reach the hospital, which is a series of 1960s institutional-style buildings up on a fenced-off bluff overlooking the water. Half a dozen deer loiter on the grass in front of the reception area, and huge oak trees bow near the dry sagebrush on the hills.

I step out and notice how quiet it is—and at the same time, it's deafening. Another contradiction.

Kurt gives me a tight smile. "You okay?"

"Not sure," I croak. "But it's … it's peaceful. Even if I'm second-guessing being here."

"Do you want me to take you back to my house? I don't want to do that, because I'm not equipped to take care of you, but if you insisted, I would. I'm not going to check you in against your will."

"No. Don't take me back. I'll … I'll figure this out."

"Okay, babe. Then let's get you checked in."

We walk inside, and Kurt addresses the admissions nurse. "Um, hi. Our therapist called over and said you had a bed available for my husband, John Haskell."

Why is it that every time one of us says the word husband it thaws my frozen heart a bit more?

"That's right," she says kindly. "We do. Why don't you fill out these forms and let me have your insurance information?"

Kurt digs in his pocket for his insurance card, explaining that we just got married and he'll guarantee payment. He's arranged to take some time off—obviously, since he's spent all day with me—but his work acknowledged the coverage in an email he shows her.

I park my ass on a leather couch and try not to worry about how expensive this place must be. I'm grateful that Kurt's filling out the forms, because my address is now his, and I don't remember what it is.

"Any dietary restrictions?" she asks. "Allergies?"

I shake my head. "No, ma'am."

After she reviews the forms and enters the information in the computer, she says, "Okay, John. Are you ready? If you have any personal property like a cell phone, wallet, or keys, you'll likely want to give it to your husband, because you won't be allowed access to it while you're here."

Everything about going into a mental hospital is unnerving, but this still hits hard. It feels like they're stripping away my last connection to the outside world. I guess because they are. With only a few seconds' hesitation, I hand my phone to Kurt and tell him the passcode in case Mama calls. I watch as it disappears into his pocket.

Most people worry about the photos that someone might find on their phone, but with me, it's the opposite. There are so many images out there of me doing a wide variety of sexual acts that my phone's basically storage for photos of sunsets, horses, dogs, my mama, and my sister—and now a couple of Kurt from Vegas. I've got nothing to hide—or, rather, little that Kurt doesn't know about already. He seems to figure out my deepest, darkest secrets without me even telling him, and he knows I have a lawsuit going, even if he doesn't know why. But I'm giving him access to even more of me when I give him the phone.

I think I *like* giving him access to me. No one else has ever had that. It's intimate. I'm slowly letting him see every part of me. The real me.

He must be a loser, too, if he wants to know me.

Anger flares within me at that thought. No way am I letting my fucked-up brain insult Kurt. *Take it back.*

Fine. Just, no one'd want to get to know you.

Whatever.

"I'll give you a moment to say goodbye," the nurse says, and again the paradoxical combination of nerves and calmness washes over me. I've never been in a place like this before, but I assume it'll change me. I have a chance to get better, but I don't know how that's gonna happen.

Kurt looks up at me, his warm brown eyes concerned. "What do you want me to tell your mom?" he asks. "If she calls."

"If she calls, tell her I'm busy and I'll call her the next chance I get."

"Anyone else I should tell?"

"Can you get a message to my lawyers? Ask Sam to tell them I'm here, so they'll understand if I don't reply to an email or something?"

Weird that the people who'll know I'm checking myself into a mental hospital are my husband of, what, two and a half days, and my lawyers. But that's all I care about. Ace can wait.

"You got it," Kurt says. "Is this a secret as to anyone else? I'm not planning on blabbing, but I want to know how much I can talk about it."

"I don't want it getting spread, but I trust you to tell the right people. Need-to-know basis."

"Got it."

I appreciate the fact that he pulls out his phone and adds a reminder to call Sam. Kurt has a million things going on, but this matters to him. *I* matter to him.

Kurt takes a piece of paper and scribbles down his phone number for me. "In case you can call out." He gives me a smile, which thaws some of the ice inside me, and even though I'm still numb, I'm so darn grateful he's here. "When are visiting hours?" he asks the admissions nurse.

She tells him, and he enters the information in his phone. Again, my heart thumps. He's going to visit me. I don't have to do this for days on my own.

"Can I come tomorrow?" Kurt asks.

"Assuming that he's out of the locked ward, yes," she says, and I freeze up again.

Locked ward? *Shit.*

My brain starts picturing every single TV show I've ever seen that had someone taken away in a straitjacket. Do they still use straitjackets? Are they going to use one on me if I get too mouthy?

"Locked?" I ask. Is this hospital stay a good idea, or am I giving up freedoms I don't wanna lose?

The nurse gives me an efficient nod, which makes me feel better, since it seems like this is all routine. Or else she doesn't care, which would be bad. Contradictions and paradoxes. "It's protocol. You'll be in a locked ward until you meet with the doctor. That's usually about twenty-four hours, but it might be less."

I'm inching closer and closer to Kurt. Should I pull the plug on this? I'm checking myself in, and I can check myself out ... right? I don't dare ask that, now that I've gone this far. Instead, I ask, "And the doctor will decide if I'm safe to be in the regular ward?"

"Exactly." She looks at me expectantly, which means, I guess, that it's time to go.

I dig in my pocket and hand Kurt my mostly empty wallet. "Won't need this," I say. Now he has every material thing I own except the clothes on my back and whatever few photos my mama has.

I'm entrusting myself to Kurt. And I really hope that's the right call, because if things here go haywire, I don't know how I could get myself out of this mess without him.

"Don't worry," Kurt says. "I'll take care of everything for you." His voice is husky, and it seems he's catching the same feels as I am. He gives me a kind smile. Then he opens up his arms, and I step into them.

He smells clean and sexy and already familiar, and his body feels perfect against mine. I cling to him while the admissions nurse waits patiently. He whispers in my ear, "You got this. I care about you. I'll come visit you. You're going to get better. The only way out is through, babe. You can do this. You can live."

I'm going to get better.

The only way out is through.
I can live for one more day.
I'm trusting myself to the right people. The right person.

I lean down and kiss him, and unlike most of our other kisses, this one's sweet and closed-mouth until I get a little desperate at the end. We break away from each other, and as I wave goodbye, alarm hits me.

What if I never get to leave? What if I'm so fucked up that I have to be locked in here for the rest of my life?

Shit, this was a bad idea.

But as I follow the nurse deeper into the hospital, I remind myself that I *have* to get better. I just have to.

CHAPTER 19
Kurt

I drive away from the pastoral hospital with a churning stomach and restless limbs. I just left Johnny in the care of a bunch of strangers. He's my *husband*. My brand-new, I barely know him husband, but my husband nonetheless.

I drive on autopilot, lost in my thoughts. I've had my dream man for such a short time, and I let him be taken away from me for his own good. I miss him already.

While I know he needs professional help I'm not qualified to offer, it feels wrong to be driving away from him when I really want to watch over him. He should be with me. I should be able to just lean in and touch him.

It's ridiculous for me to feel this strongly about him when I've only just met him, but he's a big guy with a big personality who's made a huge impression on me.

Thank fuck I met him before he harmed himself.

The first person I call once I get into better cell reception is Sam. After chatting for a moment, I ask if he wants to go to dinner tonight. We agree to meet at a chic restaurant near his work, and that's one thing off my list.

Now I have to figure out how to fit Johnny into my election

plans. After that, I'll worry about what he and I are going to do once he gets out of the hospital.

I call Paige next. She sounds pissed when she answers. "Oh, now you're talking to me?"

I flick my eyes to the car ceiling, even though she can't see me. "I'm sorry, okay? Look, I know I've made your job a lot harder, and we'll have to deal with the press, but I like my husband, and I don't want to hide him."

There's only a brief silence. She's probably already got three contingency plans outlined and is just trying to decide on the best one. "Well, we'll need to get him some media training, and then he can come to a press conference," she says. "What's his availability this week?"

"Um." I pause. "About that."

"What?" Her voice is sharp. "What aren't you telling me?"

"I had to check Johnny into a hospital. It's none of your business, but he needed to get some help."

"Oh my god, is he on drugs? Holy shit, Kurt. Just when I thought you couldn't be a bigger PR disaster, you have to marry an addict?"

"He's not an addict," I say quickly. "And even if he were, addiction's a sickness, and getting help is a good thing. Be nice."

"Sorry," she mutters. "I'm on edge. That was rude of me. I wasn't thinking."

"Fine. In any case, he's in the hospital for a different reason. I'm going to respect his privacy. Just know that it will be a few days —likely until next week at the earliest—before he can go out in public. Maybe longer."

"Fine. Good. I'm glad he's getting better."

"Thank you. Are you making progress with managing my mess?"

"Kind of. I should've gone into fashion design," she mutters. "Fabric doesn't talk back."

"I know our marriage seems random"—*because it was*—"but

either I win the election with him, or I figure out something else to do. That's all there is to it."

"So the election is unimportant all of a sudden? You couldn't have, I don't know, waited a few months to get married?"

I take a deep breath and hold it as I turn from the windy mountain road onto the highway. "There are other elections and other positions I could run for if I don't get this. I'm shooting for the moon right now, but if I don't make it, that doesn't mean I can't be on, I don't know, the local school bond committee or something."

"You don't have a kid."

"They need members of the public. And that's beside the point. All I mean is, he can be integrated into my campaign."

And my life.

"Fine. Whatever." She heaves another sigh. "We'll talk about it when we meet next. We also have to get you ready for the pre-primary debate. When can we schedule you for debate prep?"

"Whenever," I say. I've emailed my boss and HR to take time off to care for Johnny, and in any case, I've scaled down to part time during the campaign and can set my own hours as long as I get the work done. So I should be okay for the time being.

Part of me is wondering if I should just give up the day job anyway. It's not like it makes me all that happy. Sure, I like graphic design and nerding out on fonts, but I could do that on my own. I can find another option for health insurance.

"Where'd you go?" Paige asks.

"I'm on PCH."

"No, I mean where did your brain go? You got quiet."

"Sorry. Just thinking. Yes, schedule a meeting, and we can go over talking points."

"Fine." My phone beeps with another call.

"Paige, my momth—er, Melissa—"

"I'll let you talk to the lieutenant governor," she says, and hangs up.

"Hey," I say to my momther as I signal to pass a Prius.

"Hey yourself," she says. "I hope you're well. We have a few things to discuss."

"I suppose," I say, trying not to be rude.

"Surprise, we're headed to Southern California this weekend. Can we meet your husband?"

"I want to say yes, except he's not with me right now. It will have to be next week at the earliest," I tell her.

"Oh? Is he busy?"

"You could say that." I realize I'm not going to be able to keep this from her even if I wanted to. "Mom, he's got some issues—not substance abuse or anything violent—and I've checked him into a hospital."

Her voice immediately takes on a caring tone. "Oh no. Is he okay?"

"I think he's going to be. I hope so. But he's going through some personal stuff, and he needs a chance to recover. Can you give him that?"

"Of course, honey. I'm sorry. We'll schedule when it works for him."

"Thanks. I appreciate it."

I want to tell her that he was so close to being another Andrei. That I couldn't go through a loss like that again, even if I didn't care about Johnny as much as I do. And that I feel like I know him already, in part because he's been part of my intimate life for so long.

None of that's appropriate to tell my momther. So instead, we talk about her schedule, and when I hang up, I call my assistant and give her a list of things Johnny will need while he's in the hospital. Good thing I know his sizes and preferences now. I remember a book I read a year ago that I liked, and I ask her to add it.

I drive back home.

The condo feels emptier than usual, even though Johnny was

here less than a day. He's got such a big personality that his absence looms large. I set his phone and wallet in the dish on the counter by mine and study them. His worn leather wallet reminds me of him. It's something a cowboy would carry around. His phone is an older model, which doesn't surprise me. They somehow look right next to my YSL billfold and new iPhone.

My pulse quickens at the memory of making out with Johnny in the living room just a few hours ago. When I wander upstairs, there's his suitcase and bag of new clothes in the corner of my bedroom, his towel on the rack, his indent in the pillow.

Dammit. I miss him.

I could look at him anytime I want to, on my phone or laptop. But the thought of watching him on my favorite porn site now feels slightly icky, even though I remind myself that he willingly puts himself out there for people like me to ogle and that he's been a part of my sex life for basically my entire adulthood.

Some people might think that I'm imagining the connection between us because I've objectified him in his videos, but I don't see it that way at all. Johnny was never simply a sex object to me—he always seemed so sincere and down-to-earth. So human and real. I always wanted him to be real for me.

Now he is.

It's just been me, my right hand, and my imagination (combined with a premium subscription) for a long time. Oh, sure, I've had a few dates and hookups, but no one's sparked the kind of interest in me that one evening with Johnny did.

Hell, I wanted to marry him after a few hours together.

And I still want to be married to him. It feels like I have some claim on him, and—as weird as it sounds—I feel possessive of him. I'm clearly delusional, since there are likely plenty of fans who feel the same way.

But I've got his phone and wallet, and his signature on a marriage license.

In that sense, Johnny Haskell is *mine*.

* * *

When I called Sam to schedule dinner, I wasn't planning on him bringing his boyfriend, but I understand why Jules is here. Sam has to manage his public image for Jules's sake. And having dinner alone with his "ex" is a recipe for disaster. Good thing Jules is terrific.

We're in the back of the restaurant, away from prying eyes, although when Jules leaves, there's sure to be photographers at every exit.

I want to be careful of Johnny's privacy, but these two are as trustworthy as it gets. Jules knows what it's like to have his privacy invaded. He has no desire to talk about anyone behind their back. Sam doesn't, either, plus he's part of Johnny's team of lawyers and is required to keep things secret.

Sam also has connections everywhere, because his grandfather is the governor of California, and he always seems to have a commonsense solution to problems.

"I need some advice," I say without preamble, after we've ordered.

"Oh?" Sam says, breaking off a piece of bread and dipping it in olive oil. "How can we help?" Sam's gorgeous, and his style is rather twee, what with his bow ties and suspenders. He's got pale blond hair and cerulean eyes. Jules is lean, dark-haired and dark-eyed, and covered in tattoos. They somehow match by being complete physical opposites.

"Did you see the news about me?" I ask.

"We don't go online too much," Sam admits. *Oh*. He and Jules would stay away from gossip, because they wouldn't want to see what's being written about them—and especially about Jules.

"Well. Um. I got married over the weekend," I say.

Sam's jaw drops before he gets the bread to his mouth. A blob of olive oil hits the tablecloth. "For the love of David Bowie, you did not."

Raising my hands, I say, "It was not planned. I was ... very, very drunk."

"Who's the lucky guy?" Sam asks. "Do I know him?"

I squirm. "Actually ... it's Johnny Haskell."

I wouldn't have thought his eyes could get wider, but I'd have been wrong. "Velvet the Cowboy?" he whispers.

I nod.

Jules chuckles. "Velvet the porn star?" His British accent sounds so posh.

"The same." I sip my water.

"Nice," Jules says, and Sam gives him a playful shove. Jules shrugs. "What? He's a gorgeous man."

"I didn't know you knew him," Sam says to me.

"I didn't. I met him Saturday night in Vegas, at a bar. And I recognized him—though, let's be real, I'd have wanted to talk with him in any case. He's even more handsome in real life than he is in his videos—as you know. I think he recognized me from some of our old PSAs, not sure."

"You met him on Saturday, and now you're married to him," Sam says flatly, then shakes his head. "Sorry, I don't mean to judge. I'm just surprised."

"Surprised the hell out of us, too," I admit.

"Well ... congrats? Shelby, our receptionist, had a spontaneous marriage, and he's doing great and totally in love with his husband, so you're in good company."

Do Johnny and I have a chance long-term? It doesn't matter right now. "I wanted to talk with you because he's got some issues. And so does his mother."

"Okay." Sam clearly doesn't know where I'm going with this. How could he?

"Johnny asked me to tell his lawyers about what's going on with him," I say, "so, Sam, can you please make sure to share this with whoever is working on his case?" He nods. I turn to Jules. "And I can trust you to keep a secret?"

Jules smiles. "Of course, mate."

I let out a breath. "Johnny checked himself into a hospital for a few days, because he was having a mental health crisis."

Sam's brows furrow. "I'm so sorry to hear that. Can he have visitors? Would he want us to visit him?"

"I think so," I say. "Maybe not immediately, but I'll let you know."

"I'm sure the guys will visit him, then. They really like him."

"Yeah. I do, too." I sigh. "Okay, so that's part of it."

Sam bursts out laughing. "Holy shit, Kurt. There's more? You go from no news to lots of news."

"Yeah, I know. The other part isn't as surprising, I don't think. I wanted to ask if you had any ideas about how to help his mother. You guys do some insurance law, right?"

"We do."

"That's what I thought. The thing is, his mom's health insurance denied her a transplant that she needs. Do you know anything about appealing insurance decisions?"

"Sure. Those matters usually go through the company's utilization management department. It's illegal for them to take cost savings into account when making medical coverage decisions, but they do it all the time." He tears off more bread with a growl.

"That's terrible," Jules says. "You Americans have the worst health system. It's unbelievable."

"I know, right?" Sam says. He grins at me. "Maybe your mom can fix it when she gets to the White House."

"That'd be nice. At any rate, would you mind looking into it?" I ask. "I mean, I know insurance companies are the worst, but still. It seems weird that she's so sick, yet they won't pay for her transplant."

"Insurance companies cut corners, because they have to turn a profit," Sam says. "There's pressure to show increased shareholder value quarter over quarter and only so many ways they can make money—especially with rising costs. That doesn't make it right," he adds. "I'm just saying that it doesn't surprise me. I expect she already tried internal appeals. Most people who've had to deal with health crap know their way around the process. But we can go further—file a complaint with the Department of Insurance if need be. That is—I'm assuming she's in California?"

"Yeah."

He nods. "Just let me know her information, and I'll see what I can do."

"Her name's Sue Ann Haskell." I saw her name on the envelope Johnny gave me, the one he meant her to get after he was dead. Thinking about it makes my stomach hurt. I give Sam the name of her insurance company, which Johnny told me, and her phone number, which I pulled off his phone.

"I'm happy to help if I can."

"Thank you," I say, feeling a little lighter.

"Anything for my favorite ex," Sam says with a smile.

"So, what have you two been up to?" I ask, and Sam launches into a story about their recent trip to Italy.

I listen, glad Johnny is getting care and missing him all the same.

* * *

After dinner, I'm restless, so I end up doing a few hours of design work after all. But when I rub my bleary eyes sometime after midnight, I know this is too much: election, work, Johnny. I've already decided Johnny has to come first. Even if our marriage isn't real—though it feels realer every minute—he's a good man with a soft heart, and he deserves to be cherished. It seems like he's gone way too long without anyone showing him how much they appreciate him.

I'm going to do my best to fix that.

A quick check on my phone shows that, sure enough, the gossip sites are running headlines like "SPICING IT UP? Rocker

Julian Hill and boyfriend Sam Stone dine with Stone's former lover Kurt Delmont—with Delmont's porn star husband nowhere to be seen." There's a photo of Sam and Jules holding hands as they duck out the back of the restaurant. I sigh at the comments speculating that we'd make a great threesome. Or foursome.

I log on to my computer again and send in an application for more time off from work, including details about my time-sensitive projects so they can be transferred to other designers. When I'm done, I go into my bedroom, which—after sharing it with Johnny for only a few hours—feels so, so empty.

I wonder what Johnny's doing right now. I hope he realizes how brave he's being, taking the steps to get well. It was easy to see that the idea of a locked ward scared him. It scared me, too, even though I know he's in a modern hospital, not something out of *One Flew Over the Cuckoo's Nest*. He's not being tortured. He's there to get the help he needs.

I wish I could see him, though. Just for a minute, to know he's okay. To tell him I miss him.

CHAPTER 20
Johnny

The porn version of a strip search is much sexier than the real thing.

After Kurt leaves, a male nurse walks me to the locked ward and into a room containing a bare bed with no sharp edges that's bolted to the floor. I freeze, wondering if it's there so they can strap down unwilling patients. There's literally nothing else in the room: no sheets or other bedding, no chair or nightstand, no curtains. Through an open door off to the side, I can see a bathroom with a roll of toilet paper on top of the sink. It doesn't even seem to have towels or a mirror—just a sink and a toilet.

The nurse hands me a hospital gown with snap fasteners and says, "Put this on, opening in the front. No laces are allowed. No strings on hoodies or sweatpants. No belts. No weapons. Take off everything you're wearing, and put it on the bed." Although he gestures toward the bathroom, I'm not feeling the need for privacy. Which is just as well, since I doubt I'll have much of that in here. There's no handle on the bathroom door, let alone a lock. I shuck off my shirt and put the gown on, then unbuckle my belt and drop my pants and boxers per his instructions.

He makes me open the gown and turn around so he can see my

whole body. "No tattoos," he murmurs. "No cuts or burns." Next, I open my mouth so he can poke around inside. He checks me everywhere and then marks something on a clipboard, seemingly satisfied, before squeezing my clothes, feeling through every pocket and all the way down the arms and legs to make sure, I guess, that I haven't snuck in a knife or something. He finds the slip of paper with Kurt's phone number and places it on the mattress.

He's making sure I ain't got nothing I could use to kill myself.

As the violins start up in my brain again, I want Kurt. I want to be able to talk with him about being strip-searched. I want to talk with him about how I feel. I've been lost in my head for months, and the past couple of days, having someone to be honest with, has really meant something. I miss *him*.

The nurse finishes with my clothes and tells me I can get dressed, but he keeps my boots and belt. He hands me some thick socks with tread on the bottom, then leaves the room, giving me some semblance of dignity now that he's taken away anything I could use to hurt myself.

This is so weird. I put my T-shirt, boxers, and jeans back on, and when I'm ready, I knock on the door—because I'm locked in—and the nurse returns to let me out. I follow him down the hall into the section where, I guess, the other inpatients are. We pass a room where someone is screaming, and two large, burly nurses go racing past us and scoot in there.

I really am in the locked ward of a mental hospital.

Is this where I belong? Are my problems the same as that person's?

I deserve to die.

As we continue on to the main area, other than there being nothing loose that we can use to harm ourselves or each other, it ain't much different from a regular hospital or dorm. It feels institutional, with terrazzo flooring and windows in all the doors.

The nurse shows me to my room, which has two twin beds and—continuing what seems to be a trend—nothing else, not even a dresser or chair. "Your roommate uses a sleep apnea machine, so you'll be under supervision all night," he says. I must look puzzled, because he adds, "The sleep apnea machine has wires," and then I figure it out. Whoever I'm sharing with needs the machine, but they don't want anyone using a cord or whatever to kill themselves.

"Okay," I say quietly, staring out the window. It's early evening, but the sun hasn't set yet.

"Someone will come get you when it's time for dinner," he says.

"What do I do until then?"

He gives me a small smile. "Just try to relax."

Relax? Without a phone or a book or anything to do? He's gotta be kidding.

But I try. I sit on the bed and stare out the window. It looks out on a mountainside, so there's not much to see but dry brush. For the next however long, I think about why I'm here and whether I can get better. *I can, because I decided to.* Trying not to panic that I can't leave this building or even this room, that's an interesting mind game.

How long will it be until I see Kurt again?

It's idyllic here, away from the city. Quiet. In some ways, it calms me, and in others, it creeps me out. It's like the people running this place know that everyone here is on edge, so they need to put a damper on all the inputs to avoid triggering an explosion. We're not safe enough for a regular, noisy environment.

As day turns to dusk, I keep watching the outdoors, since I have nothing else to do. I'm finally zoning out from the lack of any stimulation when, out of nowhere, a mountain lion appears right outside my window, sending my heart racing. The big cat's *right there*. There's a pane of glass between us, but he's not more than five feet away from me. I want to call out to someone to come watch with me, but who? I don't know a soul in this place, and my roommate hasn't showed up yet.

So I sit there and watch alone. The mountain lion swishes his tail and prowls just like any other cat, except he's huge. His paws are probably the size of my hands. After a little while, he freezes, then stares down a small hole, still as a silent night. I hold my breath as I watch him watch the hole. Then the cat pounces, and he's got dinner—a rodent of some kind. Unlike the way a person eats, he just chomps that little critter in half without pausing to ask permission.

Well, hell. *That's* not something you see every day.

There's meaning here, but I'm not sure if I'm the mountain lion or the gopher.

I want to call Kurt, the folded piece of paper with his number burning a hole in my pocket. But I don't want to seem needy, and I don't know what the rules are for the phones, anyway. I want to know how my mama is, but I don't want her to worry. I want to get better, but I don't think that's going to happen instantly.

Heck, my brain spins out fast.

The only way out is through.

A knock on the door interrupts my thoughts. "John Haskell? You have a delivery," a new nurse says as she enters the room.

I frown. "I do?"

"It's been cleared." She hands me two full paper bags, and inside I find a bunch of new clothes in my sizes with the tags cut off, plus toothpaste, a toothbrush, deodorant, body wash, and shampoo. Everything's obviously been processed by the hospital, since the hoodies' strings have been removed. There's also a book of cowboy poetry.

"Who brought this?"

"Your husband had it delivered," she says. Damn, Kurt really is a fairy godfather. The toiletries are my favorite brands, so even if he just asked his assistant to take care of this, he must've had some kind of personal involvement.

That man. He's walloping my heart, I tell you.

I look at the book until yet another nurse comes in and says it's time for dinner. He escorts me into a common room that has four picnic tables off to the side, as well as several couches and a television playing some show I don't recognize. A few people are lounging around, and some are eating, but none of us are talking to each other. I sit at one of the tables and pick at the lasagna and salad and garlic bread a staff member brought me. It's surprisingly tasty.

Before Kurt, how long had it been since I'd eaten well?

All the patients around me—maybe eight or ten—are wearing sweats or pajamas and have a beaten-down look about them. I probably look the same way.

We can't all be in here for the same thing, though. And it dawns on me that I have no idea of these other people's circumstances and experiences. One young woman shuffles by in fuzzy slippers, an enormous sweatshirt, and Minion-patterned pajama pants, laughing. She goes down the hall and I guess into her room. She comes back a few minutes later, and now she's crying. Then she repeats the circuit, laughing.

Should I do anything about her? Is she okay? No one seems to pay her any mind.

I haven't been looking much past the end of my own nose lately—except as to Mama—but there's a big world out there full of other people and other problems.

I finish my meal and watch the boring TV show until I can't stand it no more and return to my room.

As they warned me, a huge, tattooed male nurse sits in a chair, his arms crossed over his chest, staring at my roommate, who's already in bed with a mask over his face. The sleep apnea machine makes a constant noise, so it'll be hard to get to sleep. That's on top of the fact that I'm in a new place and have a guard who's gonna be watching me all night.

There's no privacy. I guess I should be getting used to that. Kurt certainly wasn't giving me much privacy since he discovered my plans.

I nod to the nurse, who gives me a cursory nod back, and put my new sweats on. After taking a leak and brushing my teeth—grateful for the familiar flavor of my usual toothpaste—I crawl into the cold, narrow bed covered in thin blankets and stare at the ceiling. This is the exact opposite of where I want to be. Last night, I was sleeping with a warm Kurt in my arms.

Except ... as I lie in the hospital bed, a calmness does come over me. Being cut off from the outside world is helping my mood. The horrible pressure that I've felt for so long is ... not gone, but held at bay. While I ain't forgotten about my mama by any means, and the violins are serenading me in the dark, I'm not as desperate as before. Perhaps because there ain't nothing I can do. I can't text her. I can't talk with her. I'm stuck.

I think about what Kurt said, how I'd be hurting her by killing myself.

Yeah. Maybe. Okay, *yeah*. That would've happened. I would've hurt her. I can see that now.

I couldn't keep trouble from visiting—no one can—but I went a step too far when I invited it in for a drink and made it my guest of honor.

Kurt seems to think I can get better. Can I?

That little sweet spot for Kurt in my sour heart is getting bigger and bigger.

Thinking about his gorgeous face, I drift into a restless sleep punctuated by the noise of the apnea machine.

In the morning, I'm bleary-eyed, but I get up and do my usual exercises: push-ups, crunches, planks. Just because I'm stuck in here doesn't mean I can let myself go, and I've already taken too much time off, what with the bender in Vegas. I'm itchin' to go for a run, but unless I want to do laps up and down the hall, that's not happening. So I content myself with body-weight exercises. I may have no job prospects now, but maybe I have a smidgen of hope I will in the future.

They bring us breakfast, and we eat it at the picnic tables in the common room. We aren't even allowed out to go to the cafeteria, which is in a different building. I literally am locked up. Going to get our own food is a privilege reserved for those in the unlocked ward. Sunshine and fresh air are privileges. It's like I voluntarily put myself in prison. I'd laugh if it were a laughing matter.

Thankfully the doctor comes and sees me first thing after breakfast. He's a younger guy, seemingly harried, but with a patient manner, and when I talk, he studies me intently.

"I was planning to kill myself so my mama could get the money from my life insurance," I say, and explain what happened.

"I'm so sorry," he says, and he sounds like he means it.

After he asks me a few questions along the lines of Christian's yesterday, he says, "This is the wrong ward for you. You don't need this level of supervision. I'll have you transferred to the unlocked ward."

"I 'preciate that," I say faintly, surprised at how relieved his words make me feel. The admissions nurse had said everyone started off here, but in the back of my head I was scared that the doctors would say this was where I belonged—like, forever. So that's one thing going right.

One thing besides Kurt saving me, that is.

The doc and I talk about medication. "I ain't a fan of drugs, but if it will help, I'll try it," I say. I guess I really am beaten down. "Better living through chemistry?"

He nods and smiles. "Are you in?"

I think about Kurt and my promise to him to stay alive. I think about my mama and my need to take care of her. I think about my sister and how she's sacrificed her dreams for Mama, too. I think about Christian saying that to decide is to cut off all other options.

The only way out is through.

"I'm in," I say, and he smiles.

"Good. You're on the road to recovery." Shortly after he leaves, a nurse brings me a few pills, including one for anxiety, and while I understand some of the meds will take weeks to kick in, that one hits me almost immediately and is more calming than weed.

Okay, I do feel better.

While I wait to be transferred, I look again at the cowboy poetry book Kurt sent. The break from my routine's given me a different perspective.

Helplessly watching my mama get worse backed me into a corner so I felt like I had to fight my way out. And while I still feel like that, I'm thinking that there might be some other way to help her.

I'd felt so alone. But I'm not alone anymore, thanks to Kurt. Something as simple as him sending me clean underwear and a book to read makes me feel ... seen. Cared for.

Almost hopeful.

I start thinking about what I have to live for. Mama, May Ella, Kurt. And maybe myself.

Pretty sure that's enough.

CHAPTER 21

Johnny

It takes longer than I'd expected to move me to the new ward, but at last I can step outside and feel the sun on my face. I've surely spent some long days indoors, but I've never been barred from going outside. Being locked up has been an exercise in patience and moderating my thoughts. In a way, I feel stronger, like I can handle anything, even after just one night.

The new building's not all that different from the locked ward, except there's more furniture and things to do. A nurse helps me move the paper bags of my belongings into my new room, which has a chair and a dresser.

"There's a group session on codependence right now," she says. "Want to go?"

"I mean," I say, "why else am I here, other than to show up for what y'all are putting on offer? Not that I'm codependent."

She gives me a kind nod, likely thinking I don't know what I'm talking about. Which is true. I've heard the word 'codependent,' but I haven't got a clue what it means.

The group session's started already, and the leader—therapist?—is talking. I take a seat in a chair at the back of the room, and he smiles to acknowledge me but doesn't point me out.

"Recovery is an emotional time, a volatile time, and it's easy for people to get bonded in situations like that," he's saying. "I'd suggest that you be cautious about getting too close to anyone while you're healing. People come and go over the course of a lifetime, and the reasons why they are in your life now may not be valid later."

Is that why Kurt and I are getting so close? Because I'm depressed?

I don't like to think that.

But I literally met him Saturday, and today's Tuesday. So I maybe need to watch out and not read too much into how I feel about him.

The leader asks, "How many of you have heard of the term 'codependence'?"

Most of us raise our hands.

He nods and asks, "How many of you have heard of it *and* know what it means?"

A lot of hands go down.

"It's a term that gets thrown around a lot, and, like with many psychological terms, it's often used incorrectly. There are several definitions, but one I like—and that author Melody Beattie uses—is that people who are codependent let another person's behavior or situation affect them to the point where they're obsessed with controlling it. The other person may or may not be responsible for the situation—they could have a substance abuse problem, they could be emotionally unavailable or abusive, they could be physically or mentally ill or have other problems. But the codependent is preoccupied with gaining control over that behavior or situation. Stopping it. Fixing it. The codependent thinks the other person's life is their responsibility."

I sit up a little straighter. Wait, what?

"A lot of codependent people have lived through events that are traumatic and out of control. They respond to that by trying to find something they *can* control. Not in an intentionally harmful way, but as a means of feeling safe. They try to solve problems that aren't theirs to solve. They feel responsible for another person's happiness. If that person is happy, then they're happy. If that person is upset, then the codependent gets upset until that person feels better."

I'm not codependent. He ain't describing me.

"Codependents can exhibit a wide variety of behaviors. They can be anxious, depressed, repressed, angry, and controlling. Being codependent can result in all kinds of problems, from tolerating abuse in an attempt to keep a relationship going to being a martyr with long-term resentment from an unfulfilled desire to be recognized for their sacrifice."

I want to leave. I don't want to hear this.

I move to get up, but then he says, "Codependents are constantly trying to prove that they are good enough to be loved."

I feel like someone just smacked me in the chest. I can't get any air.

"A codependent person overdoes and attempts to be responsible for things that aren't their responsibility at all, or they can be extremely irresponsible when everything gets to be too much. They're trying to get their needs met in a way that doesn't work. Often, they're doing the wrong things for the right reasons—or the right things for the wrong reasons."

Good thing those meds are taking the edge off, or I'd be jumping outta my skin right now.

As he keeps talking about different types of trauma, my lip trembles. Every word he says feels like it applies to my life, and I want to get the fuck outta here. He's reminding me of nights after we left the ranch when we were drinking hot water for dinner. Mayonnaise sandwiches. Sleeping in the footwell of our car so my sister could have the back seat. Mama cryin' and not wantin' us to see, so she'd say she had allergies. Desperately wanting her to be happy so that I could be happy, too.

After what feels like hours, but is likely more like fifteen minutes, the therapist finishes his talk and offers us some books on codependency in case we want to learn more. I wanna set them on fire.

The only way out is through.

I take one of the books with me to my room and open it up. It might be the bravest thing I've ever done.

* * *

We go to breakout sessions after lunch, and I have an hour to meet with a therapist named Chantal in a private room in the ward.

After introductions, Chantal points to the codependence book I brought in with me. "Did you attend the session this morning?"

"Yes'm."

"And what did you think about it?"

I sigh. "They said a lotta stuff to think about."

"Like what?" She gives me a gentle, encouraging smile. That doesn't mean I wanna start chatting.

Shifting in the uncomfortable plastic seat, I stare at her for a while. Finally, I say, "I get the idea you're gonna just keep askin' questions, and I have the choice to either shut my trap or start singing. And since my husband's paying for this here place, I figure he should get his money's worth." *The only way out is through.* I pinch my nose. "Here goes. When I was a kid, we were very poor, and there was a time we were homeless. This was when my mama got sick. And when that leader was talkin' about codependency, all I could think about was how much I had to do to care for mama when I was a kid. That's different from caring for her now, mind."

"Did you want her to be caring for you instead?"

"No. I ain't selfish."

"In here, it's okay to be selfish. Or what you perceive as selfish. What did you think about having to be so responsible at such a young age? Did you resent her?" Chantal presses.

"Hell no," I say immediately.

"It's okay if you do, or did. Or if you resent the situation. It doesn't make you a bad person. Tell me some more about your childhood."

I stare at the wall. There's a poster about STDs and a faded photo of Yosemite National Park next to each other. I tell Chantal the things I already told Kurt about growing up and then about why I'm here.

When I'm done, she says, "I'm wondering what your identity is, other than caregiver. Who are you, Johnny?"

"No idea," I mutter.

"How did the presentation on codependence make you feel?"

"Pissed me off. 'Cause Mama's sick. She was sick, and she is sick. Chronic kidney disease. It made me feel like I was doin' somethin' wrong when I was doin' everything I could to get money to her. We were dumpster diving, and outdated food from the back of Walmart was too expensive. What else was I supposed to do?"

Chantal waits for me to finish my rant. Finally, she says, "I think you need to honor what you did to survive. But think about what you gave up. I'm not talking about blaming your mother for getting sick. The situation was the situation. Johnny, you were forced at an early age to be the parent. At a time when you were supposed to be worrying about math homework and the kid at school who caught your eye, you were worrying about putting food in your belly. And not just yours, but your mom's and your little sister's."

"Yeah. I was."

"So here's the thing. Some of what you were doing was being responsible. That's honorable and necessary, especially when you're caring for a sick relative. Where the line is, though—and I think we can agree that you crossed it or were about to—is thinking you should kill yourself so she could have surgery. Do you agree?"

I don't answer, and she lets me sit with my thoughts. Finally, I say, "The guy leading that session said a lotta things that bugged me, and some of what he said sounded like my situation and some didn't, and I don't know what's what."

Chantal tilts her head thoughtfully. "Part of recovery is sifting through information to determine what advice applies to you and what doesn't. There are a lot of explanations for why people feel the way they do, and deciding what fits for you can be complicated. If what you hear helps you and you connect with it, then see if it's useful for your recovery. If it isn't, it's okay to reject it." She leans forward in her seat. "With you, we know that taking care of your mother is noble and kind, and you have been very responsible for her, which is generally a good thing. But you need to understand that suicide would be taking it too far. You didn't answer me before, and this point is crucial. What are your thoughts on it?"

"Most of me still thinks the world would be better off without me," I admit.

"Then maybe we have more to talk about than your mother's illness."

I raise an eyebrow. "I know I got more going on. I filed a lawsuit for sexual harassment. My career's in the toilet. Things aren't going well."

"Then whatever you'd like to tell me, I'll listen. I think the biggest question is, are you focusing on your mother's illness to avoid something going on inside yourself?"

Later in the afternoon, I'm back in my room when there's a knock on the doorjamb. I found out real quick that if I closed my door, they'd open it every ten minutes or so to check on me, so it's easier just to leave it open. "You have visitors," a nurse says with a smile.

"I do?" Is it Kurt? He said *visitors*, though. Plural.

"Do you want to see them? Come on."

I follow him down the gleaming hall into a common room

with seating and low tables and come face-to-face with three tall men wearing suits and ties.

Thankfully, I like all of these well-dressed men. They're my lawyers: Danny Villaseñor, Noah Weston, and August Ramirez. Noah and August are the founders of the firm. Danny's my lead attorney. All of them are the sort of people you wanna know. Them being here must, again, be Kurt's doing, and I'm obliged to him for telling them what was going on so I didn't have to.

"Johnny," Danny says, and he holds out his arms. While I suppose it could seem weird that I'm hugging my lawyers, I'm told that lawyers are people, too, and I believe it. At least with respect to this particular firm. "How are you doing?"

I raise an eyebrow. "I've been asked that a lot in the past little bit here, so I hope all y'all will excuse me while I come up with an answer. The truth is, not great, because, well, I'm in a mental hospital. That must mean that something's wrong." I pause. "But I think I have hope."

As I say it, I realize I might actually be telling the truth.

Noah's eyes visibly well with tears, and August, his husband, reaches over and takes his hand.

"We discussed it in the car on the way here, and we feel like we let you down," August says. "You're going through all this turmoil with the lawsuit, and we should've referred you to a therapist. We're truly sorry."

"Don't be sorry. My mental health ain't your responsibility."

"But we could've predicted that this would be challenging and done something about it, and the fact that we didn't ... that's bothering me." Noah's sincerity is breathtakingly sweet. I'm not sure how someone so innocent got to be a lawyer—and a damn good one, too—but I guess anything is possible.

"Well, nothing happened," I say. Then I cringe, because a lot of bad stuff damn near happened. "Okay, that's not a hundred percent true. But it ain't your fault. Even if you'd told me to get my head shrunk, I probably wouldn't have listened. Don't blame yourself for my issues."

"It's hard not to. We know how difficult the depositions and hearings have been on you," Danny says.

"It's okay," I say. "Y'all are trying to help. I'm grateful you're here. Not sure many lawyers make house calls."

"More than you'd think. We visit a lot of people in the hospital or at their homes if they can't come to us. We just don't talk about it much," August says.

We sit down and chat for a while. "I still can't believe that y'all came all the way up here to see me," I say after a bit.

"We were in the neighborhood," Danny says with a grin.

"We're your friends, and we wanted to make sure you were really okay," Noah says. Just then, there's another knock at the (open) door.

Kurt's standing in the doorway, smiling at me tentatively. He's so handsome and sweet and ... *there* for me. Fuck that "don't form bonds during recovery" bullshit. Far as I'm concerned, that only applies to me getting close to other patients. I *wanna* bond with my husband.

He's positively edible in his dark blue flat-front slacks and light blue dress shirt with the sleeves rolled up. Especially with his mop of hair and sexy forearms. I always thought your heart going pit-a-pat was an exaggeration, but apparently not.

"We won't keep you," Noah says.

I realize I'm on my feet. The three lawyers get up, too, and all shake my hand, then hug me as well. "You got this," August says. "We're rooting for you."

"Oh!" Noah says. "Sam mentioned that your mom's been having issues with her medical insurance. We want to look into that. Do you mind if we talk with her?"

I swallow hard. "No, I don't mind. Thank you." Once again, Kurt's doing his magic.

They leave Kurt and me alone in the room. Kurt stands there

awkwardly for a moment, and I bound over and pull him into a hug. "You came back," I whisper against the top of his head.

"Always," he says, squeezing me around my middle. He already smells like home.

He looks up at me, and I kiss him as naturally as if we're an old married couple. He seems surprised but kisses me back. "I missed you," I say.

I don't deserve you.

Damn. I'd hoped those mean thoughts might've gone away with the anxiety drugs. Seems not.

"I missed you, too," he says, gazing into my eyes. "And you kept your promise."

"Still alive, yeah."

"Promise me again?"

No. I should just finish the job. "I promise to stay alive until I see you again," I tell him, trying to keep my voice level.

Kurt nods in approval. "Thanks, babe. I'll hold you to it." We sit down where I'd been sitting with the other guys. "Tell me how things are going."

I'm a loser.

"Better with a change of clothes. Thank you kindly." I get him caught up with the events since I checked in, including my close (but behind glass) encounter with the mountain lion. Someone yells from down the hall, and I wince, feeling self-conscious. "Aren't you weirded out by this place?" On his way in, I'm sure he passed by people talking to themselves and all kinds of other behavior that doesn't fit with societal norms.

"Why would I be?"

"Well, the people here act kinda different," I admit. "I hate to say it, but there's a reason for the stigma around mental illness."

I suck. I'm wrong. I don't deserve to live.

Kurt shrugs. "They're still people. Probably trying their best to get through the day, just like the rest of us."

"Maybe I'm feeling a little ashamed I'm here ... and that I

brought it up," I say. "Like I wanna separate myself from them, say I'm not as weird as they are. How many stigmas can I have at once? Gay porn star locked up in a mental institution—it's almost the punchline to a joke."

All I've ever been is a joke. I really should just kill myself.

As usual, Kurt treats me with more care and generosity than—well, than anyone I can think of. Certainly more than I give myself. "That's a natural inclination. I'd rather you be honest about your thoughts and feelings than shove them down. When we censor ourselves too much, we end up repressing feelings we need to process—and that keeps us from healing. One of the things I want to talk about in my campaign is better mental health care. Our brain chemistry is no different from any other physical ailment, and yet we treat it with such secrecy and, like you say, stigma."

I nod. "Very true."

The more Kurt talks, the more ... almost normal he makes me feel, even in circumstances so far outside my regular life. He makes me believe I could get better. That this might work. I'm fighting those voices that want to tear me down, that want me to remove myself from the earth.

And none of it would be happening if this amazing man hadn't sat down next to me at that bar Saturday night.

CHAPTER 22
Kurt

After just one night in the hospital, Johnny seems more relaxed. There's less tension at the corners of his eyes, and he's smiling more. They told me what I could send for him to wear, which was mainly sweats with no strings, and while he should look sloppy in them, this is Velvet the Cowboy we're talking about. Even in plain gray sweats and a white T-shirt and looking ill at ease, he's still beautiful.

"They're trying some medication," he says. "It's supposed to take a while to kick in and get the dosage right, but we'll see how that goes. I'm also learning about codependency and childhood trauma. Tips on mental health."

"That's great," I say. "I mean, I'm not glad that you're having to go through all that, but I *am* glad that you're getting help."

"Yeah. I'm still numb, but ... kind of hopeful. Sometimes. Like, I ain't better yet, but there's the *possibility* of improvement. And that possibility's everything."

"I'm so glad to hear that." I hold his hand.

"They gave me something for anxiety, too. I felt *that* right away. The nurse scared me about it—telling me not to take it too much, but the doctor said he thought it'd be fine."

"What do *you* think?"

"It made me feel ... not happy, precisely, but it kept me from feeling bad for the first time in a very long time. Not bad is a massive improvement."

"Excellent." I lean over and kiss him again. "I miss you. I mean, not right now, when I'm here. But when I was home. From the minute I left you here yesterday."

He tilts his head. "Really?"

I nod.

"I miss you, too, precious."

My cheeks heat, but I need to confess something. "What would you think about ... What would you think if I watched one ... or some ... of your videos while you're here? Too creepy? You know I'm a fan. I'm proud of you. I've always liked the way you present yourself in them. And it ... it makes me feel closer to you. Even before we met, I've never thought of you as an object on the screen, but just ... hot."

Johnny gives me a rare unreserved smile. "I think I'd be honored."

"Phew," I say. "Because I watched a favorite one last night." That makes him chuckle, and given how depressed he's been, that chuckle seems like a full-on belly laugh.

"You do what you need to do to make yourself feel good until I get outta here and I can act out those scenes for you in person. Sound good?"

"Yes." The promise in his voice makes me tremble. "I don't want to force you, though. If you're not feeling it, you don't have to, well, *perform* on my account."

He shrugs. "I can still take care of you."

"You don't have to."

"What if I want to?"

I smile. "Then I'll accept whatever you want to give."

"And I'll not mind a bit if you need to get your hot self off." He closes his eyes. "Now that's a pretty thought."

My face flushes more, and I kiss him to make him quiet.

* * *

I visit again the next day, and we talk about how Johnny had some time with a therapist one-on-one and that he's been trying to be as open as possible, but it's hard. I'm so curious, but I don't want to push him to tell me more than he wants to. I'm here to support him any way I can, but I'm not his doctor. I have to keep reminding myself of that.

"What have you been doing?" he asks me.

"Ugh, so much. Fundraising. Doing mailers. Coordinating volunteers. Prepping for the pre-primary debate—that's a big one. It'll be televised. And while I think most people ignore those, since I'm now notorious, I suspect there's going to be more interest than usual, so I need to be ready."

"Notorious? You mean because of ... us?"

I nod. "It's ... a media shitstorm. The conservative press has latched onto the story and is using it against the entire party." My cheeks heat. "We were in a lot of other people's selfies in Vegas, so we're popping up all over the place." I sigh.

"What?"

"I don't wanna pile shit on you when you're busy getting better."

"I'd rather hear the truth," Johnny says. "Keeps me from making up stuff."

"Well ... Santangelo—the incumbent—is using you against me. I hate that society thinks that way."

He shakes his head. "I'm used to it. Maybe it's weird, but I was never ashamed of being in porn." He grins ruefully. "I'm ashamed of plenty of other stuff, but not that. Don't let it bother your pretty head."

"I'm trying not to. But it's hard, because the criticism's everywhere. You'd think that, with both of us in the same political party,

Santangelo wouldn't be so harsh ... but nope. I guess it's fair, since I'm challenging him, but it still feels crappy. Maybe I'll get him in the debate."

"How are you feeling about that?"

"Disillusioned. I can talk passionately about issues for days, and I've worked with my campaign strategist and Paige on the talking points, so I have them down by heart. We practice with them lobbing questions at me on a variety of topics." I sigh. "But I'm so far behind in the polls that I don't think there's any chance of winning."

"This coming from the optimist?" he says.

"Yeah. This coming from the optimist. I have to try, though."

"You don't, actually. I'll support you in whatever you want, but Mama says there's no shame in quitting if the deck is stacked against you."

"She sounds smart."

"I think her actual words were 'You can warm your socks in the oven, but that don't make 'em biscuits.'"

I snort. "How did you get 'There's no shame in quitting' from that?"

"Some things just ain't what you want, no matter how much you wish they were," Johnny says.

"Wow. Isn't that the truth?"

"But I don't mean to discourage you. Is there some way I can help?"

"You just focus on getting better," I say. "That's your only job right now. Promise me you'll stay alive until I see you again?"

He nods. "Yeah, all right. I promise. And if you need to post something about us, you have my permission to say whatever you need to that will help your career."

My throat grows thick. "While I'm grateful for that, I care more about helping you get better."

"You're already doin' that. And thank you." He gives me another look. "You sure divorcing me won't help your campaign?"

I shake my head. "I have no idea, but I don't care anymore what people think about it. And my mom's election is still two years away. I don't want to divorce you. Do you wanna divorce me?"

"No," he says quietly. "I don't."

* * *

I'm sitting in my campaign headquarters, which is a nondescript office space in the San Fernando Valley, with Paige. She's an energetic twenty-nine-year-old who interned for my mother and worked on several other campaigns before becoming my campaign manager. But she's still grouchy at me for going off script with Johnny.

"Should I post something about the wedding on Ad/VICE?" I ask. "Or other social media? The hubbub's not going away."

"Yes, we need to talk about that." She stares at the ceiling and seems to mutter a prayer. "The way I see it, you have several choices of how to respond—not react, *respond*. Let's evaluate which one works best. First, there's always the no-action alternative."

"Meaning no comment?" I shift in my seat. "I kind of like the no-action alternative. It's none of their fucking business, and I like being married to Johnny. Let's leave it at that."

She raises an eyebrow. "The advantage of saying nothing is that you imply it doesn't matter. The disadvantage is that you don't get to make the narrative go the way you want it to."

"Okay. And I assume you want to control the narrative."

"I always want to do that. So if we throw out the no-action alternative, the question is what kind of public statement you want to make. Are you acknowledging the marriage? Saying that you're getting a divorce or annulment?"

"No divorce. No annulment. He and I agreed."

"Okay, I thought we were evaluating alternatives, not rejecting them out of hand, but this is your campaign."

"We're evaluating alternatives for what we say. Not alternatives for what I *do*. I'm not leaving Johnny, so you need to give me possible statements that work in that reality."

"Fine," she says unconvincingly. "Then your statement should be along the lines of you're pleased to announce your surprise wedding to John Haskell, and that you were dating a long time but decided to formalize the relationship recently."

That makes my stomach dip in a really unpleasant way. "I don't want to lie, either. I was required to lie about Sam for years. And I don't like playing into the idea that a relationship isn't legitimate if we haven't been together a long time."

She stares at me. "You don't make my job easy."

"You're good at your job. You don't need easy," I say. "Can't we just keep it simple?"

"What, like, 'The Kurt Delmont campaign congratulates Mr. Delmont on his marriage to John Haskell last weekend. Mr. Delmont is looking forward to a long life of happiness with his new husband'?"

Her words make warmth and happiness bloom in my chest. "Yeah," I say huskily. "That works for me."

Paige puts her face in her hands for a few seconds, then sits up with a sharp breath. "Okay, then let's not waste any more time." She pulls up my official account, then pauses. "Do you have any photos of you two where you don't look wasted?"

I roll my eyes and forward her the email from the wedding chapel.

She scrolls through the images. "Good lord, you did indulge last weekend, didn't you?"

"No comment."

"Ah. The no-action alternative." She smirks. "Well, if I crop the photo to show your rings and use a black-and-white filter, that should class it up."

"Thanks," I say dryly. "I'm glad you can make me classy."

"You know what I mean." With a few taps on her phone, she sets up a post and then holds it out for me to review.

I have to admit I'm impressed. By focusing on our hands, she's made what could be construed as a drunken mistake look like something with way more dignity and romance. A lump forms in my throat. I nod. "Post it."

Paige's finger hovers over the button. "Done." She smiles. "Now let's work on the rest of your campaign."

* * *

On his third full day of inpatient care, Johnny tells me, "A lot of shit has come up. Will you come with me to one of my sessions with Christian after I'm out of here, so I can tell you both at once? I've already had to tell the story too many times to the lawyers, and it's ... hard. For me."

I really want to know what he's talking about—now, not sometime in the future—but I won't press. I don't want to make things more difficult for him. Besides, it sounds like this is something private, and we're surrounded by other patients visiting with their loved ones. "Of course. Anything you need."

"Thanks."

"I know you've been asked a lot, but how's your mental state? I was pretty shocked when you told Dr. Gray how much you think about suicide."

"Yeah, that's not goin' down that much. Maybe a little bit. The meds help. It's like those bumper things at the bowling alley—they keep me from falling into the gutter."

"They don't stop the thoughts entirely?"

"Nope." He scrubs his face. "It's hard to explain how shitty it is to be plagued with a recording in my brain that tells me, over and over and over again, to kill myself. That the world'll be better off. Mama'll be better off. That I'll show them, and they'll all be sorry."

"What do you mean they'll be sorry? Sorry for what?"

"Hell if I know. Maybe that they pushed me to this. That they're bad people."

"Who are bad people?"

"I'm talkin' about shit with my lawsuit again. And it's all a mess inside my head—suicidal thoughts, thoughts that I guess are just depression, I dunno what else. I dunno if it's from my childhood or from more recent shit. I just ..." He holds up his hands helplessly. "I don't have it all figured out."

"You don't have to," I say.

"I keep repeating to myself, 'the only way out is through.'"

"Is that helping?"

"Definitely." Johnny's eyes look a little red, and he leans closer. "Can we talk 'bout somethin' other than me, please? I'm getting a little tired of that topic."

"Sure, babe. Anything you like."

"Then, how's the campaign going?"

"Paige posted this press release." I hold out my phone. "Hope that's okay. Sorry for doing it without asking."

Johnny stares at the black-and-white image for a while. Paige had disabled comments, but there are tens of thousands of likes.

He clears his throat, his cheeks pink. "It's mighty fine with me."

I smile at him, lean over, and kiss him.

When we left Vegas, I thought I had to fix Johnny. I don't feel that way anymore. It's more like he's simply someone I'm dating, who I care about a whole lot.

But does he see me like that? Or am I imagining things that don't exist?

He's starting to look healthy. I hadn't realized how defeated and wan he was before, since that's the only way I knew him. Now, though, he's got rosy cheeks and his eyes are brighter, even though he has a few days' worth of stubble. He's more animated, and he mentions wanting to get a part-time job so he'll have something to do once he's out of here. We start brainstorming possibilities that won't bore him to tears.

"You like working with horses, right?" I ask.

Johnny nods.

"Then let's see if we can get you work on one of the ranches in Hidden Valley. That's not far from our house." I look at him. "I guess I'm making assumptions, and I shouldn't do that. But I have some friends who have horses, and I can ask them if they know anyone who's hiring a ranch hand or someone to help with riding lessons. Do you want that?"

"That'd be mighty kind of you," Johnny says.

When I call, I'm delighted to find out that they do have a need for him whenever he wants to start. *Excellent.*

* * *

The next day, though, Johnny's still in bed when I arrive, and it's the middle of the afternoon. When he gets up, his posture's sagging, his feet are shuffling, and he's got a vacant stare that worries me. I kiss him, but he seems utterly listless.

This is part of his illness. The part he doesn't show anyone. The part where he withdraws.

I try starting a conversation about something unimportant, a TV show I watched last night, but he's just not responsive.

Rather than force him to talk, I sit with him on a bench outside and watch the birds flit around and the deer amble on the main lawn. I hold his hand. At the end of visiting hours, he kisses me on the forehead and says, "Thanks, darlin'. Sorry I wasn't up to it."

I hug him tight, trying to will strength into him. "That's okay. I guess some days are going to be like this. I'm still here for you. Just please promise you'll still be here tomorrow."

His voice is dull, but he promises.

* * *

After five days of inpatient care, the hospital deems Johnny ready to be discharged. When I arrive to pick him up, he's waiting for me at the reception desk, holding four paper bags filled with the clothing and toiletries and books that I've brought him, and my eyes sting with tears. I'm so grateful I get to take him back home with me.

"Hey," I say, relieving him of two of the bags.

"Hey, darlin'." Johnny leans down and kisses me, and even though we've been kissing more and more, this kiss feels like a victory. He's not magically cured or anything, but he seems stable. For today, anyhow. That's a win. "Can we get these filled?" He hands me several prescription slips.

"Of course." I drive us to the nearest pharmacy.

He's going to have to go to outpatient care every day for a couple of weeks, then back to Dr. Gray. This is going to be a lot of work. But I have faith that he can feel better.

He's kept promising to stay alive for just one more day.

I'll still be watching out for him, of course. Besides, I want to keep him close to me for other reasons—as in, the fact that I like him. That I want to have a relationship with him.

He looks around the condo when we walk in, and his eyes catch on where I put his lifetime achievement award up on a prominent shelf in the living room. He swallows hard but doesn't say anything.

"Let me know if there's anything you need," I say. "Also, you can use the Volvo to go to the job interview. After that, we can get you a different car, if you'd rather, or a truck—"

"Hold it, hold it," he says. "My tab is getting way too big."

"What tab?"

"I'm gonna pay you back for all this you've spent on me."

While I want to wave my hand and go "pfft," I know he wouldn't like that. Instead, I nod. "Okay. Just so you know my position, I don't care if you pay me back or not. But I can tell it matters to you. We can keep the spending low, so it's manageable. Right now, it's not much—an increase in my car insurance, a few deductibles, and the therapist until insurance picks it up. How does that sound?"

"It's more than that, but okay, yeah. Thanks. I 'preciate it."

Johnny has a pride streak a mile wide, I think, which is why he had to get so low before he asked for help.

In fact, he never actually did ask for help—but he accepted it, and that's what matters.

Johnny takes a shower and puts on some of the new clothes I got him. (Oops, I suppose he'll add that to his tab, too.) I cook some steaks and grilled veg. Alcohol might not mix with his meds, so I pour us tall glasses of seltzer rather than beer, and we eat dinner outside on the balcony, looking at the highway and the ocean.

This is all I've ever wanted. Someone to be with me.

"It may be too early to tell," I say, as we watch the sunset, "but do you think it was a good idea to check yourself in?"

"It was the best idea," Johnny says sincerely. "I didn't know how tangled up I'd gotten until I sat still for a moment and looked at the knots."

"I'm proud of you for going. It takes a lot to set aside all the shit and face your demons."

"Pretty sure I haven't even started to face my demons," he says. "But I do think I'm headed in that direction."

"Looking forward to the next step?"

He shrugs. "Kinda? It's scary, too. I'm not sure what to think."

"I have faith in you," I say. "I know you can do it. And I'll stand next to you and slay whatever demons I can."

We fall into bed in each other's arms, but we're both exhausted. Before I even have a chance to think about asking to do anything, Johnny's snoring quietly behind me, one big hand on my waist.

I love having him home with me.

I grin into my pillow and fall asleep.

CHAPTER 23
Johnny

Every morning for the next ten weekdays, I'm picked up by an official van and taken to the hospital to attend a group session for a few hours. Every other afternoon, I attend a therapy session with Christian. Sometimes Kurt comes with me to those, sometimes he doesn't.

The violins are still making a racket in my mind. Sometimes I wonder where Kurt put the gun. I've stared too long at some railroad tracks, and every time I'm on the road I wonder what would happen if we just ... veered into oncoming traffic and got it all over with.

Focusing on my brain is hard work, and some days I feel like I've been beaten with a meat tenderizer by the time I'm done. But I told Christian and Kurt that I made the decision to get better. Some days it feels like that promise is the only thing that motivates me to get off the couch.

Staying fit helps with my mental state. There's a gym at Kurt's condo complex, and he comes with me to work out. He complains, but in a cute way. He complains even worse when I make him join me for a run ... but he comes anyway. Makes me all soft and sweet on him.

Kurt took time off from his job to be with me, but he's still busy working on his campaign. He has a million meetings and is always going to fundraising dinners, taking phone calls, reviewing numbers and charts. He asked me how much I wanna participate in his public life, but we agreed that for now, he should do the campaign stuff alone. I'm far from being healthy enough to be out in the public eye. Better for both of us if I keep focusing on my recovery.

I wish I could help out with the campaign, because I do like being with him. I know our marriage is mostly about him not wanting to blow up his political chances even more—and putting me on his insurance, because he's too generous—but if I had my druthers, it would be more than that. I want him to be *mine*.

It's too bad that I'm such a damn mess.

If things were different, if I were worthy of him, I'd want to be with him for real. But he's already done too much for me. I'm keeping track of every single penny he spends on me, but I don't know how I'll ever repay him.

I know the political stuff's getting him down. He's always looking at his phone and cussing. It's clear he ain't doing as well as he wishes—because of me—but I dunno any way to help him. I figure the only thing I can do right now is get better. I'm doing that as much for him as I am for myself.

Since I'm still having suicidal thoughts—and Kurt asks me about them all the time—he's set up a babysitting system of sorts for when I'm at home and he's out. He didn't call it that or tell me he was doing it, but that's what it is. He makes sure there's always someone around. It pissed me off when I first figured it out, but now I think it's cute. How can I not be charmed that he's keeping watch over me? Some days he'll send over our neighbor or their kid. Or Paige, his campaign manager—I bugged her for tips on how to help him. His assistant, Wendy, or his housekeeper, Galen.

Today, it seems my babysitter's Julian Hill, the biggest pop star in the world. I'll admit to being a wee bit starstruck, even though I don't listen to his music.

He saunters into Kurt's condo wearing tight, ripped gray jeans and a plain black T-shirt. He's lean and tall, with tattoos everywhere. His hair's an artful mess, and his face is impish and gentle. "Hey," he says with a grin, holding out his hand. I shake it, my mouth dry. "I'm Jules."

I nod. "Johnny. Nice to meet you."

"I'm a fan," he says. Why, of everyone who has ever seen my videos, it takes Julian Hill to make me blush, I have no idea. Maybe because of his fancy British accent—it makes him seem snooty, even though he's clearly not.

"Thank you kindly," I manage to get out. "I havta be honest with you: I only listen to country, so I ain't sure what songs you sing. My sister might've listened to you, though, when we were growin' up."

Jules laughs. "That's refreshing, actually. Then we don't have to talk about music or any of that bollocks. What would you like to chat about instead? Tell me: What's your favorite thing on earth?"

Kurt.

"Besides my mama and sister?" I ask.

He nods.

"Dogs," I say. "And horses."

"Dogs are the best," he agrees, and he becomes my favorite pop star, even though I couldn't tell you one song he sings. "If you were to get a dog, what kind would you get?"

"Well, I like all dogs, but you can't go wrong with a goldie. Or a German shepherd. They're so smart and loyal."

"Agreed. I've always wanted to adopt a retired greyhound. They're sleek, and I figure that they could use some love after being forced to race."

"Ain't that the truth." I walk into the kitchen, and he follows me. "Want something to drink, since you're forced to be here?"

"Oh, I wouldn't say forced. I'm happy to do it. And I'd love a cuppa." It takes me a moment to figure out he's talking about tea. He helps me make him a "proper" mug.

I end up talking with Julian Hill for two hours about all the dogs we've ever wanted to own.

* * *

When Kurt gets home from the Rotary Club meeting, Jules and I are sitting on the balcony, watching the waves and the surfers. We go inside and chat with Kurt for a moment, and then Jules hugs us before being whisked off by his driver.

"How'd'ja get Julian Hill to babysit me?" I ask once we're alone.

Kurt shrugs out of his jacket and slips off his tie, setting them on a dining chair. "It's not babysitting. More ... just making sure you've got company and are okay. I asked Sam if he could do it, and he volunteered Jules."

"It was nice of him, if unexpected."

"People care about you." That statement makes me want to squirm, but Kurt leans over and kisses me. "As they should."

"Yeah, maybe," is the most I can get out.

"Are you tired of people asking you how you are?" he asks.

I shake my head. "No. Or ... maybe yes, but it's still a valid question. My mood is all over the place. Sometimes I'm feeling pretty good, and other times I'm wondering where you put the keys to the locked cabinet."

Kurt winces. "It's still that bad?"

"We agreed to be honest. It's not like going to the hospital was magic. It stabilized me, sure. Kept me from getting worse, definitely. But getting back to normal, or something like that?" I bite my lip. "That's gonna take a while."

"Then I'll be patient."

We move to the couch on the balcony and settle down to

watch the waves. Kurt puts his head on my shoulder. I love that. I love his warmth next to me on this cool evening. And I'm trying to be aware of these moments of happiness and pleasure so I can remember them when things aren't as good.

"You know, even if there's no magic cure, I'm still proud of you for going," he says. "And grateful, honestly. I wasn't there in time for Andrei, and seventeen years later, I'm still fucked up about it." He pauses, then adds, "Sometimes, now, I have these nightmares where it's his bloody body, but your face."

That makes my gut clench, but I don't know what I can say. "I'm so sorry y'all went through that."

"I keep thinking, if I'd been a better friend, a better boyfriend, would it have been different? Did I make things unbearable for him? What was wrong with me that I couldn't stop him?"

"Even though I wasn't there, I can guarantee there was nothing you could've done. If someone wants to do that to themselves, they can't be stopped."

"I stopped you."

"You did, but I also let you. And honestly, I still wake up every morning questioning whether I want to go through with it."

Kurt turns to me with pain in his eyes. "Fuck. I'm sorry."

"Now, see? That there ain't your fault. It's some chemistry in my brain that's making me feel that way. The meds haven't all kicked in yet. I have hope, but if I get too far ahead of myself, I spin out. The only thing I can do is bring it down to this moment. Today. Do I want to live for today? Maybe, maybe not. But I promised Kurt I would, so I do."

"I knew this was hard, but I hadn't realized how hard," he says, squeezing my hand.

"Sometimes it's really damn hard, darlin'." I stroke the top of his head and then kiss it. "Andrei's suicide wasn't on you. That, I know for sure."

"How do you know?" Kurt asks quietly.

"Because I know you. You're kind and loving. Look at the care you take of me, and I'm next to being a stranger. Even if you were a punk kid—which I don't think you were—you didn't want your boyfriend to die. Y'all couldn't have stopped him if he was that determined."

Kurt tilts his head up at me. "That's what my therapist keeps saying."

I chuckle. "I know for a fact that sometimes things need to be repeated many, many times before they can settle in. Speaking from someone deep in the thick of it, his death was not your fault. Period."

He sighs and cuddles into me. We don't move for a long time, and I look at him to make sure he's not upset or nothin'. But he ain't. He's just staring out at the beach.

This couch has big cushions, and there's a chaise lounge at the end of it. I shift us over so I'm spooning him and he's looking out through the glass, our heads on a pillow. I pull a blanket over us.

"Can I tell you something?" I whisper, holding him close, my lips against the back of his neck, my whole body aligned with his.

"Of course," he murmurs.

"Sometimes I need this more than I need to fuck."

Kurt shudders against me. Then he turns around and slots a leg between mine, his arms around me, his head on my chest. He rearranges the blanket so it's still covering us. "Sometimes I do, too."

* * *

After my outpatient care is done and I feel okay enough to try my hand at working, I start up Kurt's Volvo one morning and drive to his friend's house in Hidden Valley. I'm as out of place as an armadillo at prom, because everything's so, *so* expensive. Despite being close to Los Angeles, the area's rural, with acres of pretty, fenced-in fields, oak trees, and a quiet sense of seclusion. Oh, and the houses are huge, with big barns and proper riding facilities.

It's the first time that Kurt's trusted me on my own, but I promised him I'd stay alive. And I'm feeling more and more like I don't want to kill myself. The violins have longer and longer periods of silence.

Mostly I'm just ... blank. Numb. I'm not sad, but I'm not happy either. I think the meds keep me from getting too deep, but I'm never unicorns and rainbows either. I'm still battling painful, intrusive thoughts.

I pull up the long driveway where the GPS tells me, and I almost turn around and head back to Kurt's place. No way can I work here. It's not for someone like me. It's too ... polished.

But then a wiry woman comes out of the barn, flanked by two dogs. She's got long, dark red hair plaited into one braid down her back and is wearing a western shirt and old boots. She looks like she's tough as nails and knows what she's doing. At her heels are two border collies, full of mischief. Then I see the horses in the corral, and I draw in a breath. They're utterly gorgeous. Stunning American Quarter Horses with glossy coats and a healthy look about them. They're well cared for.

I let out a sigh of relief. I might have issues with people, but animals are animals, and I know how to deal with them. Okay. I can do this.

Getting out of the car, I step over to the woman and tip my hat. "Howdy," I say. "I'm Johnny Haskell. I'm looking for Bronwyn?"

"That's me," she says. "Welcome. You good with mucking out stables?"

Despite my generally down mood, I chuckle. Because this isn't a hazing question. Mucking stables is an essential part of caring for horses. "Sure. Just set me to work. Mind if I pet the dogs?"

"Go ahead." Bronwyn gestures to the dogs. "The bigger one is Maggie, and the smaller one is Sally."

"Hello, Maggie," I say, squatting down so I can scritch behind her dark, fluffy ears. "You're a good girl, aren't you?"

She licks me, and I say hello to Sally, too, who's also a good girl. The dogs hop all over me and lick my face, and it makes me smile more.

The smile's starting to get less creaky.

I glance up, and Bronwyn nods. "You'll do."

"How's that?" I ask.

"You gotta get along with animals around here, and you take to those dogs like you're one of them."

Standing, I hook a thumb in my belt loop. "I may be part dog, that's correct. Can I meet the horses?"

"Follow me."

With the dogs at our sides, we walk over to the first horse, who's shiny in the sun. The scent of hay and horse manure is all around us, but to me that's as natural as salt in the sea.

"This is Stacy," Bronwyn says. "She's four. Her sister Betty Lou is in the stables. I took Stacy out this morning for a trail ride, and she's had some cooldown time. We'll need to groom her, then Betty Lou needs some exercise, too. I'll take her out, and you can muck."

I nod. "Sounds good to me. How many horses do the owners have?"

"Eight, plus they also board a few for other people, so there's usually ten or twelve here at a time. Sometimes more. I'm full-time, plus there are some other part-timers. But we can always use more help. Let's go meet Pepper, Jan, and Lucky."

I get introduced to all the horses, and Bronwyn gives me a rundown of their personalities and special needs or quirks. For some reason, it's easy for me to remember things like this—their names, their needs. While I pull out my phone to take a few notes, I know I won't need to refer to them. Bronwyn hands me a clipboard, and I fill out some tax forms, needing to look up my address on the phone. But I get it done.

We stop by the tack room, and Bronwyn shows me where the

food and other supplies are. Then she puts a lead on Betty Lou and asks me to muck out the stables while they're gone.

Fine by me. I grab gloves, a broad shovel, and a wheelbarrow and get to work. It's a cool day, but I work up a sweat, and ... I don't know. Being out in the fresh air and sunshine, working around these big, gorgeous animals with dogs at my side, makes me feel centered. Even though we're not that far from the traffic of Los Angeles, it's quiet here. It feels like a different world. One where I could actually be happy. I understand why people pay so much money to live here. It's my idea of heaven.

The hours pass quickly, and I can look back and see what I've accomplished: neat stalls that are clean, with everything stocked up for later. The horses are all groomed and fed, and I feel productive in a way I ain't felt in a really long time.

Back when I was working on a set, I could tell when we were getting footage that was going to work, and I could often predict when it'd be a video that would take off and be popular. But things didn't always go right, and sometimes at the end of the day, I'd go home sore and not feeling like I did much.

Here, though, there's no question about what I did, from getting the trail dust off a horse to making sure everything's tidy and in good repair. Taking care of horses is the work that feeds my soul. I haven't done it since my early teens, but I love it.

Kurt figured that out about me, and like a present, he gave it to me. I *really* like that man.

CHAPTER 24
Johnny

After a few days of working in Hidden Valley, I get into a rhythm of going there either early in the morning or very late in the evening, depending on their other staffing and my therapy schedule. When I get my first paycheck and can buy groceries, I feel capable—like I'm actually pulling my weight for once. I realize that's barely a drop in the bucket compared to everything Kurt has spent on me, but ... it's not nothing.

One afternoon, I walk into the house after I'm done for the day feeling kinda beat. I look for Kurt, but he ain't in the kitchen or great room. Maybe he's at work in his home office, and I shouldn't disturb him. I need a shower, though. I walk up the stairs into the bedroom and stop short.

Kurt's lying on our bed with his shirt rucked up and his hand on his cock, his laptop propped next to him on the duvet.

And I recognize the soundtrack. Because it's my voice saying to someone—have to remember who—"Bring that hard cock over here, darlin'."

Holy crap. He's watching my porn.

Maybe I should be weirded out, but it's the opposite. I

watch his strong hand fist his cock, his dark blue pants down around his ankles, and I get turned on like I haven't been in a while.

Just when I know he's getting to a good part, I clear my throat, and he freezes. "Shit, you scared me!" he hisses.

"Oh, don't let me interrupt," I say, raising an amused eyebrow. "This is mighty entertaining."

He's beet red. "I'm so fucking embarrassed. Oh my god."

"Don't be. This is in-person feedback on my work." I come closer. "Keep going."

When I see myself on the screen, I usually feel separated from it. Like, that's Velvet. I'm just Johnny.

Right now, though, I'm taking in Kurt's nude form and having very interesting thoughts.

We've fooled around a bit since I came back from the hospital, but not much. He's a very beautiful man, though, and seeing him like this makes me wanna do more.

"What if I do what I'm doing in the video to you?" I ask slowly. Which is rather cheeky, since Kurt and I haven't gone further than a few hand jobs and a quick blow job or two.

Kurt bites his lip, and I can tell he's tempted but doesn't want to say yes for some reason. Probably because I told him sometimes I'm not in the mood.

"We don't have to," I whisper. "But you look so sexy right now that if you're up for it, I am."

He'd paused the video and thrown a blanket over his lap when I first spoke. He's still lying there, body tense. "Okay," he says after a moment. "Please, I want to see you naked." There's an edge of desperation in his voice that I appreciate. I take off my shirt, and Kurt eyes me hungrily.

"I'm covered in dust," I say. "Give me two minutes?"

He nods.

I strip hastily and speed walk into the bathroom to take the fastest shower ever. When I'm done, I return, still trying to dry myself with the towel. "Take off your own clothes," I order, "all the way."

He hurries to comply.

I'm going to kiss his mouth before I kiss his cock, even though his cock is right there, waiting to be sucked. I straddle him, cradle his chin, and kiss him softly.

Kurt deserves some sweetness. He deserves to have things not be so difficult all the time. He deserves to be treated with affection. I can bring the heat, but I think Kurt may need something more. Something different.

One kiss morphs into another and another, neither of us wanting to stop. I'm holding his face in gentle fingers, but he's now tugging my ass to him.

And my skin feels tingly in a way it hasn't in a long time. My heartbeat's quickening, and my pulse is in my throat—in a good way. It feels this way when I hear a beautiful song or see a horse galloping, strong and free.

When I'm *moved*.

I almost sob—I'm finally feeling a big emotion other than sadness. Kurt's kisses are affecting me in a way I didn't expect, and I can't complain about it at all.

His cock's hard between us, and as a connoisseur, I can attest that while it's not the biggest, it's truly lovely. A bit of a curve, which I think is mighty fine. It's sticking straight out from him like a javelin buried in the ground.

I run my fingers down his throat. "Want me?" I murmur against his lips.

"Yeah." His voice sounds husky.

"Good."

I suck on his lower lip. "Look how beautiful you are, baby. Damn."

Kurt blushes. How often does he hear praise? And more importantly, how often does he get attacked? By his political opponents, by members of the public who don't understand what a treasure he is, how lucky they are that he'd even consider working on their behalf.

I trace a hand down Kurt's bare chest. He's got a dusting of hair across his pecs, and I scratch my nails through it, then down to his happy trail.

He rumbles like a purring cat, relaxing his arms by his sides and exposing his whole body for my exploration. I'm enjoying this: lazy, naked, get-to-know-you time.

I linger on his arms, letting my fingers trail up and down, up and down, watching as the fine hairs rise and stand on end.

His eyes are closed, but he smiles. "That feels so good," he slurs. He reaches out for me, but I tsk.

"Let me," I say. And he obeys, putting his hand back on the bed. "Good boy," I whisper, and his cheeks flush.

Interesting.

"Do you know how handsome you are?" I continue, playing with my theory that he likes to be praised. My lips follow the pattern my fingers began. Kissing his upper bicep, then down, into the inside of his elbow, along his forearm. When I get to his palm, I drop an open-mouthed kiss there, then take his thumb into my mouth.

His cock is stiff against my thigh. I suck hard on his thumb, then draw back and do the same thing to his index finger.

Kurt moans. "Fuck, that feels good. Why does that feel so good?"

I'm busy sucking on his middle finger now, so my answer's a shrug. I move so one of my legs is between his and his cock is pressing against my hip bone. I keep going, sucking on his ring finger. I pause for a moment to spin the ring on that finger with my other hand, then keep going to his pinkie.

"It's like you're giving me five blow jobs," he whines.

"Are you complaining?" I say, my voice guttural.

"Absolutely not." Kurt arches into me, and I take pity on him, stroking his cock, using his precome to smooth the way.

"Fuck," he moans again. "Please. More."

"Be patient, like the good boy you are." I watch for his reaction, and yes, he stills, letting me have his body as a playground. I smile against his collarbone as I kiss my way across his chest, aiming for his other arm.

He reaches a tentative hand up to stroke my side, and I let him. Damn, this is so sensual. It's slow, patient, attentive. I kiss the pulse point under his neck, then kiss down his arm, repeating what I did on his other side, including sucking his fingers one by one.

When he's wriggling under me, I push his legs farther apart and settle between them, then continue my slow torture down his torso. I linger on each nipple, licking and sucking until he's groaning with every breath.

Then I kiss down the middle, and when I finally, finally get to his cock, I dart out my tongue to taste his precome. He shudders, and that does something to me. Because he's not acting. He's not exaggerating his responses for the camera.

This is just him and me. This is real.

I glance up from between his legs, and he's gazing down at me with an expression that's nothing short of adoration. A warm bubble in my chest expands, and I grin at him. "More?" I'm teasing, but his need is intoxicating.

"Yes. More. Please."

"I love it when you can only say one-syllable words." Without waiting for a response, I swallow him down, and he arches off the bed.

"Mmmfhgh."

I give him a good hard suck and then pop off to ask, "You wanna come this way?"

He nods urgently. I pretend to think about it, just to see his reaction, and he doesn't disappoint. "Please, Johnny."

"Since you're so good." I kiss the tip of his hard cock, then engulf him in my mouth again, swallowing repeatedly around him.

"Sweet hell."

I keep going, deciding not to torment him further. I like his O-face. I buckle down, devoting myself to bringing him to orgasm. Letting myself deep-throat him as much as I can—which is quite a bit—and not backing off until he's coming with a shout.

Sucking him even while he's returning to earth, I slow down, cradling his cock in my mouth. He reaches down and runs his fingertips through my hair. "Oh my god, that was amazing."

A low chuckle rumbles from my chest. I suck a final time, then pull back onto my knees.

He looks debauched. There's no other word. His hair is bedhead sexy, and his brow is shiny with sweat. He's panting, and his cheeks are flushed. Instead of saying anything, he hooks his ankles under my armpits, pulling me up for a kiss.

I comply readily and enthusiastically. "Such a good boy," I whisper when we pause, and I look at him. "Do you like it when I say that?"

Kurt stiffens, then bites his lip and nods. "Yeah."

"Then I'll be glad to keep doing it."

"Please." He gives me a sly grin. "Can I return the favor?"

I scurry to the side so fast that he laughs. I lie on my back and flop my arms out. "Be my guest, darlin'. Do whatever you want."

Kurt licks his lips. "God, you're beautiful."

I blink. I'm used to talk like that as part of a scene, but that's acting. It's meaningless. He's being sincere. "Thank you. You are, too."

Kurt pounces then, straddling me and kissing me, and I kiss him back. "What do you want me to do?" he whispers against my neck.

"Touch me. Lord, please," I groan. I'm not faking my enthusiasm, either. His touch lights up my skin, and just being around him makes me ... happy.

It's been so long since I've been happy, but I'm starting to remember that I used to be that way. Before ...

I shudder. Best not to think about that.

"You okay?" Kurt asks.

I yank myself back into the moment. "With you? Never better." I just went a long time without any crappy thoughts. *Hallelujah.*

He crawls down my body and lowers his mouth to my cock, then hesitates, looking at it. It's intimidating. That's not bragging, it's just a fact.

"You don't have to perform, darlin'," I tell him. "Just do what you like, and it'll feel good."

Kurt swallows and then opens his mouth, sucking in my tip.

"Oh, bless, that's good," I say. He's got the suction right, the location right, his tongue is massaging the underside of the head just right.

I put a hand in his hair, just gentle, like petting a cat. "I like you down there, servicing my cock. You're so good at it, and you're so beautiful. Having you—oh Lord," I say, as he gets in an extra-good suck. "Yeah, precious boy, you've got that down. Oh, damn. So good. Oh, baby, yes."

I can tell he's pleased by the relaxed but determined set of his shoulders. He uses his hands to massage my balls and press into my taint, and then he starts jacking me. He's choking on my cock—but, again, determined.

"Look at you. You're amazing," I say, all warm inside.

This man. How was I lucky enough to find him? He's so in tune with what I like, and whether that's intuitive, or he's paying attention, or he *really* studied my videos, I don't much care. All I know is that he's sucking me in a way that feels fresh and new and so damn pleasurable.

"You keep that up, I'll come," I say. "You wanna make me come right now? Or do you want to just keep my cock in your mouth?"

"You don't wanna come?" Kurt asks. His lips are swollen, and his hair is messy, and I love it.

"I do, but I also like having your mouth on me."

He tilts his head. "I notice that you don't come as often as I do. Do you think that's because of the ..." He gestures at my head. "Depression?"

"Could be."

"Do you think you'd feel better if you did come?"

I bite my lip. "Right now, what I want most of all is to be close to you. I don't feel the need to finish." My erection's flagging as we talk. "I guess maybe I am having issues with it? Maybe the meds are messing with me. All I know is I crave having your body next to mine. And your mouth on me is a big bonus."

"And I like having something to do that keeps me from thinking about all the shit going on in my life."

"Then warm my cock, baby. Let's take a little nap, and you can suckle on me while you sleep." It's early evening, but we've been going a long time, and we were both up before the sun this morning.

His eyes widen, and I wonder if I've gone too kinky for him. But then I realize he's *excited*.

I prop some pillows behind my back and sit up, and Kurt curls up by my side and takes me into his mouth. I'm still about half-hard, and his tongue and lips feel amazing.

"You make me feel like I don't have to perform," I whisper.

His eyes widen and he pulls off enough to say, "You never have to perform with me."

"Thanks," I whisper. He suckles on me, and I groan, running my fingers through his hair. "Precious boy, you keep this up, and I may never be able to let you go."

He sighs happily, and we fall silent.

Eventually, he stops sucking, and I realize he's fallen asleep with my cock in his mouth, just as I suggested. I cover him with the blanket and fall asleep myself.

I love this. There's another thought behind that, a bigger one, but I let it slip away before it can scare away this moment of peace.

CHAPTER 25
Kurt

My life's changed, and I'm not entirely sure how that happened. I really like it, though.

My attraction to Johnny grows with every moment we're together. I wouldn't have thought that was possible. It's not just that I'm living with my absolute crush, whose essential goodness comes through even when he's not feeling great.

During the month-plus since our night in Vegas, my husband has spent five days in a hospital, two weeks in outpatient care, and the better part of ten days split between therapy and his new job on the ranch. And somehow he's also started doing all these things for me that I didn't even realize I needed.

Tonight, I walk in the door after running an errand, and he has index cards spread all over the dining room table. He's standing and studying them, moving a few around.

"What'cha doing?" I ask, snaking an arm around his middle and kissing his shoulder.

"Figuring out which zip codes y'all need to focus on to win," he says in his low drawl. Like it's obvious that he'd be helping me with this.

I raise an eyebrow, scanning the demographic data on the cards. "How'd you get this information?"

"I talked with Paige. Got the info from her spreadsheet. If we know how many registered voters there are in each zip code and how many of them normally vote, then we can figure out the best places for you to focus your campaigning. I was just lookin' at it all, trying to see how I could help."

"Shit," I say, pressing my palms to my cheeks. "You're a political strategist."

"Never said I didn't understand politics," he says with a wink. "Just that I didn't like politicians. Save one."

"I always liked porn stars," I say. "Well, one in particular."

He stands up, draws me close, and kisses me. "Did you watch my porn because you had a crush on me?" he teases, nipping at my lower lip.

I nod. "Yeah, in part." He's told me so many truths that I might as well share one of mine. Taking his hand, I pull him down to the couch and snuggle in next to him. "The other part was that I was lonely. I couldn't date anyone, because I was supposedly dating Sam. If I tried to hook up, I'd have to trust the guy to keep his mouth shut—which is a lot to expect from a hookup. I threw myself into my work so I didn't have much time for anything else. It's amazing how busy you can stay if you try hard enough. If you're scared of not having anything to do."

"Darlin' ..." he starts.

"But I like sex. The only way I could get it without risking some scandal was alone with my screen. It's not the same as having someone to kiss and hug and touch, but ... it was better than nothing."

"I understand loneliness." He sighs. "I was scared of future loneliness. Of the pain of losing Mama. That's how I got myself so messed up."

"That's a trauma response," I say. "Don't judge yourself for how you reacted when she's been so sick."

"Yeah, okay. The codependency thing. But that's not all." He sighs, and it sounds like it comes from all the way down in his toes. "I have an appointment with Christian tomorrow. If you come, I'll tell you both then. I will. Just don't wanna say it more times than I havta, 'cause it sucks."

He's made comments like that before, and in contexts that make me think something happened at the studio. But what? Did someone get rough with him? Did he have to fuck someone he didn't want to fuck?

And will talking about it make him want to get the pills and the gun again?

I haven't moved the gun since I locked it up. I hid the keys in the pocket behind the passenger seat of my car, where I don't think he'd look for them.

"I think you and I both have lived in the past a lot," I say, "and with this campaign, I'm living in the future. But I'm really interested in the now."

"Yeah, me, too." He peppers kisses along the back of my neck. "Though I do like getting to know you, so I like hearing about your past."

"Me, too. I mean, about yours. What was it like growing up?" I ask.

Johnny pauses with his lips on my skin, then draws back. "My daddy was a seasonal worker. He was there for a summer at the ranch and got together with my mama, and then he went on to his next job without knowing that she was pregnant. She wrote to him at the address of the camp where he was going—that was before everybody had cell phones—but apparently he never got the letter, so when he came back the next summer, it was 'Surprise, you have a son.' Anyway, he decided to stay on and work at the ranch year-round, but it was tough living for them. Mama got pregnant again with my sister, and after a few years, my daddy took off. Still, things were okay. Even after Mama got sick, we were getting by, mostly, until the owners decided to sell up."

I'm quiet, just letting him talk. But I'm feeling very protective of his mother, his sister, and little Johnny, who didn't ask to be born in circumstances that were so spare.

"Like I told you before, we headed to Fresno. Took us a while to get there. We got in Mama's car—it was a beat-up old thing—and we'd drive as far as we could on a tank of gas, then see where we could sleep for the night. Most of the time we couldn't afford a motel room, but sometimes we'd find a place that would let us stay in exchange for working."

I squeeze his hand. "Where did you go to school?"

"I didn't, for a long time. When we finally ended up in California, I enrolled in school, but I was way behind. Mama had tried to teach me reading and arithmetic, but there are only so many hours in a day, especially when you're lookin' for work. Eventually, though, I did okay. I was a big kid, which helped. My daddy was a big man, I think. When I was little, he seemed big, anyhow. I could hold my own in a fight, and that kept kids from making too much fun of me."

"Were you in fights a lot?" I don't want to move from where I'm leaning against him, but I want to see his expression, so I turn and face him.

Johnny scratches his chin. "I'd say I was in fights just enough to let folks know not to mess with me."

"Makes sense."

"I told you about my sister. Someone at the ranch had a fiddle, and she took to it immediately. Then she learned to play softer songs. Sadder ones. Mama didn't have money for lessons, but May Ella'd just teach herself." He shakes his head. "She's incredible. I hear her playing in my head all the time." He pauses. "Actually, I'm hearing it less these days. When I hear it, all I can think is how much I still have to do to help my mama."

"You know that she's not your responsibility."

"But she is," Johnny says so earnestly my heart breaks. "Who else does she have? Family's got to take care of each other."

"Family can ask too much of you sometimes," I insist. Then I hesitate. "Well, I don't know your family dynamics."

Johnny holds out his hands in an "exactly" gesture. He gets a faraway look in his eyes. "Although this is the codependency stuff they were talking about in the hospital."

"What's that?"

"That I've been trying to fix things I can't ever fix."

I hug him. "It sounds like you've been through a lot. I guess the real question is, where do you want to go from here?"

"I ain't figured that out yet. I'm still focused on getting better and tryin' to get my mama taken care of."

"I wonder if Sam, or the firm, has gotten anywhere with the insurance company. Something sounds wrong to me. If she's otherwise a good fit, why isn't she getting approved?" I cock my head. "Could I be a donor?"

"What's your blood type?" I tell him, and he shakes his head. "Nope. I don't think that's compatible."

I renew my commitment to help him help his mom. I could just send her the money—I *want* to just send her the money. But doing that without Johnny's consent would feed his feelings of inadequacy. I've seen the little pad of paper where he's adding up every single thing I've bought him. I'm not willing to jeopardize his mental state by adding a big-ticket item to that list, especially when his mom's illness seems not to be an immediate crisis.

I don't know how to tell him that he's worth every penny in my bank account. That I don't care if he pays me back. That I don't *want* him to pay me back.

I don't know how to tell him that I want to protect him. That I want to take care of him. I don't know how to tell him how lonely I was before he came into my life and how integral he's starting to be for me.

"Are y'all ready for the debate?" Johnny asks, clearly wanting to change the subject.

"I think so," I say. "I'm never going to be perfect, but I want to do the best I can, so Paige and I have been practicing with a consultant."

"You're going to be amazing. Want me to come and be in the audience, clap for you?"

"You think you're up to it?" This isn't about me—I'm ready for Johnny to come out of the shadows anytime he wants to.

"I do." He pauses. "I'm gettin' used to feelin' my feelings and talking about them instead of just pushin' them down until they explode." He clears his throat. "So ... you comin' with me to therapy tomorrow?" he asks. "Do y'all have time?"

I nod. "Of course."

* * *

When we get to Christian's office, Johnny doesn't get out of the car right away. He stares out at the ocean, then looks down at his lap, then gazes up at the office building.

"Today's gonna be hard," he says. "I think I'm ready, but it's ..." He scrubs his face with his hands. "I'm scared you're gonna look at me different."

"I won't," I promise.

"How do you know that? What if the ... stuff I have to say is awful?"

"You're not the type to ever do anything truly awful, and if something awful happened to you, it's not your fault."

"Okay, yeah, I get it." He doesn't sound entirely persuaded. "I'm just nervous."

I give him what I hope is a reassuring smile. "That's probably why you need to talk."

"Maybe. Yeah. Okay."

We get out of the car and hold hands as we walk into the office, then settle side by side on the couch when it's time for his appointment.

Christian leans forward with a professional and kind smile. "What would you like to talk about today?" she asks.

"I wanna talk about what happened to me that day at work," Johnny says. "And why I brought my lawsuit. Even if I'm fucking petrified what Kurt's gonna think of me afterward."

CHAPTER 26

Johnny

If Kurt and I are gonna be together for real—and I want that more and more every day—he needs to know everything about me. Even the ugly stuff that I've tried to hide.

Christian is a professional. It's her job to listen to this sort of thing and not react. But this may make Kurt look at me differently. Make him think less of me.

My stomach feels hollow and empty, and my mouth goes dry. I start looking for the exit—which is the door. It's right there. I could run.

"Are you sure you want to talk about it?" Kurt asks, breaking through my nerves. "I'd never force you to."

Honesty.

The only way out is through.

I can do this.

I scratch at my face. "No, but yes. I don't want to, but I'll have to talk about it again at the trial, anyway. The thing is, I'm afraid you ain't gonna like me no more, Kurt."

"That's never going to happen," he says, lightly stroking my forearm. I want to lean into him, but I've gotta be strong or I'll never get through this.

"Johnny, in these sessions, you don't have to say anything you don't want to. So why don't you start with what you *want* to tell us?" Christian says.

I scrub my cheeks and start twisting my wedding ring. "Y'all know I've always been a top, right?" I look at Christian. "You understand gay sex terminology?"

She nods. "Yes. Why are you exclusively a top?"

"That's what I like. I tried bottoming once, and it hurt, and I didn't like it. I try to make it good for the people I'm with, but it's not for me."

"You have every right to set boundaries that work for you, regarding sex and elsewhere in your life," Christian says.

I clear my throat and rub my hands over my jean-covered thighs. "Okay, so, well. I've worked for a lot of different studios. The one I usually worked for had a founder who was big on ethics and consent. He got sick, though, and left a new guy in charge. And this new guy—well, he's a veteran in the industry, so he's not new, just new to me—he's known for being … edgier. He brought in his own company, where he jointly produced and directed, and started to take over different planned productions. More than once, he asked me to do some scenes outside my costar's limits. I said no, and he got pissed. I did the scene the way I thought it needed to be done. He chewed me out something fierce afterward, but I wasn't gonna do what he asked. Then he asked me to work with another actor who I guess was a buddy of his, who called me a sissy for respecting my costars' boundaries. Anyway, a few weeks later, I got called for a job, but the director sends me to his studio. I'd worked there before, though it wasn't my favorite. That day we were gonna film on a sound stage with a bed and some props. Nothing too unusual. They told me we'd be filming an orgy scene. I've done plenty of those, and this time I think there were maybe eight guys? I didn't think anything of it, and that was my first mistake."

I can tell that Kurt doesn't like where this is going, but he doesn't say anything. A sour taste rises in my mouth, and I swallow hard.

"What happened?" Christian asks softly, putting her notepad down.

"Well, I get there and they hand me my usual bottle of Gatorade, and it's open. I figured it was just my brain tricking me. You know how that happens, like you think 'Did I open it already, and just forgot?' I guess I wasn't really thinking straight or wasn't suspicious enough." I shake my head. "There are some sketchy people in porn, and I know better than to trust anyone I don't know well, but I didn't think I'd need to check my drink at a place where I'd worked before, for damn sake." My stomach rolls. "And I always had Gatorade before filming."

Kurt makes a soft, hurt noise.

"At any rate, after I drank it, I started to feel woozy. Wrong. Loose. Dizzy. And then I was in this kind of—I don't know how to describe it, but I couldn't control what was happening. I don't bottom, Kurt," I whisper. "Not ever. I'm good with a lot of sex and kink, but that's a hard limit for me."

He takes my hand, not squeezing, just warm and gentle.

"It's like I was out of my body. I could tell the cameras were rolling. I could tell that the other actors were messing around and making fun of me. Making fun of the fact that here's this big cowboy who don't bottom. They handcuffed me to the bed and spread my legs, and I couldn't really fight back. And then there are periods I remember and periods I don't. But I remember guys ramming themselves up my ass. Taking turns. Laughing at me."

I'm starting to tear up, which I don't do. "I mean, I'm a big guy, and I'm fucking strong, but I ain't strong against seven or eight guys, not drugged, not handcuffed. I kicked and screamed to the extent I could. What I thought was going to be a fun scene was … I can't describe it. It was like being in hell."

I can't bear to look at Kurt, so I'm laser focused on Christian, who has a kind look on her face. "I dunno if the other actors knew that I was drugged. It might have been—I hope it was—just the director. I'm pretty sure he's the one who roofied me. He was pissed at me for questioning his authority. The other guys said later that he'd told them I was going to resist and playact like it was a rape scene. Only it actually was. He wanted my genuine reaction. He wanted my fight. Well, he got it." My eyes are hot. "I'd told him I'd never bottom. And he wanted *Velvet Finally Gets Topped*."

"Johnny," Kurt says, and I finally turn to him. He gives me a reassuring nod and looks like he wants to hug me but doesn't know if he should.

"Don't pity me. Please. I don't want it. I don't want you to not touch me, either."

"I'd never—" he starts, but I interrupt him. I want to get the rest of this out and over with.

"I had to take myself to the hospital the next day, because they didn't stretch me properly, and I had … injuries. Tearing and bleeding inside. Bruises and scratches all over my body from where I fought. Where they held me down. I couldn't stop them. I'm a strong guy, but not when I'm shackled to a bed." I'm repeating myself, but I don't know how else to explain it. "I feel so damned ashamed about the whole thing. How could I have been so stupid, to let this happen? I should've known better than to trust them. That studio was known for its grittiness. I should've been smarter."

Christian's started taking notes again. Kurt's got tears in his eyes, and he scoots closer, putting one arm around me.

"The doctors treated me, but I got funny looks from some of them. I guess word got out."

"Jesus," Kurt mutters. "This keeps getting worse and worse."

"The police came and took a statement. They did an investigation, but I'd waited too long and the hospital didn't run drug tests right away, so the shit was outta my system. No charges. So I talked to a lawyer. Your buddies, Danny and Noah and all. It took me a long time to tell them everything. I didn't know—I mean, I wanted to just forget it had ever happened, but I *can't* forget, and what if I didn't say anything and he kept doing that to, to other people, and ... anyway, they filed a lawsuit for sexual harassment and sexual battery. That's been going on for a while. Only no one believes me, because I'm a porn star, so I'm supposed to have my body used however by whoever." I can't keep the sourness out of my voice.

"Babe," Kurt whispers.

"All the witnesses they deposed said that they thought I was acting. That I'm a veteran in the industry. That they were doing what they were told was supposed to happen. No matter how hard my lawyers have worked, I ain't got no evidence other than my word, the medical reports—which can be interpreted as a natural consequence of a rough scene—and the video, which could be me being a really good actor. Then the company sued me back, but the lawyers got that tossed out. So that's where we are," I finish.

The room's silent. My eyes are hot. My body's drained.

Christian's watching me, letting me feel the bad feelings, I think.

Finally, Kurt asks softly, "Were you taking those sleeping pills to deal with the trauma from the rape?"

I nod. "I wasn't taking them. But that's why they were prescribed, yeah."

Kurt's rubbing his leg, and his muscles are jumping under his skin. Then he clenches his hands into fists, and his face crumples. "Babe," he whispers. "I'm so fucking sorry."

I stiffen. "Don't be sorry for me. I hate it. I hate people feeling bad."

"I know," he says. "But I want to help you however I can."

I want to roll my eyes, but here's my pushy husband. Who I'm quite sweet on, if I'm being honest. He's a catch.

I wish he were my husband for real.

"Don't treat me as if I'm damaged because of what happened," I murmur.

"I promise I won't," Kurt murmurs back. "And I'll never ask you to talk about this again if you don't want to. But who was the director who did this to you? Tell me his name."

I look everywhere but at him. Finally, I mutter, "Gary Pinkerton."

Kurt blinks. Gary's famous enough to be known outside of porn circles. Along the lines of Hugh Hefner or someone like that —someone famous for being a smut peddler.

"I thought he only made straight porn," Kurt blurts.

"Oh, he'll film people having sex with anything that moves. And some things that don't."

"What's going to happen to him? He should be in jail."

"Like I said, there's no criminal case. The lawsuit's plugging along, for whatever that's worth, but I ain't likely to win. There's no proof that I was roofied other than my word. There ain't no one else to testify that I didn't consent, because they were told I did. There ain't no one who cares, because I'm just a fucking porn star," I say bitterly.

"Do you believe you couldn't be raped, because you're a man?" Christian asks.

I nod. "I know it ain't right, but yeah. That's part of it. I'm big. Strong. A cowboy. Ain't no one who can violate me." I cough. "But they did."

"And how does that make you feel?"

"Like a fuckin' loser!" I explode, pounding my fist against my thigh. "Sheee-it, I ain't weak." I glare at her, my lips curled in a snarl. My cheeks burn, and my breath hitches.

"But having your control over your body taken away like that makes you feel weak?" Christian asks.

"Fuck. Yeah. Like I'm ... helpless." I let my overgrown hair flop into my face.

We all sit in silence as the room recovers from my hollering.

"Can I say something?" Kurt asks.

Both Christian and I nod.

"Now that I know all of this—and it's horrible, babe, and I'm sorry. I don't have words bad enough to say how fucked up it is. But I have another concern. You have nightmares sometimes. I've seen you touch your wrists, and now that I think about it, you were careful when I handed you drinks in Vegas. So I'm scared I'm going to accidentally trigger you. That I'm going to do something —just something innocent that I don't even realize—that makes you think you're back with those monsters. Do you think I could mess you up like that?"

"Maybe," I say, my throat thick. "I do get flashbacks sometimes."

"If Johnny reacts when you touch him without meaning harm, Kurt, what are you going to do?" Christian asks.

"I guess talk to him, remind him what's real and what isn't," he says.

"That's a good start."

Again, the room goes quiet. After a moment, Christian says, "Johnny, it seems as if you may lack the levels of safety and security many of us take for granted, and you've got some shame piled on top of that. You've been relying on yourself for a long time, being the primary resource—financial and, in earlier years, physical and maybe emotional—for your mom. Who took care of you when you were growing up?"

"Didn't need no one," I mutter. My head is starting to hurt.

"You didn't need someone to care for you?"

I shrug, and she nods. Not in an agreement way, more a moving-things-along way.

"Now you're a provider and a caretaker, and it seems like you think you have to do it on your own. Does that sound right to you?"

"Sometimes," I mutter.

"But it's okay to let other people help if they want to," she says.

"Shit." My jaw hurts. I wanna get out of here.

"Babe, you might have some toxic masculinity," Kurt says.

"Possibly," Christian says. She turns to him. "We don't have to label it as toxic. We're all products of our environment."

"Sorry," Kurt says. "I didn't mean it like that. You're also a softie."

I put on a smile that falls with Christian's next words.

"Let's speak plainly. You were violently assaulted at work, on camera," Christian says. "Not only was your body violated, but the fact that it was recorded, there's documentation of it that others might see—that perpetuates the violation and keeps it fresh. It's natural for you to feel like you need to protect yourself against further harm by not letting anyone get close to you. It's a sign of healing that you've let your husband in to hear about this."

"I'm fucking scared he's gonna leave me, now that he knows," I say, my eyes wet.

"Never," Kurt hisses. "What happened at that studio wasn't your fault. Period. And if you try to judge yourself for it, I'll ... well, I'll tell you as many times as you need to hear it that you have *nothing* to be ashamed of. The fact that it happened and that asshole isn't being punished, though, that's making me ragey."

How does Kurt always break through my defenses? Instead of running, I want to curl up in his warmth.

Christian notices when I move closer to him. "It's important that you have someone like Kurt," she says. "He supports you. Can you feel it?"

"Yeah," I say. "I feel like we've always been together."

"I do, too. Even though that's so far from the truth," Kurt says.

"What do you mean?" Christian asks. "How long have you two been together?"

I turn to Kurt. "I don't want to minimize what you've done for me, but she should know that we only just met two days before we first came to see her." I turn to her. "We've known each other a little over a month. It was one of these get-drunk-and-married-in-Vegas things."

"I didn't know that," she says, her eyebrows raised. "Does the length of time you've known each other matter to you?"

"No," I say. "I feel like Kurt's exactly what I need."

He glances at me, and his expression makes me feel like I've just downed a cup of hot cocoa on a cold day. "I'm so glad to have Johnny in my life," he says. "I liked him before I met him"—he coughs—"um, from his videos, but now that I know him as a real person, know how complicated and caring he is, it's ..." He shrugs, apparently at a loss for words.

"Forgive me for asking, but with such a ... spontaneous marriage, did you ever consider dissolving it?"

"Yeah," Kurt says. "I did, at first. But ... well, this sounds awful, but I thought that it would look bad for my political career if we divorced immediately. And then I got to know him, and now the last thing I want is to split up."

Kurt's not one to fib, but is that true? Seems too much to hope for.

Will he still want to stay with me even if his political career doesn't take off? Because I've seen the poll numbers, and ... he's a lovely man, but the race isn't close. No matter what he says, I'm still not sure he's with me by choice. I've trapped him, in a way.

"What do you think?" Christian asks me.

"I think I like Kurt a heck of a lot. And I'm grateful he's helping me through this. I'm scared, though, that we're only bonding because I'm a mess—the folks at the hospital said sometimes that happens, and I want something real."

"It feels real to me," Kurt says, which makes my pulse flutter in my throat.

"I'm scared you're gonna change your mind about me after the election." I laugh humorlessly. "For a marriage that wasn't even meant to be real, I'm really hung up on you."

"The election has nothing to do with our marriage," Kurt says. "And for what it's worth, I'm really hung up on you, too."

Christian gives us a warm smile. "It sounds to me as if you both care deeply about each other, despite your relationship being very new. And that's good. We all need people who we can rely on, especially in times of stress. Now, outside of this room, there are things happening in your real world," she says. "Kurt, you have an election coming up. And Johnny, you've got your lawsuit."

"Yeah."

"How's your stress level with that?"

"Pretty fuckin' high," I admit. "And it's not just the lawsuit. I've been jumpy. After the ... the incident, I started carrying a gun for protection. I also had some fantasies about making Gary Pinkerton go away permanently." I quickly hold up my hands. "I'm not a murderer. I just needed to feel safe, you know? My plan B, back in Vegas, was going to be either him or me. But when it came down to it, I didn't think I could shoot someone else. Not, like, out of the blue."

"The gun was for him?" Kurt asks. "I didn't know that."

"Or me. I was gonna take the pills, then use the gun if I needed it."

Christian looks at me for a long moment, apparently trying to figure out if I'm a danger to society.

"I locked up the gun," Kurt assures her. "Even though I'll admit hearing his story makes me feel violent, too, and I'm not a violent person."

"Are either of you two going to do anything with the gun?" Christian asks.

"No," I say.

"No," he says.

"If that changes, you call me."

We both nod.

She looks satisfied. We get to the end of the session, and she says, "I don't know what the 'right' outcome for your relationship is. You got together in highly unusual circumstances, and while the immediate crisis has passed, Johnny, you're still working through a lot of difficult issues. In any case, you didn't come to me for relationship counseling. But whatever path or paths you two end up walking, as I said before, it's clear that you truly care for each other."

I nod and smile at Kurt. "I think that's true."

He nods back. "Definitely."

CHAPTER 27

Kurt

Johnny said he was worried that I'd look at him differently because of his assault, and I promised him I wouldn't. I'm going to keep that promise, but I'll admit it's difficult. Not because of anything he did or didn't do or because I think he's weak. But because that level of betrayal has to mess with his head. No wonder he was in such a bad place. Add that to his mom's chronic illness and the unstable situation in which he grew up, and it's amazing that he's as together as he is.

When we get back into the car, there's a slightly awkward silence. I think he might feel like he overshared.

But I feel closer to him, like he opened up this part of himself and let me see the scary things that he hides from everyone else.

He's the bravest fucking man I know. I don't blame him for any of the horrors that were inflicted on him, but they do help explain some of his behavior. The fact that he came out of that not hating all of humanity is a testament to his gentle nature. Everything I find out about him just makes me like him more.

My dominant reaction, though, is a thirst for *revenge*. Gary Pinkerton can't get away with this. There's Johnny's lawsuit, yes, but ... a bad part of me says a financial judgment can never be enough.

I'm going to do something about it, even though I've never done anything like that before.

It makes me sick that Johnny suffered, and learning about it activated something protective inside me. Something that demands to tear down the people who hurt him. I want to keep him safe from everyone and everything.

Of course, that's not possible. No one can ever be safe from everyone and everything.

How can I at least prove to him that he matters? What can I give him to heal his soul?

I come up with an idea. Or two.

"Let's drive up and see your mom for Thanksgiving," I say. "Would you like to do that?"

Johnny swallows thickly and rubs the back of his neck. "More than anything. You really wanna go all that way, though? Shouldn't you be with your own family for the holiday?"

"You're my family now," I tell him. "And Thanksgiving was never a huge deal for the Delmonts anyway." I smile at him, and he leans over and kisses me. "Pack a bag so we can stay somewhere overnight. Or let's take the whole long weekend. Visit her and then see where else we want to go."

Johnny calls his mom to make sure that she's going to be around, and we make plans to drive up the Wednesday before Thanksgiving. Before then, I have something else to take care of, and I need to do it in person.

When Johnny's at work the next day, I call Sam, who readily agrees when I ask if I can come over. I know he won't judge me. I'm just hoping he can help.

At his—Jules's, originally—secluded beach mansion, Sam gives me a hug and invites me to sit at a table outside, taking advantage of the view. "Jules is recording, or I know he'd want to see you," he says apologetically.

"That's fine. What I want to ask is ... Well. The fewer people who know, the better."

He tilts his head. "Okay," he says slowly. "That sounds ominous."

"Johnny told me about the assault ... the reason why you guys are suing on his behalf."

Sam draws in a quick breath. "It's fucking awful. I saw the video, and it's ..." He looks ill. "Horrible."

I close my eyes, not wanting to imagine it. "What are the chances of him winning anything? Is justice going to be served?"

"No criminal charges were brought, so the only way to get anything like justice is if we get a big punitive damages award. Otherwise, it's ... nothing. Nothing will happen to Pinkerton." Sam's voice is bitter.

I hit the table with my fist. "That's unacceptable." I lower my voice. "I've never asked for anything like this in my life, but is there anyone you know who would be connected enough to ... make sure Pinkerton gets what's coming to him? Or at least part of it?"

Sam's first response is to shake his head. But then a light flashes in his eyes. "Okay, there is one person. And just so you know, I understand. If someone did something like that to Jules, I'd slice their dick off inch by inch and feed it to them."

"That's ... vivid. And also basically what I want." I look at him expectantly, even though my stomach's churning.

"One of the lawyers in my office, Charlie, he's kind of with this guy. I mean, I guess they're dating. Who knows? They have a strange relationship." One side of Sam's mouth turns up in a smile. "Rowan is ... interesting."

"How so?"

"Feral fucking gremlin. Pretty sure he met Charlie at knifepoint. I bet he'll know who to contact. Or, honestly, he might do it himself. He scares the fuck out of me."

I can't believe I'm doing this. "Sounds perfect. Do you have his number?"

"No, but I have Charlie's, and I can introduce you." He smiles. "Beware. Charlie's a bit of an asshole. But he's definitely met his match in Rowan."

"Is there any reason why he'd do me this favor?"

"Rowan? This might be sport to him. No harm in asking." Sam coughs. "No harm to you, that is."

I've never had a weirder conversation, but at the end of it, I feel like I've made progress toward getting what justice I can for Johnny.

* * *

The day before Thanksgiving, Johnny and I load up the car for our trip to Fresno. He's been antsy all week, so I head for the passenger seat and let him get behind the wheel.

"Do you want to pick the radio station this time?" Johnny's tone is teasing, and I appreciate that more than he knows. Because it signals that his mood is up.

"I'm good with country."

He looks at me in disbelief. "Really?"

"Sure. It makes you happy, and I don't mind it."

"That might be the secret to a happy marriage: giving the other person what they want when it doesn't harm you to do it."

"Exactly."

While the route out of Los Angeles is hilly and pretty, once we get into the Central Valley, it's nothing but agriculture: fruit and nut trees, row crops, cows. Johnny seems to get more tense with every mile we drive, his jaw tightening, fingers tapping on the wheel.

"You okay?" I ask. "I thought you'd be excited about this trip."

"I am excited, but I'm damn scared Mama's gonna be worse than the last time I saw her."

Silos flash by. "I suppose that's possible. We won't know until we get there. What will you do if she's gotten worse?"

"Feel like shit."

"And you kind of feel like that now, no? I mean, you're already imagining it."

He sighs. "Yeah. You're right. I'm borrowing trouble, and the interest rate on that's way too high. Okay. Maybe she's gonna be good."

"Is this more of me being an optimist and you being a pessimist?"

Johnny flashes me a quick smile. "Likely, yes."

"No matter what, it's gonna be okay. Want me to drive so you can relax?"

"Yeah, maybe," he says. "I mean, I'll try to settle myself. But maybe you can drive after the next rest stop."

He's starting to admit when he needs help, which is good. And he's not being so stoic. His rule about honesty is fucking refreshing, given that I've been around politicians all my life. Of course, he and I don't carry the baggage of having known each other—apart from our public personas—prior to Vegas, so that makes it easier.

I take over the driving after we stop for a quick lunch at a diner an hour south of Fresno, and when we get into town, he directs me to his mother's house.

We pull up to the driveway of a one-story home in what looks like a pretty nice part of town. New houses, tidy yards, new cars.

"Is this ..." I ask. "Did you buy her this house?"

"I did." Johnny's chest swells with pride. "All paid up."

Ever since he was a kid, he's been working to care for his mother. I'm not sure how I feel about that. It's kind, loving, and honorable of him, of course. But part of me thinks, well, that she's an adult. Surely she could do some things for herself.

Then again, maybe I'm being an insensitive jerk. I haven't had to deal with someone I love being chronically ill. And I've certainly never had to worry about how to keep a roof over my head or food on the table. Maybe I need to just let Johnny live his life the way he wants to and stop judging things I don't understand.

We get out of the car, and he offers me his hand with a smile. "Come and meet my mama." His hand's steady, but his voice wavers slightly.

He walks up to the door, which is adorned with a fall leaf wreath, knocks, and walks in. "Mama?"

"In here, Johnny," she says, her voice a quiet drawl.

We walk into a sparkling clean living room. Does he pay for a housekeeper, too?

His mom's sitting in an upholstered chair, with another woman seated nearby.

"Mama, Denise, this is Kurt Delmont. He's my husband. Kurt, my mama, Sue Ann Haskell, and her caregiver, Denise."

His mom's tiny, with pretty pale eyes and a generous smile. She seems frail but warm and friendly. "It's so nice to meet you," she says. I go to move toward her, but Johnny stills me by setting a hand on my bicep as she stands up and comes over to me. Her steps are sure but slow.

"Likewise," I say, smiling and shaking her small hand.

That intuition I have kicks in again, and I can see why Johnny has given up everything for her. She's *gentle*. *Kind*. She's *trying*. You can tell by the determined set of her jaw and the way she's kept everything around her as nice as it can be. The house's furnishings aren't fancy or expensive, but they're treated with care.

It makes me understand him a lot better. It makes my heart beat faster for him, that he's this protective of her.

She's the kind of person you'd give things up for.

He's the kind of person *I'd* give things up for. Like the fucking election, without a moment's regret.

"Where's May Ella?" Johnny asks, after he hugs his mom and helps her back to her seat.

"She's at work, but she'll be home in a little bit. Can I get you some iced tea? Or lemonade?" Sue Ann asks.

"I'll get it," Johnny says, encouraging her to stay put while he goes into the kitchen and gets us all drinks. Denise goes with him, and I hear them chatting in low voices. I'm guessing Johnny is quizzing Denise on Sue Ann's condition.

I don't know what I was expecting. Maybe because of Johnny's description of his early life, I'd imagined us going to a depressing place, perhaps in a trailer park littered with trash and weeds. Instead, his mom is being well taken care of in a sparkling, cheerful home, while Johnny made do with the bare minimum he needed to survive. That thought hits me harder than anything, because I can see that his sacrifice to her was complete. Even though he thinks he's a failure, he isn't.

She needs a new kidney, yes. She's on dialysis, which clearly affects her life. But she's living comfortably thanks to him.

A surge of pride rushes through me at the same time I get inordinately sad. Because this has come at what cost to him?

Now that I see how much he's given her, I'm torn. Part of me wants to take him away so he doesn't have to worry about anything ever again. Part of me wants to celebrate what a giving person he is.

One thing I know: If I try to change him, it'll backfire. Johnny thinks it's wrong to keep things for himself. He's always giving—money to his mother; pleasure and support to me; amazing care to animals, based on what Bronwyn has told me.

I need to come up with a way to give Johnny something just for himself. And help him understand that he's worth treating just as well as he treats his mom.

* * *

After Johnny and I visit with his mom for a while, his sister comes home. She's pretty, like Johnny, but seems a bit beaten down. Maybe it's from being on her feet all day. She says hello, then excuses herself to go freshen up. I hear a shower turn on. I imagine managing a Taco Bell leaves you feeling pretty grimy.

She's back before long, damp hair in a braid, still looking tired but smiling. She downs a glass of water, and the four of us chat for a few minutes. Denise is always nearby, and she occasionally contributes to the conversation, but mostly she stays in the background.

"Will you play for us, May?" Johnny asks, after May Ella's had a little time to relax.

May Ella grins. "Sure." She goes out of the room and returns holding a violin. Settling it under her chin and on her shoulder, she holds the bow up, poised for a moment, and then just lets fly.

Holy shit, I get goose bumps. I've been to the symphony, of course, and it sounds to me as if May Ella's good enough to play in a major orchestra. She's got the passion and skill, and her music rips your heart to pieces and then sews it up again.

I glance at Johnny, and he's watching her, rapt, his eyes welling with tears. This is his childhood, I realize. While teenage Johnny probably did more manual jobs, this is how May Ella would get people to give them money for food. This is one of the ways that they were able to support themselves—with the art that she's creating with her instrument. It's soul-deep.

I hadn't thought that visiting Johnny's mom would be so emotional for me. I'd thought that we were taking this trip for him. But maybe that's not all there is to it. Maybe this was something that I needed to see. To help me get to know him better.

We stay the night in a hotel and come back the next day to cook Thanksgiving dinner. Johnny takes charge of the bird, and May Ella and I handle the sides. His mom tries to help, but she's just too frail, so we settle for her supervising.

Sitting around a Thanksgiving table with my husband, my new in-laws (what a concept!), and Denise, a wave of gratitude passes over me.

Gratitude that Johnny listened to me when I told him not to kill himself. Gratitude that he came home with me. That he helped his mama. That he's now getting help.

That I have a new family, even when I didn't intend it.

We wash the dishes and watch some football, and then it's time to leave for our hotel. It's been a long day, and Sue Ann's clearly tired.

After we say goodbye and promise to visit again, she takes one of our hands in each of hers and says, "It's so good to see you boys making each other happy. I love you both, and I hope this is just the first of a whole lotta holidays together."

"We love you, too," I say, and Johnny looks at me with hearts in his eyes.

As we pull out of the driveway, I tell Johnny I have a surprise for him. "Tomorrow, we're gonna go out to the coast," I say. "I know a place that I think you'll really like."

CHAPTER 28

Johnny

It seems Mama's doing fine, which is all I can ask for. I hate seeing her so frail and sick, but at least she's got help and everything she needs ... apart from that damn transplant.

Her house ain't big enough for all of us to stay, given May Ella has a room and so does Denise, so Kurt made us reservations at the nicest hotel Fresno has and told me I wasn't allowed to put it on my IOU list. I'm not sure I agree with that, but I gotta admit it's been nice these past couple of days having a quiet, comfy place to unwind after all the visiting. I love my mama and sister so much, and I'd be with them all the time if I could ... and I'm also used to having my own space to be alone. Or with Kurt, which is like being alone, only with someone else there.

I'm currently curled around him in bed, after we exchanged very enjoyable blow jobs. For once, I wanted to come, too—and he readily obliged—so I'm feeling that post-orgasm elation.

"I'm so damn grateful for you, precious," I whisper.

"Grateful for you, too," Kurt whispers back. He pauses, then adds, "I brought something with me that I wanna wear tomorrow."

"What's that?"

"A butt plug."

I choke out a laugh, then kiss him. "Does that mean you want me to fuck you?"

"Yes. If you're up for it. If the time comes and you're not in the mood, just say so."

Even though I just came, my dick's rallying. After months of being uninterested in sex, he's making me *want* him. And that's got me feeling more back to normal than anything else going on. "Hell yes, I wanna fuck you. Count on it."

I fall asleep to the pleasant image of Kurt bouncing on my dick, riding me hard and fast.

After room service breakfast, Kurt drives us southwest, and we end up at a place on the coast south of San Luis Obispo. A bed-and-breakfast run by someone Noah knows. It's gay friendly, and the guy who runs it—a small, artsy type—has an elegant boyfriend who's significantly older than him. But they seem like a good couple.

The place is an old Victorian, but it's not too fussy. We check in in the early afternoon, and the room we get is upstairs, tucked away from everyone else. Even better, I notice that some sound-proofing has been done, because once the hosts show us in, I don't hear them leave down the stairs.

That's a very good thing, since all I want to do right now is fuck my husband.

My sex drive's returned with a vengeance, and I could cry in relief. Back to damn normal.

I go to Kurt and cradle his face in my hands. "You're amazing," I say. "Thank you for taking the time to come see my mama."

"Oh yeah?" He gives me a cheeky smile. "How are you thinking you might show your gratitude?"

"Hmm." I kiss his mouth, and he kisses me back hard. I love how he can't seem to get enough of me. There's zero routine with Kurt. None. Every time with him feels like this explosion of passion, or sleepy comfort, or need. So much need.

But up to now, it's mostly been me wanting to get him off. Now I'm ready for some pleasure and enthusiasm of my own.

I start undressing him, unbuttoning his shirt as I kiss his neck. He lets me slide the fabric off his shoulders, and my hands roam all over his back as he fists my hair. Then I drop to my knees in front of him and unzip his pants, pulling out his cock.

He's not hard yet, but I suck on him, and his knees buckle. "Oh, god." He whines, which I love. I take his balls into my mouth, one at a time, as I shove his pants down. He toes off his shoes and steps out of them while I wait impatiently to get my mouth on him again. When he's stark naked in front of me, it's all I can do to not pick him up and throw him onto the bed.

My cock's as hard as his, and I'm longing to be inside him. I reach down between his ass cheeks and don't find a toy. "You're prepped," I say, sliding a finger into his slick hole. "But no plug?"

"Yeah. I, uh, was wearing it earlier. I took it out when we stopped for gas. Didn't want to meet the hosts here with a partial erection." He pauses. "I want you. But I'm a bit intimidated by your cock."

"You can handle it, baby boy."

Again, I'm testing to see what he likes. He seems to unravel at the 'baby boy' comment, so I'll keep that up.

Kurt takes a deep breath. "I hope so. I really want to."

I tug us back toward the bed, undoing my pants as we go, and strip in record time. "Do you need more prep? I'm sure you do. Let me check."

He rolls onto his stomach, and I use a lubed finger to probe his hole gently. It's easy, because he's pretty loose.

"Enough," he says, squirming.

I smack his ass. "I'm in charge."

He huffs but doesn't argue. After a little more prep, I pull out a condom and hand it to him while I position myself against the headboard. When I'm settled, he rolls the rubber onto me. I love the care he shows in everything he does. Then he squirts half the bottle of lube on my dick—okay, kidding. But it's a lot.

"Ready?" I whisper, and he nods. "Good. Then ride me." He hovers over me, lining my hard cock up with his entrance.

Slowly, he sinks down, his body stretching to accommodate my girth. He's vocal, moaning and groaning, but it doesn't sound like he's in real pain. His dick flags some, but that's common.

"You got it," I murmur. "Such a good boy. Take my cock."

"I want to. Oh my god, this is. Oh my. *God*. Fuck. Yes. Oh, wow."

Watching my cock disappear inside *my husband* is the sexiest thing. "You're so fucking hot."

Kurt nods, biting his lip, holding his breath. Finally, he gets all the way down so his ass is against me, and I smile at him.

"Make yourself feel good, darlin'," I urge. "Find the spot."

Slowly, he rises up, then lowers himself, little by little, changing the angle until he's crouched over me and suddenly moans long and loud.

"That's it. You got it. Take it, baby boy. Fuck yourself. Keep going." I reach out and start stroking him, and soon he's hard again. He looks angelic, like he's in some kind of trance.

"Talk to me," I whisper. "I'm used to communication."

"Oh my god, Johnny. You're so big. It's so hard. It feels so *unghhh*. Hurts ... good."

"*Yes*. Keep going. Keep talking to me."

"I can do that." He speeds up, now fucking his ass on my cock and fucking his cock in my hand, and I'm letting him use me in the best way possible. I love how this feels. I'm already nearing orgasm, but I'm going to hold on until he comes.

My other hand is on his hip, and I'm guiding him faster and faster. Soon, he's going so fast that he's popping out of my hand, and he takes over jacking himself off. Sweat is streaming down his forehead and dripping onto me.

Over and over again, he slams himself down, then pulls up and does it again. I'm thrusting into him, and we're in sync. It's bliss.

I can tell he's heading for an O, and I wanna see it. Now.

"Be a good boy and come for me, Kurt."

And he does. His body tightens, and he's holding his breath, and then he's coming loudly, his body shaking.

I let myself go, almost blacking out as I thrust so hard into him that he winces. I don't want to hurt him, but I can't help it. He feels so amazing.

I feel amazing. Like I'm rebooting my system—my brain is clear and my body's exhilarated.

Once I come down from my high—which seems to go on and on and on—we ease him off me, and he lies down at my side. I yank Kleenex out of the box on the bedside table, clean him up, and deal with the condom. Then I tug him to me.

"C'mere," I whisper, kissing his head. Kurt snuggles into me. "You good?"

"So good."

I smile. "Perfect."

He looks up at me and kisses me. "I've never been fucked that well before."

"Darlin', that was all you. Had to give you a chance to get used to me. Next time, it will be me."

"*Fuck.*"

I adore this man.

* * *

The next day, Kurt drives us to the beach, where we rent horses so we can go riding on the sand.

I hadn't realized how much I missed being on a horse until Kurt sent me to Hidden Valley. Now, riding one just for fun ... it makes my heart happy. The wind whips my face as we gallop down the wet, hard-packed sand where the tide's just going out. I watch Kurt, and he's laughing as the freedom of riding gets to him, too.

God, he's so pretty, with his hair wild in the breeze and his smile shining brighter than the sunshine bathing our faces.

The salty spray, the sound of the waves slapping on the shore. The way his cute ass bounces in those dark wash jeans. The squeak he lets out as his horse goes faster, perhaps, than he wants her to.

I realize with a start that I could fall in love with him.

I ain't never been in love before. Not even close. There wasn't any time for it, and I hadn't found anyone I clicked with.

With Kurt, though, from the moment I met him, we've had that spark. He's precious.

And even though I knew he represented the enemy—politicians are about half a step up from insurance executives in my book—he seemed genuinely into me. And not just because I did porn.

He seemed to like ... *me*.

Not even for sex. I'm used to meeting people and fucking them right away. So when Kurt and I had time to get to know each other, it felt like *more*.

I shake my head. Maybe I'm just falling for the first person who's treated me like someone other than a cock to ride.

Maybe this is me getting way ahead of myself.

But all I can think when Kurt turns around, laughing and gesturing me on, is that I'm in deep trouble.

I *really* like him.

In the evening, we go to dinner in a tiny restaurant in an old home in Santa Ynez, where the downstairs is set up as several small dining rooms with white tablecloths and real candles and efficient waiters in crisp white aprons.

"I don't see the prices," I say, looking at descriptions of a bunch of dishes I've never heard of before, but Kurt waves a hand.

"Let me treat you. It's a fixed-price menu. The only thing that costs more is the wine."

I suspect that it's incredibly expensive, but I let it go. Little by little, I'm learning to let him spend money when he wants to, because he has it, and it's not a big deal for him. I'm learning that it doesn't mean bad things—like I'm not keeping my end of the bargain or that I have to give him sex in return. Our relationship feels ... normal. I think Kurt would call this progress.

I mean, I still have a list of things I need to pay him back for. But I decide this fancy dinner doesn't need to go on the list, because I feel like we're building a partnership where he gives me what I need, and I give him what he needs.

What he needs—what we *both* need—is attention and care. And we've been giving it to each other in bucketfuls.

I'm not sure how I survived long enough to meet this man.

Come to think of it, I almost didn't.

CHAPTER 29
Kurt

In the car coming back from our Thanksgiving trip, I think again about the things I realized sitting in Sue Ann's living room.

Before I met her, I'd been judging Johnny: He was too selfless. A martyr. Giving too much to her, when he should've been treating himself better.

But now I've seen how much that care means to her, and there's something about feeling that love—from him to her and back again—that makes me understand.

Johnny's a caregiver. A provider. He's done it all his life, despite not having the resources that I do.

I want to figure out a way to give that kind of care to him. Because in his own way, he's giving me just as much.

I'm falling for him. Maybe that should scare me. But it doesn't.

As we near Ventura, he brings up the lawsuit, telling me that Danny mentioned some breakthrough on the evidence but won't give him any details yet.

"When do you go to trial?" I ask. "It sounds like it's been pending a long time."

"It has. Trial's set for late March. We have mediation early next year." He sighs. "It's a chance to settle it, they tell me, maybe get some money and not have to go through the hassle in the courtroom. But all I can think about is that I'm going to have to be in a room with Gary again. The idea makes me want to hurl. He didn't lay a hand on me, but he damn well violated me just the same."

Anger flares within me, and I vow to contact Sam's friend ... Colleague? Colleague's friend? And make Pinkerton hurt.

"What happens if you don't settle?" I ask.

"We go to trial, and the whole story comes out. I'm torn. Part of me wants to tell every gruesome detail. Get out the video and play it." His cheeks redden. "It's just so fucking embarrassing."

I gulp. "Have you seen it?"

"No. But my lawyers have a copy."

"So they've seen it."

He nods. "And they had pretty grim faces after. I'd assume that none of them are prudish, so I don't think it's the porn that set them off. But the circumstances—knowing it wasn't consensual or even CNC ..."

Shit.

Johnny's shown me all the parts of him that he wants to hide from the world. His broken parts that are precious and vulnerable, soft or fragile or bruised.

Johnny's an amazing person, and I want to prove that to him in as many ways as I can. I want to give him anything he needs.

I'll get in touch with Rowan about justice, but there are other things I can do right away.

"I was wondering something. You said you sold your truck. What kind of truck was it? Something special?"

A wistful look crosses his face. "Special to me. It was just an old F-150, but I liked it. It suited me."

"Who did you sell it to?"

"A neighbor." He whips his head around to face me. "What are you thinking?"

"Do you wanna get it back?"

"If *I* get the money," he says, emphasizing the I, "*I* can buy another truck. You don't need to go tracking down my old one. I can save money from my job and get one in time."

"But …" I sigh. "Okay." I drop it for now. Still, I'm resolved to figure out where his truck went or to get him another like it.

The rest of the trip passes in amiable chatter and easy silence.

When we get home, Johnny stops me at the foot of the stairs before I can even take off my shoes. "Wha—?" I say, before his mouth crashes down on mine.

I grunt in happiness as he pushes me against the door, caging me in with his hands on either side of my head.

Yes. He's reclaiming this part of himself.

He licks and sucks at my lips, making me hard for him. Making me want him.

When we break apart, I chuckle. "Um. Wow. I. Yes. Thank you."

"Do you know how much it means to me that you took me to go see Mama?" he growls.

I shrug. "It seemed like the right thing to do."

Johnny rolls his eyes heavenward. "'Right thing to do,' he says." He fixes his gaze on me. "You have absolutely no idea how much I needed to see her and how much it meant for me to check on her in person. Thank you."

"We could move there. Or get an apartment near her. Something—"

Again, he cuts me off with a kiss, only this time one of his hands goes roaming, cupping my pec, then sliding down my side to my hip and grasping my butt.

I love the fire in Johnny. The depression had banked it for so long, but now I'm seeing the intensity, the passion that always came across on the screen. Only it's directed toward me.

"I want to fuck you again, darlin'," he says in a quiet, almost dangerous voice. "You ready for that, or do you need to wait?"

I'd optimistically done some extra cleaning that morning in the shower. "Stretching and lube," I say.

"'Kay." He picks me up like I weigh nothing.

"For fuck's sake, I can walk," I yelp.

"Not after I'm done with you," he mutters darkly, and that makes my dick go from curious about the proceedings to fully hard and busting out of my zipper. I laugh as he carries me up two flights of stairs like I'm a sack of potatoes. He's barely breathing hard.

When we get into the bedroom, he tears off my clothes and his. I've never seen him this animated before.

I. Fucking. Love. It. I love that he's getting back to who he really is. And if this is the beginning, I can't wait to see how happy he'll—we'll both—be when he gets a little more recovered.

He tosses me naked onto the bed on my back, then lies on top of me, his hard dick rubbing against mine while he kisses me deeply, slowly, passionately.

Judging by his movements, what we're doing could end up a hard fuck or a slow bone. Either way, I'm fully on board.

Johnny kisses me one more time before shifting over so I can roll onto my stomach. Then he reaches into the nightstand drawer for the lube.

"We really should just get a big bottle with a pump dispenser," I grumble.

He laughs, but two fingers coated in cool liquid are soon nudging at my entrance. Apparently he doesn't want to waste any time.

I gasp at the intrusion, but I fucking love it. I love the fullness and the hint of pain. I love how he brushes against my prostate every once in a while. It's clear he knows he's doing it, but he doesn't want to make me come. Not yet.

While he expertly stretches me, he's murmuring how gorgeous my ass is. He's kissing my skin. He's reaching a hand around to stroke my cock, and then he's taking a break and rubbing his cock between my ass cheeks like he can't help himself.

"I want you inside me," I say, trying to make it more of a demand than a whimper.

"Patience, baby boy. It's for me to decide when you're ready, and you're not ready yet."

"Whatever," I mumble into the pillow, not sure why I'm being bratty but knowing it's okay for me to be that way with him. That I don't have to be a mature adult when I'm in the bedroom. That I can rely on my husband to give me what I need when I need it.

After two fingers, he stretches me with three, and then a fourth. I'm dying here.

I say so.

"Patience," he says again, and slaps my ass. He seems mesmerized by the way it moves, given the way he gets quiet and then does it again.

I look over my shoulder. "You okay back there?"

"Fuck, your ass is so smackable." Another slap, and while it stings, it's not hard enough to do anything other than create more want in me.

"It's also really empty, and I want you inside me now," I say.

He smacks my ass again. "I'm in charge."

But he does dribble on some more lube, and I can tell that he's putting on a condom and slicking his cock, too. Then he runs his cock up and down my ass crack, which just drives me bananas. "Put your cock in me."

"Fine," he says, and he lines up the head and nudges it against me. My body resists, like it always does, but he steadily presses his way inside.

I need to scream. I need to yell. But he's just spent all this time prepping me, and I don't wanna complain after all my bravado about being a size queen. Turns out I can't always immediately take my porn star husband? The one I've wanted my entire adult life?

Johnny, of course, reads me and stops. I can tell his muscles are contracting as he holds himself above me. "Talk to me, Kurt," he says. "Tell me how you're doing."

"It's a lot," I admit. "Give me a moment."

"'Course." He leans down and kisses my shoulder, and as he does, my body gives way a little more just from gravity, and he edges deeper inside me.

"Fuck!" I shout.

"Do I need to pull out?"

"Absolutely not," I snap. "I fucking love your cock." He waits, a bead of sweat dropping from him to my back. My muscles release and let him in.

Johnny slides forward all the way, his pelvis meeting my ass, and we both groan in satisfaction.

"Holy fuck, that's it," I whisper.

"Almost," he says.

I freeze. "You're kidding."

He chuckles. "I'm kidding. I'm all the way inside your gorgeous ass, and you're taking me so well, baby boy. Look at that pretty hole swallowing my cock."

"You can." I swallow. "You can take a picture. If you want."

Johnny's silent for a moment. "Yeah?"

I nod. "I want to see it."

He pulls out, which makes me reconsider my life choices, then returns with his phone. "Tell me if you want me to stop," he says.

"Just stick your cock in me again," I grouse, and he does. My eyes widen as he pushes steadily and my body takes him like it's where he's meant to be.

I don't know how he's filming and holding himself up at the same time. He's pretty damn coordinated.

"Want me to fuck you?" Johnny murmurs.

"Yes. God, yes. Please."

Johnny starts a rhythm that's slow and deep and hard, and I'm at his complete mercy. I fucking love it. I'm scrabbling at the mattress, loving that he's just taking over, using my body to get off, that he's both taking what he needs and giving me the best prostate massage ever.

"Gonna have to turn the camera off," he mutters. "I wanna rub your cock."

"Just put it off to the side on a pillow," I beg, so he does, setting it near my head. In the selfie mode, I can see what we look like. My big, hot husband—boyfriend?—mounting my ass expertly, his face set in concentration and so fucking sexy. His lips parted, eyes intense. He adjusts our angle, tugging my hips back so he can reach around for my cock, and now he's banging me at the same time he's jacking me off, and the noises I'm making are obscene and loud.

But no one can hear us, and this is what I've always wanted. To be fucked by Velvet the Cowboy.

No. I wanted Johnny. At any rate, Johnny's who I want now.

It's even hotter than I could have imagined, because I'm watching him fuck someone on a screen, only the person on the screen is me. My wide brown eyes are watching the scene. I'm the one whose ass he's pounding into the mattress. I'm the one he's cooing to, who he's saying is such a good boy, who he's telling to take his cock just a little longer.

"Fuck!" I snarl, because if I don't swear, I'm going to blurt out something else. Like that I'm in love with him.

Because I fucking am.

Johnny again changes his angle, and now it's pure, perfect torture. Utter bliss. He's got me at every pleasure point he could, and I'm not going to hang on much longer.

"Come for me, darlin'," he drawls, and I lose it. My brain fuzzes out as my body stiffens and my legs lock up and my back tenses and my abs get tight and my dick starts gushing come.

"Such a good boy," he murmurs into my skin, and before I come down, he's shoving into me hard and groaning this deep, delicious sound of pleasure. I can feel him pumping into me, the way he shudders and his hips undulate against my ass. "You make me come so damn hard. Damn."

Then he collapses atop me, kissing every part of me he can reach. The back of my neck, my shoulders, my upper back, the top of my head. I turn so he can kiss my cheek, and he manages to find my lips before his softening cock slips out of me. He reaches out and shuts off the camera, and I turn onto my back so he can settle over me again. He kisses me fiercely but slowly, with measured intensity. It's passionate but not frantic.

"Damn," I whisper. "I loved that."

"Best fuck ever," he says.

I raise an eyebrow. "Thanks for the compliment, but let's be real. You can't be serious."

"I can."

"I mean, it was for me, no question, but for you—"

He cuts me off. "Precious, you have no idea what you mean to me. And between that and how gorgeous you are, it was the best. No question."

That makes me feel warm inside and out, and the only thing I can do is kiss him some more.

Eventually we get out of bed and clean up ... pretty much everything, since we've made quite a mess of ourselves and the sheets. But when we're settled back in, he spoons me, his big arms around my body, and for the first time in my life, I think I know what it feels like to have a lover. Not some random person to get off with every once in a while, but a real lover.

CHAPTER 30
Johnny

I'm tired and raw.

I'm at therapy by myself. Kurt's gone to his campaign headquarters, because I told him I didn't need him here.

That was a mistake. I thought I was on a high from feeling so close to him. Feeling like I was understood.

But it's all crashing down. Seems I'm not out of the woods yet. My brain ain't all the way untangled.

The problems started when Christian asked, "When you went to visit your mom last weekend, did you tell her that you'd planned to kill yourself?"

A violin shrieks in my head.

I cough and look out the window, then decide I'm being a coward and face my therapist. "No."

"Why is that?"

Because no matter how hard I try, I'm not good.

"I don't want to talk about that with her. It's dark. Bad."

"So you don't want to hurt her."

"Yeah, that's part of it. And ... I still feel fragile. I hate saying it that way. But I don't feel totally right every day, all day."

She smiles. "Not many of us do."

We look at each other.

"Y'all want me to tell my mama, don't you?"

"I think that she might have something to say about it. And sometimes the things we don't want to hear are the most important ones."

I nod. "Yeah, okay. I guess. But can you tell me what's going on? Was it the rape that got me all fucked in the head? Or was it my childhood? Am I codependent, or depressed? What the fuck is going on, excuse my French."

Christian studies me. "I'd say it's all of that, although I wouldn't use the term 'fucked in the head.' I think you have a history of needing to care for a parent and facing financial uncertainty, both during some formative years. You couldn't control what was happening then, and in response, you've put all your energy into controlling the world around you. Give yourself credit for the big responsibilities you handled. Are handling, rather. Your mother is truly sick, has a chronic illness, and you've helped her immensely. But you went too far when you considered suicide as a solution. You'd spent most of your life doing the best you could under tough circumstances, but then after the assault, you got off track. That feeling of control was taken away. You couldn't help your mother the way you wanted to, *and* your personal world, the privacy of your body and your sense of strength, wasn't safe anymore. You also had some chemical imbalances, likely, with lower dopamine and serotonin levels. A few other things going on, too, I imagine."

Just hearing her list out all those problems is overwhelming. "Can I ever be fixed?"

"In some ways, yes. With proper treatment and care, suicidal thoughts will lessen, depressive mood will improve, you can feel healthy more of the time. But mental health can fluctuate, just like physical health—and like physical health, after a serious illness, you need to monitor it even more closely. It can be steady for a while but then get off track, and we need to bring it back around."

"Kurt says the only way out is through."

"Then this is more of that 'through'," she says.

"I havta say, 'through' sucks."

She chuckles. "Give yourself credit for showing up to do the work."

* * *

The following Saturday, Kurt asks, "Want to go have lunch with my folks this afternoon? They're in town, and they want to meet you."

That's kinda intimidating. The lieutenant governor of the great state of California wants to meet ... Velvet the Cowboy, porn star? I've gotta be brave, though, so fine. I nod and ask, "How much time does your mom spend in Sacramento?"

"A lot. She's down here seasonally—when the legislature isn't in session, and during vacations, and so on."

"How does that work for your dad?"

"He can work anywhere. Usually, he's where she is." He smiles. "They have a good marriage. I think you'll like them."

"Okay, then. Let's meet your folks." I look down at my jeans and western shirt. "Should I put on something else?"

Kurt smiles and shakes his head. "Nope. I think you should be exactly who you are at all times. I don't want you to change anything for her whatsoever."

"If that's what you want," I say, but I'm still nervous.

We drive to his parents' house, which is in Brentwood, and it's immediately apparent yet again that Kurt comes from a different world than me. The half-timbered house is like something from a fairy tale, with gates and luscious lawns. Flowers. Fountains. It's decorated for Christmas in a very restrained style.

Aww heck, I *really* don't belong here. I get this itchy feeling all over my skin, and the violins—which had been generally tending more toward quiet—start up again with a loud, discordant symphony.

"This isn't my childhood home," Kurt says as he turns off the car and reads my face. "You know that, right?"

I shake my head.

Kurt squeezes my hand firmly and looks into my eyes. "I'll give you a tour of the old neighborhood sometime, okay? It's not at all like this. You and I aren't that different."

I look at him dubiously but choose not to argue.

"What does your dad do?" I ask.

"Computer shit that I don't understand. Hence the early investment in Amazon. Mom was a marketer. Between hard work and a lot of good luck, they really hit the jackpot."

We walk up to the large, ornate front door, where his mom greets us. It's apparent that Kurt gets his coloring from her—she's got the same kind brown eyes.

Those eyes alight on me, and either she's an astonishingly good actress, or she doesn't actually mind having a porn star for a son-in-law. I think it's the former, but I can deal with that.

"Hello, ma'am. Pleasure to meet y'all," I say, holding out my hand.

Melissa Delmont smiles warmly and shakes my hand, her grip somewhere between businesslike and friendly. "Johnny. Welcome. And welcome to the family. It's nice to meet you."

I'm watching her carefully, looking for any sense of insincerity, but I suppose that ain't giving her a proper chance. Still, I think she suggested Kurt should get our marriage annulled, so maybe I'm not out of whack. But I guess she's decided to embrace me—politically speaking, of course.

Kurt's dad, Ron, also greets us. He sizes me up more coolly, but he's not rude at all and shakes my hand firmly. I think he's just reserving judgment, which I can completely understand.

Melissa has us all come into the kitchen, where trays of cold cuts and cheeses, various types of bread and condiments, and bowls of salad are set out. It's way more low-key than I was expecting. I'd been worried about which fork to use. But this is almost like a picnic or a cookout. In fact, it's the way my mama used to set out food for the hands when I was young.

I immediately feel more at home. We get drinks, fill our plates, and sit down at the kitchen table.

"I know you've worked in the adult industry," Melissa says, not beating around the bush. "That's not a constituency that I come in contact with all that often, so I hope you'll forgive me if I take the opportunity to gather some information. I'm wondering if there are any reforms that we should be looking into. Anything to keep the performers or other people involved safe?"

I'm floored. I'd have been content with polite tolerance. Instead, she's asking how she can help?

I swallow.

"Well, ma'am, I think the laws that are in place are pretty good. The problem is the people who don't follow them. So I think it's more of an enforcement thing rather than a legislative thing. Maybe there could be some stricter penalties for people who don't follow the rules."

She pulls out her phone and—Lord bless her—starts taking notes.

Kurt is looking at her as if this is totally normal behavior. It may be for her, but it's sure enough not what I was expecting.

"Don't you feel uncomfortable talking to me?" I blurt out.

She gives me a patient look. "No, Johnny. I'm not uncomfortable. You're a person, and you're someone my son is apparently quite taken with. While your relationship is less than ideal for his image—for him to get married out of the blue, and, yes, to a sex worker—I think we need to have less shame around issues of sexuality and intimacy. I can't say that in public too loudly, because I'd be stoned. But pretending that people don't have sex has caused a lot more problems than accepting the fact that they do and making how they do it safer for everyone." She closes her eyes. "I don't need any specifics on my son's bedroom activities, mind you. That's a line I'm never going to cross. But I'm happy to champion the rights of workers everywhere."

That sounded a little practiced, but I'm not going to be mad about it.

"And you, sir?" I say, addressing Ron.

He clears his throat, then looks me in the eye. "I'm wary about trusting anyone with my son, but I can tell that he cares for you very much. The bottom line is, I'll support Kurt in anything that's good for him. If that describes you, then I'm happy to have you in the family."

"I'll be good for him," I say, and it sounds like more of a vow than our wedding vows—which, admittedly, I don't remember. I reach out to Kurt and hold his hand. "I'll take care of your son. I promise."

Kurt snorts. "I don't need taking care of—"

"We all do," I say.

I think my honesty gets to him, because he nods and puts his hand over mine. "Yeah, okay. I understand."

"How is your mother doing, Johnny?" Melissa asks. "I'm told she has kidney issues."

"Insurance denied her coverage for a transplant, which meant she got taken off the donor match list even if we could find the money to pay for it ourselves. Neither me nor my sister are matches. Guess there's some kind of treatment you can do to let someone donate anyway, but it means the risk of rejection is higher, and I want her to have the best chance."

"I'm not a match, either," Kurt says. He tells her Mama's blood type.

"Well, I wonder if I am. That's my type," Melissa says.

That floors me again. "What? Why?" I start. "You don't know her—"

"I'm told that donating a kidney can help you to live longer," she says with a half smile that I recognize, because I've seen it on Kurt's face. "Let me talk with her and her doctors."

Kurt's looking at her, his eyes wide. But they're soft, too.

"I'll take any help we can get, ma'am," I say.

She nods. "You're family now, Johnny."

I don't know what to make of that statement. When my mama said it about Kurt, it felt normal. When the lieutenant governor says it—in the context of *potentially donating an organ*—it's extraordinary. But I'm sure not going to complain.

After we finish eating, Kurt takes me upstairs to his old bedroom. It's packed with art.

"Do you really think your mother would donate a kidney?"

He nods. "She's pretty determined. If it can be done safely, I'm sure she will." He stares hard at me. "No black market shit."

"I wasn't gonna do something where they, like, stole a kidney. It was just more ... people who needed to sell an organ for some reason. It's not legal here, but I figured my mom could fly somewhere else for the surgery. But your mama's giving me hope." I clear my throat. "It doesn't always feel right to have hope."

"Maybe not, but remember you're talking with an optimist. We're going to make things better for your mom, one way or another."

He goes to move on, but I reach out and grab his elbow, looking him in the eye. "Thank you." I try to let him know how much it means in those two words, but it's hard.

I think he gets it, though. "You're welcome, babe." He kisses me, and I kiss him back but pull away before we get too hot and heavy for his parents' home.

"We gotta get you to do more art," I say, gesturing to the colorful paintings everywhere. "It's obvious it's part of you."

"I know." He sighs. "I don't think I've created anything original since I gave Sam one of my paintings and Jules ended up using it on an album cover."

"That's super cool."

Kurt smiles, but it's a little sad. "I've just been so busy with work ... and my mom's campaigns ... and then my own campaign."

"And me," I supply. "But let's see if you can make some time to do this. You're talented. If it's something you like doing, then you should do more of it."

"I'll try to find some time for it, then. Thanks." Kurt rubs his face. "Can I confess something?"

"Always."

"I'm thinking about quitting the race."

I raise an eyebrow. "You are? That's not just jitters ahead of the debate?"

"That might be part of it. But I'm also wondering ..." He sighs. "I'm wondering if I'm really cut out for this. Campaigning, and even legislating, seems so far removed from the action. I want to be helping people. And spending my time asking for money or making speeches seems like the opposite of that."

"You'll get there, darlin'. But you know I've got your back, whatever you decide to do."

I just hope quittin' the race doesn't mean he's quittin' me. He says he won't. But can I count on that?

CHAPTER 31
Kurt

Johnny and I go back downstairs, and my momther gives me one of her looks that makes me feel like a specimen under a microscope. "Kurt? Can I speak with you a moment?"

"Sure," I say.

"I'll go show Johnny the backyard," my dad says. Did he and Momther discuss what's on her mind already, or is he just picking up on her cues? Either way, Johnny, after a silent "Are you okay?" with me, strolls outside with my dad, leaving me and my mom in the TV room.

Once we're alone, she studies me. Really studies me, so much so that I want to squirm.

"What's going on, Mom? How are you?"

"I'm busy helping run the state, but right now I'm more interested in how my only son is doing."

"I'm fine," I say. I think that's true.

"I'm not so sure. You married someone on the spur of the moment, and he's distracted you from the election." She pauses. "To be clear, I care more about you than any election."

While I know she loves me, sometimes that gets lost because of her political ambitions. The idea that she would choose me over the White House is nice, although I'm not entirely sure it's accurate. Maybe she thinks she can have it all.

"Thanks. I love you, too. But he's important to me."

"That came out automatically," she says. "How do you really feel?"

I catch her eyes, then look around the room. It's the most comfortable one in the house. The furniture is older and shabbier than the other spaces, which were put together by a top interior designer. But this room's the real us. Dad's old Barcalounger, which he insisted on keeping when they moved here, still holds pride of place.

"It's complicated," I finally admit. "But I'm not pretending. I really, really like him."

"Good. In that case, let's talk about the campaign. You know I'll back you all the way, but I have to ask, are you sure this is the right path for you?"

I take a long breath. "I don't know. But I'd be letting everyone down if I didn't keep trying. I have the time, the money, the interest, the ability to be a politician."

"I agree that you have all those things, but there are many ways to affect public policy. You don't have to do it from Washington." She tilts her head. "Sometimes just having a one-on-one with someone can do more good than a speech before thousands or even millions."

Her words remind me of what I told Johnny about choosing to take care of him even if it might damage my campaign. And thinking about the fact that—apart from Johnny—the things I've been spending my time on are things I'm doing more out of a sense of duty than passion makes me realize that everything I do is about trying to take care of people.

I've been judging Johnny for going to extremes to care for his mother. Am I doing the same thing? Focusing my whole life on trying to make up for the person I didn't save?

And even if that's a valid choice, should I maybe be doing it in a way that fits my personality better than politics?

While Momther doesn't know what's going on inside my head, she can tell I'm putting some pieces together.

"So that's something to think about," she says. "Whatever you decide about the campaign, you'll have my support. Now, back to your husband. He seems very nice. But I imagine whatever he was being treated for when you first got together isn't the sort of issue that goes away overnight."

"I'm not going to betray his confidence," I say. "He's had a tough life, and yes, he's dealing with some challenges right now. But he's somehow stayed soft and good despite everything."

"Is he good for you, though?"

I don't hesitate. "Yes. I know it seems rash, but he and I clicked from the moment we met." I pause. "I don't usually believe in this kind of stuff, but I think sometimes that he's *the one*."

Her eyes widen. "Oh, wow. That's not the sort of thing I ever expected to hear from you."

"I wouldn't have expected it, either."

"You do seem happy with him. Well, I'll support you all the way if he's the one you truly want."

My mom's my mom. She loves me and has always been there for me. But now she's explicitly saying that she's willing to risk her squeaky-clean image—and her dream of the White House—for my happiness. My heart feels like it's crammed tight in my chest. "I know we haven't been together long, but he is."

When Johnny returns from the garden tour, he gives me another questioning look: Are you okay?

I smile and nod. Even with everything that's on his mind, plus the stress of meeting my folks, he's concerned about me. That's how I know that what's between us is real.

* * *

Johnny's having dinner with his lawyers to go over some details about his case, so I go to Jules and Sam's beach house for dinner on Tuesday. They've decorated for Christmas with tiny white lights everywhere and a tree hung with seashells. It looks magical.

"I have news!" Sam says. "We investigated and discovered that the utilization department for Johnny's mom's insurer had been doing illegal cost savings. That's why they denied her care when they should have approved it. We brought a complaint, but because it's such a strong case, their attorneys already contacted us to offer a settlement. She should be getting enough to pay for her care and then some."

My jaw drops. I'd hoped for some good news, but I hadn't dreamed it would be so simple or so fast. "That's wonderful. I can't wait to tell Johnny."

Just then, my phone buzzes with a text.

JOHNNY

Mama's gonna get insurance coverage! Noah just told me!

KURT

I know, babe! Sam just told me too. Congrats!

JOHNNY

If only we can find a donor.

KURT

Maybe my mother will be one.

JOHNNY

I hope, I hope.

Over dinner, I mention I'm questioning whether politics is the right career for me.

"Not everything that sounds good on paper proves to be what we want," Jules says. "I'd thought a traditional record deal was the ultimate goal, but going indie and doing my own thing has been so much better than I could have imagined. You'll find what's right for you, too."

"Yeah, I guess. Are you working on a new album?"

"Always. I just need a spark," Jules says. "I'm thinking of trying something new. I like contradictions—happy music with depressing lyrics, or vice versa. Or the juxtaposition of modern and classical. Like violins with a drumbeat."

"You should get Johnny's sister to play for you," I say.

"Oh? What does she play?"

"The violin. She's very good."

Jules raises an eyebrow. "Does she have a website? Or a demo I could listen to?"

"I doubt it. She's had to back-burner the music in favor of earning a living. But she played for us when we were there for Thanksgiving, and she blew me away."

"All right. I'm intrigued. Put me in touch with her so I can hear what she sounds like?"

"I'll do that," I say, and make a note to get her number.

"How's Johnny doing?" Sam asks. "Better, I hope?"

"I think so. He has good days and bad. The intensive therapy definitely helped, but he's not all the way ... I don't know if he'll ever be fully recovered."

"Those sorts of things take time," Jules says. "I think it's possible."

Sam nods. "Though maybe also, no matter how much we've dug, no matter how many therapists we've talked to, no matter how far we've come or overcome, there's still always more to do. More to dig. More shit to clear in our psyche. I don't know why we make such a big deal about needing to talk about what's on our mind."

"Yeah, I suppose."

Eventually the conversation returns to the subject of the campaign.

"I'm so far behind," I say. "I'm pretty resigned at this point to the idea that I'm not going to win. I'm just wondering whether I can still do some good if I stay in the race until election day, or whether I should concede and be done with it."

"There's no shame either way," Jules says.

"My mom pointed out that politics isn't the only career where I can help people," I admit. "It just seemed like the obvious one."

Sam clucks thoughtfully. "She's right, though. There are plenty of things you can do to that same end. Ways you can help without having to cater to voters."

"What are you thinking about?"

"How about working for a nonprofit? Noah and August started one to help LGBT+ youth, and they could likely use some help. It's small now, but it could grow."

I raise an eyebrow. "Nonprofit work?"

"Sure. I think you'd be good at it, and it could be good for you. You've got all this drive and energy, and you care about our community. You could see the results of initiatives a lot faster there than in the Senate. It would be on a smaller scale, but ... a kid who has a bed for the night. A teen who doesn't hurt themselves. Those are important, too."

Visions start swirling in my head. Helping people individually rather than through lengthy attempts at legislation. Working with colleagues who share my values. That sounds ... not awful. Satisfying, even. "Hmm. Interesting idea."

"I'll ask Noah about it next time I see him," Sam says.

"I mean, for now, I've still got the campaign," I say, shifting in my seat. "But, yeah, let me know. I'll see what Johnny thinks, too. He might have an opinion on it."

Sam tilts his head. "Sounds like you two have more of a relationship than 'We met in Vegas and whoops, I fell on his wedding ring.'"

"Yeah. We do. I mean, I liked him before I met him, because I thought he was damn sexy—I don't need to tell you guys that—"

They both grin.

"But the real him is more complex. Sweeter. I ... I think I might love him."

Sam's smile goes all soft, and his eyes instinctively go to Jules's. "Does he know that?"

"He knows I care about him."

Sam leans forward. "But have you told him that it's ... more?"

I shake my head.

"Then tell him, mate," Jules says. "I bet he needs to hear it."

CHAPTER 32
Kurt

To my surprise, Johnny isn't back yet when I get home from Sam and Jules's. That doesn't do anything to settle my nerves. I'm feeling faint, and I've got a headache coming on.

I want to ask Johnny if he'd consider doing this thing—relationship—for real, but I feel like a kid asking his crush to go to prom and not knowing if they'll say yes.

Except ... what we have is real. Isn't it?

If he's going to turn me down, I don't want it to be in my living room, where I'll have to relive the rejection over and over *and over* again. The beach is right across the way—we just have to put on shoes, go down to the light and cross the highway, and we're there. That's a safer place to do it.

Who's the optimist now?

I keep pacing in the hall, waiting, and when he finally walks in the door, it's all I can do not to jump on him.

"Did you have a good dinner?" I ask.

He nods and kisses me. "Yeah, thanks. Got a lot to think about."

"Want to go for a walk on the beach?"

"Yeah," he says. "That sounds nice."

His cowboy boots aren't great for walking on sand, but I bought him some blue rubber shower shoes for the hospital, and he's taken to keeping those in the front hallway so they're convenient for walks like this.

My husband's wearing dark blue Wrangler jeans, a tight heather gray T-shirt, and a black zip hoodie, and I want to climb him like a tree. He's let his hair grow out so it's a bit long and wavy, and the front flops down over his brow. I want to brush it out of his face. He has no business looking so effortlessly sexy.

I put on my own flip-flops, and we walk down to the state beach.

The ocean is silver and gold where the last of the sunlight glints off its surface, and since there's been some rain recently, clouds on the horizon range from vibrant deep orange to bright pink. Does that mean more storms? I can't tell what to expect, and that seems like a metaphor for everything in my life right now.

We stop for a moment, watching the waves lick up on the shore. There's a breeze, and the water is choppy.

I clear my throat, and Johnny turns to me, his eyes neutral. "So, I'm considering something."

"Oh? What's that?"

"I'm kind of thinking of quitting the Senate race. Maybe see how the debate goes, but if my numbers don't improve after that, drop out."

His face falls. "If that's what you want, then you should do it."

"Hey," I say, stepping forward and taking his hand. "I didn't think it would upset you."

"It don't upset me none."

"Then why do you look like that? Like I kicked you."

He's silent for a moment, lips pressed together. Then he says, "Do you have any use for me if you're not running? Didn't we stay together because you needed your image to be ... not volatile?"

My jaw drops. Is that what he's been thinking, still? That this is some kind of publicity stunt? Or that it's transactional, what we can do for each other?

I think of his list of expenses that he intends to pay me back for. He's started cashing his paychecks and putting money in an envelope for the clothes and the therapy deductibles, but I haven't touched it.

I shake my head. "That's not what this is for me. I've been feeling like," I gesture between us, "like we're in a relationship." His shoulders go ramrod straight. "And I really like you." More than like. But I can't say that, not with the way he's reacting so far. I stumble onward. "So I was wondering if you, I don't know, wanted to try giving a real relationship a shot. Being my boyfriend in addition to being my husband."

A sad look passes over Johnny's face, and he shakes his head. My stomach lurches. I'd tried to prepare myself for this, but on some level, I'd believed that he liked me—in *that* way—too.

But maybe this has been one-sided, nothing but fan worship. Where I've tricked myself into thinking it's real.

His next words surprise me, though. "You don't want me."

I narrow my eyes and fold my arms over my chest. "What? I just told you I do."

He drops his chin to his chest. "I come with more baggage than an airline."

"We all have baggage. And I'm pretty sure I know what I'm getting into with you. We haven't known each other long, and I know this is a weird situation. I like you, and I thought you liked me, too, but I guess you don't. So I'm sorry, now I've gone and made this weird. Fuck!"

He puts both arms on my shoulders and faces me head on. "Wait, darlin'. This has nothing to do with me liking you. I like you more than you'll ever know."

"Okay. Then you just don't want to be in a relationship?"

"That's not what I said. I do. But you deserve so much better than me."

"Oh, stop that bullshit," I snap. "I get to decide who's good enough for me and who isn't. If that's even a thing. I want *you*, Johnny. I want you to be mine."

"Guess that's hard for me to believe. I've had it in my head that we were quittin' when you were done with the Senate stuff. Like you said in the car when we came here from Vegas."

I run a hand down my face and look up at some seagulls circling overhead. "Well, believe me, right now, that I want you, and I want to try it. Try being boyfriends."

"I want you more than anything," he whispers. "You see me, the real me. Not just the character I used to play."

"Then give us a chance." I hate that I'm begging. I'm pretty sure I've never begged for anything in my life. But I want him, and I'm not afraid to look weak in front of him. "Will you go out with me? Be my boyfriend? Try this for real?"

"Yes," he says so quietly I almost miss it, but when I leap into his arms, he catches me and kisses me soundly. "Yes, this is real," he repeats. "I want to be real with you. Boyfriends. Exclusive boyfriends." He smirks. "And husbands."

A shiver runs through my body at his words and the way his hands feel cupping my ass. My legs are wrapped around his waist, and I'm holding on to his shoulders so he doesn't have to support my full weight. Even though I know he's plenty strong enough to do so easily.

I don't care that we're in public in a very popular area of Los Angeles where a photographer could pass by at any time.

Whatever. I'm kissing my husband. Who is now my boyfriend. It's a free country, and, I realize, this is *exactly* what I'm fighting for as a politician. I'm fighting for the right to love who I want to love. Yes, I'm pretty sure I'm in love with Johnny, even if he's not in love with me. I can try. I can see if this can develop into love.

He brushes his lips over my mouth one more time before gently lowering me to my feet, and we grin goofily at each other. "Boyfriends?" he asks.

"Yeah. Boyfriends. You good with that?"

"Giddy," he admits. "Been a long time since I've felt giddy. What in tarnation?"

"I think that's dopamine or something. Knowing someone likes you a lot and wants to try being real with you can make you feel good."

"It certainly is making me feel better."

I squeeze his hand. "I know a way I could make you feel even better," I say pointedly, looking at the growing bulge in his tight jeans. His dick is almost always visible, it's so big, but right now there's a pole going down his leg, as graphic as a Tom of Finland drawing. In fact, Johnny's right out of one of those vintage pictures, with his classic hypermasculine looks and cowboy persona.

He leans down and nips at my neck, then wraps a hand around my waist. "Thought we were going on a walk."

"Ugh. We are. Fine. But when we get back? We're getting naked."

Johnny grins and kisses me. "Okay, precious. Lead the way."

I walk with my boyfriend on the beach, the cool sand giving way under our feet as the water licks the shore. And when we get home, Johnny makes me see way more stars than were visible in the sky tonight.

I have a boyfriend—a real one—for the first time in my adult life. I couldn't be happier.

CHAPTER 33
Johnny

A few days after Kurt and I decide to be boyfriends, I'm outside on Kurt's ground floor patio, using his sleek, shiny barbecue.

To be honest, I ain't sure that I'm not dreaming this whole experience of being with him, because from where I was, this is a complete U-turn. I don't recognize my life right now.

I'm flipping a big hunk of brisket when a throat clears behind me—one I recognize. I'm glad he knows not to startle me. Then two arms slide around my middle. I link my left hand with his, rings sliding against each other, as he puts his cheek between my shoulders. "What'cha doing, babe?"

Babe. I like his names for me almost as much as I like calling him precious. But he's so precious he has no idea.

"Thought I'd make you some brisket," I say. "It's been cooking on low for hours. Should be gettin' real tender. Wait until you try Mama's special sauce."

He sniffs appreciatively. "It smells great. Thanks. Need some help?"

I shake my head and turn around to kiss him. Kissing, cooking, all these kitchen gadgets. It feels established. Not permanent, but more than temporary. I've always kept my own places pretty spare, so I could pick up and leave whenever I needed to. So being surrounded by all Kurt's appliances and extras makes me feel settled. Like I'm putting down roots.

Also, cooking seems to make the violins go quiet.

Kurt makes the violins go quiet, which is more important than an air fryer, my mental voice scolds. But this is all so new, and my brain is in such turmoil, that I think I should cut myself some slack. If what I can do is grill a brisket, well, then, maybe I celebrate that.

While the food cooks, Kurt comes out with glasses of water, which reminds me of something I've noticed. "You don't drink the beer in your fridge," I say. "Is that because of Vegas—one hangover too many?"

He shakes his head. "Not that. I decided not to drink around you, since I figured you couldn't have it while they were tinkering with your medication."

My heart swells at his thoughtfulness. "Drink your beer," I say. "If you want one. I think I can have one every once in a while. But I'm good without it, too." I sip the water. Something else dawns on me. "You got rid of the Gatorade, didn't you?"

"Yes," he whispers.

"Thanks."

We eat on the patio with the dull roar of Highway 1 below us. Just beyond the row of houses on the other side of the highway is the beach, where all kinds of people are out—surfers, folks sitting on the sand, people walking their dogs. One dog's pulling its owner like it's mushing on snow, and I point it out to Kurt.

"Would you want a dog?" he asks, and danger bells go off in my brain. Because he's the sort who would come home with a puppy if I asked for it.

I do want a puppy, but I ain't gonna burden him with one.

"Never had any of my own," I say. "But on the ranch, there was a pack of them. I loved them all, even the unruly hounds."

"That's kind of a nonanswer."

"I feel like if I say yes, a dog's gonna show up here."

"It could. Would you want one? What kind? A mutt or a purebred?"

"I couldn't support one of them puppy mills. Yeah, there are reputable breeders, but I think I'd want to adopt one from the pound. I feel like I'm not in a position to be able to take care of a dog, though, and I'm not sure there's enough room for one here."

"Okay. Got it." He tilts his head. "What if I brought one home anyway?"

I open my mouth, but no words come out.

He smiles even broader. He got me. He knows I'd love it.

"I see. Okay. What kind of dog?" Kurt asks.

"I like 'em all. Bigger dogs, probably, but I care more about personality. Not sure there's enough room for a big dog to run here, though they could go on the beach."

"Where would you want to live if you could live anywhere?"

I bark out a laugh. "You'd best not be planning to come home with *a new house* for me, darlin'." I'm joking ... mostly. This is Kurt, after all, and who knows what ideas he'll get in his sweet, pretty head.

"We're just talking," he says, shooting me a smile. "Didn't you ever play that game when you were a kid, making up around-the-world trips or planning out your dream house? I wanted a pool and a trampoline and an art studio and a separate freezer just for ice cream. I mean, not all of that is ridiculous, I suppose, but the point is, it was a fantasy."

I don't rightly remember any such imaginings. Before Mama got sick, I wore myself out running around on the ranch with the dogs and the horses and the goats, not thinking up things that were never gonna happen anyway. And after ... I was busy trying to do extra chores anywhere I could, to help out with the bills. "If you say so," I tell him. "Well, I don't need a big house or a fancy one, but I wouldn't mind having a bit of land and privacy," I admit.

While the condo is up high and not so easy for people to see into, it's still in the middle of a city.

"Like in Hidden Valley?"

"That's too expensive."

"Setting aside the price," he says.

"Then, sure. I mean, yeah, open space and fields and trees. That's more my speed."

He nods. "That makes sense. You definitely seem happier out in nature, and with animals." He takes another bite of brisket and makes a happy noise before telling me about a meme Sam sent him earlier in the day, and we talk about this and that as we finish our meal.

I hope it's ridiculous to imagine he'd think about moving on my account. Everything he's already doing for me is too much. A house would be ... well, I don't know the words for how *much, much* too much it would be. Even if he says he don't need to be paid back, I still feel wrong being a kept man. I wanna contribute, and I'm only just now barely starting to feel like it's a possibility that I ever could.

After we finish eating, Kurt does the dishes, shooing me away when I try to help. I look around his great room and realize the place is starting to feel like home to me. When I first got here, everything was so ... *him*. Which made sense, it being his house. But now there are little touches of me all over the place, too: my hat hung up on a peg, my boots by the door. The cowboy poetry book he gave me on the coffee table. A to-go coffee mug he bought me sitting on the drainboard. My award on his shelf. He even framed some old photos of mine that were in the bottom of my suitcase.

I do like it here, even if it ain't the country.

"Do you want to watch a show?" Kurt asks.

"Don't mind if you want to," I say. "The shows that just manufacture drama annoy me, but I trust you to pick something good."

"Well, let's see what you think of some better-written shows."

I plop my ass on the couch and spread my legs, and Kurt settles between them. I decide immediately that if watching TV means curling up with him on the couch, I'm on board.

He puts on *The Last of Us*, since I'd told him I hadn't seen it—though he warns me it covers some tough subject matter. Once the story gets going, I'm enthralled.

"Wow. This is ... wow."

"I know," he says. As the drama (good drama) continues, I think about the way the show portrays society. About how there are still individuals trying to do the right thing, even when the institutions are going to hell.

When we get to the episode with the same-sex couple who lives a beautiful, ordinary life in the middle of the zombie apocalypse, though, I'll admit it. My eyes get hot. Dang. "Why're y'all making me watch this," I huff. "You coulda told me it'd hit me in the feels. I'm not just talking about the heavy stuff at the end of the episode. I'm talking about the part where they get together at the beginning."

"I know. The actors said the intimacy coordinators really helped their performance."

"Intimacy coordinator. I've heard that term, but I ain't come across one."

"They should be standard in porn, and I bet there are some. Just not at the studios you worked with, I guess." He gives me a small smile. "You'd be a good one."

"I wonder what I'd have to do to become one," I say. "Then that could be my job when you're out being a senator or graphic artist or whatever else you decide to do. Since I'm not gonna do porn no more."

"I'm sure you can find out."

"Now that you've had a moment to process it, what do you think about being married to a porn star?" I ask. "Or former porn star." I'm kinda afraid to hear his answer, but I guess the masochistic part of me wants to know.

He gives it some thought. "I guess my knee-jerk reaction was just that. Sex workers have such a stigma in this country, and most everywhere. But why is that? Because they're evidence of our bodily needs? Or is it that we like to feel better, higher, bigger, more important than someone? Is it our Puritan heritage that wanted us to renounce all things related to the flesh? It doesn't totally make sense to me."

I nod.

"I do think, though, that I may have some internalized issues with it," he continues. "Because if I'm married to a porn star, then that means I like porn. Or people assume I do, anyhow, and since they happen to be right ..." He shrugs. "I admit that's not something I wanted the whole world knowing."

"Internalized ... ?"

"Criticism. Judgment. Because no matter how much therapy I've done or how open-minded I think I am, there's still a part of me that thinks that sex is taboo."

"Yeah. I get it." I sigh. "Question: What would you think about it if I were still doin' porn? Would it piss you off?"

Kurt looks at me intently. "I've been able to sidestep that, since you retired before we met."

"So I'm pushin' ya. Not sure there's a right or wrong answer. Just curious how you really feel."

"I'm feeling pretty damn possessive of you, so the idea of you touching anyone else ... wouldn't make me too happy. I understand that it's a job—that someone goes and performs, and it doesn't necessarily have anything to do with emotions or cheating or shit like that—but I just ... don't want to share you."

I squeeze his hand. "I don't wanna share you, either. While I enjoy sex, I like that I have a different job now." That reminds me of something I've been thinking about, and it's the perfect opening. "I know you say I don't need to pay you back for all the money you've spent on me, don't need to keep track. But I still want to. It's gonna take me a while to earn my keep financially, though, what with going to therapy all the time and the ranch not paying that much. So I thought of another way I could maybe even things out a bit." I raise a playful eyebrow.

"For the record, I don't feel like we're uneven, but based on your expression, I'm intrigued. What are you talking about?"

CHAPTER 34
Kurt

A shiver runs through me at the promise in Johnny's eyes.

"What do you think about letting me take over in the bedroom?" he asks. "Be a ... dom, kinda. Would you trust me to give you an escape? Time when you don't have to think about what you need to do and who you need to do it for?"

He hasn't even finished speaking, and my body's already flooded with ... I don't know what kind of hormones or whatever. It's like I can feel my blood pressure relax and my mind start to clear. "Fuck," I say. "Yes. Please. My brain's so full of ... shit so much of the time. I love it when you tell me what to do."

"You know I'm a stickler for consent," he says.

"You have it. I'll tell you if I don't like something or don't want to do it. But I can't imagine you doing anything that would pass my limits."

"Then just you wait, baby boy. I'll rock your world. Bring that pretty cock over here and let me suck it." Johnny tugs me to him, wrapping his arms around my waist and brushing his lips against the skin behind my ear.

He runs a hand down my side and into my pocket.

I love it when Johnny takes over. He's so much bigger than me.

It's not that I'm little. He's just *so* big. I can imagine I'm overpowered, and it's a turn-on. He could throw me around, but he doesn't.

Power that he chooses not to exercise. Restraint.

Him being in control.

Me not having to be.

It's hot. Fucking hot.

I turn around and join my mouth to his, kissing him as he slides his other hand under my ass cheek, pulling me closer to him. When I part my lips, he licks into my mouth, and he tastes so good.

"Fuck," I whisper.

He rubs his erection against mine, and I want to please him even more than I want to feel his mouth on me.

"What is it?" he asks, in tune with what I'm thinking, as usual.

"I want to suck *you* off."

He chuckles, then smiles against the crook of my neck. "Oh yeah?"

"Please?"

"I'm not sure I should be lettin' you call the shots, precious, but since you asked so nicely, maybe just this once." He gives me his best dom look. "Be a good boy and get down on your knees."

That command, in his gentle twang, makes the little hairs rise on the back of my neck. *Yes.* "I love it when you order me around."

"Good boy," he says as I position myself. He runs a hand through my hair, tousling it. I reach for his pants, but he clucks his tongue. "Nuh-uh. Hold on."

He pulls back and studies me. Something about that makes everything even hotter. Because I could be embarrassed sitting here. Like, why am I kneeling before him? But he makes me feel special. Like I'm doing something praiseworthy.

"You look so beautiful," he whispers. "I just needed to see you."

I wait, patiently, as he watches me. He lifts my chin up with one finger, and his big eyes, full of heat, meet mine.

"Fuck, you're so beautiful," he repeats. "Okay, now suck my cock like a good boy."

I reach for his belt buckle. But he's better at taking that thing off than I am, so he helps me.

Then I ease his dick out of his pants. His porn star dick: long, thick, huge. It's fucking pretty, the way he's pretty. It's unlike anyone else's I've ever seen, just ... perfect. That's what Johnny has. A perfect dick. It's huge, but it's not *too* thick, not *too* long.

And he always smells good. Even when he's been working and is a little musky, I like the natural scent of his skin. I like the hair on his thighs and around his dick. I like the trail of hair under his belly button and the hair he's letting grow on his chest.

I open my mouth and he puts his dick into it, and I sigh with happiness.

"Look at you," he whispers. "You take my cock so well, sweetheart. You're such a good boy. Lick it. Yeah, that's it. You know I like it that way. You're so good at this. The best."

Johnny's praise fills me up inside in ways I never imagined. I wouldn't have thought I was starved to hear things like that. For validation. But Johnny's words make me feel like I *am* good. Like I can please him. Like this is important, and like together we can make something beautiful.

He also makes me feel like I can't do this wrong. Like if something isn't right, he'll correct me gently instead of resenting or judging me.

I take more of him into my mouth, relaxing my throat and then swallowing around the tip of his dick. He's too big for me to take all the way. *He's* the porn star, not me.

But even though I think I'm doing just okay, that's not what he's telling me. "You make me feel so good, sweetheart. That's it. So, so good. You look gorgeous choking on my cock. Fuck. Absolutely the most beautiful boy."

Johnny's so big, it takes him a while to get fully hard, but he is now, and it's intimidating.

But.

I keep sucking, tears rolling down my face as I take him deeper than I can comfortably, but he lets me.

He's groaning, and these are his private groans. They're quieter than Velvet's. Sexier, in my opinion, because they aren't practiced. They just come out.

Soon he's pulsing down my throat, and I swallow his bitter, sweet, salty release.

Thank fuck he's starting to get his sex drive back. And I get to help him with it.

"Okay, baby boy. Now it's my turn." He grabs me by the waist and hauls me over his shoulder, depositing me on the couch, where he proceeds to make me come using only his tongue.

* * *

The day before Christmas, I walk into the house doing my best to hide my excitement. Johnny's sitting on the balcony looking out at the ocean. We put up lights and decorated a tree, but I can tell he's still struggling with the blues.

"Babe?" I call as I walk outside.

"Hey." He sounds listless.

"How are you doing?" I sit down next to him, though I don't want to settle in for too long.

Johnny shrugs. "Not sure, honestly. It's one of those days. Some are good, and some are ... tough."

While I'm not happy he's down, I'm heartened that he's being forthright and telling me about it. That's massive progress. I put my head on his shoulder. "Is there a particular reason why it's tough right now?"

"Maybe the holidays? Not sure. I called Mama, and she's doin' about the same as she was at Thanksgiving. I want her to be better."

"I know you do." I kiss him. "I'm sorry today's not so good. I have something that might brighten it up a bit, though. Can I give you your present?"

"You didn't have to—"

I kiss him again to silence his protest. "I know. Wait here. Or, actually, come inside. I have to get it out of the garage."

"Okay," he says, looking dubious but interested despite himself. Maybe he's picking up on my enthusiasm. I tell him to take a seat on the couch and head downstairs.

In the garage, I open up the puppy crate and pull out the wriggling bundle of fur, holding her securely in my arms as I climb the stairs. I open the door and call out, "Close your eyes."

"Sure, darlin'," Johnny says, and as I walk up to him, I can see he's obeyed.

The squirming puppy yips as I drop her into his lap.

Johnny's eyes fly open, and his hands go around her immediately, as she jumps up and starts licking his face.

His face softer than I've ever seen it, he looks up at me and asks, "Who is this?" as if he daren't hope she's for him.

"Your Christmas present," I say with a smile.

Johnny's expression is indescribable. He seems so bowled over he's about to cry. "Is she ..."

"Yours. Ours."

"I told you that y'all didn't need to get me a dog," he says, but he's grinning.

"Yeah, I heard you. I just ignored it, because if there was ever a man who needs a dog, it's you." I pause. "She's a rescue. Jules found her, actually. He said she'd be one you liked. They say she's likely part golden retriever, part German shepherd, which makes me think she'll be sweet and loyal."

Like you, I think.

"I've always wanted my own dog," he whispers, as he pets her floppy velvet ears and lets her climb up his chest.

"I know. And I think when she's a little bigger, she'll be able to go with you to work."

I wouldn't have thought he could get more excited. "Oh, yeah, she can definitely come with me to the ranch. You'll be a help with the horses, won't ya, girl?" he coos, stroking her belly and playing with her paws.

"You keep an eye on her. I've got more stuff to bring in," I say, and go out to the garage.

When I return with my arms full, he laughs. "What didja do, buy a whole pet store?"

Grinning, I shake my head as I empty the bags on the table: a collar and leash, puppy chow and dog bowls, toys and treats.

"What do you want to name her?" I ask, coming over and scratching her ears.

"She doesn't have a name yet?"

I shrug. "Whatever they called her at the shelter, that doesn't matter. You're her dad, so you get to name her."

Johnny studies her, his face soft and happy. "Well, I reckon she's a little lady, so I think that's her name, isn't it? Lady. I know it ain't an unusual name, but it seems like her."

"Then Lady it is." I go to leave, but Johnny reaches out and snags my wrist, tugging me to him for a kiss.

"Thank you," he whispers fervently. He snuggles his nose into Lady's fur and inhales what I know is that sweet clean-puppy smell. "This is the best thing anyone's ever done for me. I've just always ... I've always wanted a dog."

"And now you have one."

"I've always wanted a boyfriend, too."

"You have one of those, too."

I kiss him again, and he whispers, "Thanks," against my lips.

"I'm glad this was a good surprise," I tell him. "Her crate and bed are still in the car. I'll be right back."

As I scoot off to the garage, I hear him tell Lady, "Your other daddy's spoiling you, isn't he? You deserve to be spoiled, though, don't you, pretty girl?"

I return with the bed and crate, as well as puppy pads and more toys, and Johnny chuckles.

"Dogs require care," I say defensively, as I set the dog bed down by the couch.

"I'm just teasin' you. I love that you're taking care of her like this. I think I'll get her used to the house, then we can take her for a walk on the beach."

"Sounds good to me."

There were so many reasons to give Johnny a dog—it will help with his recovery, distract him from his trial, give him something to focus on besides himself. But the bottom line is, I knew it would put that smile on his face.

That night, Johnny makes love to me, then lets Lady into our room and up on our bed. I roll my eyes and point out the perfectly good dog bed I bought.

"She's stolen your heart," I say.

"Yeah, but you stole it first."

* * *

My phone is ringing early in the morning, and it's my momther. We spent Christmas Day with her and my dad, but we're now in that dead zone between Christmas and New Year's where everything blurs together.

"Hey," I say, my voice gravelly from sleep. "Is everything okay?"

"I just got news that I had to share." Her voice is pitched high with excitement. "I'm a match."

"Come again?" I squint at my phone.

"I'm a match for Sue Ann Haskell," my mom says louder. So loud that Johnny must hear her. He stirs behind me and sits up, blinking.

"Are you saying what I think you're saying?" I ask.

"Yes! I can donate a kidney to her."

"Holy shit, Mom. Thank you."

"I'm happy to do this for my son-in-law's mother. Everyone deserves to have the best possible quality of life."

I look at Johnny, and his eyes are red. "Okay, then," I say. "What do we need to do next?"

She tells me the plan, and I hang up, feeling overwhelmed. And if I'm feeling that way, I have no idea how Johnny is feeling.

"Did you catch all that?" I ask.

He nods. "Your mama is gonna save my mama."

"Pretty much." I nod. "You good with that?"

"I mean, yeah, because I want Mama to be okay. It just … means that the Haskell family is going to be in debt to the Delmont family for the rest of our lives."

I rear up and haul myself around so I'm sitting on his thighs. Then I get right in his face. "You listen to me, and you listen well, John Haskell. Life's not a tit for tat. Someone giving you a gift does not mean you have to reciprocate. This is not some deal where your mom gets a kidney, so you have to donate a liver."

"It still feels wrong."

"What's wrong is stopping someone from willingly helping your mother. Are you going to do that?"

Johnny sighs and shakes his head. "'Course not."

"Then let's celebrate that she's a match. Okay?"

He nods.

We have breakfast in the great room, Lady curled up at Johnny's feet, and I smile at the framed photos of us he gave me for a Christmas present.

Things are looking up.

CHAPTER 35

Johnny

Not wanting to keep the good news from Mama—and since I need to see her expression in person when we tell her—Kurt and I drive up to Fresno the following morning, bringing a few late Christmas gifts with us. And Lady, of course, even though that means lots of pit stops, as well as cleaning up once when she gets carsick.

As we head up the interstate, I'm excited to see Mama, like I always am, but that doesn't keep my own stomach from clenching as I think about the other thing I have planned for this visit. Kurt notices, like he always does, and asks me what's wrong. He puts a warm hand on my thigh, and that helps me get my words going. "I'm troubled," I say.

Kurt tilts his head. "You are? Why? This is what you've wanted—your mom could be completely healthy again soon."

"Yeah, but ..." I blow out a breath. "I have to tell her what's going on with me."

"You mean about your mental health issues?" Kurt asks.

I nod. "Christian said I needed to fess up to Mama. Well, she didn't say it that way, but she said I should be honest, even if it's hard. But ... it's gonna upset her. Disappoint her. And that's gonna hurt, 'cause I never want to make her sad." My throat closes up.

He gives me a little squeeze. "Babe, she loves you as much as you love her, if not more. She'll want to know what's really going on with you."

"It just sucks to have to bring it up. I wanna let it be. Why ruin Christmas? Or New Year's. The holidays."

"There's no law that says you have to tell her, but I think it's a good idea. She should know. You're not ruining a holiday by being honest."

I know he's right, even though thinking about making my mama cry has me wanting to turn the car around and drive in the opposite direction until we run out of road.

Mama's happy to see us, of course, and she takes to Lady right away. My good girl somehow knows to be extra gentle with her, and soon we're all sitting in the living room, Lady curled up on her lap, Kurt next to me. Mama looks about the same as always—frail but smiling. Trying hard. Fierce. May Ella's fussing in the kitchen.

We've exchanged presents. Mama gave me a new brass belt buckle the size of Montana with running horses on it, which I love, and she gave Kurt a little book of my baby photos, which got him all melty. Kurt and I gave her a new bathrobe and slippers and May Ella sheet music.

"I can't get over what a treat it is to see you both again so soon," Mama says. "I hope you had a good Christmas with Kurt's family."

Kurt looks at me, and I nod. "We did," he says. "It was the best Christmas I can remember, because I had him to share it with. But then yesterday we found out about one more big present—and it's for you. My mom's a match."

Mama turns her head slowly between Kurt and me. "A ma— Are you serious?"

"Oh, Mama, that's wonderful!" May Ella says, and a tear slides down her face. I reach over and hold her hand.

"You really hadn't heard?" Kurt asks Mama. "I asked my mom not to call you and spill the beans, but she was pretty excited, so I wasn't sure."

Mama shakes her head. "Not a peep since the doctors contacted me to get permission to share whatever medical information. As if I could have sat here with y'all and not said, if I knew! You two boys! Between you sorting out that nonsense with the insurance company and now this, it's ... I don't know what to say." She dabs at her eyes with a tissue. "Come here and hug me. I am truly blessed."

I wrap my arms around her, trying not to think about how very tiny she is, and Kurt hugs her gently, too, and then we settle back down on the couch. "It's good to see you happy." I smile, but it feels forced. *Tell her the bad stuff, too, Johnny.*

"A new kidney," Mama whispers. "Finally. It really is a Christmas miracle."

"We have another surprise," Kurt says. "This one's for you," he tells May Ella. He digs in his pocket and then hands her a folded piece of paper. "This is Julian Hill's phone number. Do you know who he is? He asked me to ask you to give him a call so you could play the violin for him. Maybe you can do a video call at first, and then if things work out you could take a road trip and visit him in LA. He's writing his next album and mentioned that he wants to have violins on it, so I thought of you."

May Ella's eyes are wide as dinner plates, and she's holding the piece of paper like it's a diamond necklace. "You're joking," she says in a harsh whisper.

I shake my head. "No, he ain't. He's friends with Jules. Nice guy. Likes dogs."

May Ella flushes. "I cannot believe we're talking about me playing for Julian Hill. Julian Hill the pop star. Who used to be in the boy band I listened to when I was a teen."

I tilt my head. "I told Jules I couldn't name any of his music, but I thought you might've listened to it. Guess that was correct."

"Oh my dear Lord in heaven," May Ella says. "This is too much."

"So you'll call him?" Kurt asks.

"Yessir," she whispers. "Right away. Though why would he want to listen to me, when he could get any violinist he wanted? Ones who're actually trained."

"Formal training isn't everything," Kurt says. "I heard you play, and I know he's going to love your passion. He likes keeping his inspiration down-to-earth. He used one of my paintings for an album cover, and I'm not exactly Van Gogh."

May Ella is shining as bright as a new penny, and I don't want to spoil this moment. But Christian's right—I gotta face this and get it out of my system. It's gonna eat me alive if I don't.

"It's all so wonderful," Mama says.

Kurt catches my eye, and he gives me a nod like he knows what I'm thinking.

That man. Having his encouragement is everything.

"Mama, I have to tell you a few things that aren't so wonderful."

"Oh?"

"I'm sorry to be bringing this up now, but there really ain't no good or right time to do it, so ..." I just go for it. "I've been struggling lately. Mentally, I mean. A while back, I had a bad thing happen at work—I got assaulted."

Mama's face drops, and she reaches out to me. "Oh, I'm so sorry, Johnny. Are you okay?"

"Of course," I say automatically, and then, "I mean, physically I'm fine. But no, I'm ... I'm not okay." I clear my throat. "The assault sent me into a pretty bad mental state, for a lot of reasons. I felt weak and ashamed. And I couldn't get work, so I couldn't help you when you were denied for the transplant that last time."

She watches me carefully but doesn't say anything. May Ella's doing the same.

Might as well get it all over with.

"I decided to kill myself, Mama, so you could get the money from my life insurance and use it for the medical stuff."

Mama gasps in a breath so sharp I worry, and her hand flies to her mouth. Her forehead wrinkles, and she starts to cry. "Oh, Johnny. No. Baby, no."

"I'm sorry. I didn't want to tell you. But yeah, that was my plan. I wrote you a note. I even wrote an obituary. I'd found a way to get you a kidney, from a place where they buy them from people. It wasn't necessarily aboveboard, and you would've had to go outta the country. They told me they could find a match—they have lists of people who are willing to sell their kidneys for the right price, I guess. It seemed like the only way to help you."

"John H. Haskell, there's always another way." She starts scolding me, and for some reason, her anger makes me feel better. "I can't believe ... My goodness, son. I don't know what to say."

"Johnny, I'm so sorry you felt so bad," May Ella says. "I'd had similar thoughts—at least about trying to get her the money. I don't have life insurance, but I thought about doing ... other things."

Mama turns to her. "No, baby girl, oh my goodness. You children, you do not have to take care of me like that."

"We do, Mama," I say.

"But I couldn't live without you," she says. "I'd never want you to sacrifice yourselves for me. Your lives or your principles. I'm just grateful you came to your senses."

"Actually, I didn't. But Kurt found out and stopped me."

Her head whips to him. She beckons, and he moves over on the couch to where she can reach him. She takes his hand and holds it tight, saying fiercely, "I owe you my life, then. Because you saved my boy."

Kurt swallows. "Anyone would have done the same thing."

"No, anyone wouldn't. And anyhow, that's not the point. The point is that *you did*."

He gives her a smile. "I was really worried about him. Still am, sometimes." He looks over at me with those big brown eyes, and it's my turn to fess up more.

"I had to go to a hospital for a while," I say. "I did inpatient and outpatient therapy. And now I have regular sessions with a therapist who asked me if I'd told you these things. When I said no, she gave me a look like I knew you'd give me. So I'm sorry to ruin Christmas."

"You haven't ruined anything. I'm just so sorry you felt that bad," Mama says. "I hope you're getting all the care you need so you'll get better."

"He is. At least I think he is," Kurt says. "I'm doing everything I can to make sure of it."

Mama opens her mouth to say something, then stops and shakes her head, closing her eyes. A tear drips down her cheek, and I feel like utter shit.

"I'm sorry I planned to kill myself," I tell her. "I'm sorry I couldn't think of another way to save you. I'm learning that it was my depression telling me that killing myself was the only option."

"We would've never forgiven you!" May Ella says.

I give her an apologetic look, then turn back to Mama. "Kurt said that killing myself would hurt you worse than having bad kidneys, but that sort of logic is hard to believe when you're in the middle of depression."

"He's right, though." Mama gives me a watery smile. "I love you, Johnny. Don't you forget that. Don't take yourself away from me, ever. I'll not have it."

"It's a little easier to tell you this, knowing that we're gonna get you your transplant," I admit.

"But I bet it was hard anyway," she says quietly.

"Yeah. It was."

"Then thank you for telling me, and I'm so sorry it got that bad," Mama says. "Let me know if there's anything I can do to help you heal." She looks at Kurt. "And thank you for saving my son. You're a hero. I hope you know that."

"I think my mom's the hero, actually," he says.

"Yeah," I say, my voice hoarse. "She's a keeper, too. Just like you."

* * *

That night, lying in the hotel bed in Fresno, tracing a line down Kurt's back with my fingertips, I sigh.

"What's up?" he asks.

I don't answer right away.

"Honesty," he reminds me. I grumble, but I know he's right.

"Why don't I feel better?" I finally ask. "I've done all the things I'm supposed to do. I got therapy, and I'm taking my meds. I fessed up to Mama. She's gonna get the care she needs. I have an amazing boyfriend, a job working at a beautiful ranch, and a fancy home to come back to every night. And a dog sleepin' at the foot of my bed. So why do I still sometimes want to end it all? Will this ever stop being so hard?"

He pulls me closer to him. "Recovery isn't linear. And shaming yourself for not feeling better is counterproductive. What's the line about 'If you're in a hole, stop digging'? Piling bad feelings on top of bad feelings just makes a bigger pile. You don't have to feel great on any kind of schedule."

"I wish I could, though. I wish you didn't have to watch over me like a hawk."

"I choose to do that," Kurt says with a little edge in his tone. "Because I like having you around. I like it a lot. If you need reminding that your life has value, I'll remind you."

"I don't want you to have to remind me. But okay, yeah. That's piling bad feelings over bad again, isn't it?"

He shrugs. "It's okay, babe. You don't have to be anything other than who you are."

"Where did I find you?" I ask wonderingly.

"In a bar in Vegas."

I chuckle. "That was pretty smart of me."

"It was."

He kisses my palm, and we lie in the darkness for a while. All my spinning, secret thoughts are rising to the surface, despite my attempts to banish them.

"Do you feel like you're in crisis?" Kurt asks.

"I'm not sure. I don't think so. Maybe it will be better after the trial," I whisper. "Or if we can settle this thing at mediation."

"We can hope so," Kurt says. "But that's still a ways off. If you need an emergency session with Christian, or to go back to the hospital, just say the word. I'll support you. Whatever will help. Do you think you're a danger to yourself as things stand?"

I do a mental check. "The thoughts about guns or pills or whatever still come, and they scare me. I still hear violins, but not all the time. I don't feel so much in the dumps. I get happy sometimes. I get horny sometimes. It's … better. But not back to normal. I do like my job. I wish I had more hours at it, honestly. Bronwyn and I get along great, but I'm not the only part-timer there."

"Is it the money that concerns you? That you feel you're not earning enough?"

"In part. But more that I want somethin' to do. Pass the time. Occupy my thoughts."

"Maybe we should be looking more into getting you an intimacy coordinator job. I bet you know someone who could get you an interview. You could ask your agent. Or a friend in the industry."

"That's a good idea."

"I don't mean to push you before you're ready," he adds. "Just, I think it might be something that would make you feel good. You'd be helping people."

"You're right."

He snuggles into me.

"Why do you want to be with me?" I blurt, out of nowhere. "I'm a damn mess."

Kurt pushes me onto my back and straddles my waist. "John H. Haskell, I want to be with you for more reasons than I can list, but let me try to articulate as many as I can. You're honest and caring. You love your family and dogs and horses. You're genuine and sweet and selfless. You're sexy and confident and wise. I love your funny sayings that, when I think about them, have a kernel of truth." He swallows hard. "I can keep going, but the bottom line is, I just like *you*. I like how you've opened up to me, even about the things that scare you. How you don't lie about the bad stuff, even when you want to. There's a lot about you to like, Johnny, and I hope before too long you can believe that about yourself."

"Damn."

He leans down and kisses me. "What do you like about me?"

I grin. This is the easy part. I flip us over and lie between his legs, framing his face with my hands. "Everything. I like every fucking thing about you, Kurt Arden Delmont. I like how deeply you care, not just about me, but about everything. How you're not content with the status quo, but you wanna make things better, even if you haven't figured out how. I like how damn hot you are. I like that you're artsy, and even though you're all buttoned up, you have a wild side. I appreciate how you refuse to let me self-destruct. I like that you're pushy and don't let me get away with my bullshit. How safe you are to open up to. How you keep your promises."

"Wow," he whispers. "You make me sound pretty special."

"That's because you are."

We end up kissing for a while after that. When we're both breathless, I flop down next to him, but we can't keep our fingers off each other.

Kurt whispers, "That part where you say I refuse to let you self-destruct. I *couldn't* let you—not after Andrei. But I care about you independent of that. You know that, don't you? It's not just a savior complex or something. I care about *you*."

I nod, though I'm not sure I always believe that. It's still nice to hear.

He hugs me tight. "I'm proud of you for telling your mom the hard shit. Proud of you for facing your demons. I'm proud of you, always."

"Thanks, babe. Thanks."

CHAPTER 36

Kurt

It's mid-January, and I've been busy with the campaign in advance of the primary. Practicing for the debate. Cold-calling voters. Canvassing neighborhoods. Going to fundraising dinners.

Despite all my efforts, I'm falling farther behind in the polls, which feeds the part of me that thinks I should concede. Maybe Santangelo's not that bad—and even if he is, it's up to the voters if they want to keep him. I don't need to single-handedly solve all the world's problems. I have enough to do, taking care of Johnny and myself. If I drop out of the race, I can follow up with Sam's partners about the nonprofit they started. See if that's more up my alley.

But then I'll see a news story about some state making a law that belongs in the eighteenth century, and I'll be invigorated again.

Johnny taking over in the bedroom is helping clear my mind. I love that there's one area of my life where I don't have to think. And he seems to be enjoying the dynamic. So at least both of us are winning somewhere.

* * *

I'm standing at a lectern in a Los Angeles hotel under hot spotlights. There's a small in-person audience and multiple cameras trained on the proceedings.

The Democratic field started out larger, but it's now down to just Santangelo and me. Guess everyone else was smarter than I am, knowing the incumbent will be hard to beat.

But I'm going to see this through.

"We're here today with Herb Santangelo and Kurt Delmont, contenders in this year's Senate race," the moderator says from behind his desk. "This is an opportunity for the public to get to know the candidates before the primary the first week of March. This debate will be a modified town hall style. We've selected questions from audience members, and I will relay them to the candidates. Answers will be timed, and each side has a total of thirty minutes. Shall we begin?"

I straighten my spine, trying to look more intimidating—or at least confident—than I feel. Because this isn't my thing. I like debating issues, sure, but not as a performance. I like it to be real.

This isn't going to be real at all. The layers of makeup I'm wearing tell me that.

Johnny sits off to the side, but in my sight line, wearing a western-style suit and a bolo tie, his white hat in his lap. Whispers broke out when he walked in. Now he gives me a small smile as the bright lights make sweat bead up on my hairline.

"The first question comes from Lori in Camarillo: 'What are you going to do about the traffic on the 101?'" The moderator chuckles. "Quite a Southern California question. Mr. Delmont?"

I hadn't planned on answering questions about traffic. I figured it was a given, like the weather.

"Traffic and Los Angeles have gone hand in hand for decades," I say, trying to come up with something. "The traffic engineers are working on the issue, and I trust them. But I do think that better public transit will help ease congestion and get people to where they need to go."

"Thank you," the moderator says. "Mr. Santangelo?"

"My opponent wants to take away your cars," Santangelo begins, and I seethe. Because no, I fucking don't want to take away anyone's car. But this is politics. Take what a person says and twist it to rile people up. Aim for the jugular.

I can't help it. I roll my eyes. I know I'm not supposed to react to his pettiness, but I can't let the audience think I agree with what he's saying.

I glance at Johnny, who gives me a supportive thumbs-up.

More questions are asked, and I answer them as best as I can. Santangelo takes a few potshots, including pointing out that my "adult entertainer" husband is here.

It's time for me to publicly stick up for Johnny. "My husband is well-versed in the issues affecting the citizens of this state, and he brings common-sense support to my life. I couldn't ask for a better partner."

Johnny beams, and that unreserved smile makes this entire circus worth it.

While Santangelo gets in more digs wherever he can, it feels like the audience is actually listening to me when I speak. Or maybe they're simply being polite, I don't know. At any rate, I make it through each question without needing to change my shorts, and I figure that's a win.

"What is your number one goal should you be elected—or reelected?" the moderator asks.

"I will continue my efforts on the Energy and National Resources Committee to ensure Californians have access to affordable fuel to power their vehicles. I will also work with my colleagues across the aisle to rein in the excesses of extremists within our parties," Santangelo says with a pointed look at me, and I almost roll my eyes again. Because that's just code for supporting oil companies and opposing progress on civil rights. As he blathers on, it's hard for me to believe we're in the same political party.

When it's my turn, I say, "I have a three-part plan to ensure that every American has the rights that are basic to society and won't get hit in the pocketbook." I talk briefly about ensuring basic rights, enhancing access to health care, and improving education. It's a miracle, but I manage to get out all my talking points within the allotted time.

After the moderator wraps things up, I hurry to the green room, and Johnny's there. He opens his arms and enfolds me in a hug. "Great job, darlin'. You sounded so confident, and you made a lot of points that will resonate with the voters."

"I hope so," I say.

* * *

When we get home, though, I've seen the exit polls, and I'm grumpy.

"Why the fuck don't people want to protect civil rights?" I grouse, kicking off my shoes and yanking at my tie. Lady whines from her crate, and I smile at her. "We'll let you out in a second, girl." Then I turn back to Johnny. "Why do they buy into all that traditional bullshit? It's just doublespeak for oppressing minorities and fucking over the poor."

"People do a lot of things because they're scared or sad," Johnny says. "They don't think through the issues the way you have. And we don't all value the same things. All I know is you did good up there." He sets his beat-up boots by the front door next to my shiny shoes, which sums us up perfectly.

"I should've prepared more. Wowed them. Attacked him. Made it so everyone watching knew that I was the only possible candidate. That they'd be fools to vote for anyone other than me."

Johnny pulls me to him by the waist and kisses me so deep it takes my breath away. I relax into him immediately, loving the taste of him, the warm, wet intimacy of his tongue in my mouth. "I was really proud of you, precious," he whispers when we break apart.

"Thank you. I just wish things were different. I want to make them different. *Better*." He holds me as I go back to bitching at him about American voters and the political process.

When I wind down, he grins at me, raising an eyebrow. "You done?"

I nod.

"Darlin', you need to remember that you gotta take people for who they are, not who they ought to be," my brilliant husband says, then kisses me again.

I sigh. "I know. It's hard, when I want so badly to improve things. I'm sorry I'm being a grouch to you. You don't deserve it."

"You can be a sourpuss. I can take it."

"Thanks." I want to crawl into him. He's just so comforting—this solid guy. His mental state has been fragile, but physically, he's a powerhouse. I can lean on him. "You act like I'm something special," I blurt.

"I should hope so, because you are. Don't you feel it when we're together?"

I do, but I still have lingering doubts, because I've seen how he is on camera. And I'm cranky, so my fears come spilling out. "Am I? Because it seems like you're like this with everyone." I wave my hand and huff. "You call them all darlin' or precious or baby."

Johnny shakes his head. "Darlin', yes. Baby, maybe. But you're the only person I've ever called precious."

My knees give way, and he catches me. "I am?"

"You are." He kisses me again. "Don't you realize ..." He steps back and scrubs a hand down his face. "I wish I had better words to tell you how much you've done for me."

"It's my parents' money—"

"I don't mean the money. Or rather, that's part of it, sure—and I'll pay you back—"

"I don't want you to—"

"Stop. This is getting all messed up." His eyes drill into me, intent. "What I'm saying is that you had the strength and presence of mind to save me from myself, even when you knew I'd be ornery about it."

"You weren't that ornery."

"Dammit, Kurt, let me talk. You saved me—and my mama, and maybe my baby sister, too—but that's not why you're precious to me. You're precious because of your big ol' heart. You're precious because you have this inner goodness. Because you're burrowing in here." He puts his hand over his chest. "It has nothing to do with your money or how goddamn handsome you are and all to do with who you are inside."

"Who is that?" I whisper.

"Someone incredible."

I try to let that sink in for a minute. Try to believe it the way I want him to believe he's important and worthwhile and, yes, precious. "Is there some way I can get you to stop trying to pay me back?" I ask, because talking about all the compliments he just gave me is more than I can handle. "Any way at all?"

"If there's a way you can understand how much you mean to me." He pauses. "Also, stop worrying about the election. Whether you wanna quit tonight or take it all the way, no matter what, I'll support you. If you win, good. If you don't, fine. We'll find you another meaningful job."

"Thanks." I grin at him. "Now I know what you mean about words being inadequate."

He nods and kisses me again. "Let me take Lady out for a walk. Then I'll show you how hot you were when you were advocating up on that stage."

He does as he promises, devouring me in our bed, and I love every minute.

CHAPTER 37
Johnny

The following Tuesday morning, Kurt drops me off in front of an office tower in downtown Los Angeles. He gives me a quick kiss and a "You got this" before I get out of the car. I smooth down the lapels of the new suede jacket that he bought me, which I'm wearing with a white western shirt, a bolo tie, tight black jeans, and my old boots. I feel physically comfortable, but my nerves are swarming like bees emerging angry from a hive.

I walk into the lobby to meet Noah and Danny. Today's the day this case is scheduled for mediation. But all I can think is that it's the day I have to face my fucking rapist.

Even if he never actually stuck his dick in me, he's the one who orchestrated the whole thing. It makes me sick. No matter what his legal defenses are, he's a goddamn criminal.

I dunno how much therapy I'm going to need when this lawsuit is over. Because I goddamn know the assault wasn't my fault ... yet I still blame myself for letting my guard down. For not making sure that I knew every single thing that was going to happen. For letting myself be tricked. I feel like a damn fool.

My lawyers are waiting for me, and we take the elevator up into the sky. At the top of this big, tall building, I feel removed from the real world.

I need my husband. My dog. I need to get out of here. I need ...

"We won't do a joint session," Noah says as we step out of the elevator and into the foyer of the mediation company, or whatever it's called. "You likely won't see Gary at all. We'll be in separate rooms."

I cough. I'm glad. Relieved. I never want to see his evil face again. But at the same time, it seems, I don't know. Like I'm taking a shortcut. Like I should face the one I'm accusing and look him in the eye.

But I doubt that would do any good. He's rotten to the core. Me telling him what I think of him isn't going to change a damn thing. The only way we could ever hurt him is in his pocketbook.

That's if he hasn't hidden his money so it's impossible to get to anyhow.

"I don't wanna talk to him," I say, feeling like a coward.

Noah seems to read the look on my face and gives me a reassuring nod. "That's fine. It's standard for you not to see the other side, because they know it will just drive you farther and farther apart."

That makes me feel sorta better, but this whole thing is shit, because he's never going to admit what he did.

We go into a conference room and wait. And wait. And wait. Eventually the mediator comes in.

"Mr. Pinkerton is offering to settle for $15,000."

I stand up. "Let's go. This is a waste of time."

Noah makes a "sit down" motion. "There's a thing in mediation called the 'insult-outrage round.' That's where we're insulted they offered so little, and they're outraged we're demanding so much."

"We haven't demanded too much," I grumble. "If this goes to trial, I'll be wanting a lot more. I'm willing to take a discount just to get this over with."

"Suffice it to say," Danny says to the mediator, "the offer is declined."

The mediator takes this in stride. "Do you have a counter?"

We'd discussed this ahead of time, and Danny tells him our counter is $350,000. The mediator nods. "Honestly, that's a reasonable number," he says, "given what I understand about this case." He smiles. "I'll see what I can do."

For the next hour and a half, Noah, Danny, and I stare out the window. Talk with each other. Order lunch.

"Why's it takin' so long?" I ask.

"The mediator could be laying into him. Telling him the weak parts of his case. Trying to get him to see our point of view," Danny says.

"Yeah, I can see that happening ... never," I mutter.

"The mediator's probably trying to get him to offer something that isn't an insult. Let him take his time," Noah advises. "From what I know about Gary, it'll take some convincing to get him to offer more than a token amount."

Finally, the mediator returns. After explaining the other side's position and their defenses—namely all the shit I already know, like how I'm a porn star and getting fucked is part of the job, although he doesn't say it that crassly—he gets to the point. "Mr. Pinkerton is offering $69,000."

I stare, my jaw dropping. "Does he think that's funny?"

The mediator purses his lips. "To tell you the truth, I don't think he's taking this case seriously enough, so yes, I think the number is him being ... a smart aleck."

Danny looks pissed. "More like a jackass." He tells the mediator, "Let us talk with our client," and the mediator leaves.

Noah looks at me. "How are you doing?"

"Not that well. What do you think about that number?" I ask.

"I think it's a lot of money, but it's nowhere near what your case is worth," Noah says. "The mediator's right that our initial request was reasonable. Your case is worth more than $350k. Ask people if they'd take $69,000 to be gang-raped and drugged and lose their livelihood. Given your former earnings, how you haven't had work in months, how you don't have prospects of future work—it's pennies on the dollar. Plus, you've had to go through the drama and expense of a lawsuit. But it's your call, because $69k is still a significant chunk of change. The risk is that you lose at trial or the jury awards you less than that, and then you'd be kicking yourself for not taking the offer."

"Fuck," I say, scrubbing my face. "I don't like this. I don't like having to decide." Because it is a lot of money. I haven't been able to send my mama hardly anything in months, and this would help with that.

But it also seems like I'd be selling myself cheap.

I'm at war with myself. I don't like the idea of being a greedy plaintiff seeking millions, but I was really, really fucking hurt—physically, financially, psychologically—and no amount of money would ever be able to make up for that.

Also, if I settle, no one will know. That's one of the reasons why these settlements exist—to avoid a public trial where everyone is going to parade their dirtiest laundry out in front of the world.

That's what I deserve. For everyone to see what a loser I am.

I'm tempted to settle. To take what they're offering, even though I think it's insulting. To get rid of some debts, move on with my life, pay my lawyers, and have some closure.

But then it'll feel like Gary got off without any serious consequences.

I want fucking consequences.

So I call Kurt.

"Babe, I don't know what to do." I summarize the negotiations. "It's not what I wanted, but it's still a lot of money."

"It is and it isn't," he says. "It's a little bit like my election. Sometimes you have to go in and fight the fight to be able to live with yourself. Even if it means you get a reputation you didn't entirely want or deserve."

"You're right about that. As a porn star, I already had a certain notoriety, but the one who goes to trial over the wrong kind of sex on screen? That's when I become ..."

"A legend?" Kurt supplies.

"Or the least smart porn star who ever walked the earth. One with nothin' under his hat but hair. Lord, what if the jury sees me as a body to be used and decides that what I agreed to doesn't matter?"

"Then you need to educate them about boundaries and consent. So much of this stuff is education. Once people become more aware of how there are others who may not necessarily behave like them or think like them, but they're still human beings worthy of respect, the world becomes a much more accepting place."

"Hmm." I think about it, and Kurt stays quiet. Finally, I say, "I think I ain't gonna settle. I didn't go this far down this path to be quiet about what he did. If they'd offered me enough that I felt like I was being compensated for the actual harm he caused—to my career, to my body, to my psyche—that would be different. And I feel like such a tool, because I know $69k is a lot of money. But looking at my career and what I need to help my mama, it's barely enough to get by on, and it's nowhere near what I'd've made over the next however much longer that I worked. I know, as things turned out with you and all, you're glad I'm not filming anymore, but that wasn't my original plan. Porn stars don't get pensions, so I was gonna work as long as I could."

"I support you, babe," Kurt says without hesitation. "You have to do what's right in your heart, and if that's not enough for you to settle, then you need to say no. There are nonfinancial alternatives, I suppose. You could see if they'd do something like a written apology or a video saying that what they did was wrong. But it doesn't sound like this guy wants to admit anything."

"Exactly," I say. "That'd make me feel better, but when we've suggested things like that in the past, they've been nonstarters. I'll bring it up again and see if they go for it. But otherwise, we're walking out."

"That's fine, babe. That's why we have the court system. When someone hurts another, it's one way to get redress."

Sure enough, the apology idea doesn't go anywhere. That means we're going to trial, and all my horrible experiences will be out there in public for the entire world to comment on.

I feel sick thinking about it, but I know I had to make the decision that would help me sleep at night. And I couldn't sleep if I let Gary Pinkerton get away with thinking he can fuck over porn stars —figuratively and literally—for his own gain.

Kurt picks me up in the same spot where he dropped me off and gives me the best hug he can from behind the wheel. "I'm sorry they weren't more reasonable," he says.

The violins wail in my head. "Yeah. Thanks."

"Do you have time to go for a short drive? I want to show you something."

I shrug. "Sure."

He drives me to a part of South LA I've never been to. It isn't the nicest. He pulls over beside a row of old houses with graffiti on the walls and bars on the windows and gets out of the car.

"This is where we lived when I was little," he says. We're standing on a street littered with broken glass. The small houses have overgrown front yards with sunburned grass. The air smells of weed and exhaust.

"But your family's rich."

"Like I told you, my parents got lucky with some investments when I was a kid. But they didn't come from money. They came from … this."

I look around.

"With you growing up on the ranch, I think you might have had it easier than I did," Kurt says. "At least until Amazon took off and my parents were able to cash out some." He takes my hand. "I have a condo with a view and a nice car and everything else because of their investments. When they got lucky, I suppose they could've given all the money away. And they do give to charity—that's always been important to them. But it made their lives—and mine—better to keep some of that bounty and use it for our own comfort."

"You're saying that I ain't accepting help," I say.

"You are and you aren't. I think you're getting better at it. But I also think you have trouble internalizing that it's okay to have some good things for yourself."

"Like you?"

"Like us, together." He squeezes my hand and gives me a sweet smile. "So ... does this help you understand that I really think of money as mostly a matter of luck? I mean, sure, people should do something productive with their lives if they can—and you do. But if what you do from here on out is never as lucrative as your old career, that isn't going to make me think you're any less successful. And since I have plenty for both of us, can you maybe stop trying to pay me back for everything? My parents hit it big, and our lives changed. But that doesn't make me any different from you."

I think about his words as hard as I can for a minute, then nod. "Yeah. I can try."

He kisses me. "Good. Then let's get out of here."

When we get home, I fall into Kurt's arms, needing comfort but not wanting to admit it. This lawyer crap is hard, but going through the ups and downs of a lawsuit alone was so many times worse.

Lady sleeps at our feet, as usual, and I'm grateful to have her there. I need all the help I can get.

CHAPTER 38
Kurt

Since his failed mediation, Johnny's been working with his lawyers to prepare for trial and throwing himself into his work out at the ranch. I think spending more time with the animals helps keep him from worrying about whether he should have settled this thing ... or dwelling on how, soon, he's going to have to get up and tell his story to a group of strangers.

As for me, I'm still trying to make up ground in time for the primary. I've been to every Optimist Club, Soroptimist Club, Rotary Club, Toastmasters, and Kiwanis Club meeting in the areas Paige and Johnny identified as targets. I've spent endless hours on the phone, asking for money and votes. I've extended my leave of absence from work, because there's no way I can do all this *and* my regular job.

But every night, Johnny and I are together, and most nights he's ordering me around exactly as I want him to. Some mornings, when he's left early to go take care of the horses, I bring up the video he shot of him slow fucking me and watch it on my phone, because it's the hottest thing I've ever seen. He'd sent it to me when I asked, then deleted his copy. I usually don't let myself come while watching it, because it's more fun to edge and edge and edge.

I'd rather Johnny be the one to take me over the cliff. Now that I have him in my life, I want him more and more.

Watching the video makes me feel like he's here even when he isn't. When I mention this to him over dinner, he grins. "Good boy. Get yourself hard for me. I'll do it again any time you like, you know."

"It's more than that," I admit, passing him some coffee. "I've always wanted to film myself. Not just the impromptu sort of thing we did before, but a full video, complete with the perfunctory script and everything."

"Now, darlin'," Johnny says slowly. "Not to be too critical, but I think that's the worst idea I've ever heard. You're running for office, and your mama's the lieutenant governor. Making a sex tape with a porn star ain't a good idea."

"I know you're right ... but I still think it would be hot," I insist. I drop my eyes. "It's not like I don't have one with you already. There's no reason it should get out—it would be just for us. I won't share it or upload it anywhere."

Johnny reaches across the table and lifts up my chin with his fingers, studying my face. "This matters to you, doesn't it?"

I nod.

"Then let's make it happen, darlin'. We'll put passwords on it or we'll leave it on the camera. But if we can bring your fantasy to life, let's do it."

"I'll feel bad about it," I tell him.

His shoulders stiffen. "Then, never mind."

"No," I say quickly. "That—that's what I want. I want the feeling that I'm doing something I shouldn't. Like I'm gonna get caught." I inhale sharply. Because just thinking about it makes me shiver.

He sees, and his eyes heat up. "Then be ready. We'll do it soon."

"Sounds good." I grin. "Sounds better than good."

He tilts his head. "So, apart from your fantasy life—which, by the way, I highly approve of—how have you been doing, precious? We haven't seen as much of each other lately, outside of nighttime."

"I'm okay. It's just ... a lot. I mean, I'm not complaining. I know you're dealing with a bunch of hard stuff, and I don't—"

"Hard stuff isn't something we need to compete over," he says. "My shit doesn't make yours any easier to deal with. You're worn out. You've been going a million miles a minute since before I met you—that has to be exhausting." He thinks for a second, then says, "Come with me to work tomorrow."

"Not sure that's going to make my schedule any easier."

"I get that, but you gotta find time to relax somehow. What if you come toward the end of the day? I want to show you the horses. Want to go riding?"

I smile. "I do." I love seeing Johnny in his element. He was beautiful riding on the beach that day. I bet it'll be even better with horses he's gotten to know.

But I have something to do first. Something I didn't want to rush into ... but it's time to get the ball rolling.

* * *

Charlie Cooper, Sam's coworker, is prickly when I call him the next morning after Johnny leaves. But when I explain who I am and why I want to meet, he and his boyfriend Rowan agree to meet me at a bench over by the beach, where no one can hear our conversation.

I get there first and sit, feeling out of sorts. I'm looking forward to seeing Johnny later, but this meeting has me on edge. Two men walk up a few minutes later. The tall one, who must be Charlie, is breathtakingly handsome, with dark hair and dark eyes. He doesn't quite have a sneer, more an RBF. It doesn't detract from how good-looking he is.

He's holding the hand of a tiny man with short, bright pink

hair and tattoos everywhere—Rowan, based on Sam's description. Rowan's clearly rich (or has a sugar daddy), since he's wearing Cartier love rings on every finger and designer everything. His smile seems a little ... what did Sam say? Feral.

I stand and shake their hands. "Hi, I'm Kurt. You're Charlie? And Rowan?"

"That is correct," Charlie says, taking a seat next to mine. Rowan perches on his lap, and Charlie anchors him by the waist. I almost laugh. Rowan's clearly got Charlie wrapped around his bejeweled pinky.

"Charlie said you need some ... assistance." Rowan smirks.

"Yeah." I sigh. "I don't know where to start. My boyfriend—or rather, husband. It's a little confusing."

"Sounds like my brother Cam," Charlie says.

I nod. "I heard about that. Yeah, kind of the same thing. Well, I'm married to Velvet the Cowboy."

Rowan's eyes nearly do a full cartoon pop. "Holy fuck, he's the hottest."

Charlie glares at him. "Thought that was me."

"It is you. But I can still have porn."

"Maybe," Charlie says with an edge.

I watch them, distracted and amused by their dynamic, then turn my mind back to the sickening reason I'm here. "The short story is, a porn director orchestrated an assault ..." I feel like I'm violating Johnny's privacy by telling his story, but I need them to understand. And it's all going to come out at the trial, anyway. "He drugged Johnny and had him gang-raped. I want vengeance."

"Say no more," Rowan says, pulling a switchblade from his skintight sea green jeans. "I'm in."

Charlie looks up at the sky. "You had to bring up violence."

Wringing my hands, I look at them. "I'll pay you whatever you want. I just need him dealt with. Not yet—there's a civil trial coming up, and I don't want to do anything that could rebound on that. But after." I shiver. "I'm not a murderer. Don't kill him.

Or try not to. I'm not going to lose too much sleep if there's an accident. But I want to make sure he won't rape another person, *ever*."

"It will be my pleasure," Rowan says. "No money required. This will be fun."

I've never done anything like this before, but Johnny deserves more retribution than the justice system is going to provide. And so do I, if I'm honest. No one fucks with what's mine. Even if he wasn't mine back then, he's mine now.

* * *

In the evening, I drive to Hidden Valley and the expansive ranch where Johnny's working.

When I get out of my car, he saunters over to me, Lady at his heels.

I nearly swoon at the sight.

He's truly a cowboy. Long legged, with tanned skin and a cowboy hat. He looks like he was born in those boots. And then there's his handsome face.

I melt.

This man is so special. Not Velvet the Cowboy, no matter how much I enjoyed watching him on my screen. But Johnny, the outdoorsman who truly cares for animals. Who has ties to a long tradition of working with them. Who takes equally good care of me.

I go up on my toes, and he leans down to kiss me, and I get lost in his pale eyes.

"C'mon. Let me introduce you to this side of the family," he says with a grin.

Holding hands, we walk into the stable, where there are horses in most of the divided areas. This is super fancy. It even smells nice. Everything is shiny and gleams. The horses look exceptionally healthy.

"What kind of horses are these?" I ask.

"They're American Quarter Horses."

"They're beautiful," I say, admiring their chestnut brown coats and glossy manes.

"Ready to go for a ride?"

"Sure. Do you have one that's good for me?"

"Sure do. Come meet her."

Johnny stands beside the horse he's chosen for me—Lucy—as I swing into the saddle and look at the world from this taller perspective.

After securing Lady in the barn, Johnny mounts his horse with ease and clicks with his tongue, and we head off. He leads us out of the arena to the fenced pastures of this property. There are huge old oaks, along with sycamores and some other trees I can't identify. We're nestled in a peaceful valley, and all I can think is how at home Johnny seems here.

I make a mental note to check out real estate in this area. I know he objected to the cost, but this is where he belongs—somewhere with horses and dogs.

I'm going to get him everything he wants and needs, whether he realizes it or not.

"What's your horse's name?" I ask.

"Sadie. She's a sweetheart. Well, most of 'em are."

I watch my husband, in his tight Wrangler jeans and white cowboy hat, expertly maneuver his horse next to mine. While I feel comfortable enough on horseback, he's one with them. Like he thinks, and the horse moves the way he wants them to.

As we ride, my phone buzzes in my pocket, and I feel secure enough in the saddle to pull it out and check it. There's a link from Paige. It's a news story: "Lieutenant governor takes leave of absence to donate kidney."

I smile and put the phone away, riding with Johnny in the afternoon sunshine.

CHAPTER 39
Kurt

The primary's in two days, and I'm looking at projections and data from mail-in ballots, and I don't have a snowball's chance of winning.

"I should concede," I tell Johnny. "I have to. I've been thinking about it, and I should."

I'm a failure. I'm an impostor. I'm never going to help people. I've got no life's work. All I'm ever gonna do is design junk mail.

"Why do you wanna quit now?" Johnny asks. "It's so close to the election."

"Because I'm not going to win, and this is stressing me out, and it's not actually what I want to do."

"I dunno 'bout the first one," he says. "But I don't like to see you stressed, and I definitely don't want you doing something you don't want to do. I'll support you, whatever you decide."

"I'm annoyed. Why isn't this easier?" I huff.

He grabs me and pulls me to him so my face is pressed against his hard collarbone and his big biceps hold me tight. "Because you're doing hard shit. If it were easy, everyone'd be doing it. They aren't. But that don't mean you have to."

"I'm trailing by twenty points. I'm not going to get elected without a miracle."

He leans back and puts a finger under my chin, his face full of concern. "Did I do this? Keep you from being elected? How much of this has been 'Don't vote for Kurt, because he's fucking a porn star'?"

I don't want to lie to him. "Some of it. But fuck them. Fuck everyone who doesn't want to accept you."

"I dunno," he says. "You don't have to force your preferences down people's throats, either."

"Why do they think I'm doing that by just existing? For fuck's sake, I want to *help* people!"

"Maybe they don't trust your judgment."

"Ugh! I'm sure they don't trust my judgment, but I know what I'm talking about when it comes to public policy. Don't do bad shit that hurts people. It's pretty simple, really."

"I know, precious. I'm sorry. And I'm sorry if I made you lose the election."

"Don't be," I say fiercely. "I'd never trade these past few months with you. I'm just fucking disappointed that the world isn't the way I want it to be."

"That makes two of us," he says.

"Look." I blow out a breath. "I'm venting. I'm sorry for taking my frustration out on you. I can't change the world, even though I want to. I wish your former profession didn't matter to people, but it does. But that doesn't change how I feel about you."

Johnny nods. "I think, at this point, you might as well get through the election. See what happens. If you don't get elected, you concede like a gentleman and then go back to your graphic design job or go work for Weston & Ramirez House. Sound like a plan?"

I shrug. "Yeah, I guess."

"Or you could just do your own art."

I stare at him. "I forgot about that."

He smiles at me and kisses me. "I didn't. Why don't we go for a walk? Get some fresh air."

"Yeah. That sounds good."

We put a leash on Lady and walk her along the beach. I don't feel better, exactly. But I feel heard, and in some ways, that's the same thing.

Two days later, on election night, I'm at a nearby hotel holding a press conference attended by a dozen or so reporters, plus Johnny, Sam, a few other friends, Paige, and some volunteers. My statement is brief: "I congratulate Herb Santangelo on his win tonight and look forward to voting for him in November. I want to thank everyone who voted for me and who supported me in this election. I'm now looking forward to having time to focus on other interests, including campaigning for my mother, Melissa Delmont, as she runs for president. And enjoying my marriage with John Haskell. I'm lucky to have him at my side every day. He's the best person I've ever met."

There's silence at first, which morphs into applause.

More important, I feel like applauding.

In a way, it's a relief that I lost. I talked myself into going into politics, but I never really had the drive to be a politician. I just felt like I had to do something meaningful with my life.

I might be able to give back more, though, in a different way.

And I'm fucking proud to have claimed Johnny publicly. I married a porn star. So what? I adore him.

Sam comes up to me when I step down from the podium. "Noah and August want to offer you the policy director job for Weston & Ramirez House. The salary is low, but they'll add you to the office health insurance, and you get great benefits. Are you in? Do you need to do it part time, because of your day job?"

"I'll quit," I say without hesitation. "I'd love to be involved."

I've been getting out of bed for the election, and then to help Johnny.

But now I'm truly looking forward to a new challenge and the next phase in my life.

* * *

A few days later, Johnny and I get a video call we've been not-so-patiently waiting for.

"Okay, they're here!" May Ella whispers, her face in the camera as she walks to the front door of the house in Fresno and opens it. On the stoop are my momther and dad, smiling. "Hi! Come on in! So nice to meet you. Mama and I are so happy y'all took the time to come by."

"It's a pleasure to meet you, May, as well," Momther says.

"Kurt and Johnny are here," May says, holding up the phone.

"We didn't want to miss this," I explain.

"Wonderful," Momther says. She follows May Ella into the living room where Sue Ann stands.

The camera gets shaky, but the look on Sue Ann's face is one I'll never forget—a softness combined with an irrepressible smile. Her eyes well with tears, and she holds out her hands. "So you're Melissa."

Momther walks right over and hugs her so tight Sue Ann lets out a little gasp. "You're going to get better," Momther—err Mom —says. "You have a lot of living to do."

May bursts into tears, and even Dad seems to be rubbing at his eyes.

"Thank you," Sue Ann says. "You have no idea how much I will be in your debt."

"No debt," my mom says. "Family takes care of each other."

"Would anyone like some iced tea?" May Ella asks, and they settle in to make plans for the surgery. After a bit, Johnny and I sign off.

I kiss him. "That went well."

He whistles. "It's amazing."

* * *

A few weeks later, I'm sitting in the Santa Monica Courthouse with Johnny as the lawyers ask questions of potential jurors. All of us are dressed up in suits, Johnny included. Danny and August look stylish and competent, but there's tension at the edges of their eyes. The stress of prepping for trial is surely getting to them.

I know it's gotten to Johnny. I wish I could do more to help him. He's been waking up with nightmares again, and I don't know if it's from remembering the event or from anticipating the trial. There's just so much uncertainty.

"No matter what happens," I whispered to him last night, "you're getting a chance to tell your truth. It's important that you do this."

"I guess," he said, sounding unconvinced.

"No, it is," I insisted. "And you know it."

It takes an inordinately long time to pick a jury, and when the judge announces a short break, Johnny murmurs, "I don't think I'm imagining the amount of weird looks and open hostility I'm getting."

Unfortunately, I think he's right. "I don't think they like Gary much, either, so at least that's a plus," I say.

"Hmm. Could be."

Gary Pinkerton can't seem to keep his mouth shut, no matter how many times his lawyers shush him. If I want to strangle him, I can't imagine what Johnny wants to do to him.

"Either way, this is going to be hard on them. We're taking them away from their lives so that they can decide your case."

"Now I feel even worse."

"No," I say. "This is how our society works. Jury service isn't fun, but it's an important civic duty."

"I s'pose."

The day gets worse, though, when we hear each side's opening statement describing the case and what the jury is going to hear.

Listening to Danny outline what happened to Johnny is awful. It's even worse when the defense gets up and lays into Johnny, portraying him as a greedy porn star who complains about having to do his job.

Regardless, at the end of the day, I gather Johnny up in a hug. "You're doing the right thing. You've got this."

I'm worried about him, though. This is going to be a rough ride.

A little while after we arrive home, there's a knock on the door, and I accept a fragrant bag stamped with the name of Johnny's favorite barbecue place.

"I thought you'd want some comfort food after being in court all day," I say, after the delivery guy leaves.

Johnny looks like he wants to cry. Instead, he grabs me, holding me tight. "Thank you. That's mighty thoughtful of you."

* * *

Around two in the morning, Johnny starts thrashing and screaming like he did the first night here.

I don't want to touch him until he wakes up and knows where he is, so I turn on the bedside lamp and gently call his name.

"The system. It's letting me down," he whispers, holding me tight.

"The only way out is through," I whisper back.

"I have all these fucking thoughts," he says. "Like I want to go find the gun."

Panic hits me hard, even though I know the gun is safely locked up. "Thank you for telling me, but I'm not going to let you do that. Can you please promise me you'll stay alive for the next twenty-four hours?"

"Yeah, precious. I promise."

"Do we need to stop the trial and send you to the hospital?"

"No," he whispers.

"Would you tell me if the answer was yes?"

Johnny pauses, then says, "Yeah. I would."

"Thank you. I'm proud of you. And I'm so proud of you for going through with this trial. I'll be with you every step of the way."

* * *

The next day, Friday, it's his turn to testify, and whenever his lawyers aren't asking him questions, his eyes are on me. It takes a long time for him to get through the story, with a lot of objections from the other side. But eventually it's done.

When the defense cross-examines him, Johnny's forced to describe his other sexual experience where he was on the bottom—it's been fifteen years, he says. Pinkerton Studios' trial lawyers treat him like he's lying about everything, and every question is delivered with attitude. I guess Johnny's attorneys got the judge to throw out some of Pinkerton's defenses and an entire bullshit lawsuit they brought against Johnny, but even with the defense attorneys reined in, it's still painful to watch.

I sit in the audience and watch, trying to send him strength through the power of my mind. I wish I could leave, because hearing him describe how he felt when he was helpless breaks my heart. But I would never abandon him like that.

Next they play the tape.

"I know it's rough," Danny said to us when we discussed this before the trial. "But it's direct evidence of what was done to Johnny. I think it's what will persuade the jury. If you really don't want us to show it, we won't, but I think you'll have a better chance of winning the case with it. Without it, you're more likely to lose, I'm sorry to say. The choice is yours."

Johnny said yes.

The court closed the courtroom to the public, given the sensitive nature of the video, but as the plaintiff's husband, I was allowed to stay.

Seeing the recording is so much worse than hearing Johnny talk about it. He didn't repeat all the horrible things the men said while they violated him. He didn't say how much blood was running down his legs. He didn't talk about the extent of his humiliation.

I'm so frozen with horror that I only realize I'm crying when tears drip down my neck and wet the collar of my dress shirt.

If Johnny was feeling suicidal last night, I can't imagine how desperate he is now.

I'm not letting him out of my sight.

CHAPTER 40
Johnny

As soon as the video ends, I bolt from the court and throw up in the nearest bathroom.

Kurt follows behind me and pats my back as I retch. He brings me wet paper towels to wipe my face. He finds a bottle of water to rinse my mouth and holds me as I shake, not letting me go.

But my brain is going haywire.

I'm no good for him. I've gotta save him from me. He shouldn't be stuck with some worthless piece of meat—someone who couldn't defend himself. Someone weak. Someone who could be violated like that. Someone so fucking stupid.

Distantly, something tells me I'm thinking shit I shouldn't, but I can't stop myself. My thoughts are spiraling down the drain, and they just keep coming and coming, and I want to hit my head against the wall to get them to stop.

Loser.

Victim.

Weak.

Couldn't save my mama. Had to have other people do it for me.

The violins have been quieter for months, but they're *screeching* now.

He lost the election because of you.
You have no money.
You owe him everything.

And it's only going to get worse. Gary Pinkerton is testifying on Tuesday, when the trial starts up again. I don't know that I'm going to be able to handle that lowlife spewing his lies about me.

Though maybe they're not lies. Maybe I deserved all of it. Maybe I asked for it when I said yes to that first producer back when I was eighteen.

Kurt murmurs quiet words, but I barely hear him.

He drives us home. I don't remember the ride.

He makes dinner, but I don't eat. He doesn't even let me go to the bathroom alone.

He holds me all Friday night. We don't talk much. There's nothing to say.

On Saturday, we stay in bed most of the morning, only going outside in sweats to walk Lady around the neighborhood.

"Are you still spiraling?" Kurt asks.

I don't say anything. Eventually, I nod.

"Do you want to go to the hospital?"

I shake my head. Because what are they gonna do? They can't fix this. "Just stay with me," I whisper.

"I'm not letting you out of my sight," he says fervently.

I wish I could feel the squeeze in my heart his words usually give me.

Right now, though, I'm worse than numb.

I'm negative. I'm nothing. I'm radio static. I don't exist.

On Sunday, we lounge around watching television. I'm not even sure what show Kurt put on. We take Lady for a walk, and her velvet ears do get to me a little. As does her sweet puppy scent. When we get back, Kurt says, "Are you gonna be okay if I take a shower? Or do you want to come in with me?"

While I wanna tell him I'll be okay, I know that's not true, so I get in the shower with him. He washes me carefully, his hands caressing me everywhere. And while it feels good, it doesn't stop the intrusive thoughts running around my head.

I can't stand this.
I don't want to be here anymore. I can't do this.
I want to rip out my hair.
I want to be gone.

I take a deep breath.

"It's fucking hard, Kurt. Things had been getting better, the thoughts were quieter, but now they're shouting."

He nods, his eyes soft and sad. He kisses me, and I kind of kiss him back. His presence is keeping me from fully drowning.

We get out of the shower, dry off, and get dressed and return to the couch. Kurt's mom calls, and he answers, checking in with how she's feeling post-surgery.

While he talks with her, I go into the kitchen.

The keys have to be around here somewhere. Kurt said not to go looking for them, but he didn't say that they'd be particularly hard to find.

I start opening drawers like I'm looking for a spatula or something, but I don't find any keys.

Then I remember the day we first got here. When he came back from hiding my gun, he'd been going up and down the stairs.

I grab the BMW key and go out to the garage while Kurt's got his back to me, listening to his mom. I beep the locks open and open up the console in the middle, but there's nothing in there except a few quarters and some lip balm. I look in the glove compartment and take out the manual and Kurt's sunglasses. Nothing. Then I check the pockets behind the seats. And there I find a set of small keys.

My heart is pounding. Hands shaking, I hastily put everything back to rights.

Kurt has a few locking cabinets—all shiny gray lacquer—but it only takes two attempts before I get a key to work in one. I open it, but it's full of paperwork. I lock it back up and try the next.

Pay dirt. Inside is not only my derringer, but everything else Kurt has deemed dangerous: razors, a Swiss Army knife, medications. My note to Mama.

Still trembling, I pull the gun from its holster and check the ammunition. It's loaded.

Kurt didn't take out the bullets. Maybe he didn't know how.

Then I slide my ass down to the floor, staring at the gun, feeling its weight in my hands.

I hold it to my temple. The metal is cool against my skin.

They say your life flashes in front of your eyes when you're about to die, but all I see is Kurt's face.

He cares about me enough to lock up all this shit that I could use to hurt myself.

He took me to see my mama and May Ella. He got my mama the surgery she needed and May Ella a chance at a job doing the thing she was born to do.

He got me a job working with horses. He got me the sweetest dog in the world.

He's paid for all my care.

He stood by me through losing the election and never blamed me.

He claimed me, sounding proud and happy.

He watches me without complaint when I'm sad, when I can't give him back anything at all.

He's let me be myself—all the parts of me, even the ugly ones that I don't want to show anyone else.

I gently place the gun down by my hip. Then I put my face in my hands and start sobbing. Ugly sobbing. Chest heaving, inhuman noises coming out of my mouth.

I'd thought I'd been low before, but this is it. A time when even though I have everything—love, because yes, I damn well love Kurt, and despite all the reasons he shouldn't, he seems to love me;

a mother on the way to good health; a safe place to live; a good job—I still can't function.

"Fuck, damn," I hiss. I try to wipe away the tears, but they just keep coming, and I curl up next to the wall. I manage to pull out my phone, because I promised Kurt I'd call him if I was like this. Before I can place a call, though, the door from the house opens, and Kurt races in.

I go stock-still, like he's ensnared me in the net of his panicked gaze. I'm caught and unable to move.

He flies over to me. "Johnny! What's wrong? What are you doing? Are you hurt?" He shoves the gun away with his foot, metal scraping along the floor, and pulls me to him.

I put my head on his shoulder and sob.

"Hey," he says huskily. "Hey, it's okay. I'm here with you. We'll fix it. You can make it through. I'll do whatever you need. We can solve it together."

"I'm in love with you," I blurt. "I goddamn love you."

Kurt stills, his arms around me. Then he squeezes me tighter. "I'm in love with you, too. I love you so much."

"I'm sorry I'm such a damn mess."

"You can be a mess with me," he whispers. "I can take it. The only thing I couldn't take is you not being here."

He leans back, and I kiss him. It's a messy kiss—snotty, full of tears, with zero finesse. But it's the best kiss of my life.

I love him.

And I know I'm strong.

I've faced my demons, and they keep coming back. But I can fight this fight.

Kurt has tears in his eyes, too. "Were you sitting here with the gun, thinking about aiming it at yourself?"

"I did," I whisper.

His face falls. "Oh, babe. No. No, then ... we need to get you some more help."

I sniffle. "Sure, yeah. Okay. But I realized something."

"What's that?" He looks so stricken I wanna kick my own ass.

"I don't actually want to kill myself. I'm in so much pain, and I'm desperate for help—but you help me. And I fucking wanna—I wanna be with you. I don't want to leave you."

"I want to be with you, too. No matter what." He huffs a laugh. "We got married, and I have no idea what our vows were. But aren't wedding vows usually like, 'I will be with you in sickness and in health, for richer and poorer,' all that?"

"Yeah."

"Well, call this the sickness part. Or maybe the worse part of 'for better and for worse.' But no matter what, I'm staying with you. For as long as you'll have me, I'm yours. I'm so in love with you, Johnny, you have no idea. I couldn't fall in love with the man I saw on my screen—he wasn't real—but I have fallen in love with *you*. Messy you, who calls me precious and who treats me like I'm exactly that. Who enforces honesty even when you don't want to. Even when it's so painful to do."

I blink at him. "I dunno what to say."

"You don't have to say anything. I think this is the pressures of the trial and the election and all kinds of shit piling on top of each other. It's not surprising that you're feeling really bad right now. But, babe, you know that mental health isn't just magically fixed. You're going to have days like this."

Looking over at the gun, I mutter, "I hope not. This hurts too much."

"If we need to check you back into the hospital, then that's what we do. It's okay. You're going to be okay, and all you have to do right now is decide to stay alive for the rest of today. Can you do that?"

"I can," I say.

"Fuck, you scared me," Kurt says. "I thought this was going to be Andrei again. Except worse, because I'm utterly in love with you."

My stomach clenches. There's no way on the green earth of the

Lord that I wanted to make Kurt feel bad. I was only thinking about myself. "I'm so sorry."

He lifts up my chin. "Do *not* feel guilty."

"Of course I feel guilty. I never want to hurt you."

"Then ... let's go talk to Christian again."

I smile at him. A creaky smile, but a smile nonetheless. "I think that's a wise idea."

"Do you think you're ready to get out of the garage? The floor is cold, and Lady's probably worried about us."

"Yeah." I stare at the gun. "Can you put that away somewhere?"

"Of course." He sighs. "I don't know where to hide the keys, though. That was my best hiding spot."

"It wasn't very good. It didn't take me long to find it. I guess 'out of sight, out of mind' is what we'll have to do for now."

"Okay. Wait for me just outside the door," he orders.

I raise an eyebrow. "You the dom now, darlin'?"

"Never."

I kiss him. "I'll wait."

He meets me in the hallway after a minute, and we go up the stairs to the living room. "This is the scariest fucking day of my life," he says. "I'm making an appointment with Christian for first thing tomorrow morning."

"I'm sorry," I say again.

"It's your mental illness. People don't understand how much that can take over. But I do. I have infinite patience for you, okay, babe? We can get through this. Would it help to tell me what was going through your brain? Or would you rather be distracted?"

"Both, I think," I say.

"Then tell me, and after that you can have your pick of distractions. Your choices are a mindless movie, playing with your puppy, or fucking me into the mattress."

"I'll take D, all of the above," I say.

And, while I'm still feeling raw and out of sorts, I slowly start to unclench. I tell him what went wrong in my head. We walk Lady. We watch *Must Love Dogs*.

By the time Kurt's naked and writhing under me, I feel ... not normal. But like I can live for another day.

And that's all I have to do.

CHAPTER 41
Kurt

First thing the next morning, I'm sitting with Johnny in Christian's office as he tells her about the past few days. Thankfully, she agreed to see us before her scheduled sessions for the day, and court isn't starting up again until tomorrow.

Christian looks concerned as Johnny speaks, but she listens quietly.

"I just can't get these damn thoughts out of my head," Johnny is saying. "When it hurts so much, I just wanna ... make it stop. Turn off the light switch and let everything go black. It's overwhelming. I'd thought those feelings had gone, because of the meds or the therapy or ... I don't know. I just thought I was done with them. But I'm not, and I'm ... I'm fucking pissed that my brain still does that." He sniffs. "I feel like a little kid saying this, but it ain't fair. I don't want those thoughts. I wanna feel better."

She nods. "It's hard when we think we have to police all of our thoughts. But that's just not possible."

Johnny looks at her, utter devastation on his face. "It's not? You mean I have to be like this for the rest of my life?"

"No, I don't mean that. The thoughts should lessen. We

should evaluate your medication and also see if you'd benefit from other therapies like meditation or journaling."

"At this stage, I'll try anything," Johnny says. "Anything to stop these thoughts, because when they come, they come. And I don't wanna hurt Kurt. Or myself."

Christian nods. "To be fair, you were triggered by reliving an extremely traumatic event in a very public manner. Give yourself some credit for living through both—the event itself, and then the vivid memories viewing the video brought back."

"You really have gone through more than you should be expected to," I say, reaching out to hold his hand. His skin is cooler than usual, but his grip is as tight as ever. He's developed new calluses from working at the ranch, and I love the strength they represent.

"Pay attention to what you can control and what you can't," Christian says. "You can't control your past, and to a great extent, you can't control your thoughts. But you can become aware of them, and you can notice when you're having intrusive ones."

"Which is all the fuckin' time some days," Johnny says. "Excuse my French."

"You're a good person, Johnny. Just because you have some uncomfortable thoughts every once in a while—or even often—doesn't change that," she says.

"Yeah, sure."

Christian holds up a hand. "I want to make a suggestion. I think you would benefit if you could stop fighting the fact that you're a kind, strong person with good qualities."

"I don't do that. I mean ... Shit. Do I?" Johnny looks so genuinely bewildered, I want to hug him.

"How often do you give yourself a compliment?"

He thinks about it for a moment and then laughs. "I'm gonna have to say never." His face falls. "I've treated myself like shit. Why did I do that?"

"That's an interesting question, and one we can explore during future sessions if you like. But for today, I think it's most important that you realize you've done it, and now it's time to change the script. There's no point in blaming yourself for what's already happened. Part of treating yourself well is forgiving yourself for treating yourself badly in the past."

"I suppose. But how many times do I need to do that? I keep having these fucking negative thoughts. I can't seem to keep them out of my head. It's frustrating as hell."

"It is frustrating," she agrees. I like how she validates how he's feeling. Then she tilts her head. "Have either of you two ever heard of the concept of l'appel du vide?"

"No," I say, and Johnny shakes his head.

"Maybe it will give you some comfort. It's a French phrase that means 'the call of the void.' It's when you think you could just ... veer into oncoming traffic. Or jump off a cliff. It's the momentary allure of playing with danger. Wondering what would happen."

I raise an eyebrow. "That's a thing?"

"It's a thing. Knowing that it's a thing, that other people experience it, really helped me," she says. "We all have intrusive thoughts from time to time. But you don't have to believe everything in your head or act on it. Talking about those intrusive thoughts, shining a light on them, making sure that people know it's okay to talk about them and about their mental health—this is important. You did the right thing when you told Kurt what was going on, what your brain was saying to you."

Johnny and Christian talk a while more, and I can tell he's more relaxed. His shoulders aren't hunched, and the panicky look is gone from his eyes.

When we leave, he grabs me in the parking lot and kisses me hard. "I love you," he rumbles. "Thank you for standing by me."

"Stop thanking me. It's what I mean when I say I love you, too: I'm gonna stand by you."

"Maybe we should make up some new vows," he says. "Ones

that mean more to us than whatever we said in Vegas. Since, you know, we can't remember those."

I nod. "Deal."

* * *

The trial continues for three more days, and it's hard to tell whether it's going well or not. I think it is, and I think Pinkerton looks like a shit, but that doesn't mean that the jury is going to agree or award Johnny any money. The parade of porn star witnesses has drawn some media attention, but the judge has barred television cameras, so it's only the mess of reporters outside that's a disturbance.

Every night, Johnny's clung to me in sleep, but he's been peaceful. Like he's passed over one watershed and into a new one, where the view is different.

Meanwhile, I'm still plotting with Rowan. Letting him know the status of the proceedings.

On the last day of testimony, while the jury is still out in the hallway on a break, Danny says, "Your Honor, we have one more witness. A rebuttal witness."

"There are no other witnesses on the list," opposing counsel snaps, holding up a sheet of paper and shaking it.

"True," Danny acknowledges. "But we're allowed to bring in a witness to impeach the defendant's direct testimony."

"Well, I object," opposing counsel says.

"On what basis?" the judge asks.

"Unfair surprise."

Danny shakes his head. "The witness was disclosed during discovery, and opposing counsel had plenty of opportunity to take her deposition. If they chose not to, that's not my fault."

"Offer of proof?" the judge says.

"Me-too evidence. The defendant testified that he'd never

given anyone Rohypnol, but we have a witness to impeach his credibility."

"Who is the witness?" the judge asks.

"Sandra Nguyễn."

"Objection overruled." The judge nods. "You may proceed."

Johnny's eyebrows knit together. I lean over and whisper in his ear, "Do you know who that is?"

He mutters, "No, I do not."

But then the courtroom doors open, and his whole demeanor changes. A small, pretty Vietnamese woman with long, dark hair walks in, and he takes in a sharp breath. "Tawni?"

"Who's that?" I ask.

"She's an actress," he whispers. "And she's my friend."

Sandra—or Tawni—looks nervous, her hands shaking and her lips trembling, but she's got a determined set to her shoulders. She's wearing a pastel blue suit and sky-high heels, but she looks more adorable than femme fatale. She gives Johnny a quick wave but sticks her chin up in the air as she passes Gary to take the witness stand.

The judge turns to the bailiff. "Let the jury in."

Once the jury is seated and the judge indicates to Danny that he can go ahead, Tawni is sworn in. After she gives her name, he asks her, "Do you know Gary Pinkerton?"

"Yes," she says. Although she still looks scared, her voice is clear.

"How do you know him?"

"He's produced at least a dozen of my films."

The jury is now looking interested.

"Those films are pornography, correct?"

"Yes."

"Have you ever experienced any scenes where Gary Pinkerton took actions that went beyond what was agreed to in your contract?"

Tawni nods. "Yes."

Danny's voice is low and careful. "Can you describe what happened?"

Taking a deep breath and straightening her back, Tawni tells the court a story of how, after she had finished a scene, Gary called her to his office and had sex with her. She didn't want to, but she didn't say no.

Something similar happened after a later scene, and she testifies that, that time, she told him no, and he got angry, but he let her leave.

Then, the next time he called her to his office, he'd given her some Gatorade. She testifies, "I passed out and woke up later with semen on my legs, and it wasn't from the scene."

"How do you know that?"

"Because he filmed it," she says. "In his office. He filmed himself having sex with me." A shudder goes through the courtroom. "He showed me it later on his phone. He was proud of it."

"You say you passed out. Do you believe he had given you any drugs?"

"Yes, I do."

"And on what basis do you have that belief?"

"I went to the hospital for a test, and they found Rohypnol. That's certainly not something I would have taken knowingly, and I felt fine when I entered his office. Here's the screening." She pulls out a piece of paper. The bailiff takes it from her, and the document gets marked as an exhibit by the clerk.

"No further questions," Danny says.

Gary's lawyer attempts to cross-examine Tawni about how much sex she's had during her career, but her testimony is clear: "I know what I consent to and what I don't. I did not consent to have sex with Gary, and he drugged me so I couldn't say no."

After court is done for the day, Tawni's waiting in the hallway. Johnny wraps her in a hug, kissing the top of her head. "I didn't know," he says huskily. "I didn't know Gary pulled that shit with you, too. I'm so sorry it happened to you. And I'm so darn grateful you came and supported me."

"When Weston & Ramirez interviewed me, they said you had no evidence that he roofied anyone, and I knew I had to speak up," she says. "Guess the other side underestimated me. But Gary's a turd. I know people think just because we agree to have sex on camera, it means they can do anything to us. But it doesn't."

"No, it doesn't."

"Thank you," I say. "You were magnificent. It was very brave of you."

She shrugs and turns to Johnny. "You'd do it for me, wouldn't you, Velvet?"

"Yes. That I would. Wanna go to dinner with us tonight?" Johnny asks. "And maybe a drink?"

Tawni grins. "I'd love to."

* * *

The next day, Danny gives a devastating closing argument, reminding the jury that Johnny was horribly assaulted, causing physical and emotional trauma, in addition to which he was deprived of his livelihood due to Pinkerton's derogatory comments about him—and for this, he should be compensated. Danny also asks for punitive damages for Pinkerton's extreme and outrageous behavior. He tells the jury to punish Pinkerton and send a message that sexual assault is always unacceptable. Johnny then has to sit through opposing counsel telling the jury that a porn star is paid for having sex, and that's exactly what Johnny did.

The judge sends the jury out to deliberate.

And then we wait.

But unlike last weekend, Johnny's calm. When we get home, I ask him how he's doing, and he says, "Got my story out. That's what I wanted. The rest ain't up to me."

CHAPTER 42
Johnny

The jury's been deliberating for two days, and I don't know if that's a good sign or a bad one. If I lost, they'd make the decision fast, right? So maybe they're debating how much money is right to punish Pinkerton Studios? That may be wishful thinking on my part, but I'm a big fan of wishful thinking.

Then we get the call to head back to court, because the jury's made its decision.

"All rise."

I stand next to Danny and August and my husband–boyfriend–love of my life. I ignore everyone in the courtroom associated with the studio. They don't matter one bit.

"Have you reached a verdict?" The judge is addressing one of the jury members. I guess she's called the foreperson.

Kurt takes my hand and squeezes it.

"We have, Your Honor."

My heart's beating so hard, I think I'm going to explode. This can't be healthy.

Please have believed me. Please have believed me.

The judge starts reading the verdict out loud, and the language is so convoluted that I can't quite tell what's going on. But then he says that they find for the plaintiff, which is me, and then he says the amount, and it's $500,000.

I blow out a good long breath. More than I was gonna settle for. Take that, Gary.

And then he keeps going, and he says punitive damages are awarded in the amount of $20 million, and I blink.

That's the amount to punish the bad guy, Danny had explained. And if that's what the jury's saying, then they're *really* pissed at Gary.

"You won," Kurt whispers, and I turn and hug him, burying my face in his shoulder. A tear trickles down my cheek, but I get myself together as the jury files out, trying to keep a poker face.

But in reality, I'm dazed.

A few members of the jury smile at me, which makes my chest expand.

"They believed me," I murmur to Kurt.

"Of course they believed you. You told the truth," he whispers back.

"I've gotta call Tawni and thank her." Giddiness breaks through the fog of my last few weeks.

"You do that, but while she helped, you're the one who did this." Kurt pauses. "Along with your lawyers."

"They're great, aren't they?" I stand, and Danny holds out his arms.

"Congrats, Johnny," he says. "Justice was served."

I'm still keeping it together, but I want to fold inward. Nevertheless, I give August a hug, too, and we gather up all their boxes of stuff and file out.

In the hallway, Gary storms by us without a word.

"Holy shit, I won," I say, sitting down hard on the nearest bench.

"Do you think he's going to appeal?" Kurt asks Danny, and my heart continues on its goddamn roller coaster.

"He could, but it's going to be difficult for him to win, and he'd have to post a bond for the amount he owes first," Danny says.

Truth be told, I hadn't been counting on any money. I'd just been so hurt that I wanted Gary brought to justice. Is this what justice feels like?

Twelve strangers agreed that bad shit happened to me, and that Gary should be punished.

I suppose I shouldn't be as blasé as that. It does feel good to be believed.

It's finally over. Unless he appeals, which I ... am gonna choose not to think about. Not right now. There's nothing I can do about it, so go away, bad thoughts.

"Assuming he doesn't appeal, how long until I get the money?" I ask.

Danny sighs. "That's the thing. We have ways of collecting, but it's not automatic. The court doesn't supervise payment. And I think Gary won't pay unless he's pressed. Don't worry, we'll press him. Just ... be prepared to not see the money for a while."

I nod, but Kurt has a strange expression on his face. "Do you mind giving me the firm's wiring information?" he asks Danny.

Danny raises an eyebrow but says, "No, I don't mind. I'll have Alden send it to you. He's our bookkeeper." He blushes. "And my partner."

* * *

When we get home, I feel like a zombie. All the emotion of hearing that verdict come back has burned out of me, and I am ... done. As we leave our shoes by the door, Lady jumps up on me and gives me kisses, which wake me up.

"Let's put her in her crate, and I'll take you to bed," Kurt says.

It's not even seven, but fine. She's got a comfy crate, so I don't mind putting her in it.

"I'm not sure if I'm in the mood for sex," I admit.

"That's not what I had in mind," he says.

"No?"

"I figured you might need to decompress."

My face crumples. I've been working so hard to hold it together, and the fact that Kurt sees that, sees me? It makes me love him even more.

We take off our suits and climb into bed in our underwear. Kurt pushes me onto my back and then climbs on top of me, kissing me and wrapping his arms around my neck.

"I love you," he whispers.

"I love you, too."

After a few minutes, he rolls us so he's the one on his back, and I shift over so my ear is on his chest and I can hear his heartbeat.

That steady beat is prettier than any noise I've ever heard. And I realize I'm not hearing violins anymore.

I burst out crying. "Fuck," I whisper. "This was a whole lotta shit to go through."

"I know, babe. Get it out. Get it all out."

Clinging to Kurt, I cry out everything. I cry out the hate and anger. The rage. The shame. I cry out how fucking hurt I was at being assaulted and then at not being believed. I weep for the shame of being a sex worker—when people want sex workers. I cry for my mama and her illness. I cry in relief for her body seeming to accept Kurt's mama's kidney.

I cry for the sweet support of my darling husband, who's stayed by my side, even when it got tough.

He's as loyal as they come.

He doesn't say anything. Just holds me and gives me the freedom to let out all the feelings I've been caging up for months ... years ... decades.

At the end, when I'm all cried out, I have a damn headache. Kurt brings me pain relievers and takes me into the shower, where the hot water washes away all the crud.

Then he orders pizza.

I realize I'm ravenous. Don't remember the last time I was actually hungry.

After dinner, we walk Lady on the beach, and I feel like a human being for the first time in I can't remember how long.

In the middle of the night, I wake up feeling giddy. "Holy crap, it's over," I whisper in the darkness.

Kurt stirs. "Hmm?"

"Sorry to wake you, baby," I say. "But it's hitting me again and again. I'm done with those bastards forever."

"It's okay. I'm happy it's over, too."

"I feel ... free."

"Good." He climbs onto me. "But you're stuck with me."

"That's a kind of freedom I'll happily give up."

* * *

Ace, my agent, calls me the next morning. "I hear congratulations are in order. That's a big award."

"Thanks. Yeah, it is. I dunno if I'll ever see a dime of it, but it's vindicating, you know?"

"I do." His voice drops. "Johnny, I'm sorry you had to go through that. If I'd have known that those things were going on with that studio, I never would've booked you there. I know people think agents are leeches, but I genuinely care about you, and I'd never want you to be hurt. I'd never want you to be drugged. And I'd never want you to lose your livelihood." He pauses. "Now that you're retired, I suppose you have no use for me, unless you want to try acting in regular films or TV."

"Not acting, no, but, there is something you could maybe help me with. I want to try becoming an intimacy coordinator."

It's quiet on the line, and then Ace says, "You know, I think that's a great idea. Let me see what I can do."

"Thanks very much."

I hang up and see Kurt standing there with a refill for my coffee. "Your agent's going to help you find work?" Kurt asks.

"Yep. Isn't that great?"

He nods, but his lips are turned down.

I kiss him, then gesture at his long face. "What's wrong?"

"I'm balancing wanting you to be happy with wanting you to quit trying to pay me back."

Ah.

That.

"Thank you for the reminder. I need to do something."

"What's that?"

I stand and go over to the table with the notepad where I've been keeping track of everything Kurt's bought for me. I hold it up. "Do ya mind if I tear up this here paper?"

"Thank fuck. Please do," Kurt says. "Get rid of that. Our relationship is so much more than a tally sheet."

Ripping it into tiny pieces, I toss it in the trash, then take him in my arms. "That it is, precious. That it is."

CHAPTER 43

Kurt

"This is the address?" Rowan says, sitting in the driver's seat of a plain white Suburban, looking around at the plain warehouses in the San Fernando Valley where the porn studios are clustered. His eyes are bright with excitement, and his hands are trembling with what I assume is adrenaline. Since I've got the same thing coursing through my veins.

Scraping a sweaty hand through my hair, I check the map on my phone. "Yeah. You've dealt with surveillance? Security?"

Rowan smirks, and it's disquieting. I don't know much about this guy except that the prospect of violence seems to turn him on. "It's taken care of."

"You're sure?" I clear my throat. My knee's bouncing.

"Even the plates of this car can't be traced. We've looped traffic cameras. It's fine. I'd swear it on Charlie's life," he tells me solemnly.

Given the sincerity on his face—and how those two seem to be joined together with superglue—that seems like the biggest vow he could make.

"Okay," I say, letting out a breath, and follow him out of the car, my heart rate skyrocketing. I'm wearing a plain gray hoodie that I borrowed from Johnny's closet. It still doesn't have strings in it, and it's too big for me, but it manages to hide who I am.

Rowan has a tattoo on the back of his neck that says "Baby Boy." He pulls a black hoodie up to cover it and his distinctive pink hair. He hands me gloves and a medical face mask and slips a gun into the back of his jeans. Johnny's derringer is heavy against my side, making me feel faint.

"I thought we didn't need to hide," I say, biting my lip.

"Can't be too careful."

I'm doing this for Johnny. I need to get out of my own head. I close my eyes, center myself, and nod, then put on the gear.

We're joined by some ... muscle, I guess, who Rowan knows, and they're wearing masks and gloves and are armed, too. I have barely any clue what to do with a gun. After his latest crisis, Johnny gently informed me that I should store his bullets separately from his derringer, so that if things ever got bad again, he'd have to get into two hiding places, not one.

I agreed and bought two proper safes. He doesn't know the combination to either, and the bullets are in one, the gun in the other.

He also took me to a shooting range, and we took a gun safety course, but I still don't feel comfortable with a weapon. I'm queasy, but I feel queasier when I think about what was done to Johnny. And I'm the one who can fix this situation.

Rowan's bouncing on his heels and humming to himself. He's energized, and it's fascinating to me how different we are.

Johnny and I are comfy naps and walks on the beach with the dog.

Rowan's relationship with Charlie seems like they're willing to bring the other the hearts of their enemies.

Apparently they're willing to bring me the heart of my enemy, too, and I'm grateful for that.

In general, violence is not at all my thing. But revenge for hurting my Johnny? Yes.

Despite my determination to do this, I really don't want to end up in prison ... or tank my momther's career for good. So we'd better not get caught. But Rowan seems to know what he's doing, so I'm letting him take the lead and hoping for the best.

The studio is quiet. It's not quite four in the afternoon on a Monday, and there's only one car in the parking lot besides ours. We timed it this way because during the trial I learned it's Gary Pinkerton's habit to watch footage when no one's around, and they generally don't film on Mondays.

At Rowan's nod, the muscle kicks in the back door of the building, and we waltz into the office where Gary sits all alone, monitor on, a mess of invoices and notes all over his desk.

In a flash, Rowan has a gun cocked and pressed against Gary's forehead.

"What? Who the fuck are you?" Gary hisses. Then his eyes widen as he recognizes me. He holds up a middle finger. "Oh, fuck you. Tell Johnny boo-hoo. We're gonna appeal."

"You will never say his name again," I snarl. "You do not know Johnny Haskell or Velvet the Cowboy. You do not mention him or do anything to so much as inconvenience him. Ever."

He rolls his eyes, but given there's a gun pointed at his head, he wisely doesn't move.

In a quiet voice, I say, "You are going to log on to your accounts—and we're fully aware of the one in the Caymans and the two in Geneva—and make a series of transfers to the client trust account of Weston & Ramirez. Now."

Gary flinches. Then he sneers. "Why on earth would I do that?"

"Because if you don't, my friends here are going to remove your body parts one at a time." The two big dudes move forward so there are now two more guns cocked at Gary's head, which makes his complexion turn gray.

Since the other guys have Gary covered, Rowan puts the safety on his gun and shoves it in his waistband, then pulls out his switchblade, flicking it menacingly. For such a tiny dude, he's fucking sinister. "Should I start with a finger or a testicle?"

"Fuck you," Gary spits, then stiffens when the guns at his head press in tighter.

One of the big guys moves like lightning, pinning Gary's hand to the desk. Before I can process a thought, Rowan slices off the tip of Gary's finger.

Gary howls. "The fuck? You fucking bastard!"

"Transfer the money," Rowan orders.

Gary opens his mouth to spout off, but I can see the moment he changes his mind. Maybe he catches the light in Rowan's eyes. How Rowan is getting off on his pain.

How he won't be getting out of this as easily as he thought.

I'm fucking sick to my stomach, but not enough to leave. Not enough that I'll fail to see this through. Johnny deserves the compensation he was awarded.

With trembling hands, Gary opens a browser on his computer, holding his pinky tight to his palm and wincing. With a few keystrokes, he's in. "Where am I transferring it?" he asks sullenly.

I pull up the email from Alden and recite the account number for Danny's law firm.

Gary pinches his nose. "I don't have all of it in one account. It will take me a bit."

"Then make multiple transfers. Fast," Rowan orders. Gary makes a move toward him, and one of the big dudes cocks his gun.

"Fuck. Fine," Gary hisses, his keystrokes shaky. After a moment he pulls his shoulders back. "Look. Five million transferred."

"You left two million in that account," Rowan points out.

"I'll get it from another account."

Without another word, Rowan slices the skin at the top of Gary's ear.

Gary screams as blood pours down his face. "Motherfucker!"

"Transfer the funds."

"Fine," Gary spits. With a few more keystrokes, he transfers $2 million more. Then he logs in to another account and transfers $9 million.

"Where's the rest?" I ask. "You are paying Johnny every penny you owe him. Don't forget interest, which is more than $5k a day. Every day, he lives with the memory of you drugging him and making those men rape him. You took away his right to choose what happens to his body. Fuck you. You lost. Pay up. We know the production company has the funds. And you control the accounts."

Gary sneers at me, but Rowan presses the knife to his throat hard enough that red beads start sliding down his neck. "Watch how you move," Rowan warns him. "You draw back, they pull the trigger. You lean toward me, you get your throat sliced."

"If I die, you won't get the money," Gary says cockily. But it feels like false bravado.

"We'll figure it out." Rowan starts reciting an account number, and Gary's jaw drops.

"How did you know about that account?"

"We did a thorough skip trace on you. We know where you've hidden all your assets. Come on, transfer the rest of it from the Caymans. Let's go."

Looking defeated, Gary logs on to another bank account, and, now bleeding from three wounds, he transfers the remaining money into the Weston & Ramirez bank account.

"Check with Danny to see if the money's hit the account," Rowan says.

I move to the side and call Weston & Ramirez. After talking with their chirpy receptionist, I'm transferred to the bookkeeper, Alden.

"I'd like to know if you've received payment in full earmarked for John Haskell," I say.

"Um, let me check the account," Alden says. I hear a few keystrokes. "Yeah. Okay, wow. Yes. The money's here."

"Thank you," I say. "Please let Danny know."

"You got it."

I hang up with Alden. "Now you need to post on AD/Vice that you're sorry."

"Not fucking sorry—" Gary snarls.

"Rowan?" I say.

Rowan presses the knife harder against the worm's throat.

"Okay, okay," Gary says. "Fuck. Fine. Let me pull it up." He navigates to his social media account and glares at me.

"Type the following: 'I want to apologize to Velvet, Tawni, and every other actor I have ever done wrong to.'"

Gary opens his mouth to protest but thinks better of it. He starts typing, muttering something under his breath that I choose to ignore.

"What I did was vile and unforgivable. I sincerely regret my actions, and I am very sorry," I dictate.

He types.

I put my hand on my hip. "Post it."

Gary can't resist another eye roll before he hits post. I pull up the AD/Vice app to make sure it's on his account and public. It is.

"So what do we do now?" Rowan asks.

"We let him go," I say, then face Gary fully. "You're not gonna tell anyone about this, are you? It'd be much, much worse for you if you did."

"Are you gonna tell anyone?" Rowan asks.

Gary spits at him.

"That's not an answer."

"Of fucking course not," Gary sneers. "But I'll get my payback someday, little man."

Now it's Rowan's turn to roll his eyes. "Whatever. I'd like to see you try."

We all take a step back. I don't trust Gary, but I also don't know how else to end this. I look at Rowan, and just then, Gary rises from his seat and grabs for Rowan's knife.

A gun goes off, loud and startling, and a body falls to the floor.

Gary lands to the side, eyes open wide, mouth slack. Wetness is splattered beside him, and I nearly throw up. Pieces of bone, blood, gray matter. It's sickening.

My vision whites out. A pool of blood slowly starts leaking from the body.

"Shit," one of the big guys says.

"You were defending me," Rowan says. "I saw it. We'll handle this."

I start stuttering, "He ... he ... he's dead. That fucking asshole. He ... he raped my husband."

"I know," Rowan says quietly.

I race outside into the sunshine. Footsteps sound after me. It's Rowan.

"What the fuck ... what do we do?" I wanted vengeance. I didn't want *this*. Did I?

"Deep breaths," Rowan says. "Is that the first time you've ..."

"Seen someone die? No. I mean yes. I mean ... My high school boyfriend, he—with a razor blade—I saw the aftermath. His parents discovered him, but I'd come over just after. I saw the blood."

"I'm fucking sorry about that."

"But what do we do?" I say louder.

"The guys have supplies. We'll torch the place. Make it look like a suicide. With the apology and his body destroyed, it'll work."

"Are you sure?"

"Yep," he says, sounding confident. "Go wait in the car. We'll take care of it." He presses the keys into my hand.

I walk over to the car, my legs shaky, and fall into the passenger seat, putting my face in my hands. And I burst into tears.

Fuck.

I don't wanna cry over that asshole. But I also don't like having his death be my responsibility. I put this into motion. I ... I ... *fuck*.

The wind rustles the trees outside the window. I sit, staring blankly, until I see smoke, and then three men come running out of the building. The big guys head to their SUV, and then Rowan's next to me, in the driver's seat. He starts the engine and pulls smoothly onto the street.

He drives to Charlie's house and parks in the garage. We strip off what we're wearing and put it all in bags to burn, and then I take a quick shower and change into the other clothes I brought. I'm still stunned and horrified, but a small part of me is relieved.

Justice was served. Johnny's demon was slain. Literally.

"You guys okay?" Charlie asks, wrapping Rowan in a bear hug when Rowan comes out of the shower with a towel on his head.

"It was perfect, my love," Rowan says, and Charlie kisses him.

I shudder. "Perfect? He died. I didn't want him to die. I don't think I wanted him to die. I'm not sure." I'm shaking again, wondering if I'm going to vomit.

"Kurt needs aftercare," Rowan says. "Let's get him home."

"Thank you," I say to both of them with as much gravity as I can manage. "I owe you."

"Nah," Rowan says. "That asshole deserved it. I know what happened wasn't your scene, and I'm sorry you had to see it, but for me ... I can be antisocial. It's good for me to vent that in a ... healthy way. And I rarely get such a good excuse to set a nice big fire."

"What about money? The arrangements you made, the security ..."

"I don't need it."

"What do you mean you don't need it? I can pay. I have plenty."

"I've got more." He grins at me and flashes me the lock screen on his phone, which is a photo of him practically climbing Charlie. But the wallpaper is a famous coat of arms. "My family crest."

Rowan St. Thomas. As in the St. Thomas dynasty.

Holy shit.

Yeah, he has more money than me. A hundred times as much.

So what the fuck is he doing with Charlie? How did they meet?

I have so many questions. "I should pay the guys, at least," I say.

Rowan shrugs. "I can cover it as part of their salary, but feel free to give them a bonus."

I make arrangements to send money to his trust fund to pay his big, muscled assistants.

"Well, if you need help with anything in the future, feel free to call me," I say. "I don't know what I could do, but I'm in your debt."

It's probably a bad idea for me to be in debt to him, but it's worth it for Johnny.

Rowan shakes his head and gives me his wide, evil grin. "Just come hang out sometime."

"I will." God help me, I will.

Charlie insists on driving me back to my house in my car, and Rowan follows. We say goodbye in the driveway, and I walk up the stairs into the living room, still a little shaky, but trying to hide it.

As I enter, Johnny is putting down his phone, looking stunned.

"What's up?" I ask.

"That was Danny. He says that Gary Pinkerton wired the entire amount owed, plus interest. He paid it all. Danny took my bank information so he could forward me the proceeds."

I manage a smile. "That's awesome."

He stares at me. "You don't sound totally surprised. Wait, have you been crying?"

Joining Johnny on the couch, I climb into his lap and tuck my face into his neck. "I have to confess. I had something to do with it."

"What happened?" Johnny's voice is wary and concerned.

"I ... found someone who went with me to see Gary this afternoon. I wanted to punish him for what he did to you, and I was planning some kind of revenge. But once I found out you won, I wanted him to pay. Literally pay you."

"Which he did."

"And it went too far." I swallow hard. "Gary's dead."

Johnny sits bolt upright. "*What?*"

I nod, a tear sliding down my cheek. "It was awful. I feel like utter shit. I put the plan in motion, but I didn't realize ... I didn't *let* myself realize how bad it could get. He tried to hurt one of the people I was with, and ..."

"Gary Pinkerton is dead?" Johnny's eyes are wide and scared.

"Yeah."

"Fuck."

"Yeah," I repeat.

"What about— I don't want you going to jail, darlin'," Johnny says.

"I'm pretty sure we won't get caught. My friend is next-level as far as access to resources, and he didn't seem worried. And ... this definitely wasn't the first time he'd been involved in something ... dark."

Johnny holds me tight, and we sit there for a moment, quiet.

"I'm glad he's dead," I admit, "but at the same time, I wish it hadn't happened. I feel sick knowing I was involved."

"I'm horrified that you had to do something like that on my behalf. It's terrible. It makes sense that you're upset." He pauses. "At the same time, is it evil to say I'm glad he's not here to hurt anyone else?"

"I dunno right now. All I know is I wanted completion. I wanted to put all of this to rest. I wanted it to be done. And now it is, and ..." I shudder. "I don't know. I guess I just have to try to make sense of it somehow."

More silence. Johnny's arms are strong around me, and I let his warmth melt away the unreality of the day.

We hold each other on the couch for a long time. Finally, I whisper, "I guess I slew one of your demons. For real."

"Thank you," he whispers back, squeezing me tight. "Holy fuck, it's over."

A news report the next day says, "Pinkerton Studios CEO dead in apparent suicide after expressing regret for sex crimes."

I keep waiting for the police to show up at my door, but they never do.

And as days turn into weeks, I stop holding my breath so much. Maybe justice really was served.

Johnny's demon didn't respawn.

CHAPTER 44
Kurt

A few weeks later, Johnny corners me in the kitchen while I'm doing dishes, nibbling on my neck as he embraces me from behind.

His big hands run along my body from my thighs to my nipples, and I groan. Damn, I love it when he's like this.

"Need a break?" he asks.

"Yeah," I say, leaning into him. When Johnny's in the mood, I jump on it. He doesn't have to always be that way, but I love it when he is. And the more he recovers, the more he's getting back his sexual appetite.

"A while ago, you mentioned an interest in making a film," he murmurs in my ear. "You still up for that?"

I nod vigorously, my dick firming up, and I push my ass into his hardening crotch. "Well, you're feeling good today."

"So good." He grips my hips tight. "Let's have a little fun. Create new, positive memories. On camera. You're okay with that?"

"Yes. So much more than okay."

"Then are you my boy who's been away at college and has been sleeping around on me?" He sucks on my neck. "Do you need to be taught a lesson? Or are you the homeowner who needs help with your pipes and calls the plumber? Or the pizza delivery guy?" He smirks.

"I want to be the amateur with the porn star," I blurt. "I want you to coach me through what you like. I want you to teach me how to make a porno."

"Dang, that's hot," he whispers, his hand reaching down between my legs, cupping my balls over my jeans, then slowly stroking up my cock. "Okay." He nods. "Set up the camera."

Holy shit, we're doing this. I have a little tripod that I bought a while back in a misguided attempt to do Ad/VICE videos, so I set up the camera in our bedroom and make sure it's on and has plenty of battery and memory. Then I arrange it so it can see the whole room.

Johnny's waiting in the doorway, watching me with heated eyes. "How you doin', darlin'?"

"Almost ... Okay, it's ready." I rub my hands down my thighs, wiping off the nervous sweat. "I'm ... I'm ready, too."

"Then let's get started."

I whisper, "Okay." I hover my finger over the button. "And ... action." I walk out in front of the camera, not quite knowing what to do or where to look or how to hold myself.

Johnny strides over to me, and he's put on his confident, porn star persona. While it's still him, it's him ... turned all the way up.

I'm a puddle on the floor. I *love* this. Love *him*.

"Hey, baby," he says in a low drawl. "I hear you've been having a few fantasies."

I swallow hard. "I have."

"And what are they?"

He's making this easy on me. Damn. "I've always wanted to be fucked by you. On camera."

Johnny grins his sexy smirk. "That can be arranged. Have you ever been with someone as big as me?"

Of course, the truthful answer is that I've been with him

before, so I know what I'm getting into. But for the camera, I say, "No one's as big as you are."

My cock is hardening even more in my pants. And my ass is clenching, wanting that painful, overfull feeling of having him inside me.

Fuck. I want Johnny inside me. I want him dominating me and taking me over.

"You're so handsome, precious," he says. He traces his finger down my nose, bops the tip, and then traces along my lips, first the top, then the bottom.

He smirks. "Suck."

I open my lips and suck his finger.

Then he pulls it out and leans down and kisses me while that finger goes exploring inside my pants.

I moan.

He hasn't undone them, so they're a tight fit, but oh, god, it feels good.

And the kiss. This is part of why I always loved watching Johnny's videos. His kisses always seemed so good.

They are.

It is.

His tongue delves deep into my mouth, and he takes over, one hand exploring between my ass cheeks, the other around my upper back, tugging me to him.

Somehow, knowing that this is being recorded makes it hotter. Like, who's watching? I know it's no one, but still. I could watch it someday.

"Hey," Johnny murmurs, lifting up my chin so I'm staring into his blue-green eyes. "Where'd you go, precious?"

"Sorry," I say. "Got lost in my own head a bit."

"Want to turn off the camera?"

"Not on your life." I grin.

"Then maybe I need to do my job better." Johnny reaches down between us and cups my erection, stroking me carefully.

I groan. This. This is what I want. Relief from the pressure. Not just sexual pressure, but all the pressures on me. I want relief from all of them.

All. Of. Them.

And Johnny gives that to me.

"You've never been with a pro like this, have you?" he asks.

I shake my head.

"Then why don't we start with you getting me hard. Wanna drop down on those knees for me, baby?"

I do so immediately, and Johnny, clearly knowing where the camera is, turns us so my head won't be blocking the view. He puts his hands behind his head, posing. "Have at me, darlin'."

My hands are trembling, but I manage to undo the button of his jeans and slide the zipper down.

I push his jeans down on his hips and pull out his big cock. Even not fully erect, it just keeps going, and I instinctively bury my nose at the base, inhaling his scent. While he still manscapes, he's gone a bit more natural than he was when he was working on camera. So he's got neatly trimmed pubes rather than being fully shaved.

I suck on one of his balls and then the other, and his cock hardens further. Meanwhile, Johnny's keeping up a steady stream of praise, telling me how beautiful I look, how amazing it feels, what a good boy I am.

Finally, I lick all the way up his cock, laving attention on it. I'm getting it as wet as I can, and when I get to the tip, I do my best to swallow him down. I have no idea how anyone could ever deep-throat him unless they were one of those snakes with a jaw that unhinges. Regardless, he seems to like what I'm doing, and I get him fully hard—and all the while, he's cradling my jaw and whispering to me how well I'm doing.

He takes his shirt off, displaying those abs I love, and then he hauls me up by my armpits, taking my shirt off in one swift move.

We join together, warm chest to warm chest, and he kisses me deeply, his hips rocking into me in almost a dance. His hands work their way down my ass and inside my pants, and then, without breaking the kiss, he skillfully undoes my pants, making me step out of them so I'm naked.

I'm in front of a camera with my boyfriend-husband-lover, and he's got his fingers between my ass cheeks, his dick rubbing against mine as he kisses me like I'm essential for breathing.

I could come like this.

But Johnny pulls some lube out of his pocket—when did he stash it in there?—and squeezes some onto his fingers, and now he's wiggling one into me. When the angle gets so he can't go any farther, he kisses me one last time, then whispers, "On your knees, beautiful."

I drop down to my hands and knees, feeling vulnerable, because my ass is facing the camera. Johnny arranges me, kissing down my back and sliding his fingers inside me, prepping me.

It's not that much work to get me loose, and soon, Johnny pauses. "You good with no condom, darlin'? I can put one on."

"I trust you," I say.

And I so do. He's it for me, and I'm it for him. Period.

He again moves us for a better position for the camera and kisses me deeply. "You ready?" he murmurs.

I nod.

"Good. Let me fuck that gorgeous ass of yours."

I hear him lubing himself up, and then he's probing at my entrance, his huge cock nudging its way into my narrow entrance. No matter how much prep I do, it's always a tight fit, but he steadily pushes in while I groan loudly. I can never help the noises I make when he's inside me. It's just a lot to take.

But I love it. I fucking love it so much.

I bear down, and he slips in farther. Eventually, his pelvis is flush against my ass, and we both breathe hard for a moment.

"You okay, baby?" Johnny asks. "Talk to me."

"I am," I whisper.

"I'll go slow at first. I know it's not easy."

"I love it, though." I can feel his smile as he kisses along my back. Then he does an experimental pull out and thrust in, gripping my hips tightly.

The push in is overwhelming, and I miss him when he pulls out. He starts a rhythm that is somehow both deep and gentle. I'm not sure I could handle a true hard fuck right now.

He reaches around and strokes my cock hard again—it always flags when he first gets inside me. I'm loving how intense this all is. It's even more intense because of the eye of the camera on me. Thinking that someone could watch this and see how my sexy husband is seducing me and fucking me so well.

I let myself go. I surrender to him. Let him dominate me, use me to make himself feel good. I know he'll take me to the edge and over.

"You take my cock so well," he croons, pistoning into me over and over again. "You're so fucking gorgeous, darlin'. No one has an ass like yours. No one. It's made for my big, hard cock."

I love it when he babbles at me with all his dirty talk. I love his praise. I love it when he just takes over.

I fucking love him, okay? I'm sure if the camera could capture my face, it would show, written all over, how in love with him I am.

"Yeah, baby. Come for me, precious," Johnny murmurs.

His words trigger something deep inside me, and before I even realize it, I'm starting to climax. The sensation gathers in my balls and lower pelvis, then spreads to my entire body. There's a pause at the height of tension, and then it just ebbs, and I spill all over the floor.

"You're so pretty when you come," he says in his thick drawl, and then he's shoving up inside me and coming, too. If this were porn, he'd pull out and finish on my back, and the fact that he's not signals to me that this is just for us. He's doing this for me, but he's getting something out of it, too.

It's real. *We're* real.

Then he collapses on my back, and we both sink to the cool floor.

After a moment, he kisses my shoulder and chuckles. "Why don't we turn the camera off, okay, babe?"

I nod, he pulls out, and a gush of come dribbles down my leg.

It's messy, but we can clean it up. I love it.

I love him.

I turn off the camera and kiss him hard. This one's for me.

CHAPTER 45
Johnny

I put a finger under Kurt's chin and kiss him. "You good, precious?"

"I am. You?"

"Very much so. In fact, I think I got more out of that than I'd expected."

"In what way?"

"I think you got to see the best part of me. I was reclaiming a job I used to enjoy—but with you, so it meant something. Fucking you on camera felt *right*," I say. "It didn't feel like a performance. More ... that I was giving you what you wanted—and what you wanted was the true me."

"Yeah," he says, curling into me. "That sounds right. The true you is more confident than you usually let on in real life, I think."

I nod. "I'm not so aw-shucks as I come off as. I can dial up or down my country roots, although they're always gonna be there to some extent. I'm never gonna be comfortable with putting on airs. But that doesn't mean I'm auditioning to be in a western movie like my Velvet the Cowboy namesake."

Kurt has a skeptical eyebrow raised. "I think you're always

going to be a cowboy." He snuggles into me. "Did you miss it, though? Porn?"

Kissing his head, I say, "A little, yeah. I'd treated giving up porn—my livelihood—as no big deal, but it mattered to me. I wouldn't have stuck with it so long if I hadn't gotten something out of it. The true me loves sex. The true me loves to be on camera. You unwittingly combined a few things that I very much need, or at least enjoy: sex on camera, a sense of play, and sometimes ... a performance."

"And I've always liked sex as something in a movie." Kurt smiles. "This is good. We can make this work. Now we know that, when you're getting a little too low, we can maybe turn the camera on and both get our needs met." He pauses. "Do you think you'd want more than just me?"

I shake my head. "I've never needed to be promiscuous." He chuckles. "I just like to use my body this way and to give it to someone else."

"I'm happy to receive it."

"Then giving myself to the love of my life suits me just fine."

He smiles shyly and kisses me hard.

"Should we get cleaned up?" I ask.

Kurt nods. I watch his ass as he heads into the bathroom to get some towels to clean the floor, and I know I'm in love with him.

* * *

The following weekend, we drive up to see Mama, who's a few months out from her kidney transplant. We've been keeping tabs on Kurt's mom, and she's doing well, but this is the first chance we've had to see my mama since she was cleared for visitors.

Kurt had this funny thing where he used to call his mom "Momther," because he explained that she wasn't close enough to be a mom, but she wasn't distant enough to be a mother.

That's stopped now. She's just plain mom. Especially to me. Especially since she donated a kidney to my sweet mama.

As we drive up the interstate, Kurt fiddles with something on his phone. While he usually lets me pick the radio, he says, "Listen to this," and music comes over the car's speakers. Lady's ears perk up in the back seat.

It's a pop song, and I recognize the voice as that of Julian Hill. A lump forms in my throat at the violins that are rocking alongside the guitar and drums.

"Well," I say. "That's May Ella, isn't it?"

"Yes. Doesn't she sound fantastic?"

"It's amazing."

"I guess Jules spread the word about her being a contract musician, and now other musicians are wanting to work with her. They like her story, and they like her sound."

"It's a dream come true."

When we get to Mama's, she's walking around. Slowly, but she seems stronger than before.

"Hey, Mama," I say, giving her a gentle hug.

"John, you're a sight," she says. "Always so handsome. And Kurt, it's good to see you." Her eyes well with tears. "I'm sorry for gettin' emotional. I'm just so grateful for your mama."

"She's a good egg, isn't she?"

"Do you think she really has a chance at the White House?"

"She's leading in the polls right now," he says. "And I've never known her to fail at anything she put her mind to."

"She deserves every success," Mama says. "She's a keeper. Like her son."

* * *

Two months later, I glance around the movie set, which is being prepped for a shoot. The soundstage is dressed for a period drama in which a penniless stranger is going to have sex with a handsome duke.

This ain't a porn production. It's part of a scripted series on a streaming service. My job is to go through all of the movements with the actors and ensure they are completely on board with who will be touching what, and how. I've read through the contracts and know what each actor has agreed to do and not do.

"Okay," I say, flipping to the next page in the script. "In this scene, Tristan and Johan are overcome with passion and are going to have oral sex, so let's talk about how that's going to be shown on the screen and what y'all are comfortable with doing." The actors are in robes, and we lounge on the bed, talking through the choreography of their upcoming scenes.

I've got no qualms about talking about sex in a plain manner. And I'm really good at making sure that everyone is on board. That we're all speaking the same language. That they are in agreement with every touch, every kiss, every part of their body that will be shown on camera. That there are going to be no surprises and no one is going to feel that what they are doing is wrong. That no one is going to get hurt or go beyond their comfort zone.

This is the most important job I've ever had.

When I'm done for the day, it's not too far to Burbank, where Kurt's working at Weston & Ramirez House. We carpooled today, knowing that we were going to be in the same neighborhood, and I pull up in my old truck, which Kurt managed to track down, since my neighbor had sold it. He somehow found it via the VIN, but he did me the honor of not buying it for me.

I appreciate that more than he'll ever know. Even though I have plenty of money now, I still wanna have some things be mine, and since I was the one who sold it, I wanted to buy it back. It felt important, and I'm glad Kurt got that.

Weston & Ramirez House looks like a normal middle-class family home, although the area's a little gentrified now, Noah told me. I knock on the door and walk in.

My husband's standing at an easel in the living room. Two other easels are on either side of him, so the kids standing at them can see what he's doing on his canvas. Tarps cover the floor. Kurt turns around and smiles when he sees me. I recognize the two teens he's teaching, Toby and Quint, and they wave at me.

"Howdy," I say.

"Hey, babe," Kurt says, giving me a quick kiss. "I have a little more to do."

"Don't mind me. I've got all the time in the world."

Kurt continues with his art lesson, while I settle back to watch. "If you layer in color like this, you can get this 3D effect."

The two teens copy his brushstrokes on their own canvases. He does a few more strokes, then goes over to watch what they're doing.

"That's terrific," he says. "Toby, that's awesome."

"Thanks," Toby says.

The resident assistant comes in with two other teens, and the kids close up the art projects for the day.

"See you tomorrow," Kurt says, as the kids wave at him. Well, most of them do. One doesn't, and he looks somewhat sullen.

Kurt goes up and whispers something in the kid's ear. After a moment, the kid nods, and Kurt smiles.

When we get out to the truck, I unlock his door and ask what he'd said.

He pauses with a foot on the side step. "I just made him promise to stay alive until I saw him again."

I inhale sharply. "Damn, babe."

"Yeah. Some of these kids have had it real rough. We bring in medical care for them. Therapists. Counselors. All kinds of help."

I tug him into a hug. "That kid gonna be okay?"

"We have staff watching him at all times, but I think forming a connection with him, showing up when I say I will, and listening to him are the big things. Getting him medical help, of course. And making him promise me he'll stay alive until the next time.

I'm getting a chance to keep these kids from becoming Andrei," he says.

I kiss him, then go around to the driver's side. As we head home, I ask, "What was Andrei like?"

Kurt looks out the window for a moment. "I mean, he was a kid. We were in high school. We liked music and art and movies. We were trying to figure out what our style was and who we were. He had a darkness to him, an edge, and I think I found it seductive, but he also had a fun, goofy side. He liked the absurd. He didn't think that he fit in."

"Not many of us do," I say.

"Yeah. I know. But I let these kids know that not fitting in is how we all feel. Maybe that will help them hang in there."

"You're damn good at that. But remember, it's not all on you."

He shakes his head. "I know. All I can do is my best. Show up for them. Love them. Respect them. Listen to them."

He's way more suited for this job than being a senator ... or designing mailing inserts for utility bills. He's also throwing his energies into getting his mom elected. While he doesn't have the stomach for a lot of the things that go on in the background of politics, he has an interest in policy, and he can donate his skills in art and graphics.

I let him go on his rants about fairness, and when he's done, I kiss him silly.

It works. I love his passion and how much he cares.

And I love that he can be on the ground, working to create the changes he wants, but still have the ear of those who are higher up.

It seems ideal.

A year after Kurt and I met, I pause at the front doors of a Sacramento art museum.

"What's the plan, precious?" I ask, feeling relaxed and confident. I won't know many people in there, but that don't matter none, because they'll all know us.

"As far as I know, we just need to show up," Kurt says, looking dapper in a classic black tuxedo. I'm wearing a western-style tuxedo, my white cowboy hat, and my favorite boots. My good dog Lady is on a leash at our heels. She goes most places with me.

"I love the fact that you're here with me," he says. "I've done these events by myself, and it's so much better with someone else. And you're not just someone else. You're you."

"Precious, everything's better with you."

"Shall we go in?"

I give him a quick kiss and open the door. We cause quite a stir walking in. Likely because in this hat and boots I'm close to seven feet tall. But more likely because on my arm is the most handsome man in existence.

Oh, and his mom's the front-runner for president of the United States.

I've lost track of how many photos I've been in, standing behind her as she talks at a lectern. Standing next to my husband. Supporting her.

Supporting him supporting her.

The Delmonts treat me like I'm a natural part of the family. I'm Kurt's husband. Part of the group.

It makes me feel more welcomed than I ever have in my entire life.

With me at his side, Kurt goes up to potential donor after potential donor and charms them into supporting his mom. Or charms them into donating *more* money to her. To pledging more assistance. He reminds them what it is we're fighting for.

Makes me proud to be part of this family.

At the end of the night, Kurt and I are deciding whether to go back to the hotel or get a drink at one of the Sacramento watering holes.

"Do you have any plans tonight, cowboy?" Kurt asks, making me chuckle. Reminding me of the night we first met.

I kiss him. "The only plan I have right now is to spend the rest of my life with you."

Epilogue

KURT

Two years later

"Hi, babe," I say, walking into our sunny country kitchen at the end of the day. I've been in my studio. I got lost in the work, which is the best feeling. I'm painting these romantic couple portraits based on photos I've taken, and I love the way they're turning out.

Johnny's at the stove making chili. I walk up behind him and wrap my arms around his waist, putting my left hand atop his in a pose that's second nature to us now. "Checking in on you."

That's our code for "When's the last time you thought about killing yourself?"

He pauses to think about it. "I'm good. In fact, I can't remember the last time I had a suicidal thought. It's been ... a while."

I kiss the nape of his neck—which I have to go up on my toes to do, although it's easier when he's in sock feet, as he is now. "Even if you did, you know it'd be okay, right?"

"Yup, darlin'. I do. Feels good to have some space between the dark thoughts, though." Johnny smirks. "We should make up one of those safety signs like they have at those construction supply stores. 'It's been 365 days since John Haskell's had a suicidal thought.'"

His words make my chest expand until it hurts. "Has it been that long? A *year*?"

Johnny shrugs and turns around to kiss me properly, his hands around my waist. "Not sure. Maybe. It's been so long that when I do have them, my thought process is like 'Hey, I recognize you. Thanks for coming to visit, but you don't have to stay.'"

"Yay," I murmur. "I'm so glad to hear it." I look down at my paint-spattered clothes. "Let me get cleaned up, and I'll help you cook."

He waves a hand. "Ain't no bother. I think the First Son can take a break from cookin' every now and again."

I snort. "First Son. Yeah, I guess. Damn, I'm so glad she's in the White House. I love all the changes that she's making."

"I'm not usually one to be optimistic," Johnny says. "But I have hope."

* * *

"Come on, Lady," Johnny calls after dinner. He saunters out into the dappled sunlight under the sycamore trees, headed for the barn. We're going to take the horses out for an early-evening ride.

Even though he objected at first, once Johnny realized how easily we could afford it between my trust fund and his lawsuit win, we bought a ranch in Hidden Valley. The real value is in the land—there's a lot of it, and it's quiet and private. While the house is nice, it's not the biggest one out here, and that suits us fine, because what we really care about is getting him out in nature and with animals.

Lady has a friend now, named, appropriately enough, the Tramp. He's a geriatric mutt that Johnny fell in love with at the pound. I couldn't tell him no. The Tramp needs a little extra assistance with life, and Johnny gladly gives it to him.

And of course we've got two horses of our own—Nolan and Dakota. We go riding most afternoons and for long rides on the weekends. Johnny still works part time at the neighbor's ranch, too. He never looks more peaceful than when he's mucking out stalls and grooming horses and generally taking care of them. Oh, and I help out. At home, anyway. Johnny's taught me my way around a curry comb, and I've mucked more stalls than I'd ever care to. I like having our animals all spick-and-span.

Tonight, I'm following behind him with the Tramp, because I love watching Johnny work. I've always liked watching him—the way he moves is confident and sexy and oh so focused.

But right now, my pulse is racing and my mouth's getting dry. My nerve endings are tingling.

I tell myself to calm down, but my self doesn't seem to want to listen.

After we tack up the horses and take them out to the corral, Johnny smiles at me. Before he makes a move to mount up, I say, "Hey, Johnny?"

"What's up, precious?" My big, sweet, happy cowboy steps toward me.

My knees feel a little weak, so I hold on to one of the bars of the corral. "I was wondering something."

He gives me his full attention. "What's that?"

"You know that you're the love of my life, right?" Heat creeps up my neck and cheeks, and my heart beats even faster.

Johnny's eyes get brighter. "And you're the love of mine."

"What would you think about getting married?" I ask. "Or rather, since my proposal in Las Vegas was kind of crappy, what do you think about actually staying married?"

"Hon, I thought we were."

Then his eyes widen as he watches me get down on one knee, in the dirt and all. I hold out a ring. "I like our simple bands, but they were chosen when we didn't have our full faculties about us. I want to love you in the sober light of day. With nothing around us but nature. No lights, no strippers, no drinking, no dancing. Just us, the dogs, the horses, and"—I gesture—"the sunset. So, whadda you say, cowboy? I love you more than I ever imagined I could love anyone. Will you do me the honor of marrying me?"

"Yes, Kurt. I'd ... *yes*," Johnny says. He tugs me up into his arms and kisses me. "I love you," he whispers fervently against my lips, his hat sheltering me from the breeze.

"The entire world is better when you're in it with me," I say.

"I feel the same way. When do you wanna get hitched again?"

"I don't care. I just want to know what I promise you."

"Oh, precious. I know what I promise you. I promise to love you in good times and bad. No matter how good the good, and no matter how bad the bad. I just plain love you. We can talk about it more, but there's no need for talkin' when two people understand each other. And I understand you, and you understand me."

"Yeah," I whisper. "I do."

"As Mama says, there's plenty of good hay in the barn, and a smart horse finds his way home. I found my way home with you."

I kiss him hard. "Tell me what else your mama says?"

"I intend to spend the rest of my life doing that."

* * *

Leslie's MM-only newsletter includes bonus content, like an alternative scene from Chapter 22 in Johnny's perspective. Sign up here: http://eepurl.com/hD9a4r or on her website at www.lesliemcadamauthor.com

Acknowledgments

Thank you to everyone who helped me with my recovery and with this book:

For generating ideas, reading early chapters/drafts, hashing out plot, and being all-around supportive: Kristy Lin Billuni, Mary Carr, Lex Martin, Rachel Ember, and J.E. Birk.

For smelling like Johnny: Duke Cannon "Redwood" solid cologne. I have no idea how a scent could be so inspirational, but there you have it.

For saying "What in tarnation?" (without irony) in the backseat of my car and making me think someone could get away with saying that out loud IRL: My kid's friend, J.

For being quotable: Abraham Lincoln ("It has been my experience that folks who have no vices have very few virtues.") and other unknown folk philosophers whose wisdom has been passed down through the years to Johnny.

For entering me as "momther" in their phone (and my husband as "masculine parental unit"): my wonderful younger child.

For beta reading: Megan Dischinger, Katy Cuthbertson, and Karen Cundy.

For editing (and gently pushing me to do more) (and letting me vent when it got to be too much): Alicia Z. Ramos.

For proofreading: Katy Cuthbertson, Virginia Tesi Carey, and Jerica MacMillan.

For creating the cover(s): Cory Stierley (photo), Brandon Janes (model), Garrett Leigh (design), RJ Creatives (alternative edition cover design).

For being the best things in my life: My family.

For taking the time to read: You. If you enjoyed this book, please don't forget to leave a review because reviews really help authors be seen.

Also by Leslie McAdam

IOU Series (lower angst m/m)
Ambiguous (audio narrated by Hamish Long and Kirt Graves)
Studious (audio narrated by Declan Winters)
Delicious (short story)
Oblivious
Curious
Notorious
Ferocious (coming soon)

Creepin U: A Monster Romance Series (shared-world m/m)
The Nøkk and the Jock (coming soon)

With J.E. Birk and Rachel Ember (holiday m/m/m)
ILYBSM
TMI

FASTER series (shared-world sports m/m)
Off Track

Sarina Bowen's World of True North (shared-world m/m)
Undone (audio narrated by Iggy Toma and Tim Paige)
Unmanageable (audio narrated by Jacob Morgan and Teddy Hamilton)

Albrecht College Series (college m/m)
Mixed Motives (short story)

All American Boy Series (shared-world m/f)

Boy on a Train (audio narrated by Desiree Ketchum and James Cavenaugh)

Romantic comedies with Lex Martin (m/f)

All About the D (audio narrated by Stephen Dexter and Ava Erickson)

Surprise, Baby! (audio narrated by Jacob Morgan and Muffy Newton)

The Giving You ... series (m/f)

The Sun and the Moon (audio narrated by Tor Thom and Charley Ongel)

The Stars in the Sky

All the Waters of the Earth

The Ground Beneath Our Feet (audio narrated by Tor Thom and Charley Ongel)

Love in Translation series (m/f)

Sol

Sombra

Stand-alone novella (m/f)

Lumbersexual (audio narrated by Tor Thom and Charley Ongel)

About the Author

Leslie McAdam is a California girl who loves romance and well-defined abs. She lives in a drafty old farmhouse on a small orange tree farm in Southern California with her husband and two children. Leslie's first published book, *The Sun and the Moon*, won a 2015 Watty, which is the world's largest online writing competition. She's gone on to receive additional literary awards and has been featured in multiple publications, including Cosmopolitan.com. Her books have been Top 100 Bestsellers on both Amazon and Apple Books. Leslie is employed by day but spends her nights writing about the men of your fantasies.

Website: https://www.lesliemcadamauthor.com
M/M-only newsletter: http://eepurl.com/hD9a4r

www.ingramcontent.com/pod-product-compliance
Lightning Source LLC
LaVergne TN
LVHW021220080526
838199LV00084B/4293